SEEDS OF SORROW

IMMORTAL REALMS

BOOK 1

ELLE BEAUMONT
CHRISTIS CHRISTIE

Midnight Tide
PUBLISHING

Gram—

Thank you for the time spent in the gardens and for teaching me how to nourish soil, grow plants, and to eat the fruits of labor. I fancy myself Persephone now. ~ Elle

For Mom—

Thank you for supporting my independence, encouraging my first steps into the world on my own, and believing fully in my ability to do whatever I set my mind to. The strength I have, you fostered into being. ~Tiss

Prologue

Draven

The smells of blood and brimstone mingled on the breeze, followed by dark clouds of smoke billowing overhead as the village burned down around the three kings. Draven kicked roughly at the back of a monster feasting on the body of a young woman. When it fell onto its back, he thrust his sword into the beast's chest and slit it fully down the middle of its body. The creature's innards spilled out onto the ground, and Draven took a step back to protect his sandals from the sludge.

The moment of distraction was all that it took for another beast to catch him unawares. The sharp prick of claws digging into his back was the only warning he had before the full impact of the creature sent him staggering to the side.

The force of hitting the ground knocked the breath from his lungs, and with a harsh grunt, Draven rolled away from his attacker. The sharp drag of claws over his back seared his body with pain and shredded the red fabric of his tunic. He didn't have time to compose himself, however. Feeling the heat of the beast's breath at his nape, Draven rolled once more and swung toward it with his sword.

The beast roared in fury as the blade sliced through the corner of its jaw, sending a hunk of flesh and bone flying through the air. Lying on his back, Draven called on his powers and turned himself invisible. Rising up onto his knees, he used the beast's confusion over where its prey had disappeared to his advantage and brought his sword down on its neck. The monstrous head thudded to the ground, spinning away from him over bloodstained grass, and the beast's body crumpled.

Panting, Draven staggered to his feet, the muscles of his back protesting every movement. Behind him, his brothers Travion and Zryan were in the midst of dispatching their own monsters. Large fur and scale-covered bodies dropping to the ground with heavy thuds. Draven looked around him quickly, noting that the last of the beasts seemed to have been put down, and any that could be had been driven back through the Veil into the dark realm they'd crawled out of.

Swiping his brow with the back of his hand, Draven smeared a patch of black blood over his forehead. He turned to his siblings and noted that the fine linen of Travion's green tunic hung in tatters; the only thing keeping it from falling to the ground was the belt around his waist. His dark auburn hair lay plastered to his head with sweat and blood—some of which appeared to be his own. However, the sparkle of victory in his blue eyes let Draven know he was okay.

Zryan, on the other hand, stood naked as the day he was born. Running a hand through his dark brown locks, Draven's youngest brother shot him a proud smirk.

"Where are your clothes?" Draven asked, staring at him blandly.

"I shifted into a griffin. It seemed more efficient than a sword."

"Of course." In Draven's opinion, Zryan was always looking for a reason to end up naked, no matter what he was doing. Looking away from his brothers, Draven watched the humans, who were frantically trying to contain the fires as best they could. Their pitiful buckets of water did little to quell the blaze. "We should do something about that."

Travion turned to face the village. "Allow me," he grunted. Lifting his hands, Travion pulled storm clouds into the beautiful blue sky and brought a torrent of rain down on the inferno.

At first, the fire merely sputtered in agitation, continuing to lap at straw rooftops. But Travion persisted, and finally it succumbed to the intensity of his rainfall. Once it was out and nothing but lightly smoking embers remained, Travion released the clouds, and the blue sky returned. A cheer rang out from the villagers followed by many cries of thanks mixed with Travion's name.

"Of course. I bring the aid to drive back the beasts, and it's Travion who receives all the praise for a little cloud play." Zryan had come up to Draven's side, his arms crossed over his chest.

"Where credit lies is hardly of importance right now. The more important thing is what is to be done about the Veil," Draven said, eyeing Zryan.

"I'd also like to make mention that I was correct about that as well." Zryan's smirk had only grown.

3

"Correct about what?" Travion asked, returning to their small huddle.

"That Midniva was being overrun with creatures from Andhera. And no one wanted to believe me!"

"How were we to know? Nothing is meant to be alive in the dark realm," Travion countered.

Draven's eyes fell to the final beast he had slain. Its eyes were clouded and staring lifelessly into the distance. It was a monstrosity of a thing: a humanoid face with razor fangs hanging down over its bottom lip, all surrounded by a red mane, a muscular lion body, taloned paws, and a hard-shelled scorpion tail. Draven had never seen anything like it before, and a deep fear of what exactly was happening in the dark realm coursed through him.

"That was true in the beginning days," he began, waiting until he knew he had both Travion and Zryan's attention before continuing. "But there are rumors that Ludari banished all of his enemies to Andhera. There is a chance the lost souls unfortunate enough to have made their way into the dark realm now find themselves twisted beyond recognition." He pointed down at the beast. "I think this thing used to be a person."

His brothers froze, all eyes now on the monster.

"By the sun," Travion rasped.

"This has to be contained," Zryan followed. "Before the body count rises higher and it grows entirely out of our control." His shoulders had stiffened, and a dark frown now creased his brow. "There have been too many accounts of attacks on the humans living here. People bloodied, torn apart . . . *feasted* on."

Draven found the almost tangible unease coursing its way through his youngest brother an unnatural sight for one typically brimming with arrogance. His own features pinched together. He had seen some of the bodies himself during his trips here to the middle realm. The mortals were terrified. Fearful of moving anywhere in the dark lest they be attacked, and now it seemed even the daylight was not safe.

"And what are you suggesting?" Travion asked, looking between his brothers.

"Andhera needs a warden . . . "someone we can trust to abide by our rule and keep the monsters there in check."

Contemplating Zryan's words, Draven let his eyes fall to the hand still curled around the hilt of his sword. It was coated in dark blood and grime. Currently the hand of a warrior. His hands had been used to dole out punishment for as long as he could remember. Not always because he wanted them to but because that was what was demanded of him.

"A warden? Zryan, who could we trust with such a task? Would we not be setting up our own future aggressor? With such power behind them—" Travion began.

"What choice do we have?" Zryan growled, confidence fueling his vehemence. "If it is not Andhera rising against us later, it will be Midniva rising in rebellion *now* at our inaction to protect them."

Zryan does speak true, Draven reflected. Shifting the grip on his hilt, he considered what he was about to say, taking that extra moment to ensure he was certain before he spoke.

"I will go."

Both Zryan and Travion stilled instantly, their eyes leaving each other to focus on Draven instead, shock and rejection mingling in their gaze. He stared back at them, an eerie calmness settling over him.

"Draven—" Travion hissed, and dread rumpled his brow.

"You cannot honestly be—" said Zryan at the same time.

Draven held up his hand to silence them both. "I will go. Better a king than a warden."

Travion only sputtered, but it was Zryan, now eyeing him with contemplation, who spoke.

"You realize we do not know what will happen to you if you go? We have no understanding of the dark realm or what is happening there. Should you choose to live in the dark realm . . . "it may twist you in unimaginable ways." It was his turn to gesture at the dead beast at their feet. "You may no longer be fae, Draven, but something *other*. Something that Andhera chooses for you." Zryan paused, and their eyes locked. "There may be no coming back."

"I realize." There was only calmness and finality in Draven's voice.

"No!" Travion growled deeply, his pale, freckled face reddening. He reached forward to wrap his fingers around Draven's wrist. A motion that had been repeated hundreds of times throughout Travion's childhood, his thumb at Draven's pulse. "This is absurd, Draven." Travion's eyes looked deeply back into his, and Draven heard the unspoken words of his brother. Travion understood what he was trying to do, and he would not stand for it. "No one is saying it needs to be one of us, and no one is asking this of you. Zryan, do not encourage him in this insanity." He shot Zryan an imploring glance.

Zryan did not reply, simply continued to study Draven's features.

"If Andhera is left unchecked, then the inhabitants there will continue to plague the mortal realm until there is nothing left. Who better to claim the dark realm but one of our own? Who better to build a kingdom and enforce the laws that we would see fit?" Draven said, catching Travion's eyes once more and accepting the love and concern he found there but only letting it fuel his resolve rather than convince him to change his mind. Draven knew what he could be sacrificing, and he also knew he couldn't allow either of his brothers to take up the burden. Better he should suffer through hell than either of them. "I am aware of what may very well happen once I go, and I can accept that."

Travion moved to protest once more, but Zryan pressed a hand to his chest, silencing him before he could begin.

"Now, the only question left to settle is, when do I leave?"

1

Eden

The sun shone in all its glory, nurturing the soft pink blossoms that fragranced the air. Unlike most days, this one was to be embraced fully. Eden's mother was gone and wouldn't return until the night sun painted the sky a mellow orange. Without her mother there, she was free to invite whomever she wished over, and Eden was more than delighted to invite her friend, Aurelie, for a visit.

Aurelie's chestnut-colored lop rabbit had just given birth to a litter not two weeks ago, and as she'd promised, Aurelie had brought a kit with her. But that wasn't why Eden's lips twitched with uncertainty.

Eden cocked her head and eyed her friend as though she'd sprouted a third eye. "I'm sorry, did you say the Blossom Festival?"

Mischief sparked in her friend's dark brown eyes. "Your mother is gone for the day, and I can have you back before the sun settles on the horizon."

The notion was tempting. Eden hadn't been to the Blossom Festival since her father had passed away nearly a decade ago. He'd wanted her to see and experience as much of life as possible, but her mother had other ideas. After his passing, she'd all but kept her locked away from society, claiming it was for her own good.

Eden shifted on her bare feet, scooping the brown rabbit into her hands. Its nose wiggled as it drew in her scent, then lowered its head, lapping at her fingers gently. "He's precious, Aurelie," she murmured but glanced up as her friend mock-glared at her.

"No brushing over the topic." Aurelie swiped at the air, then placed her hands on the crook of Eden's elbow. "You're coming with me. I promised my brother that I'd take him to the Blossom Festival, and you know how fond he is of you."

Eden's lips twisted into a frown, and she huffed. Tamas was much younger than both of them, and he often looked at her with doe eyes and a crooked smile. A sweet, if not mischievous, youngling. But to venture to the festival . . . "

Her heart leaped in her chest. Eden wasn't known for being anxious—in fact, she'd been accused of being foolish and daring on more than one occasion. However, the idea of deliberately disobeying her mother's orders set butterflies aflutter in her stomach. Mother would be angry, and if she were angry, she'd lock Eden in her room. Not even Aurelie knew this. It wasn't something she was keen on discussing. Most fae Eden's age were finding suitors and even venturing into a lifelong union with their other half, but Eden couldn't seem to crawl out from beneath her mother's thumb.

"Eden, are you listening?" Aurelie huffed. "Stop pacing. You're making me dizzy."

The silken fabric of her pale blue gown shifted and

tumbled down to conceal her bare feet. With each light step, blades of grass tickled between her toes, but she enjoyed the feeling of being connected to the ground in some manner. Perhaps it was the fae in her, the three realms calling her closer to them, beckoning her. Or it was simply that Eden had always preferred being outdoors, nestled in the crook of her garden and bathing in the sunshine.

She dragged her forefinger along the top of the rabbit's head. "Fine. I'll go with you, but we must be back before Mama returns." Eden peered up at Aurelie just in time to catch her friend leaping up in victory.

The celebration was cut short when a bell rang from inside, one that Eden had been hoping would chime while her mother was gone.

"Come with me." Eden excitedly grabbed her friend's free hand, then ran with her toward the white lattice fence. As she approached the gate, she unlatched it and bounded to the front of the manor. Eden hoped that she would arrive behind the postman before one of the servants did; her mother always tossed invitations away before Eden even had a chance to glance at them.

The front door opened at the same time Eden halted, as did Aurelie. The brown kit sneezed at the postman, then proceeded to groom himself.

Her heart galloped, partially from the exertion of running and partially from excitement. It was a rarity that she ever intercepted the mail before her mother, and because of that, she was never able to respond to invitations. "Is that the mail?" Eden questioned, but as she did, her hand moved toward the postman's and she took up one of the missives, eyeing it closely. *An invitation from King*

Travion in Midniva? He was hosting a ball in two weeks' time.

"Oh, you're lucky. I've only been to Midniva o—"

Eden looked at her companion, brow furrowing not in a glare but as a reminder that she'd *never* been and could count on one hand how many events she *had* attended.

"Right," Aurelie amended, then bumped her hip into Eden's. "You should reply while your mother is gone."

Surprise washed over Eden's expression as she peered at her friend. But she was right; her mother wasn't present, and if she replied with a resounding *yes*, then her mother couldn't retract it without rumors spreading wildly, or possibly gaining the disfavor of one or all of the kingly brothers.

King Travion, as far as Eden had heard, was the mild brother, which was why he ruled over Midniva, the middle realm that housed mostly humans and some fae creatures. It was the realm most closely linked to Andhera, the dark realm, and the one most likely to be invaded by its creatures due to the falling of the sun.

Andhera wasn't a place anyone willingly spoke of unless it was in hushed whispers, and its king, Draven, was ruthless. A name never to be spoken aloud, and if it was, it was as a curse. He was feared, and rightfully so, as he was the king of nightmares.

But Lucem, *home*, Eden assumed nothing could compare with it. A land of plenty, warmth, and most of all, its beloved ever-blooming flora. A land where one did not fear becoming the meal of some terrifying beast hidden in the shadows. Their king, Zryan, was known mostly for his wandering eyes, but Eden had never fallen under his gaze, which she was thankful for.

Eden pressed her lips together, nodding. "Fetch me a quill and a pair of sandals." She flicked her hand at the servant, who remained rooted in place. A look of uncertainty passed in his lingering gaze. "Please?" she prompted, this time he left and returned with what she'd requested. Eden wrote down her name, as well as her mother's, and quickly handed it back to the postman.

Excitedly, she passed the rabbit off to Aurelie so she could pull her sandals on. She yanked the straps into place on her calves, then Eden beamed at the servant. "Thank you." Plucking the rabbit from her friend, she fought to remain calm for the sake of the kit. Inwardly, she squealed. Finally, finally, she was able to journey to Midniva, and for a royal ball!

"And I know just the colors for you." Aurelie waggled her fingers against Eden's bicep. "We'll have to go over the dress details tomorrow—or whenever is convenient for you. For now, we have to go before the street is mobbed."

Eden deposited her new pet in the caring hands of her servants and asked for a horse to be prepared. When it was readied, she fled the manor in haste.

Eden turned to the white horse being led to her: Aiya. The mare's kind eye met hers, and she proceeded to whuffle the air around Eden.

She took the reins in her hands, carefully situating the skirt of her dress as she settled into the saddle with the aid of the servant. "Let's not make your brother wait any longer."

"My carriage isn't here yet."

"Then, I suggest you climb up." Eden laughed, smiling mischievously. She reached down and pulled her friend up while the servant gave her a boost. "Maybe we can beat the carriage before it leaves."

Aurelie's arms wrapped around Eden's waist as the horse began to trot. "Go easy, you know I'm not as good of a rider as you." Her voice came out shakily, jarred by the horse's movement.

With a pat to her arm, Eden led the horse down her drive. "My darling friend, I suggest you hold on tightly then." With a prodding of her heels, the mare leaped into a steady trot.

By horse, Aurelie's house was only fifteen minutes down the road. Trees lined the roadway on both sides, shielding them from the sun's abrasive rays. It was almost too hot for Eden, but the wind created by the horse's movement fanned her red hair away from her face.

It felt as though they'd just begun their ride when they arrived. The carriage was readying to pull out, but in haste, Aurelie dismounted and ran to stop the driver, leaving Eden to deal with Aiya.

A young male voice called out, followed by the scuffling of feet on the dirt drive, then a boy emerged from around the corner of a massive rhododendron tree. When he spotted Eden, he stopped to pluck a purple bloom and proceeded to rush forward, presenting her with his bounty.

"Oh, this is lovely, Tamas." Eden bent down and laid a kiss on top of his curly brown hair. "It will do perfectly." She stood up, exchanging a glance with a servant before releasing her horse into his care. Eden smiled as she gently guided Tamas to the awaiting carriage.

When they were all settled inside the carriage, Eden scooped up Aurelie's hand, smiling. "Thank you for letting me come." She turned to look across the way at Tamas. His curly, dark hair framed his cherubic cheeks, and his fox-brown eyes gleamed with mischief. Part of her had always wanted a sibling to spend time with and perhaps to lessen the gnawing loneliness she felt on most days.

"Just remember, *I* get to escort Eden around the festival." Tamas glared at his sister.

"I haven't forgotten. With you by my side, who would dare misstep?" Eden offered playfully, then allowed the cab to fill with the chatter of brother and sister bickering.

The festival was less than an hour away from Aurelie's home, deep in the heart of Lucem. On arrival, the carriage parked a few streets away from the main festivities and allowed for Eden, Aurelie, and Tamas to exit without being trampled.

"Come on, Eden!" Tamas curled his fingers around her hand and tugged.

"What are we rushing for?"

"Our first dance!" Tamas shouted over his shoulder as they jogged toward the festival.

Flowers rained down from baskets being tipped from windows, voices carried joyous tunes as they celebrated another Blossom Festival. Each petal seemed to have a will of its own, for they danced on the wind, blew across the street, and spun around in small cyclones.

Silk garland hung around the shops, writhing as the same breeze caught them. It appeared as though they, too, were celebrating.

In the corner of a stone wall, two fae embraced one

another. The sheer fabric of the dark-haired female's dress had tumbled from her shoulder, revealing her tanned breast, which her blond male lover currently laved with his tongue. The sight stirred desire in Eden's core, but she didn't shy away from it. Lucem was open as far as displaying one's sexuality for all to see, and the patrons certainly weren't timid about putting on a show.

Eden yearned to taste another's flesh like those lovers. However, her mother had ingrained into her that Lucemites viewed virginity as a bargaining chip. While chastity wasn't a must, a virgin could fetch a higher ranked noble if they were intact.

She peeled her eyes away as the male's hand delved between the pair. Although she couldn't hear it, Eden imagined throaty purrs erupting from the female.

Turning her attention toward the flowers dancing on the warm breeze, Eden stuck her hand out to catch one. "This is beautiful. It is as I remember and more," she marveled out loud.

Memories rushed back to her, of her father whisking her away to the festival, parading her around the streets, and buying her as many flower crowns as she asked for. Life had been different when he had been alive, but what could she do? Dwelling on his death would only twist her into something . . . "something like her mother. Anxious, commanding, and at times, unforgiving.

Not that Eden could blame her. King Zryan had all but sent her father to his death when he'd required him to soothe an angry lower-born. Although, to be fair, none had known that the male intended violence, or that by killing Lelantos Damaris, he was sending a message to the king.

"Come on, let us drink!" Aurelie swooped in on a cart,

flashing a confident smile at the vendor. He offered two flutes of honey mead to her, then produced another with orange juice for Tamas.

Sidling up to Aurelie, Eden took her flute and inclined her head to the vendor. He glanced up at her, something she was used to. While not abnormally tall, Eden was above average in height, and in her younger years had been described by her father as 'coltish.'

Aurelie sputtered after taking a sip of the mead. "By the sun, this is strong."

Eden glanced down and took a sip of hers. The liquid spread down her throat smoothly, all the way to her stomach. "It's stronger than my Mama's ouzo." She took another sip, and heat immediately crawled up her cheeks.

In the air, the perfume of honey and butter pastries mingled with the heady scent of alcohol. It was dizzying and overwhelming all at once.

As her escort tugged at her elbow, he pointed toward a dance party. "Dance with me, Eden!"

Eden lifted her eyebrows, downing the rest of the flute's contents. "Not until you ask a lady properly." She discarded the glass, casually following Aurelie's figure as a male swept her into a quick-paced dance.

"Will you please dance with me, Eden?" Tamas bowed low.

"Oh yes, of course." She winked, then grabbed the boy's hand and led him toward the throng of individuals. With the thrum of alcohol pulsing in her veins, Eden pulled Tamas into a bouncing, energetic dance. When she spun away, her chest collided with a tall blond male. Eden hadn't seen ringlets so tightly wound against a person's head before, and his eyes were a perfect clashing of green and blue. On his right cheek, he bore one freckle, as if to accentuate how high his cheekbones were. He was positively beautiful.

His smooth hands reached up to steady her.

"I'm sorry," she blurted, unable to tear her eyes from his.

"Don't be." His gaze shifted as if he were committing her face to memory. "Are you enjoying yourself?" He lifted his pale brows and glanced around.

"Immensely. I haven't been here in years." Eden didn't need a mirror to know she was flushed. She could hear how out of breath she sounded, and there was a certain buzzing in her veins she blamed on the mead.

The male pulled his head back, and one hand came to rest on his chest. A chest that was scarcely concealed by the same sheer fabric as her gown. "Years? You don't say. We must ensure it's a day to remember." He bowed, then lifted a hand. "My lady, I am Lord Calix of House Omorphia. I'd be honored if you danced with me."

House Omorphia? Eden blinked, placing the name immediately. It was one of the families her mother was trying to warm Eden up to. They hadn't met, but the idea of marrying someone she didn't even know . . . it didn't appeal to her.

"I accept." She paused. "But I would have even if you weren't of Omorphia." She took his outstretched hand. "My name is Eden of House Damaris, and I'd prefer if you simply called me Eden."

Calix's eyes widened. "Damaris?" His other hand slid to her waist as he drew her flush against him. He smelled of sunshine, mead, and citrus. "My father knew yours well." The harp now played a soft melody, a stark contrast to the lively beat from before. Calix led Eden in a fluid dance, their bodies seldom separating. "Why have I never seen you?"

What lie could she possibly spout? Eden glanced to the side. Aurelie mouthed, *Good for you.*

"I am not fond of court. I prefer the tranquility of gardens to the vipers of society." It was the truth, even if it wasn't the whole of it.

Calix swept Eden across the cobblestone street, leading her in a circle, but she didn't move as smoothly as him and occasionally felt the hard planes of his body melding into her. Warmth spread through Eden's body, and she wasn't certain if it was due to the heat or the mead coursing through her.

"I can understand that. I'm not overly fond of it myself, although it's expected of me." Calix shrugged.

She frowned, searching his vibrant eyes. There was a spark there, something kind and playful, and she saw the truth of his words in them as well.

When the music ended, Calix slowly withdrew from Eden. "It has been my greatest pleasure to dance with you, Eden. Enjoy the rest of the festival." His fingers were the last to pull away, but before he did, Calix bowed his head and brushed a kiss to her knuckles.

Eden touched her ear; it was hot to the touch, and she knew her face was scarlet. She laughed, mostly at herself and the fluttering in her stomach.

"I leave you alone for a moment and you wind up in the arms of Lord Calix!" Aurelie gently pushed Eden's shoulder. "Unfair, if you ask me."

Her brow furrowed. "How? I bumped into him."

Aurelie cocked her head, scrutinizing Eden. "Never

mind. Let's go find some honey cakes." She twirled round, grabbing Tamas' hand.

Eden watched her friend, unsure of what had been lost on her. Leave it to her to miss something. Not wanting to sour the day, she rushed after Aurelie.

Eden spent the rest of the festival dancing until her feet were nearly bloodied and eating until her stomach felt as though it would burst.

By the time they'd found the carriage, Tamas had consumed so many honey pastries that the sugar had overtaken him, and he was dozing as they walked. Eden situated herself next to him, allowing him to crash into her and slip into a peaceful slumber. She combed his curls back over his pointed ears, then looked out the window. The sun was dipping low in the sky, where it would sit until morning before rising to its full strength. In Lucem, the sun never gave way to a moon as Midniva's did. This was, after all, the land of light.

Eden succumbed to the hypnotic sway of the cab and jingling of the horses' harnesses. She woke as they pulled into Aurelie's drive, blinking away the sleepiness. Above her friend's manor, the aged wisteria blooms cascaded down in a dancing, purple waterfall. The sweet scent invaded the cab, tickling Eden's nose.

"This has been a most unexpected day," Eden sighed as she walked toward the stable.

Aurelie twirled in front of her, brown eyes full of life

and wonder. "And that young lord who asked me to dance . . . "

Eden laughed. Tamas had done well to keep any potential mates away from her. "I don't want to return home, but I must. I fear—"

"I know." Aurelie held up a hand, then motioned to a stable hand to fetch Eden's horse. "For what it's worth, I'm glad you were able to come with us."

"Me too."

As pleasant as the ride to Aurelie's had been, Eden pushed her mount as fast as she could go, fueled by the worry of what her mother had in store for her but also by a tinge of excitement. She would still have to admit to replying to the invitation, and while Eden knew her mother's reaction would be less than approving, she didn't believe anything more than exasperation would come from it.

The sun bathed her home in a golden light, and the flowers surrounding the property had closed their blooms for the evening. Although the air still held its perfumed fragrance, it wasn't as strong as it had been during the day.

In the stable, Eden relinquished her hold on her mare, then quickly made her way inside her home. The candelabras and lanterns were lit, illuminating the hall as she wove her way to the sitting room, where her mother typically spent her evenings.

Her heart beat heavily in her ears, and color rushed into her cheeks. She stepped into the doorway, fidgeting with her fingers. "Mama—"

"Eden Damaris, I demand you explain yourself. Where have you been?" Her mother stood from the chaise lounge, rising to her full, grandiose stature. Her sharp, slanted features only added a harsher quality to her current dour mood.

At once, Eden's heart sank. "I went to the Blossom Festival with Aurelie. I didn't see any harm in it. I've missed going with Papa—"

As Naya strode forward and closed the distance between them, she cupped Eden's cheeks. "I miss him too, more than you know. To have your life-mate ripped from you is something incomparable. But it doesn't excuse your foolish behavior." She dipped her head, pressing a kiss to Eden's hair. "And that rabbit . . . " Turning away, Naya tsked, but it melded with laughter.

This was a chastising Eden could live with. It still caused her cheeks to flush with embarrassment and made her squirm, for surely she'd disappointed her mother, but it was far better than she'd anticipated. It bolstered her confidence, and in a rush, Eden blurted her next words.

"I responded to an invitation from King Travion. He's hosting a ball in two weeks' time, and I said we'd go. I've been wanting to go to Midniva for ages, and I thought . . . I thought . . . " Whatever confidence had resided in Eden dwindled rapidly as tension-filled silence rippled around them.

Naya's body grew rigid, and the slow turn toward her made Eden think of a wild cat preparing to pounce on its prey. Before she could unroot herself from where she stood, Naya lashed out, slapping her across the face. An exasperated, strangled noise escaped her.

"How could you? You reckless girl! You haven't a clue what you've done." She rubbed her hand as if it stung from the strike, then paced back and forth. "Out of my sight. Go to your room at once."

Eden had jolted as her mother's hand connected with her cheek, but it hadn't been the first, nor would it likely be the last time. She lifted her own hand, stroking cool fingers against the mark. "I didn't mean . . . "

"Go!"

Eden rushed from the room, hot tears splashing down her freckled cheeks, stinging the growing welt.

She should have known better, and yet she'd done it anyway.

Draven

"**D**on't . . . Please don't!" Kailush pleaded, hands frantically clinging to the stone frame of the door behind him. "I b-beg of you, Your M-Majesty."

The young vampire lordling's heels balanced on the edge of the opening, his trembling frame backlit by a yellow crescent moon that hung in the afternoon sky.

"Begging? Is that what we've come to?" Draven drawled. "That last one—the maiden—did she beg you for her life before the end also?"

Wind whistled through the doorway, tugging rapidly at the young man's hair and causing the torches on the walls to flicker around them. The wind, however, was not the coldest thing in the room.

"I didn't know what I was—"

Draven had heard enough. With one slight push, Kailush lost the faint grasp he had on the stone and fell back, arms pinwheeling in the air as he dropped through the emptiness. Draven stood in the open doorway, watching the body plummet from the high peak the castle sat upon down into the cavernous pit below—swallowed up by the true death.

"Is this a bad time?" a voice questioned from behind him.

Satisfied that the young vampire lord was now gone, Draven stepped away from the opening, drawing the heavy wooden door closed and locking it with the loud thud of a metal arm falling into place. With a simple tug of his double-breasted jacket, he turned to face Seurat.

"Just enacting overdue justice." Draven glanced at his manservant, taking in the windswept quality of his appearance. "You've been in the owlery." He could smell it on him: feathers, straw, and droppings.

"A missive just arrived from Midniva, Your Grace." Seurat stepped forward at the inclination of Draven's head, holding out the rolled note for him to take.

Draven accepted the parchment, his deft fingers quickly unfurling it. A frown pinched at his features as he read the hurriedly scrawled words. "It is from Travion. I am needed at once in the middle realm."

"I will prepare your things straight away."

"I'm not certain there is a need for that, nor time . . . "

"There is always time, sire," Seurat countered, and with a bow of his head, quickly left the room.

"Keep it light, Seurat!" he called after him, though was uncertain whether the man had heard or not.

Shaking his head, Draven looked at the note in his hand once more. Travion had been brief, mentioning only that he and Zryan were both in Midniva and had need of him. The haste with which the letter had been sent concerned him, and with this in mind, he set off to find General Ailith, commander of his army. In his absence, she would be in charge.

In the end, three chariots pulled by glistening black kelpies left the castle in Andhera, traveling the lone road that led to the barriers between realms, the day moon following their journey.

The party had to cross through the Veil at just the right moment in order to time their entrance into the middle realm perfectly with the setting of Midniva's sun. Should they spend too long a time in the Veil, they may find themselves lost to its empty landscape. However, if they passed into Midniva before the sun set, Draven would find himself in the throes of agony, burning from the outside in.

It was a task that Captain Hannelore, Ailith's second-in-command, took upon herself most seriously, pacing their agitated steeds as they crossed the wasteland that was the non-space between realms.

When at last the party slipped through the large stone arch into Midniva, the last rays of that day's sun were just fading beyond the horizon. Draven cast a glance to Hannelore, the harpy's smooth features wearing a relieved look.

"Be at peace, Hannelore. Night is upon us," he called out to her.

"You refused to let me cross first," she shot back, frustration now shining through the relief that had been there a mere moment ago. "We had no way of being certain!"

Draven only spurred his kelpie Rayvnin on faster, heading down the main road leading to the coast. There hadn't been a need for the extra precaution; he had known Captain Hannelore would bring them through the pass at just the right time. His people did not fail him.

A heavy beat of wings sounded behind Draven as Hannelore took to the skies. Her steed continued on its course alongside Seurat and Captain Channon, who rode together in the third chariot. The harpy flew ahead, checking their path to be certain no outlying threats awaited them.

The three black chariots arrived at the seaside castle within the hour, bright torches lining the lane and bridge up to the main courtyard, and large floral bouquets flanking the stone steps. Though hesitantly, Travion's stable hands received the kelpies, taking them to be stabled alongside nervous horses. Entering the castle, Draven swept down the corridors, ignoring a footman who bustled quickly to catch up, wishing to properly announce the arrival of the king of the dark realm.

Draven was surprised and confused to find the air in the castle was not one of hushed concern but rather festive. Servants rushed about with more bouquets of flowers, while, from the northern wing, sounds of instruments being fine-tuned caught his ear.

Taimon, Travion's steward, attempted to halt him in his quick stride, but Draven brushed him off as well, having no desire to stop and speak with the man when he was far more interested in what his brothers had to say for themselves.

Feeling rage beginning to rise up inside of him, Draven marched through the halls, his gray velvet cape snapping behind him in protest. Pushing his way into the throne room, Draven found his brothers both situated at a small table, casually having a cup of wine as they laughed. They fell silent when Draven appeared, his harpy soldier to his right and his were-wolf guard to the left. Seurat, carrying a bag over his arm, brought up the rear.

"Someone had best be dying," he spat out, sensing that the state of emergency his brothers had led him to believe was taking place was far less dire than he had presumed.

"Draven!" Zryan called out, a smile on his face as he stood. "You've arrived. When *was* the last time we three were all in a room together?"

Travion, though he also stood, had the decency to wear a mild look of guilt on his face. Which meant this had been Zryan's doing all along. "Welcome, brother," he uttered.

"You didn't tell him, did you?" came a voice from the doorway.

Draven did not need to look behind him to know that Alessia, his sister-in-law, had entered the room. She made her way to his side, leaning in to press a kiss to his cheek by way of greeting.

"Hello, darling," she murmured, her dark brown eyes offering a silent apology for whatever her husband had planned.

"Hello, Less," he growled back, his pinched features softening slightly.

On her stunning form, Alessia wore a sheer gown of soft blush that flowed down to the floor in cascading ruffles that did nothing to conceal the lean body beneath. Her dark, almost black hair fell over her shoulders, shining in the candlelight from the chandelier overhead. Gliding over to the table, she stole Zryan's wine goblet from his hand and sipped from it.

"Why have you called me here?" Draven demanded. He looked over his siblings as a coiling annoyance tightened his gut and caused his sharpened canines to prick his bottom lip. Dragging his tongue over one fine point, he considered biting a chunk out of his youngest brother simply for the inconvenience of his haste.

"Well, for you to attend this evening's ball, of course!" Zryan was wearing the smug smirk on his features that was all too common and never an omen of good fortune.

"A ball?" Draven sounded dumbfounded because he was. "You called me, last minute, to Midniva . . . for a *ball?*" His eyes narrowed on Zryan's grinning face; over his shoulder, he could see Travion shifting restlessly.

"I told you he would not be pleased," Alessia drawled, having wandered a little ways away with the wine.

"Not just any ball," Zryan continued, ignoring her. "Spring Festivus!" He clapped his hands and moved forward. Zryan's light eyes were full of mirth, and his dark hair was swept back from his face in a careless manner. He had manipulated his way into getting what he wanted, as usual.

Draven simply stared at him, his hands clenched at his sides. "And why do I care about Spring Festivus? It has nothing to do with the tidings in Andhera."

"Zryan . . . and I," Travion began, "felt it would be good for you to join high society for an evening. We see you so rarely these days, it is as if you prefer the dark crevices of Andhera to the company of family." The long sweep of his hair fell over his forehead, threatening to cascade into his eyes, but obeying some unspoken rule, it remained in place. As second born, Travion was the perfect blend of his two brothers.

In truth, Draven did prefer Andhera. This world of sunshine and growth, where springtime was celebrated and nights gave way to the dawn, was a far cry from the eternal darkness of Andhera. Draven was now as foreign a creature to this land as were his subjects.

"Think of it as a chance for brotherly affection," Zryan interjected.

"You thought a ball would be the best opportunity for this?"

"It was Seurat's idea," Zryan stated, smirking.

Behind him, Draven heard Seurat cough in a manner much resembling a gasp of horror. The dark king had little doubt this was a lie.

"I will not be attending the ball. We will return to Andhera at once."

"Come now, Draven. You're already here. What is the harm in staying?" Travion was giving him a pleading look, and Draven couldn't help but wonder what nonsense Zryan had spouted to have him agree with all of this.

"He speaks the truth, and don't make Seurat have brought your freshly pressed garments all this way for naught." Zryan was offering the charming smile that worked on so many in his court but only made Draven's desire to bite something all the fiercer—perhaps the pulse point in his throat.

At the mention of dress clothes, Draven looked back and found a shamefaced Seurat moving forward, the draped bag over his arm. "Forgive me, Your Majesty, but I do have fresh attire for you."

A muscle in Draven's jaw leaped, and he clenched his teeth together. "It would seem," he ground out, "that I am attending the ball."

"Fabulous! Be down in an hour, we wish to greet the guests together. As a family!" Zryan trumpeted in triumph.

Draven did not come down in time to greet the guests as they arrived. The thought of watching each one approach him with apprehension, eyes downcast for fear the nightmare king would steal away their soul, was not at the top of his priorities.

Instead, he allowed Seurat to dress him in a black dress shirt, with a slim-fitted brocade vest over top. It had double rows of brass buttons and leather bindings across the front. Slim black slacks covered his legs, and there was a shining pair of lamia leather boots for his feet. Seurat finished the look off with his velvet cape, looped around his neck and draped over his left shoulder.

Standing in the mirror as Seurat arranged the cape, Draven took in his appearance. The face staring back at him did not appear frightening, though it was severe. Short-cropped auburn hair cast a light shadow over his jaw and softened the rugged nature of his features. Though his blue eyes had hardened over the millennia, they did not denote the extent of the change he had undergone, if one were able to ignore the sheen of predatory light in their depths. It was the sharply pointed canines, exposed when he became angry or hungry, that belied the truth of his transformation.

Unlike his brothers, Draven was no longer a child of the light but one of the beasts that hunted in the shadows.

"Should you feed, Your Grace? Before you go down?" Seurat met his gaze in the mirror, the dark skin of the other man's features a contrast to his own pale cheeks.

"I am sure Travion will have something prepared for me." His brother was aware of the great strain being around those of fae blood was for Draven, their scent a constant, delicious temptation.

He had given in once, in the early years, when living a normal life had still seemed possible. The fae blood on his tongue had been intoxicating, and there had been no way to contain himself. He had killed an innocent that day, no better than the monsters he sought to control, and quickly realized there was no place for him here in the other realms.

"Very well, sir."

Turning from the sight of himself, Draven nodded his thanks and left his chambers. He had purposefully prolonged his preparations, wishing to wait until the majority of the guests had arrived. If he were lucky, Draven would be able to slip into the ball mostly unnoticed and spend the better portion of the night in the recesses of the ballroom.

Descending the grand staircase, Draven could hear the sounds of music filtering from the north wing, the strains a trill of happiness. Following it, he came to stand in the doorway, watching the men and women as they twirled around the dance floor. The gaiety made him snarl, and so he carried himself through the throng of people, making a beeline for the servant holding a tray that bore a single goblet ringed in rubies.

Snatching up the goblet, which he knew contained a mixture of blood and wine, Draven watched the startled servant back away in surprise and quickly composed himself.

"Y-your Grace!"

Draven didn't say anything, merely tipped back the goblet and downed the contents as quickly as he could. Discarding the empty cup back on the tray, he shouldered past the servant and headed toward the terrace. Filled with blood, at least he would be better able to cope with the alluring scents of the fae surrounding him, but he still wasn't sure he could stomach the frightened glances as people recognized him.

There was a reason he stayed away.

Stepping out onto the terrace, Draven drew a deep breath, allowing the fresh spring air of Midniva to calm him. If he stayed out here, he could enjoy being away from Andhera for an evening and avoid the strained conversations that were bound to happen inside. The humans in the ballroom tended to avoid Draven at all costs, seeing him as little more than a beast coming to feed on their life force. The fae were hardly better, gazing at him with disdain for the creature he had become. The reasons for his descent into the dark realm had long since been forgotten by most.

Walking to the edge of the railing, Draven looked down over the garden and noticed a slender form in the dim light.

The young lady, wearing a long sapphire-blue gown with a sweeping skirt that trailed behind her, was stooped over in the garden, rooting around in one of the bushes. Finding himself amused and curious, Draven turned to his

33

right, descended the few steps down into the garden itself, and made his way toward her. As he drew closer, the details of her dress became clearer. Blue sheer over a cream skirt and bodice, decorated in softly falling petals. Like a cherry tree raining blossoms on a warm spring day. The gown itself was off the shoulder, allowing for an expanse of warm, cream flesh to glow in the torchlight around them.

"What, pray tell, are you doing?" he asked, his hands clasped behind his back.

Startled, the young lady nearly toppled into the bush. Righting herself, she turned bashfully and faced him only to find the full skirt of her gown caught on a nearby bush.

"Here, allow me." Draven stepped forward, and reaching out to the rose bush, carefully unpicked the delicate fabric from the cloying thorns. As he straightened, he found a pair of bright green eyes staring up at him in a shy but open manner.

"There are little men in the flowers," she murmured quietly, as if unsure she should've said it at all.

Draven's eyes wandered down to the bush. He half expected to see a goblin tucked away beneath it. "Little men?" He looked at her once more, his features questioning.

A happy trill of laughter left the maiden, her light red hair brought to life by the firelight of the torch nearby. "Not actual men. Look." A slender hand reached out to embrace one of the green floral cups, angling it toward him.

Taking pause for a moment, Draven found himself studying the youthful features before him. Full lips, high cheekbones with a smattering of freckles, and wide, beautiful eyes that seemed to dance with life. Leaning in,

Draven gazed into the cup and smirked at the sight of white petals nestled inside that did, indeed, look like a tiny man.

"It appears he is wearing a hat," Draven commented, and it brought a truly brilliant smile to the young lady's face.

"It does!" she agreed cheerfully.

If Draven could reach out and bottle rays of sunshine, he was certain they would be similar to the happiness radiating from her. Innocence and wonder were ripe upon her, and the warm, tantalizing scent wafting from her spoke of magic. She was fae, and if he could make a guess by her gown, he would say she was one of the Lucem fae, here only for an evening of celebration. But one could never be too sure.

"Do you often wander the gardens finding flower men to keep you company rather than dancing with the actual gentleman at the ball?"

"I don't generally do either. This is the first ball I've ever been to in Midniva . . . and only my second ball in general," the maiden explained.

Draven looked at her in surprise, realizing at once that the innocence about her was not an act but simply the truth of a life yet not experienced.

"Then all the more question as to why I find you out here in the gardens and not inside." Was she also running from the crush of bodies and knowing eyes?

"And miss all of this?" Her hands lifted, indicating the garden surrounding them.

Draven found himself glancing around, and for the first time, truly taking a moment to admire what his brother had built for himself here in Midniva. This inner courtyard was a sanctuary of lush greenery and flora. Soft, sweet scents were carried on the spring breeze from the multitude of flowers bursting with life. In the corners stood lush fruit trees, heavy with blossoms, and in the center sat a marble fountain where a stone satyr danced with a water nymph.

"I must agree with you, this is preferable to anything found inside."

The young fae plucked a hanging blossom from a trellis and brought it to her upturned nose. "Besides, I was curious about King Travion's gardens."

Draven lifted his brows. "Oh? And why is that?"

"I've heard that all three kings have gardens worth coveting, and that because they're all from Lucem, each one pays homage to that in some way."

Draven was close enough to see the fluttering of the pulse in her throat. "And have you seen Lucem's palace gardens?"

She ran her fingertips along the petals of the blossom. "When I was little, my papa brought me to a fete, and I ran into the gardens."

"This seems to be a theme of yours."

Her lips twisted into a sheepish smile, but there was mischief sparkling in her eyes. They were still close enough that when she reached out, she easily tucked the white blossom into a fold of his dress jacket. "It's no secret that I prefer the tranquility of nature to the venomous members of the court." She bit her bottom lip, as if regretting her choice of words, then tapped her finger just below the blossom.

For a brief moment, they shared a smile, which was

quickly interrupted by another voice sounding out, loud and harsh. "Eden! Foolish girl, there you are!"

Draven watched the light die in her eyes as concern and embarrassment filled them instead. Looking over his shoulder, he recognized the stern features of Naya Damaris storming their way. Quickly, Draven looked back to the young woman before him. Offering a dip of his head, he excused himself and headed for the terrace once more.

Naya gave him a horrified glance of recognition in their passing, bowing just enough to be considered acknowledgement. He could just make out the hushed whispers of disapproval as she reached her daughter.

Walking to the doorway leading back into the ballroom, Draven found Zryan leaning there waiting. "I see you've met the young Eden, daughter of the ever-enchanting Naya Damaris . . . " Zryan was smirking, a look in his eyes that Draven did not feel like unpuzzling.

Instead of responding, he stepped past his brother and submerged himself into the tumult of the ball around him.

Eden

Naya wound her arm through Eden's, forcing her to march along. Eden cast a lingering glance over her shoulder at the man, who seemed to disappear into the shadows. A trace of a smile remained as she played over the small but fond moment they'd shared. Not many took time to indulge in the simple pleasures of life. How easy it was to overlook the beauty that surrounded oneself. But he, whoever he was, had done just that without making her feel like a fool.

Except, as her mother carted her back into the palace, she felt every bit a fool. If she could have willed the marble floor to open up beneath her and suck her to the depths of the underworld, well, she might have considered that.

Eden was not a child by any means. She was old enough to be considered for marriage. However, her mother insisted on sheltering her. It was only recently that Eden could endure it no more.

By the sun, I am one hundred and twenty-five years of age.

Every moment, it was as if her mother were breathing down her neck or shifting her across some invisible board of chess. Eden wanted no part of it and knew that if her father were alive, he wouldn't have allowed it either.

"Why must you be such an insolent child? You have no idea . . . " Her mother breathed out slowly, composing herself as if trying to will the red fury from her complexion. People were beginning to look their way, prodding her into calmness.

Eden lowered her gaze to the floor, pretending to occupy herself with the oversized train of her gown. The detailed fabric rustled in her grasp as she pulled it up, but rather than wait, her mother pulled Eden along and nearly sent her toppling to the floor. A startled yelp escaped her, which promptly turned into a nervous bout of laughter.

"Oh, for sun's sake, Eden," Naya ground out under her breath. "Compose yourself. The Omorphia family is here."

It took a healthy amount of self-control to not roll her eyes. While her mother didn't know she'd bumped into Calix at the festival, Eden was certain he wouldn't have cared that her gown was giving her troubles.

She fought hard to contain her nervous laughter, especially as more eyes turned to them, but she felt a particular gaze on her from somewhere in the ballroom. Not amongst the crowd but from elsewhere. She twisted her head, searching for it, and found her gaze settling on the man from the garden.

Inside the palace, Eden could see him better. Even from where she stood, she could tell his hair was auburn, and the candlelight playing off of it only seemed to enhance the red tones. She couldn't detect the color of his eyes from afar, but she could see the crinkling of a smile at the corners, not yet shared with his lips.

His clothing, unlike that of the rest of the guests, was

dark as night, save for the flower she'd gifted him. The dark color highlighted his complexion, allowing his visage to stick out most. Not a boastful costume bright in colors as many of the men seemed to don but something elegant and—as she took note, she blushed—form-fitting.

Eden smiled, trying not to laugh beneath his gaze, but as she did, the man offered a hint of a smile in return.

"Are you even listening to me, Eden?" her mother prompted, yanking her along.

"No." Eden sighed. Another lecture was on the way, of this she was certain. As if the travel from Lucem hadn't been filled with enough of that, Eden braced for more.

Except, as luck would have it, Calix approached her, saving her from another tirade. "Lady Eden, I think it was?" the male fished for her name, smiling.

Eden lifted her eyebrows, surprised he'd remembered her name when there were several other nobles vying for his attention. "You are correct, Lord Calix." Eden reached her hand out to him in greeting.

"You may call me Calix." He bowed his head, gently taking Eden's hand and placing a lingering kiss to the back of it.

Eden turned to see where her mother had gone off to. She spotted her talking to another, but for a moment, her eyes locked on Eden's, and a slow, smug smile spread across her mother's face. *But of course,* she thought. This was exactly what she wanted, wasn't it? With a sigh, Eden decided to give in to the pull of the festivities.

This was why she had longed to come, to be a part of society in some manner. And since she was here, why not experience what it had to offer?

"Very well, Calix. Would you care to dance with me?"

Eden asked, then flushed as his eyes widened. "Was that not right?" she asked quietly.

"No, I mean, of course it was. I've just never been asked for a dance first." Calix inclined his head. "It would be my honor."

Warmth seemed to cling to Calix; it burst from his skin, from his eyes, and even his voice was pleasing to Eden's ears. Yet, as he led her onto the dance floor, it wasn't his eyes she searched for. It was the man from the garden, the one who'd smiled at her from afar. But as the music played, Calix led her into a spirited dance, carefully minding the bunched-up train of her dress.

He led her through several dances until her feet throbbed, her chest felt as if it'd burst, and even the breeze coming off the ocean couldn't cool her down. When she could take no more, Eden made her way to the table of drinks and took up a glass of wine. Crisp berries exploded on her tongue, quenching her thirst but not cooling her.

While she was sipping at a second flute of sparkling wine, Eden's mother approached, her green eyes focusing on her with an intensity she was familiar with.

"I think we should leave soon," Naya murmured, scooping up one of the drinks. "I'm developing a headache, and I'm tired. We still have a long journey home, you know. It'll only tax us both." The skin near her eyes tightened, and a hint of hysteria crept into her gaze. Eden knew that look all too well—it was the one she wore right before she hurled something across the room or caused the nearby plants to wilt.

Her mother was right, of course. Whether or not the headache was made up Eden didn't know, but they did have a long way to travel, the Veil wasn't close to their

41

home, and they'd need to search for a carriage. As much as Eden may have wanted to spend a few more hours in Midniva, exhaustion already tugged at her.

Eden wished to seek out the man she'd spoken to in the garden and ask if perhaps he was willing to share one dance with her before she left. Not once had Eden seen him take to the floor or even ask anyone.

But there was something distinctly off about her mother. She appeared restless, and her pale complexion was flushed. Typically, in such a state, Eden would see the storm rolling in, and falling rains swiftly followed. In this case, she couldn't tell if her mother wanted to scream or bolt; perhaps both.

"Very well."

Her mother nodded in approval. "Let us go. I've said my goodbyes already, and I need to speak with you about what happened in the garden."

Eden set her glass down, scooping up the trail of her gown as she followed her mother through the crowd. "Mama, I know I shouldn't have been out there alone, but why are you so upset?" It was beyond her, and while Eden possessed a wealth of patience, she'd had enough of the runaround and cryptic verses.

Her mother found an alcove in the shadows of the ballroom. Her eyes darted around in search of someone. Who? Eden didn't know. But she found herself looking around too, hoping to find a familiar face, and when she did, her mother's words faded into the din of the room.

"Eden, listen." Naya placed her long finger against Eden's chin and forcefully turned her head to look at her. "That man is—"

"Ladies and lords, may we have your attention please."

King Travion stood, or rather swayed, on a platform at the front of the ballroom. Even from where Eden currently hid with her mother, she could tell he was deep in his cups. His dark auburn hair had loosened from its hold and tumbled down, clinging to his angular jaw.

"Thank you all for attending," Travion began but was cut off as King Zryan leaped up to join him. A charming smile curled his lips as his arm slid around his brother's shoulders. He whispered something to Travion, who then took a seat behind him.

Idly, Eden wondered where Queen Alessia had disappeared to. It was no secret she and her husband were often at odds, which trickled into Lucem's society. On more than one occasion, both of them had taken their marital strife out on their subjects.

"I will speak on my brother's behalf, for he seems to have enjoyed this night far too much already." Zryan winked, then smoothed his hand down the front of his shirt. His eyes scanned the room for a moment, and Eden wasn't sure if it was her imagination or if his smile fell a fraction.

Her mother reached out to Eden, slipping her hand around her wrist, and squeezed firmly. "Let us go, now, Eden."

Frustrated with her mother, she finally broke and quietly snapped. "Why? Why can I not stay? Why must you try and control every aspect of my day?" She tilted her head, assessing her mother, and something akin to fear crept into her gaze.

"Mama," Eden prompted. When it appeared she wouldn't say a word, Eden readied to leave, but her mother's grip tightened all the more. Had the man from the garden witnessed her mother's antics? Eden's gaze traveled to where he stood, but his attention was on King Zryan.

"Because," Naya began, then found who Eden's eyes were trained on. "That *man* you were speaking to is King Draven."

It was as if he'd heard his name fall from her mother's lips, because he turned from looking down on King Zryan —his brother—and homed in on where Eden stood.

Although Zryan continued to speak, all Eden could hear was the thrum of her heart as she attempted to piece every moment of the evening together. Somehow, it didn't make sense. That man couldn't possibly be the king of nightmares, the name none spoke unless they wished to curse another. The wretched, vile king who feasted on blood rather than proper food.

The very image clashed with the gentleman who had entertained her for a moment, had allowed her to gift him a blossom. Her confusion must have been written on her face because while she gaped at him, his expression began to harden.

"I didn't know," Eden finally wheezed, then let her mother guide her through the guests. "I-I didn't . . . He cannot be." Denial snaked its way through her, warring with her experience. Pressure built in Eden's head, making her dizzy as she blindly followed her mother, but they were halted by two guards.

"I'm sorry, Lady Naya, Lady Eden, but no guests are allowed to leave until after the announcement is made."

Scarlet patches mottled Naya's face. Her eyes had grown bloodshot, only adding to her frazzled state. "You cannot be serious. My daughter doesn't feel well."

It wasn't a lie, at least. Perhaps it was the wine, or maybe the latest revelation, but she felt the floor tilt. *Do not faint.*

"It'll take just a moment," one of the guards attempted to soothe Naya.

Eden burned with embarrassment, but instead of feeling heated, she felt cold to the core as fear crept up her spine. Why had King Draven sought her out in the garden? Why had he spoken to her, endured her idle chitchat? Her eyes burned with the threat of unshed tears. If her mother hadn't stumbled on them, what would have transpired?

It didn't matter, for as soon as the announcement was through, she and her mother would be on their way home. Safe.

Draven

That brief moment of sunshine in the garden had evaporated as quickly as it had come. Draven had seen the moment on the young maiden's face when her mother had informed her of who he was. He hadn't needed to be within earshot to know; it had been enough to see the dawning realization in those once happy green eyes, no longer sparkling with friendly interest. It left Draven feeling tired, as interactions with the fae and mortal realms always did.

"Draven, I'm sad to see you haven't availed yourself of any of the vibrant young refreshments present tonight." It was Alessia, appearing from some dark secluded corner, cheeks a little flushed as she slipped up beside him. "Or—did you?"

Her keen eyes flicked quickly between himself and Eden across the ballroom.

Draven eyed her dryly and reached out to tuck a few tousled hairs behind her ear, hiding the only evidence of her dalliance. He harbored no ill will toward his sister-in-law. Zryan had long ago lost any faithfulness owed to

46

him, and Draven had seen enough of the pain in Alessia's eyes.

"Hardly." While his youngest brother had turned Lucem into a land of lasciviousness and frivolity, Draven had no desire to succumb to the allure of it. Least of all with an innocent noble who would only find herself tainted by any intimacy with the dark king.

Zryan was still spouting off about friends and family, giving the sort of speech meant to incite loyalty in people, and Draven wished to be anywhere but here. On the road back to Andhera would be preferable, and his eyes sought Hannelore in the crowd, her dark feathered wings not hard to spot amongst bright colors of spring. She stood apart from them, a lone sentry preparing for battle.

Channon's blond head was lost somewhere in the throng, and instead of finding him, Draven's eyes landed once more on the young maiden from the garden. Eden. A delicate blossom just on the cusp of blooming. Across the crowded space, their eyes locked, and he could read an unspoken question in the depths of them.

Was he? Was he truly the king of nightmares?

"It is with great joy and much excitement that I announce the joining of two great houses!" Zryan was calling out. "For unwavering loyalty to our family, I wish to gift Lady Naya Damaris a crown through the union of her daughter Eden to my brother, King Draven of Andhera."

If there was a sound more quiet than silence, it filled the ballroom now. It was the steady paling of Eden's features that made Draven believe what he had just heard was true. Even though his brother couldn't have *possibly* just declared he would be wedding a young maiden without first discussing it with him.

47

The need for his presence at this ball suddenly became all too clear.

"I don't understand." It was Naya speaking. Pushing through other guests so that she could stand in plain sight of the three kings. "You think you can just hand my daughter off to the dark king?" There was a rage building inside of Naya Damaris, one which left no room for doubt concerning her thoughts on this arrangement.

With a growl, Draven moved to grab Zryan's arm, at the same time that Travion, drunk but still able to read a room, came forward, a glass of champagne raised high in the air.

"Let us celebrate! To the happy union!" Travion shouted, and the rest of the room sounded out with their own cheerful cries, more out of a sense of responsibility than any true joy.

"Don't kill him yet," Alessia muttered to Draven before moving quickly to stand beside Travion, raising her hands to clap and using her body to shield the two brothers from view.

With Travion distracting the room, Draven hauled Zryan off to the side, his face set in hard lines, eyes gleaming with the threat of violence as he met those of his youngest brother. "What in the name of the eternal afterlife are you thinking? Zryan, I am *not* marrying that young lady!" Draven hissed softly.

"You speak of her as if she were barely out of the nursery. Eden is at least a century old, if not more."

"A *century*!" Draven spat it like a filthy word. What was a century to either of them but a mere moment in the long length of their lives?

The hand that still held onto his brother's arm tightened and, fearing he may actually rip it from its socket, he withdrew himself. This sort of manipulative treachery was not unheard of for Zryan, but this was the first time in all their years that he'd ever focused it on Draven.

"Hear me out, brother," Zryan began.

"No," Draven growled. "There is nothing to be heard. You will go back out there and declare this all a farce for the sake of a good laugh."

"Draven, I can't." The joviality that typically resided within Zryan's eyes was gone. For once, he leveled a serious look on him. Stepping closer, he lowered his voice so that no one close by would hear, Alessia least of all. "I have reason to believe Naya is plotting against me. I haven't proof for you in this moment, but I am close, I am sure of it."

Draven's eyes narrowed. "Plotting? How?"

"She is seeking to undermine my marriage by informing Alessia of my . . . indiscretions. I'm not certain how she is becoming aware of them, but there are spies in my house."

Draven ground his teeth as he listened to his brother. All of this was because Zryan did not wish for his wife to hear of yet another woman he had bedded behind her back? As if she were not already aware of it all.

"And what has this to do with me wedding Naya's daughter?"

"You needn't wed her . . . Unless you wish it." For a moment, the spark of mischievous chaos returned to Zryan's eyes. "I saw the way you looked at her in the garden." A growl from Draven silenced him on this train of thought. "I need the daughter gone. Perhaps once she realizes I can disrupt her life in such a way, Naya will cease her attempts to disrupt mine and allow Alessia and I to return to our happy, blissfully unaware existence."

49

Draven turned on his heel to pace away from his brother, only to stop and storm back. "If you believe Alessia to be unaware of what you are doing, with or without Naya's help, you are an even greater fool than I thought. And I cannot take Eden to Andhera! She is an innocent waif . . . The dark realm will destroy her, and you know it. I won't have that on my conscience. Give her to Travion."

Zryan chortled, waving the notion off. "No child of Naya or Lelantos could ever be a waif. Lelantos was one of the best advisors I ever had." A look of regret passed briefly through his eyes. "She cannot reside here in Midniva, it is too close. I want her firmly tucked away in Andhera . . . with you." His eyes gleamed.

"No."

"Give me a year."

"No! In that amount of time, the powers of Andhera will have transformed her, and there will be no returning to Lucem for her. If it is her mother who has annoyed you, Eden should not be the one to pay."

"Fine," Zryan relented. "Give me six months. By then, I will have smoked out her accomplices, I am sure of it."

Draven ground his teeth, feeling the bite of sharp fangs against his bottom lip as his blood seethed with fury. Had Zryan simply come to him with this plan, they could have discussed it together. Instead, he and Travion had sprung this on him, as if he hadn't a say in the matter at all. Draven had no desire to be pulled into the immature schemes of the Lucem court, yet it would seem that was to be the case.

Zryan was eyeing him as if his happiness boded on Draven's compliance.

"Fine. Six months," he relented.

Lucem was no longer his home, and the fae there were no longer his people. It was not up to him how Zryan sought to punish his subjects, just as his brothers did not interfere in Andherian law.

"And Draven, she cannot find out."

"I am not a simpleton," he muttered. "I know." That was his final word before he swept the cape off his shoulder and strode out into the ballroom, feeling eyes upon him, both curious and abhorrent.

Snatching a glass of champagne off a nearby tray, Draven walked calmly up to Eden. Ignoring the hatred spewing from Naya Damaris' eyes, he bowed lightly and extended his hand to the maiden. He could see she wanted none of it, but clearly too afraid to cause a scene, Eden accepted his hand.

His long fingers curled around her dainty hand, feeling how they trembled with fear. It hardened him, forcing Draven to retreat into the cold facade of the King of Andhera so that he would not relent and tell her to flee. For the sake of family loyalty, he would play out this twisted charade.

Drawing the shocked looking Eden into the center of the room, Draven lifted his champagne glass. "To my beautiful bride. May our happiness ever endure!" Tipping back the glass, he drank down the sparkling nectar, feeling his stomach recoil in protest. Then, with a forceful throw, he tossed the crystal to the dance floor and motioned for the music to strike up once more.

A deafening cheer rang out as Draven pulled Eden in flush against his body, one arm tight around her slender waist, the other lifting her hand up in the air between them. The people did enjoy a good show, and what could be better than a sacrificial lamb led off to the slaughter? Eden's trembling had increased, and had it not been for his own steady form holding her aloft, Draven was certain the lady would have crumpled to the floor.

"Keep a smile on your face for the moment," Draven leaned in to murmur into her ear. "Once the dance is over and they have had their fill of this, we may speak."

Though she still trembled, Draven watched as Eden straightened her back, finding her center. There was a strength in the delicate bloom of her naivety that he was pleased to see.

"So much for innocent conversations in the garden," were the words she uttered. Soft, but filled with anger and hurt.

Having nothing he could say to explain this situation, Draven remained silent. For the remainder of the dance, he kept his eyes focused just above her head, taking note of those who watched them closely. Wondering which amongst them believed Eden Damaris was going off to Andhera to die.

As he swept her around the ballroom, Draven did his best not to inhale the sweet scent of magic coming from Eden. With each rapid thump of her frightened heart, the divine elixir flowing through her veins tempted him. Feeling the sharp prick of his teeth once again, Draven closed his eyes, taking in a deep breath.

It was a startled gasp from Eden that forced his eyes open and drew them down to her face once more. She was staring up at the indent of his fangs on his bottom lip, looking ever the picture of a timid critter caught in a predator's clutches.

"Your . . . you . . . " she stammered, searching for words.

The end of the dance saved them both, and Draven dropped her down into a deep dip to the delight of the two kingdoms watching. Righting her once more, he pulled away, placing her small hand upon the crook of his arm. With his own hand keeping Eden there, he walked her back over to where her mother awaited.

Zryan had woven his way through the crowd, with Alessia at his side, and joined them before Naya. Although he grinned, his wife coolly assessed first Naya, then Eden and Draven. "Splendid! Now that the family is all together, let's have a chat."

5

Eden

How could a room change so drastically? The ballroom, which had been gravely silent, filled with music as Draven swept Eden across the floor. He spared few words for her, but in his defense, she gave him little to work with.

Her feet still ached from dancing with Calix, but the irony wasn't lost on her, not as she recalled desperately searching out the man who held her now and wishing that, instead of the blond, it was him. Now he held her, and it wasn't at all how she'd imagined it would be. It was cold, withdrawn, and forced.

What was worse: Draven had known. He'd *known* who she was in the garden and he'd sought her out, for what? His sordid entertainment? To play with her and make her feel all the more foolish? She regretted her impulsive decision to respond to the invitation, loathed herself for escaping into the garden alone, and was kicking herself for thinking she could have one moment in her life remain unblemished. But she couldn't, because she was reckless, at least, that was what had been hammered into her head.

It was at the end of the dance, when Eden caught a glimpse of his fangs, that he truly became the king of nightmares, and her sovereign had just handed her over to him.

As she and her betrothed approached her mother, Eden saw the fury melding with fear, and it resided within her too. But she couldn't say a word; she didn't dare speak out against not one but *four* royals.

Eden kept her eyes averted from Zryan, even as he merrily declared her family. Alessia's bottomless gaze met hers on more than one occasion, lacking the warmth her husband's words possessed.

"Let us find a more suitable place to speak," Zryan offered, then slid from the ballroom without another word, although his eyes did flick to Draven once, as if silently communicating with him.

Travion had the decency to send Eden a glance, and within it, she read *I'm sorry*. But it didn't matter how sorry he was, for it was already done.

Naya remained silent on their way through the hall, but Eden felt the tension rippling from her. It was a feeling she knew all too well and had experienced more than she cared to admit.

When they had all filed into a sitting room, the door clicked shut and Naya's demeanor changed. She coiled like a snake readying to strike, her eyes frenzied with barely restrained hysteria.

"*Your Majesty*." Naya hissed the title. "You cannot marry my daughter off to King Draven. She is far too young and knows so little of our world, let alone Andhera!" She motioned to Eden, who, for the moment, remained frozen in place against Draven.

Travion flopped into a leather chair, stroking the fine red beard on his chin. Zryan's eyes filled with a clever light as he leaned against the wall, as if Naya's pleading only amused him.

Alessia remained standing in the far corner of the room, watching the entire ordeal like she was a hawk considering mice in a field.

Was this all a game to them? Eden withdrew herself from Draven, but she didn't go far. It was only so she could sit in a chair and finally breathe. *In, out,* she reminded herself. But pain blossomed in her chest from gulping down too much air, and she felt the prick of tears in her eyes, felt the heat rush into her pale cheeks.

"Actually." Zryan motioned with his hand, an arrogant tilt to his chin. "I can. You cannot call Eden a child for a lifetime. She is a young fae Lady, and it's time you treated her as such instead of hiding her and debilitating her. She *should* be betrothed already . . . " He shot a slanted look toward the corner of the room and amended his last words. "If she so pleased. But how could she, when you have her tethered like a disobedient youngling?" His cool green eyes slid toward Eden, raking her over with more than a passing glance.

"She is too weak, too naive for Andhera! She will perish in weeks." Naya stepped forward, curling her fingers into her palms. "I will not sentence my daughter to die."

Eden's brow furrowed as the words her mother spat so carelessly pricked her like barbs. Naive she may have been because of how Naya Damaris kept her daughter hidden away, but fragile? Eden was no such thing. To know how her mother viewed her as such stung.

Alessia hissed. "I'm not sure what I find more offensive:

your lack of faith in your daughter's constitution or your assumption my brother would carelessly allow her to die in his care."

Zryan hurled another remark at Eden's mother, but she didn't hear it. She focused on what her mother had said, how she felt about her daughter, and it was her words that finally broke the dam of tears welling in her eyes.

In all of her years, she'd heard nothing but horror stories of Andhera, of how it was a wicked realm where monsters roamed. Eden's king, and once her father's friend, was carelessly dumping her in a land of death and decay.

With each beat of her heart, Eden was certain she'd tip forward and black out as panic crept up her neck, but she was frozen in place.

They all were occupied with Naya, except for Draven. He hadn't spoken a word, hadn't budged from where he stood, which was still in front of Eden. She glanced up at him, assuming her expression showed exactly how she felt: full of hurt and betrayal.

Draven's eyes were blue, Eden finally took note. He had done so well to avoid her eyes while dancing that she hadn't even noticed. But now, as he stood a foot away from her, staring down at her with a furrowed brow, she saw how blue they were. At the moment, they were as dark as Midniva's turbulent waves and as unforgiving. His demeanor, coupled with the fangs she'd seen earlier, brought a chill to her.

Had he said nothing because he knew? Eden didn't want to believe it, but he must have. Why else would he find her? As her mind raced, she lifted her hands to her heated, wet cheeks and focused on the moment the invitation arrived. *Had it all been a setup?*

They were all still talking, mostly over one another, when Eden drew in a shaky breath, and on the exhale, she spoke. "When do I leave?" Draven shifted, but Eden no longer glanced up at him. She dropped her hands into her lap and looked at the others. "When do I leave?" she repeated more firmly.

Travion stood, his gaze flicking from Zryan to Draven. An unspoken sentiment shifted between them, whatever it was.

It surprised Eden how quiet Draven was. A different sort of storm appeared to be brewing within him, and it wasn't the sort she was accustomed to with her mother, loud, quick, and destructive. But Eden feared this new unknown, for Draven was the king of the underworld, and who could say what sort of destruction he could leave in his path without ever uttering a word.

"Tonight is when you'll depart." Zryan pushed off of the wall, approaching Eden and readying to inch between her and Draven, but the dark king didn't budge, which stopped Lucem's king in his tracks. Zryan did, however, kneel before her.

"Andhera has never had a queen, and it is time it had one. My brother, though fierce, cannot do it alone. He needs someone by his side. That someone is you." Zryan looked over his shoulder, shooting Naya a look of disgust. "I would be honored to have a peer of my realm, you, Lady Eden, become my sister."

Eden choked on an involuntary sob. "If I must, then so be it." For what else could she say when not one but all four sovereigns wished it?

Zryan gently patted one of her hands, then stood.

"Can we at least have a moment together?" Naya looked askance between the royals.

Travion nodded. "Of course. We can allow that, can't we?" His auburn eyebrows shifted as he glanced toward the door. "When you are through, Eden must remain by Draven's side for the duration of their time here. As his betrothed, it is expected."

After the men left the room, Eden stood and found herself looking up at Alessia. She quickly averted her eyes but gasped as the queen's warm fingers took her by the chin. "My darling, you are in capable hands. Sometimes, a life must crumble before a new one can be molded in its place." She released Eden's chin and swept a few locks of her hair behind her ear. "Be well, Eden."

Once the queen stepped outside the room, her mother rushed forward and embraced her. "I detest her," Naya whispered but silenced her next words as Eden's resolve dissolved. She sobbed into the crook of her mother's neck.

"I will fix this. I will find a way." Naya rocked Eden to and fro, stroking her long hair. "This is why I hid you away. Don't you know that the kings are nothing more than tyrants? I should have hidden you better and told you more." Tears filled Naya's eyes as she cupped Eden's cheeks.

"I'm sorry. I'm sorry I didn't listen and that I went behind your back." Oh, and she was. No words could ever hope to explain how sorry she felt for thinking herself so clever by responding to the invitation. It was a feeling far worse than the sting of a hand against Eden's cheek.

A knock on the door told Eden that their time was up.

Naya swept her thumbs beneath Eden's eyes, wiping

59

the tears away, along with any hint of kohl that may have run down her face. "In the meantime, be careful."

Eden nodded, her lips parting to say something, but the words were silenced as the door swung open. Draven glowered at Naya.

One last time, Eden watched her mother walk away, then scooped the trail of her dress up and closed the distance between herself and the king. "When do we leave precisely?" she questioned but didn't meet his gaze. Instead she looked at his shoulder.

"Now. Sunrise is soon, and we still must journey to the Veil."

Eden swallowed roughly, nodding, then mentally prepared to embark for the Veil. She wondered how an evening, which had started so lovely, could end so tragically.

Draven

Draven had considered a queen once, back in the early years of his kingdom's first peace. Before the insurrection of the shifters pairing with the lamia in an attempt to overthrow his rule had quickly wiped that notion from his mind. Andhera was a cold, cruel, and brutal place that did not leave room for the weak to obtain happiness. Any joy was hard sought and won only through pain and blood. It was not a kingdom in search of a queen, for its king would condemn no female to such a fate.

Had he chosen it, however, this was not how he would have seen it through.

Draven had gone to fetch both Hannelore and Channon while Eden took the time to say goodbye to her mother. He hadn't any words for Zryan at the moment, and if he took the time to stop and speak to him, he was certain his brother would be missing his jugular by the time he was finished. So, instead, Draven focused on gathering his guard.

"We are leaving at once. Channon, Seurat will take your chariot on his own. Shift now and go with us as a wolf."

Without question, the young were-wolf discarded his clothing there in the hall and shifted into the large gray wolf that was his other form. Standing as tall as Draven's shoulder, his cool steely eyes watched and waited for his lord to move.

"Hannelore, I am depending on you to be a vigilant eye on our travels. Eden is a novice who must be protected at every turn. She has made the journey through the Veil only once; I will not stand for any mishaps."

"Of course, My Lord. May I ask . . . "

"No," he stated curtly and turned on his heel, heading back to the study to acquire his new ward.

Seurat found him before he had made it to the door, looking downcast and worried. "I am sorry, Your Majesty. Had I known—"

Draven held up a hand to halt him in his speech, his fury too ripe to handle words of explanation from anyone. "Now is not the time," he told the other male, gazing at his dark features with their scattering of scales, the only hint of what lay beneath his flesh. "Go and have our mounts prepared. We leave at once."

Seurat left quickly, disappearing down the corridor.

Before he could knock on the door, Draven found Alessia at his side, her beautiful features pinched in a frown. She'd placed her hand on his elbow, seeking to draw his attention to her.

"Draven, I don't know what Zryan's foolish purpose is, but you needn't agree to this. You know that, right?"

He only growled in response. Draven had no desire to

be drawn into the marriage struggles between Zryan and Alessia. His brother ought to be drawn and quartered for the way he whored around on such a female as his sister-in-law.

"I am aware. But it would seem Zryan is adamant that the young lady come with me." He eyed Alessia, the truth just on the tip of his tongue.

"Darling!" The voice belonged to Zryan, coming to capture his wife's attention away and shooting Draven a warning glance. "Let's leave Draven be. He has so very much planning to take care of."

Rolling her eyes, Alessia allowed Zryan to tug her farther down the hall. The last that Draven saw, Zryan was mouthing *Good luck* to him over his shoulder.

Turning his attention back to the door, Draven paused. The blossom Eden had tucked into the lapel of his vest earlier that evening caught his eye. It was a reminder of how fresh and full of life she had been in that garden, completely unaware of what a careless ruler had planned for her. Reaching up, Draven pulled the flower from its place and crushed it in his palm, then let it flutter, broken, to the ground.

Beautiful, delicate things did not last in Andhera, and he would not have been deserving of them even if they did.

Eyes lifting to the door once more, Draven rapped briskly upon it, making his presence known to mother and daughter, and steeled himself for the journey ahead.

Only icy glares were shared between him and Naya, neither ashamed to let their dislike of the other shine through. He could only assume what Naya thought of him, the dark king who had come to steal her precious, innocent daughter away for his nefarious purposes. And Draven had not appreciated the way Naya had spoken of Eden, as if she were not but a kitten to be trodden under foot. Her daughter had more strength within her than she dared to notice.

A strength that was apparent as Eden faced him, asking for a definitive time that they would leave.

"Now. Sunrise is soon, and we must still journey to the Veil."

With a nod, Eden stepped into the hall, only balking when Hannelore stepped into view. The sheer size of a harpy was impressive. While they still bore the form of a woman, their steel gray wings stretched a full twelve feet when unfurled. Their legs finished off at the knee with the tough flesh of a hawk's leg and foot, sharp talons clicking on the floor with every step they took. Hannelore, dressed in her armored chest plate and chainmail skirt, was all the more threatening for it. Her feathered hair, plucked at the sides with only the top left to trail long down her back, was a blue streak of beauty.

"My Lady," Hannelore began. "Come with me."

Eden spared only a quick glance at Draven, barely meeting his eyes before falling into step with Hannelore. Watching them walk away, Draven reached out to brush a hand down Channon's back. The fur was soft and reminded him that the comforts of his own space awaited him at the end of this journey.

"You needn't leave already, brother." Zryan stepped up beside him, having returned from wherever he'd led Alessia off to.

Shooting Zryan a glare, Draven held in a snarl. "The sun will be up in a few hours, and I don't feel like being rushed during my trip home, as I now have another unexpected passenger to get through the Veil."

"Thank you for your aid."

"Don't thank me yet." Draven shook his head. "There may very well be blood before this is through."

Clicking his tongue at Channon, he strode away from Zryan, following after his harpy soldier and his new ward.

They were already outside, standing before the chariots, when Draven caught up with them. Channon sat back on his large haunches, panting softly as he gazed over Eden, who was now shrinking back in horror as she took in their full convoy.

"Seurat, you will take Channon's chariot. Eden, you will ride with me."

"Wh-what?" Eden stammered.

Shooting her a glance, Draven sighed wearily. "You will ride with me. Unless you think you can control a kelpie-drawn chariot for the very first time?" he asked irritably.

All he received in reply was a shake of her head. Moving to his chariot, Draven motioned for her to climb in. Once she'd clambered up with her ridiculous volume of skirts, filling almost the entirety of the space with her gown, he could only bite back words of agitation. Channon, who stood behind him, let out a wolfish bark that sounded much like a chuckle.

Draven shot him a silencing glare, and the were-wolf had the decency to bow his head in remorse.

Climbing into the chariot himself, Draven pushed aside Eden's voluminous dress as best he could, wrapping his arms around her slight form so that he could gather the reins and prepare himself.

"You will want to hold on," was his only warning before

he slapped the reins. Rayvnin reared up, pulling ahead of the other chariots and taking Draven and Eden along with him. His hands tightened on the leather as he felt the tug in his forearms and shoulders, his feet bracing firmly on the floor of the chariot to keep him upright as they raced from the courtyard.

Eden fell against his chest, the weight of her light but searing, a reminder of what he was taking back with him. She didn't remain pressed into him long but quickly righted herself, her hands clutching onto the front of the chariot.

Draven felt a flash of pride, for as they left the castle of Midniva behind, Eden kept her gaze before her, not allowing herself to look back at all she was leaving.

The trek across the middle realm took an hour, and they reached the Veil with time to spare, the horizon beyond still dark. Bringing Rayvnin to a halt, Draven allowed Channon to cease his constant gallop beside them, his pink tongue hanging from the side of his snout as he panted. Seurat, looking a little worse for wear, pulled up on his right, his dark coil of hair the only thing about him not appearing distressed.

Hannelore, knowing her place, waited until she was ahead of them before drawing to a stop. She looked to Draven quickly, then proceeded with her plan.

"Channon, you'll take my chariot now. I'll be in the air for the duration of our pass through the Veil. Seurat, you are to stay behind our master. Sire, you will take up the front, with Channon bringing up the rear."

Draven nodded his agreement. "Then let us go." Reaching to the clasp at his shoulder, he undid the cape from himself, settling it around Eden instead.

She turned her head as if to look back at him and speak. Instead, she merely pulled the cape more securely around herself.

"Should anything happen in the Veil . . . do not wander off the path. No matter what may happen."

"Wh-what?" Her words were whispered and filled with uncertainty.

"One may get lost in the void that lies within the Veil. Never stray from the path."

"Do you plan for us to get out of the chariots once we're in there?"

"No." But his words of wisdom still stood. One could never be certain of what would be waiting for them on the other side of the arch.

A naked Channon, now shifted back into his human form, stepped forward to take the harpy's chariot. Relieved of her reins, Hannelore rose into the air, claiming a position that would give her clear sightlines to anything seeking to come after them. Together, the convoy entered the Veil, quickly falling into the formation the harpy captain had set for them.

Draven had always found that passing through the arch into the Veil was like walking through a wall of water that did not leave one feeling wet. It was a space at once with light and without. Large puffs of dark fog swirled through it, casting shadows where there was nothing. The Veil looked almost as if there were no substance to it, the ground both there and fading away once looked upon.

The path, which led through the Veil to each of the arches, was one that could not be directly looked at. So Draven kept his gaze fixed on a location in the distance and traveled by way of his peripherals. Should he have looked directly down at the path, it would have disappeared, leaving him feeling as if he were traveling on nothing at all.

It was a place meant to disorientate, and Draven had no desire to be lost and wandering the emptiness for all eternity. Souls lost themselves here in a trap there was no escaping from.

It was the shrill wail from one such soul that caused Draven to realize Eden had collapsed against his form, her body slack and lifeless. Unwilling to stop, knowing it would only put her in more danger, he transferred both reins to one hand and curled his free arm around her body. He was not surprised that this was the moment that finally broke her.

Nestling her against his chest, Draven took a moment to gaze down on her ashen features, red lashes resting over freckled cheeks. Eden was a lovely creature, all elegance and grace. Andhera was not the world for her, as it was not the world for many. He wasn't certain how he was meant to keep the smile on her lips in the land of two moons, but perhaps if he gave her the freedom to explore in the way she had never been allowed to before, these months in hell would not weigh too harshly upon her.

When at last they broke through the other side of the Veil and entered Andhera, everyone took a welcomed breath of relief. Their party halted once more, and Draven took the chance to lift Eden into his arms, carrying her over to a small grassy knoll and laying her down on it. Behind them, Channon conversed with Hannelore over whether he was more useful in wolf form, or she in the air.

Brushing red strands out of Eden's eyes, Draven felt a

mounting need to keep this innocent being safe. So many things in his kingdom would try and tear her down. Would her fortitude last?

"Does she need water, my lord?" Seurat was at his side, a waterskin in his hand.

"When she wakes, yes." Draven stood, straightening his vest. "Did you know?" he questioned, voice low and dangerous.

His manservant looked shamefaced and regretful as he met his eye tentatively. "Of the ball . . . yes. But not of this." Seurat motioned to the unconscious fae. "I am sorry, sire . . . I thought only to bring you much needed interaction."

Draven felt the stern frown hardening his features, his disapproval evident on his face. "I had not thought you would set the desires of my brothers above my own, Seurat. I am disappointed in the placement of your loyalty tonight."

Seurat, looking stricken, could only nod.

"See if you can rouse her, we must be on our way." Draven left them then to join his army captain and the captain of his wolf guard.

"Your Majesty." Hannelore dipped her head respectfully as he approached them. "We think it best if Captain Channon shifts back to a wolf from here on out. I will take up my place at the back, and he will run ahead."

Draven nodded. "Agreed. Channon's nose is of more use now that we have entered the woods."

Around them, giant trees stretched toward the blue moon overhead. It cast their gnarled branches in a silver sheen, highlighting the white leaves that glowed faintly until the yellow moon of day rose and the glow was no longer needed.

"The manticores have been riled as of late, so we must make our journey through as quietly and quickly as possible."

Draven eyed Hannelore. "Did Travion not send this month's convicted?" The harpy shook her head, which drew a curse from the king's lips. "So they have not fed." Draven sighed. Of course the shipment of Midnvia's worst, sentenced to death, had not arrived yet.

The trio glanced over to where Eden now sat, Seurat comforting her as best he could and offering her a drink of water. The manticores would never dare to attack the king's convoy, not on a typical day. But what would the scent of fresh fae do to them?

"Seurat, we leave at once!" Draven called, then eyed his guards. "Keep a watchful eye on the tree line. If you see anything, do not hesitate to kill. Now is not the time for mercy."

Channon quickly shifted, and Hannelore moved to take up her position in her chariot, her bow now gripped securely in her hand. Moving to his own chariot, Draven watched Eden approach, her eyes once again set somewhere over his shoulder so that their gazes did not meet.

"My lady," he murmured, motioning to the chariot.

Silently, Eden stepped up into it once more, reclaiming her position at the front, hands already clasped around the silver rail. Climbing in behind her, Draven's arms wrapped around Eden, his senses awash with her intoxicating scent yet again. If the rarity of fae blood was such a torment to him, how much worse would it be for the true monsters in the wood? The thirst for sunshine may drive them mad.

With a snap of the reins, they were off, Channon running ahead of them. Draven could only hope that their presence would go mostly unnoticed. It seemed luck was on their side until the open landscape of Andhera came into view. From the tree line on his left, Draven could see glowing green eyes watching them from the shadow of a humanoid face. A soft gasp from Eden let him know she had seen it as well.

"What is that?" she rasped, hands tightening on the rail before her.

"Pay it no mind," he said more calmly than he felt. Behind him, the twang of a bow sounded out, quickly followed by an echoing roar of pain.

Spurring his steed on faster, Draven focused on breaking the tree line and getting out into the open where the manticore would have no place to hide, trusting the harpy to handle the beast behind them.

"Wait! It's attacking!" Eden had whipped around to look behind them, her body bent partially over his arm. "We can't simply leave her."

"Hannelore will be fine, now straighten up!" His arm jerked her, needing the weight of her torso off him as he sought to control the pull of the kelpie. Draven was surprised at her concern for someone who had already passed from living into unliving and had been deemed a monster by most.

Another roar pierced the air, followed by the scrape of claws on steel—Hannelore was now battling with the beast in close proximity. Draven wished to spare her a look, to be certain he hadn't just left her to meet the final death, but there wasn't time for it.

Once they broke from the tree line and out into the open landscape, Channon began to circle them in large loops, keeping his eyes on the hills for anything approaching. Draven took a moment to look over his shoulder, just in time to see Hannelore cleave the beast's head from its shoulders. Grunting in relief, he returned his gaze to the remainder of their journey.

In the night, the landscape was bathed in a bluish darkness that made each marker blend into the next. It was the perfect hunting time for anything looking to feast. For Draven, one of those very predators, his eyes adjusted easily enough, keeping the world in crisp detail. He could only imagine how the darkness appeared to Eden, however.

The day would be better for her. During the day, the yellow moon washed the land with enough light that one could get around outside without the need of torches, if only just.

The moment in the woods had left Eden shaking, which did not cease for the remainder of their journey. But to her credit, the young woman remained upright. It would seem she had found her backbone once more.

The first gleam of the yellow moon was just beginning to show itself as they approached his castle, traveling the long road through hills dotted with gnarled trees, jagged rocks, and every so often, a stone hut.

The castle itself sat upon a sharp cliff that pierced the skyline like a scythe. He'd built the stone fortress at the very top, so that it looked down over the valley and its sprawling city on one side and the dark crevice situated at the bottom of the cliff on the other. The crevice was a direct portal into the afterlife—a realm there was no coming back from.

Sharp black turrets rose up from the castle, lit with the faint glow of torches. The large wooden doors in the walls surrounding the structure, which could be closed to cut it off from the rest of the land, remained open. King Draven did not fear his land or his people. He had spent his first brutal century here proving to all who truly ruled this realm.

Trailing down the front side of the cliff and leading down to the land were a series of stately homes and estates. Here the nobility lived, those who had traveled into Andhera to found it all those eons ago.

As they passed through the dark cobblestone streets of his capital city, Eden remained silent, abhorring everything around her Draven was certain. He, too, stayed quiet until he'd drawn his chariot up before his castle steps and a panting Channon had morphed back into his human form.

"Welcome to Castle Aasha." Stepping down, he handed the reins to the young revenant who came floating over the courtyard, his appearance at once solid and temporary.

Extending a hand, Draven aided Eden down out of the chariot, motioning for Seurat to follow behind them. "Come, I am sure you are tired. I will take you to a room where you can sleep for now."

Draven glanced at Seurat, who understood his silent question. "The study in the east wing, sire, would be the best."

Out of a sense of duty, Draven offered his arm to Eden, who took it with some hesitation. Walking her through the halls of his home, Draven saw it with different eyes.

Though the torches brought a warm light to the gray stone walls, it was a vast, empty space, with little to offer in ornamentation. It was not a place to welcome anyone happily into its embrace.

As they reached the study, Draven opened the door and walked her in. The east study was a cozier place than most, one of the spaces that Travion and Zryan tended to inhabit on the rare occasions they stepped foot in Andhera. A large fireplace filled most of one wall, and a few red velvet armchairs surrounded it, with a desk to one side and a wall of books behind it.

Swiping a hand out before him, Draven lit the sconces on the walls so that the room had enough lighting for Eden to see.

"This is where I will sleep?" She spoke, a tremble of uncertainty in her tone.

"For now, until we can prepare a chamber of sorts for you."

"I don't . . . even have a bed." Her words tumbled out of her softly, and fresh tears followed, streaming down her cheeks, shimmering in the torchlight.

Draven was aghast and looked to Seurat for aid. Comforting weeping maidens was not his standard practice.

"I can acquire a chaise lounge for the lady," Seurat offered. "I'll have the revenants bring one shortly."

Nodding, Draven peered over at Eden. "In our land, most creatures here do not sleep. Bed chambers are not a necessary luxury."

"Luxury!" She sobbed the word, a hand coming up to cover her lips. "Please, just leave me be."

Abiding by her wishes, Draven backed out through the

door and closed it behind her. Seurat, the gentler of the two, would return soon enough and be there to answer any questions she may have.

With a weariness that was unnatural to him, Draven carried himself down the long corridors to where his own study sat. Stepping inside, he closed the door with a heavy thud, warding off any who would dare to disturb him.

What nonsense had Zryan dumped into his hands now?

Eden

The journey through the Veil had been far more taxing and horrifying than the one from Lucem to Midniva. Perhaps she'd blocked out the screeching, moaning, and feeling as though eyes were following her because she'd been so excited to reach another realm. But this time, horror filled Eden to the brim. She hadn't wanted to succumb to the dizzying feeling. She'd never swooned in her life, but everything clashed together at once. The news, the sounds belonging to distant monsters in the Veil's wickedness. There was no fighting that.

Even as she slumped, she felt Draven stir, his arms forming a steel cage around her, and her last thought had been that at least she wouldn't perish in the Veil, not as long as he kept his arms around her.

But when she woke, even the offering from a friendly face did nothing to quell the panic within. It was dark, so wretchedly dark that she could barely see beyond the male soothing her. *What had his name been?* she found herself wondering.

It didn't matter, for they weren't stationary for long. She was pulled into the chariot with Draven once more, all too aware of the hard planes of his body against hers. With his cape still around her, he invaded all of her senses. The aroma of woods and a hint of florals tickled her nose, but all thoughts of what Draven smelled like vanished the moment things became dire.

Eden wanted to believe Draven, that Hannelore would be fine, but when she glanced behind them, her hair whipping into her face, she beheld the harpy battling the manticore and wished she hadn't had the courage to do so. Whether the female behind them was of the dark world or not, Eden didn't want her to die.

Discord surrounded them, but she kept her eyes trained forward, willing herself to block out the snarling and snapping of teeth. Against her wishes, Eden trembled like a leaf in the wind, her teeth chattering. It didn't cease until they arrived in a more populated area.

Compared to Lucem's soft, vibrant beauty, this place was the exact opposite. There were no pink or yellow blooms dancing in the warm breeze, there were only gnarled trees, harsh lines, and jagged rocks. Even the homes they passed, although they made Eden wonder if they were of wealth, were dark and pointed structures. So different from Lucem's smooth stone structures that sought the light no matter which way one turned.

As they approached the castle, Eden's brow furrowed as she tried to make it out. Set against the sky, it was difficult to see, even with the moon's light shining down on it. It was situated on a cliffside, that much she could tell, and it jutted toward the sky as if it were a blade.

The closer they grew, the easier it was to discern more

than just the outline of the castle, and although it wasn't ghastly, it wasn't home either. Eventually, they made it to the courtyard, which passed in a blur as Draven escorted her inside. Although Eden still wore his cape around her, the cool air brushed against her damp cheeks, sending an involuntary chill up her spine.

There was little to comfort her in the halls. With no adornments to soften the dank interior, it matched the harsh quality of the exterior, but at least it didn't lure one in with false hope it was anything but that.

All she longed for was a bed to sleep in, to bury herself in the comfort of blankets and plunge herself into slumber in hopes of waking from this nightmare.

But it was the sudden realization she didn't even have a room of her own, let alone a bed, that truly undid Eden. What difference was this study from a holding cell? She couldn't bring herself to look at Draven, not as she blurted for him to leave and not as his quiet steps faded down the hall.

The room had been lit, but there was no fire in the hearth to warm the room, which only chilled her all the more.

"I will return, my lady," Seurat offered in a quiet voice, bowing before he left.

While he was gone, Eden paced to the bare window in the room and surveyed the steep slope below. Everything was still cast in darkness, even as the second moon rose and bestowed a muted golden light over the land. Eden's eyes adjusted, and she could make out figures moving below.

Perhaps her mother was right. It wouldn't be long before she perished in this world. How could anyone thrive in a land of darkness, where one misstep could be the end?

Footsteps outside the study pulled Eden from her thoughts. Seurat had returned with the chaise lounge as promised, and instead of blankets, there was a pile of what looked like strips of fabric.

A strangled noise escaped Eden as she fought back another bout of tears. "No blankets, either?" Eden sounded more perturbed this time, and she was, although her voice still shook with fright.

"My lady, I promise you that by the time you wake, there will be a room ready for you with a bed and proper blankets." Seurat moved toward the fireplace, situating twisted pieces of wood before he ignited them. "We fell behind in your preparations, and for that, we all apologize."

The flames cast warmth onto Seurat's dark face, revealing a smattering of calloused skin—or, no, as Eden studied him closer, they were scales. *What sort of creature is he?* She wondered but would not ask. Perhaps it was better not knowing, because if she were to have one friendly face to seek out, it was better to not know the monster beneath. He had, after all, been the one to soothe her on the knoll, offer her water, and still sought to offer her comfort now. It was more than Eden could say for Draven.

Draven.

His name echoed in her head, forcing her hands to lift toward her face. Her evening had begun so wonderfully, but now it was tainted because when she closed her eyes, she still saw *him*, his gaze unguarded, amused, and playful.

It had been a lie.

One breath, another one, then Eden lowered her hands

to her sides. "Thank you, Seurat. I need sleep. I'm so . . . tired."

He nodded in response, bowed, then left the room, closing the door behind him.

The room was so quiet that when the fireplace popped and crackled, it startled her. She turned to the lounge, picking apart the fabrics to position them into layers of blankets. Then she shoved the makeshift bed closer to the fireplace, for it was still too far from the warmth for her liking, and when she lay down on it, an annoyed sigh escaped her. The voluminous skirts were both a curse and blessing as she situated them in a way that would form another protective layer while she slept. Before she settled in, she peeled the heels from her feet, wincing when she flung them to the floor. Lastly, she tugged Draven's cape more securely around her upper half, both grateful for and resentful of its presence.

With fresh tears spilling onto her cheeks, she gave in to the pull of sleep.

When Eden woke, it was to darkness. No, that wasn't exactly true; it was that stronger, warmer glow of the moon she'd seen before falling asleep. Much to her dismay, she'd not woken from her nightmare. She shifted, pushing the layers of fabric off of her, only to regret it instantly. The room was chilly, though the fire hadn't gone out, which meant someone had come into the room while she'd slept.

Eden sat upright, finding her eyes swollen from a night

of crying. There was no mirror in the room for her to check on herself, but she must have looked tragic.

Curiosity whispered to her, pulling Eden to her bare feet and out of the study. Once in the hallway, her eyes had to adjust yet again. It was so dark, and the skirts rustling around her ankles served as a tripping hazard. In hindsight, it had been a dreadful choice for a dress, but she hadn't known she'd be condemned to spend her life in Andhera.

Eden's hand brushed against the wall, allowing it to guide her down the corridor, but movement ahead caused her to freeze. What was she seeing? A rat? Squinting, she moved forward, then made out bulbous eyes, a hooked nose, and broad, winged-out ears. As the pieces clicked together, Eden screamed in shock, which only prompted the ghoulish figure to squawk back in horror. Something scurried beside her head, then the lamp next to her lit, which illuminated a similar creature, this one with a large tear in the left ear.

A scream lodged itself in Eden's throat, unable to break free. She stumbled backward and saw another creature grabbing at her sheer skirt, wrapping it around its head and cooing in delight.

Eden grabbed it from the little beast, then turned on the balls of her feet and ran through the hall, hoping she didn't collide with some hidden creature, or worse, somehow plunge to her death.

Around a bend, she saw the golden light of the moon spilling onto the stone floor, and she ran for it, catching herself on one of the stone beams before she collided with the sill. Panting heavily, she peered outside, and from this vantage point, she saw an abyss with fog rolling around the surface.

Eden wondered what lay in the depths, which prompted the memory of her mother's words. If she were to die here, would it not be better to get it over with, rather than waste away slowly?

"My lady," a familiar voice said, startling Eden out of her melancholy thoughts.

She twisted to face Seurat, hand on her chest. Could a heart beat so hard that it leaped from its cage? Eden was certain hers was about to try.

"We have prepared your room for you, and a change of clothing. Later, if you wish, you can decide on a wardrobe." Seurat motioned toward the hall. "If you'd follow me, your breakfast is also waiting for you."

Eden blinked. "My breakfast in my room . . . ? So, His Majesty isn't going to join me for breakfast?"

Seurat had the good grace not to laugh at her or make her feel even more of a fool. "No, and for that I apologize. He will not be joining you for your meal."

It didn't matter, Eden decided. What were they to discuss? How he'd fooled her? How he'd baited her in the garden, how he'd teased her and followed her with his gaze in the ballroom?

"I won't be eating either, but thank you for your efforts." As Seurat halted at an open door, Eden ducked inside.

"His Majesty has instructed you to write a letter if you need anything from home. You may ask for any of your belongings." Seurat motioned to the quill and parchment on the writing desk.

Surprise registered on Eden's face. She pushed the black feather with her fingertip, then glanced back to Seurat. "What of my prior life would fit here? What purpose would it serve other than to remind me of what I've lost?"

All of her wardrobe would be useless in Andhera. They were flimsy dresses made for warm, sun-filled days, not meant to endure cold or wind. A portion of her jewelry would suffice, but what for? It wasn't as if she would be attending any fetes after this. There was little that Eden possessed that she could bring with her. But her bunny, she couldn't imagine leaving him behind with her mother. As foul of a mood as she'd be in, Eden feared for the little thing.

Seurat, for as kind as he'd been, seemed at a loss for words. Perhaps he knew there was nothing he could do in that moment to comfort her.

Eden nodded. "I'll be quick." She heard the door click softly, then she turned to the writing desk and penned a letter to her mother. It was brief, nothing that told of what she'd seen or how she felt, only that she was sorry still and loved her dearly. Afterward, she wrote down her list of needs and finally took notice of the room that had been prepared for her.

A lit chandelier illuminated it, and against the walls were lit sconces. Despite the castle's coolness, the room was warmer than the study, but perhaps it was the way it had been outfitted.

Instead of bare walls, deep teal drapes hung as decorations, for they weren't needed for blocking light. Gold fringe accented the edges, occasionally shifting as a draft caught them. But it was the bed which made Eden take pause, a bed framed with black engraved wood, with layers of thick blankets the same teal as the drapes.

If it weren't for the reason as to why she was here,

perhaps Eden would have been touched by how much effort they'd put in for her.

On top of the comforter, Eden noticed a change of clothing, and on the floor, a black pair of heeled lace-up boots. Unclasping the dark gray cape from around her shoulders, Eden tossed it to a heap on the floor, hating all that it represented. Deceit, betrayal, and loss. Turning away from it, she focused on the fresh garments before her.

It took some doing to wriggle out of the gown, and a few strings of almost-curses, but Eden managed. However, when she held up her new outfit, she realized there was no skirt but rather breeches. If her legs hadn't protested when the draft swept into the room again, she would have questioned the design, but perhaps they'd taken pity on her Lucem blood and decided to swath her in as much fabric as possible.

In a few minutes, Eden shimmied into the midnight blue outfit. Inside, the breeches were lined with a soft fur that kept her legs warm, and the long bell sleeves that covered her arms had the same fur too. Silver decorative buttons lined the front of the built-in vest, leading up toward the double leather collar. Once her boots were on, she scooped up the leather throngs which no doubt had kept the bundle of clothing or blankets together.

She searched the room for a mirror, and when she found a floor-length one bordered by embellished silver, she used it to pull her hair back high on her head. The female in the mirror startled Eden, for she didn't look like herself but like one of Andhera's people. Was it a trick of the glass? Hesitantly, she reached out to touch it, but it didn't ripple. She looked closer and saw the frightened, lonely fae that she was.

With a shaky sigh, Eden snatched the letter from the desk and left her room.

"The letter, as His Majesty asked." She handed it to Seurat.

He pressed his lips together, clearly warring with what to say next. "Why don't I show my lady the gardens? While not what you're accustomed to, I trust you'll find it as beautiful as we do."

As much as Eden wished to inspect it, the thought of stepping foot in a garden at this moment was the furthest thing from her mind. And yet . . . What were gardens like in Andhera? If there was no sun, no warmth, what grew?

She nodded, deciding to follow him.

Eden took note of every twist and turn of the castle, not casting her eyes to the floor but to her surroundings. She saw one of the creatures that caused her previous hysteria and pressed just a little closer to Seurat.

"What are those things?" she questioned.

"Those are our goblins. Don't worry, they're harmless, and are most happy when working. Sometimes they can be a little mischievous."

Eden blanched. "Mischievous how?"

"Harmless tricks, like stealing things."

Wonderful. Eden groaned internally. But if they were harmless, she had nothing to fear at the very least.

Outside, a cold wind whipped the strands of Eden's bound hair. There was a dampness, like it was on the verge of raining. Did it rain in Andhera? She touched her nose, feeling how cold it was.

"This way, my lady," Seurat said. "While you slept, you missed quite the bout of weather. I hoped you'd awaken so you could witness it."

What did he mean by that? "What of the weather?" Even Eden knew it was grasping for blades of grass as far as conversation went.

Seurat never did get to tell her, for as they rounded a turn, Eden met Draven's eyes.

"Another time, my lady." Seurat bowed to her. "My lord." He bowed to Draven, then left the two of them quite alone.

It felt far different than being alone with him before. As if she were more vulnerable.

Words tumbled together in her mind. She was unsure of what to say to Draven, how to greet him. "Thank you, Your Majesty, for affording me the luxury of a bed and furnished room." The words were mild enough, but they held fine-toothed barbs within. Then she lost her confidence and looked away from him.

Draven

Her words had haunted him. Enough so that when Seurat had come to request they prepare her a bedroom, Draven had handed him a heavy change purse, instructing him to acquire anything he thought would be needed to make her stay more comfortable. Seurat had chosen a handful of the maids to assist, revenants still fresh enough that the memories of their old lives, and the comforts needed there, hadn't yet faded away.

After that, he had done his best to push thoughts of the young Lucem maiden from his mind and focus on what he needed to for the day: trolls pushing onto chimera land, new revenants spotted wandering over the fields outside a village not drawn in by the summoning spell, and petty disputes between the vampire nobility. All of it seemed pitifully commonplace when Draven considered the innocent life his brothers had just decimated.

He was feeding when a trio of goblins came scurrying into his study, grumbling and grunting their discontent.

Draven lifted his head from the trembling wrist held out to him and shot a glare at the ringleader of his present pests.

"Quiet! One moment, please," he snapped, earning a big-eyed look of dismay. Huffing in irritation, he waved the mortal away. "Take him," he said dismissively to the harpy standing sentry near the door.

She moved forward to clamp a hand around the man's bicep and tugged him from the room to return him to his place in the dungeons. Rubbing at his forehead, Draven watched as the goblins hurried across the floor, crawling quickly up the leg of his desk to surround him on its surface.

They squawked all at the same time in shrill voices that made him wince. "Easy . . . easy . . . *Enough*," he growled firmly. "I can't understand you when you're all going at once."

The goblins spoke a language all their own, one that had taken him decades to decipher once the critters had snuck their way into his castle like unwanted rodents and chosen to make this their breeding ground. Castle Aasha was the safest place in all of Andhera for the tiny creatures to exist.

The smallest one, who also happened to be the loudest of the three, scampered forward to sit near where his hand rested on the desk's surface. Taking his thumb in its small hands, the goblin clung to it as it began a tale of woe. A tale of screeching in the hallways and fabulous new toys wrenched away rudely.

So, she's awake.

"That . . . is the new lady of the castle. Mmm . . . yes, she is a friend." Draven chuckled, imagining the scenario in the hallway, Eden coming across the goblins for the first time. "I'm certain she didn't mean to be rude to you and scream. Perhaps you startled her."

Draven scooped up the goblin nearest him, allowing it to sprawl over the palm of his hand as he scratched gently at its back. "Give her a chance, she is new here." He grunted as the goblin in his hand nipped him playfully, then he set it back down amongst its friends. "Be off with you now. And no taking things from her room!" he called after them as an afterthought.

The goblins were a good reminder that he had an entire new world to explain to Eden, who wouldn't be sure of anything around her. Standing up from his chair, he made his way across the room and out into the hall. Stopping a revenant floating by, he asked where Seurat could be found, only to learn that he was with Eden and that they had been spotted heading outside.

"Thank you," Draven murmured, then headed for the garden. He could only assume that was where Seurat was taking her, the one place she may be able to relate to.

Walking across the moonlit garden, Draven considered his options when it came to Eden. She needed to be made to feel at home during her time spent in Andhera. While this had not been her choice, nor his own, he wouldn't punish her more than Zryan already had by sending her here. She would also need to be kept safe. While Lucem was a land of chiffon and lust, with the scent of eternal blossoms in the air, Andhera was not. Eden had been deposited into a world where almost everything around her could, and likely *would*, seek to kill her. It was now Draven's task to keep her alive. A harpy soldier or werewolf escort may not be the worst idea.

He spotted them long before they took note of him, and

89

Draven found himself stopping in his tracks as he beheld Eden in standard Andherian clothing. Swathed in midnight blue, she strolled across the lawns beside Seurat, looking confident and strong. He found himself wondering if she could find happiness here, far away from the sunshine of Lucem, in a world of darkness that still held many wonders if one was willing to look.

Draven thought of her stooped over in Travion's garden, investigating little green blooms rather than dancing at the ball. If anyone were able to find the beauties of his land . . .

They noticed him at last. Seurat quickly took his leave, and then it was just the two of them once more in a moonlit garden.

"Thank you, Your Majesty, for affording me the luxury of a bed and furnished room."

If gentle words were arrows, Eden had just drawn them from her quiver and fired them with deft accuracy. Draven found himself frowning, which may have come off as more of a sneer as he crossed his arms over his chest, the material of his gray linen shirt growing taught over his shoulders.

"It was never my plan to deny you them." They simply hadn't been expecting the arrival of a Lucem maiden in the early hours of dawn. "I trust that Seurat has been tending to your needs?" He glanced over her outfit once again before meeting her gaze. Or attempting to—she seemed hesitant to look him in the eye.

"Yes, he has." Simple and distant.

Sighing in frustration, Draven looked out over the garden, noting that the vespertilio flowers were now in full bloom. Their dark purple petals stretched up toward the yellow moonlight, while their spray of antennas sought to attract whatever insects may be around. Their perfume, should one be close enough to smell them, held the scent of crisp mountain air just after the first snow had fallen. Clean, fresh, exhilarating.

"I have chosen a handmaiden for you. Loriah has been at Castle Aasha for a number of years now and can assist you with any questions you may have if Seurat or I are unavailable." She had also not been with them so long that she had forgotten what it was like to be human or to be alive. Loriah had been one of the revenants to aid in the decorating of Eden's room. "Loriah was employed by a noble family when she was alive, so she is wonderfully experienced in helping noblewomen prepare for the day."

"When she *was* alive?"

The horrified tone of her voice drew Draven's eyes back to Eden, and he found her staring up at him, her brow furrowed. He could see the way her mind raced behind those bright green eyes and wished he could tap into her thoughts to know just what it was she was pondering so thoroughly.

"Loriah is a revenant, as are most of my servants. Which means that once, she lived as a human in Midniva, and upon her death found herself here in Andhera because she was not ready to pass on to the afterlife. They are all given the option of serving until they are ready to meet their end," he explained.

"So . . . she is a—"

"Spirit of the dead, yes."

Eden visibly gulped but showed no other outward sign that she was concerned by what she was hearing.

"You can summon her by simply saying her name. If

you ask a question or make a request, you will be answered by whichever revenant is closest at the time. All will gladly attend to you." He watched her as he spoke, waiting for the moment when this all became too much and she looked to bolt.

"And my days here . . . What are you expecting from me?" she asked, her chin up as she posed this question.

Draven could see from the slight quiver in her bottom lip that it had taken a great deal of strength and courage for her to ask him that. Gone was the lighthearted conversation of the previous evening, demolished beneath Zryan's master plans.

"This is now your home. You are free to explore it as you wish. My only demand is that, when leaving the castle walls, you take a harpy or were-guard along with you. Your fae scent is a delectable treat to many of the residents of this land . . . and you will need the protection if you wish to explore."

"Explore? This is a land of death, what more could I possibly wish to see?" Eden shook her head, a frown marring her lovely features. "If it is anything like what I have already experienced . . . then I have had more than enough to last me a lifetime."

Her words, though fair, brought a scowl to his own face, and Draven looked away from her. "Very well then." His tone was clipped as he pushed down disappointment. Curiosity in the gardens of Midniva did not transfer over to the bizarre and dangerous beauty of Andhera, of that he was already aware. "Lastly, be cautious when on the outer walkways of the castle. The winds can become turbulent, and should you fall . . . "

Draven looked down at Eden once more, wishing yet

again that he could see into her mind and know what words he could speak to bring her comfort.

"Should I fall?" she prompted.

"The pit that lies at the base of the castle on the western side leads directly into the afterlife. There is no coming back from that death. Stay clear of it." His words were firm and important. "On that side of the mountain, you will also find a cave. Do not enter it. The cave is a dark place that elicits one's worst nightmares. It's linked directly to the afterlife, and with its essence leaching into it, very few survive the passage through to the other end."

Eden's eyes widened as she listened, his words not helping to encourage a desire to explore the landscape of this realm.

"Now, come, I will introduce you to Loriah, then leave you be to mope about the destitute life you now live."

His words must have ruffled her, for she gasped, and her cheeks burned with indignation. Cold like his realm, the king in him didn't care. She had made it very clear she had no desire to experience this world and what it had to offer; he would not hide the fact that he took offense to that.

With nothing further to say to her, Draven began to walk across the gardens, following the path that would take them through the large conservatory doors and back into the main area of the castle. If she chose not to follow, it was of no consequence to him, but he was rewarded with the sounds of her soft footfall once they reached the stone steps.

"Loriah!" he called out once they were within Aasha's halls.

The revenant appeared, her form transparent at first,

until she manifested as a solid presence. She had raven black hair that feathered around her face and pale skin that had been almost translucent in her human life.

"Your Majesty." Loriah curtsied.

"This is the lady Eden. I want you to see to all her needs and make certain that she becomes familiar with the castle. She is new to Andhera, so she will need to understand the people here. Help her learn where to find the harpies if she desires to go outside, and which of the wolves is best to deal with should she need their services."

"Of course, sire." Loriah bowed her head.

"You're not going to—" Eden began, only to be cut off as General Ailith suddenly appeared at the end of the hall and called out for Draven.

"Your Majesty! May I have a word?" Ailith, a tall woman in her life, was now a giant of a harpy, standing taller than Draven when her wings were taken into account. Her taloned feet clicked on the stone floor as she strode purposefully toward them.

Draven looked to Eden. "Loriah will see to anything you may need today. Let her know any preferred dishes you would like to have made for your meals, and we will do the best that we can do to accommodate them." With that, he turned from her to meet Ailith, who seemed to be on the warpath. "Yes?"

"Word just came from Primis," she muttered softly.

"And?" he growled, already knowing what she was about to say.

"There have been more bodies."

Seething, Draven ground his teeth. "Very well. Find Channon, tell him to round up the pack. It would seem we're going hunting."

As Ailith left him, Draven turned to peer after Eden and Loriah, already facing the opposite direction and heading away from him. Even in the midnight blue jacket and matching breeches, Eden was a bright light in a dark realm. One, perhaps, that shone far too brightly.

Turning from her, Draven called out to a revenant, demanding his cloak. Once it was fitted around him, he left for the courtyard to meet with his hunting party.

Eden

When she was alive . . . The words kept tumbling through Eden's head, even as she walked alongside Loriah, her newly appointed handmaiden. She wasn't a ghost; as they turned down the hall, the young woman's footfall echoed along the way, like a whisper on the wind.

She's undead, Eden thought. Never in her lifetime would she have imagined coming face to face with an undead being, let alone an entire world of them.

"Are you all right, my lady?" Loriah tilted her head, pausing at the door to Eden's chambers. She was birdlike in appearance, especially when she moved in such a way. As coltish as Eden may have been amongst the fae, she was nothing compared to Loriah. Humans were smaller than fae to begin with, but Eden had seen a plethora of humans at the ball, and none were as tiny as she. Frail, even.

What was she supposed to say? She was far from all right. At every turn it was as if reality fractured all over again. Instead of replying, Eden ducked into her room and lifted her hands to her face. If she squeezed her eyes closed hard enough, she'd wake from the nightmare, surely.

"Nothing is," Eden whispered. She startled as a hand brushed against her back, then realized it was Loriah drawing soothing circles.

"I will do everything I can to ensure your stay is as comfortable as possible. Whatever I can do for you, my lady, please let me know." She lowered her hand, then clasped it in front of her chest, bowing her head.

Eden's sensibilities screamed at her, telling her to run away. But to where—to death? Yet Loriah's pink lips turned into a soft, welcoming smile, pulling at the warmth of Eden's heart.

The handmaiden was trying, at least. It was more than Eden was doing. If this was to be her new existence, she'd only allow herself a few days to mourn her prior life. She was allowed that, wasn't she?

Inky tresses swept into Loriah's vision, and she pushed the stubborn strands away. "Would it help if I told you about myself, my lady?" She crossed the room, fussing with the fire poker at the hearth. Flames licked hungrily at the logs, crackling and popping sparks across the stone floor.

Maybe it was the gentleness in Loriah's tone that pulled Eden from her bout of self-pity, or curiosity that moved her, but she crawled onto the oversized bed and watched the handmaiden for a moment. "I think I'd like to know more about you."

It'd been three days since Eden had arrived at the castle and met Loriah, and in the span of that time, she'd learned much of her previous life. Of how Loriah had met her demise on the cliffs of Midniva, an end which was self-inflicted, and how she suffered whilst she was alive.

Eden had listened without judgment, but it did make her realize that while sheltered from the cruelties of the world, she'd been protected too. She had been fortunate to have a loving father instead of one who robbed her of everything, and luckier still that she had a mother who loved her and not one who ran away.

Loriah's fingers nimbly tightened the corset around Eden's waist, causing her to suck in a sharp breath. She wasn't accustomed to the fashion in Andhera and certainly was not used to being so tightly bound. Where Lucem was mostly gauzy fabrics, Andhera's clothing had substance, layers even. It was suffocating, yet she appreciated the added warmth.

Andhera may not have been as cold as Midniva's winters allegedly were, but Eden had grown beneath the sun, basked in its rays, and had known nothing other than Lucem until the ball.

"You need to begin eating properly, my lady." Loriah finished with the stays, then combed her fingers through Eden's hair, teasing the freshly unbraided strands. "You cannot keep pushing meals away or else you'll fade into nothing." She shook her head.

"I know."

It wasn't as if Andhera's food was filth or ashen. It smelled similar to the food at home. But the desire to dine wasn't there, and her nerves still clenched her throat, making it nearly impossible to swallow more than a few mouthfuls. Eden had eaten enough so she didn't collapse in the gardens, but that was it.

Eden took one look in the mirror, then sighed. A maroon velveteen dress clung to her lithe figure, but to her delight, the front portion of the skirt revealed her legs up to her knees. There were no breeches or stockings offered to her today, unlike the rest of the week, and she wondered if it was because she complained less about the cold. In truth, it wasn't even as cold as Midniva had been. Midniva's castle was situated against the rough sea, with the wind whipping around, but Andhera was warmer than she'd initially thought. Eden assumed it was largely due to her nerves settling—if only a little.

She bent to snatch her boots up when a knock sounded on the door. Loriah's eyes met hers in a silent question, and Eden nodded.

The handmaiden answered the door, and Seurat stood on the other side. "Excuse me, but the lady has a delivery." The words were barely out of his mouth when a goblin tumbled into the room, its bulbous eyes peering around in search of said delivery.

Eden flinched but didn't scream as the goblin ran toward her, sniffing the air. A snaggletooth hung over his lip as he leaned forward. She'd seen them scurrying in the hallways, chattering, and they'd kept their distance since initially frightening her.

Seurat cleared his throat and muttered lowly, "Drizz."

"He's all right." Eden kept her eyes trained on the creature as he sat down, scoping out the room. "You mentioned a delivery?"

Seurat smiled, dipping his head. "I did. The belongings you requested." He bent down to grab something, though what it was, Eden couldn't see from where she stood. But then she heard rustling and knew at once it was her newly acquired pet.

She rushed forward, sucking in a breath as the ash-colored rabbit hopped around in the cage. His eyes were wide with fear, and she couldn't blame him. "You made it." A smile tugged at her lips as she opened the wire door and extracted him. He smelled of sunshine still, and of jasmine. *Home.*

"Thank you," she murmured to Seurat, but a sorrowful chirp on the floor caught her attention. Drizz hopped around as if he were a rabbit, then wriggled his nose. It caught Eden off guard, and she laughed at his antics. *Is he trying to appeal to me?*

"Where would you like the rest of the items, my lady?" Seurat placed the cage down on the floor.

Confusion rumpled her brow. "What do you mean?" She'd only asked for a handful of things from home. Nothing much would fit here in the land of two moons. Eden didn't think the sheer gowns would go over well inside the castle either.

"King Zryan sent a chest of gifts for you."

She blinked. "Oh. Set them at the end of the bed, and thank you." King Zryan sent gifts? She wanted no part of them, and the chest would remain shut unless she needed to add something to the hearth.

"As you wish, my lady." Seurat brought the chest in first. It was ivory with gold trim, and the sun was engraved on the lid, its rays stretching toward the edges. It stuck out like a sore thumb in the room, and she half wondered if he'd intended for it to be that way.

When Seurat deposited the last of her things, he bowed his head. "My lady, if you don't need anything else?"

"No . . . you may go," she said softly, hugging the rabbit closer to her chest. If she closed her eyes and took a deep breath, she could smell Lucem's perfumed air, feel the heat on her skin, and imagine she was home again.

But that wasn't to be.

Eden knelt in the center of her room, flicking a balled-up piece of paper for Alder, so she had named him, and he hopped forward only to leap into the air and bolt away. She laughed, wondering how, in only four days, he could settle in so quickly. And here Eden was, still mourning a life she had left behind.

"Behave," she chided softly, tapping the tip of his wriggling nose as he stuck it out. "I'll return and share some of my dinner with you." When she looked up, Loriah lifted a brow. "Only a little," Eden amended, then walked out of her room with her handmaiden in tow.

In a week's time, Eden had grown accustomed to the goblins running around, squawking, and even surprising her in her room. Although she was still wary of them, she'd gifted the ones she'd startled with a bangle from home. In return, they'd cooed, squeaked, and nuzzled her calves.

As Eden and Loriah walked down the hall, she could just make out the sound of Draven's voice. Eden hadn't seen or spoken to him since he introduced Loriah to her, almost as if he were avoiding her, but that was a ludicrous thought.

She quickened her stride, following the sounds of his voice and that of the female he spoke with.

"I'll leave at once then," Draven cut in.

When she rounded the corner, she was nearly on their heels, but Draven didn't turn to glance at her until she spoke.

"I wish to join you." Eden's cheeks warmed as her confidence faltered, but when he turned around, and the harpy glanced down at her, she straightened her shoulders, feigning confidence that wasn't there at all.

Draven's eyes narrowed. "No. You'll stay here. This isn't a—"

"If I stay behind, I'll run away." It was a childish thing to say, and Eden was fairly certain she'd rather take a leap off the castle than take her chances in the woods.

"You would die," he said dryly, but then for a moment, his eyes cleared, and genuine concern swirled within, as well as incredulity.

"I wouldn't exactly call my current existence living." She regretted her words instantly. Eden hadn't meant to insult him, but it was the truth. Not once had the king of the underworld locked her in her room or ordered her to remain inside the castle. However, if she was going to spend the rest of her immortal life with Draven, she supposed she needed to grow accustomed to his way of living, and to Andhera specifically.

"Very well, you may come. But you *must* listen to me." He spun on his heel, nodding toward the harpy.

Eden clasped her hands in front of herself, then briskly walked after him. There were so many things she wished to ask him, but she didn't know how to break through the barrier between them. She wanted to know more about Andhera, and if there was more to it than the terrors on the way to the castle. Was there a semblance of life in this world, or was it all tragedy and death? Despite the many questions that tumbled in her mind, she was silent. The only noise aside from her thoughts was the hammering of her heart in her ears.

Draven wound his way through the corridor with an easy grace that Eden envied. She felt awkward in the dimly lit halls.

When they were outside, Draven was first to break the silence. He turned toward her, first ensuring that she was looking at him, then began, "It is important that you remain in your seat while I'm investigating matters in Primis." He didn't elaborate, and there was an edge of finality to his words that barred off any discussion on the matter.

Eden only nodded in understanding. Still, curiosity nipped at the corners of her mind as to what those matters could be.

The sound of wings beating against the air brought her gaze toward the sky. Bathed in the bright moon's golden light, a harpy landed in the courtyard, and even from a distance, Eden could see a hint of disgust curling her lip.

She hadn't asked to be sent to Andhera or to become its queen, and knowing Draven's subjects were less than pleased as well drove a spike of annoyance inside of her.

A familiar sound caught her attention: hooves clattering through the courtyard as the carriage arrived. Eden missed Aiya, the rides they shared together in the open fields and in the ponds to cool off.

"We must be off." With the lightest touch, Draven took Eden's hand and escorted her toward the awaiting carriage.

She realized then it wasn't just the harpy joining. There was an entire pack of were-wolves, who had already shifted. They were imposing creatures, but she supposed they weren't meant to elicit a feeling of comfort. Without another glance, Eden stepped into the carriage. It wasn't as large as Aurelie's, but she assumed it was one of many he possessed. In fact, the open carriage left little room between herself and Draven as he settled in beside her.

Eden recalled the way Draven had framed her figure in the chariot. This was different. He could see her face, see the color rushing into her cheeks as their bodies brushed together.

But the thought perished as the carriage set off, and for the first time, Eden was venturing off into Andhera.

As the kelpie pulled the carriage through the land, the castle grew distant, and so did the more elaborate homes. The road grew bumpier, and as Eden glanced down, she noticed black roots jutting upward from the ground. They belonged to the looming trees above them. To her surprise, small white blossoms hung from them. *So, some semblance of life does exist . . .*

The kelpie's hooves met cobblestone again instead of a dirt road, and as the beast pulled the carriage along, rows and rows of houses appeared. The structures were clustered together, and it made Eden feel claustrophobic.

"We are now in Primis." Draven glanced over at her so that when she turned her head, their eyes locked.

"I had no idea Andhera was so . . ."

Her companion cocked his head, as if he were truly

interested in her finishing. "Different from what you were expecting?"

"Well, yes." Eden frowned.

The carriage halted outside one of the homes, and Draven turned to Eden, knocking his knee into hers due to the small quarters. "We'll continue this discussion when I'm through." He placed the reins down and hopped from the plush seat, leaving Eden outside with the harpy who landed not far from her side of the carriage.

Draven pushed the wooden door to the home open and vanished inside. A moment ticked by, then Eden twisted in her seat. The wolves had dispersed, and only one remained in her view. She wasn't certain which one it was, but he paced back and forth, clearly agitated.

The sound of glass breaking cut through the silence in the street, followed by a woman's raised voice. Much to Eden's surprise, neither the wolf nor the harpy moved from their position.

One of the windows shattered as something smacked against it. What it was, Eden couldn't discern, but she was steadily growing more restless. What was Draven doing inside? He hadn't mentioned why his presence was needed, only that it was important.

Not able to endure it any longer, she sprung from the seat and bounded into the home. She regretted it instantly. It was imbecilic, which struck her immediately.

Inside the home, the light from the moon didn't penetrate, not until she rounded a breezeway. It shone in from the shattered window, but Eden wished it didn't. For at that moment, as she stepped through the doorway, Draven was holding a woman up by her neck in a death grip. Except, she wasn't entirely human. Below her torso, a broad reptilian body coiled. She writhed, her whip-like tail thrashing around. Eden deduced it had been her tail which cracked the window.

Eden opened her mouth to draw Draven's attention away—or to scream—but it was too late. He plunged his hand into the female creature's chest and withdrew her heart. In his grasp, the heart sputtered, spraying crimson droplets over his arm and the floor. He released the lifeless body with a shove.

Amidst her horror, a wolf darted past her and into the room with Draven, who tossed him the organ. Then, as if it were fresh honey and not someone's lifeforce, Draven dragged his tongue along the rivulets of blood on his hand. His fangs protruded; the ivory was soon bathed in red.

It was too much.

Eden recoiled, stumbling back into a wall before she screamed. It was the scream which snapped Draven's attention to her. She didn't remain in the house. Instead, she bolted as fast as she could.

The image played over and over in her mind, only encouraging her to run, which was truly what she should have done in the first place, instead of barging into the home to . . . what? To save someone from him? He was a creature of darkness. Draven was every rumor ever whispered, every fear, every nightmare that spilled into all of the realms.

"Eden," Draven called to her.

No, she would not stop. He was a monster who tore beings apart for his own pleasure, and one day, it could be her.

Eden's legs burned as much as her lungs did. She sucked in breath greedily, ignoring Draven's bellows. She could've sworn she heard him curse the wolves, and perhaps the harpy too, but she didn't listen closely enough.

"Eden!" Draven shouted this time.

Around a bend, Eden considered her options: to continue running and risk Draven's mounting ire, or to face him. He could send the wolves to tear her apart, or the harpy could dig her talons into Eden's body. But her frantic thoughts spiraled. If she were to die, at least she'd have tried to escape instead of accepting her fate.

Iron arms wrapped around her torso, squeezing her and lifting her from the ground. She flailed violently, kicking and swatting at the one holding her.

"Let me go," she rasped. Her stomach flopped as her fear turned into horror. "Let me go at once!" She continued to twist and writhe in her captor's grasp, even as her stomach lurched. Without looking, she knew it was Draven. Even amidst her panic, she could smell his familiar scent of florals and woods.

Draven's arms continued to tighten around her with every twist and movement, until he had her effectively bound against him.

"Eden, listen to me."

10

Draven

"No! You're a *monster!*" Eden screamed, legs still thrashing violently against him. "Please, just send me home," she wheezed between frantic breaths.

"Enough!" he bellowed, giving her a little shake that seemed to finally snap her out of her frenzied attempt to be free of him. Now her body hung limp in his arms while she panted. He could feel her trembling with either fear or revulsion—he couldn't be sure which. "I will let you down if you promise not to run." She should not have seen it, and it was his fault she had. Draven should have said no when she'd insisted she come along, but a foolish part of him had been pleased at a show of interest in his land. No matter how small.

A grunt was the only response that he was given. Choosing to take that as compliance, he set Eden back down on her feet and carefully unfurled his arms from around her. The moment she was free, Eden jerked away, spinning around to face him with an accusatory glint in her eye.

"You are every bit as despicable as they say you are," she spat at him.

Draven sighed, realizing what the scene in the cottage must have looked like to her, how it must still look. His hand smeared with the lamia's blood and the remnants of it across her own dress. Years of being called a monster should have dulled his senses to the disgust gleaming in her eyes, but unfortunately, Draven still found himself vulnerable to the pricks of fear and loathing aimed his way. Some things even three millennia of existence could not ward against.

"Perhaps," he replied simply. "But life is different here."

The look she gave him was almost feral. "Truly different! Your brothers don't go on day trips to kill females just for the fun of it. They aren't monsters."

"*Monsters?*" He finally snapped, her words striking too close to home for his comfort. "The true monster was that creature in there." His bloodied hand lifted to point back toward the cottage behind them. "Lamia feed on the hearts of other living creatures, but they prefer the heart of a child most of all." Draven stepped closer to her, looming over her small frame as he growled his words. "That *female*, as you call her, has been terrorizing the villages nearest here. Seven were-children have gone missing, stolen from their beds . . . grabbed while they were out playing . . . only to be found by family and friends later with their chests torn open."

Draven could see the blood draining from her face as he spoke, but still he continued, pleased in this moment to see her horror directed somewhere else. If she wanted to scream monster, he could tell her all about the ones that truly resided here.

"Here in Andhera, we believe in the punishment fitting the crime. She took the hearts of children to feed upon, so I took her heart for my wolves." He snarled, then turned from her, trying to rein in his fury. Noticing that Ailith had followed more slowly behind them, he pointed at her. "Inside, there are two human children. She must have crossed over into Midniva sometime in the last week. Go calm them, find out where they are from, and work on getting them returned to their homes at once."

Eden was visibly shaking when he turned back to her. She wrapped her arms tightly around herself, avoiding his eyes.

"And you . . . When I tell you to stay in the carriage, I *mean* stay in the carriage." He fought to keep the growl out of his voice but wasn't certain it was working. "There are things you simply don't need to see."

"Well, you've shown me none of it! So how am I to know?!" she snapped back, arms still coiled around herself.

Sighing, Draven smoothed his hand wearily over his face. He had given her every opportunity to explore his kingdom, but not *with* him. Seeing as how she couldn't look him in the eyes most days, he had thought his absence would be a relief. "Come, let's head back to the carriage." He waited for her to step up beside him, then began the trek back to where the rest of their party waited.

He strode over to the side of the house, where a small hand pump was positioned. Cranking the lever, he soon had a spray of water that he used to wash his hand clean of what remained of the blood. Drying it off on his cape, Draven turned to his men.

"Eden and I are going into the village proper. We'll be at

Matilde's. Lock up the lamia's cottage, see the children dealt with, and dispose of the body as you see fit."

Channon nodded his gray head, then made a soft wuffling noise to the other wolves. As one, they moved, seeing to his orders. Ailith was already leading two small children out of the cottage, both looking terrified yet hopeful as she soothed them.

"Come," he murmured to Eden. "If you wish to see something of Andhera that is not filled with horrors . . . follow me."

He waited to see if she would come with him. After a moment of contemplation, she nodded and fell into step beside him. She kept her distance, however, making certain that no part of them, even down to the flutter of a cape or brush of a skirt, came into contact.

"I'm sorry . . . for misreading the situation," she said, breaking the silence that had fallen between them.

Draven remained quiet for a moment, pondering his response before finally saying, "I will admit that I am a merciless king when I feel it is warranted. But I try to always be fair, and here, in a land where so many are bloodthirsty, the threat of death is the fine line that stands between whether the creatures obey my commands or not."

They fell silent once more, making their way farther into Primis, the first village that had been established in Andhera when the fae and humans had first traveled over. This had been the outpost for all those seeking their wealth in the darkest realm. Now it was a village like any other, home to a number of were-families, as well as vampires, a couple of trolls, and Matilde's house.

Walking through the streets, the lamps weren't lit yet,

111

ELLE BEAUMONT & CHRISTIS CHRISTIE

as the yellow day moon still cast enough light that those who were used to it could see perfectly well. For Eden, Draven was certain it was a daunting experience to travel always in the darkness.

Passing a number of homes and a few small shops, Draven stopped as they came upon a small two-story home. Made of stone, it sat nestled by a stream that traveled below a small wooden bridge leading to the other side of the village. There was a large tree in the front yard, one with dark red leaves and burgundy flowers that let off a soft floral scent. Hanging from one of the large branches was a rope swing, and on the rope swing, a little girl with golden hair swung listlessly.

"This is Matilde's," he said in a hushed tone to Eden. "The children here are all revenants. Children are often too confused at the loss of life to pass on to the afterlife, so we try to find them fitting homes with adult revenants who will give them the chance to live out life as they please until they're ready. This is just one of many such homes in Andhera."

Eden's eyes were wide and uncertain. Perhaps this was not the happiest of places when one first considered the need for it, but the children here tended to be full of life and joy as they lived their new unlives.

Draven left Eden where she stood and made his way across the lawn toward the tree. As his boots crunched lightly on the rough sod, the blond-headed girl lifted her head. At once, her eyes began to shine with joy and a smile lit her face.

"Drae!" she called out.

With a chuckle, he dropped to one knee before her, one

hand reaching up to grasp onto the rope of her swing. "Hello, Abilyn. Why are you out here all alone?"

"Rudyard is being unfair and won't allow me to play with him and the others."

Draven tsked and shook his head. "Well, that just shall not stand." Holding his hands out to her, he allowed the young revenant to glide into his arms. Standing up, he balanced the wee spirit on his hip. "Children!" he bellowed, a smirk on his face.

Abilyn's arms circled his neck as she nestled in happily, and as the other revenant children filed out of the house, she grinned proudly from her perch in his arms. The others cheered as they spotted him, rushing over to encircle him, hands tugging at his sleeve or shirt, others calling out questions. Why had he been gone so long? Did he bring them any presents? Was he here to play?

"Shh shh shh," he said, holding up a hand. "So, it has been brought to my attention that a certain someone has been excluding Abilyn from today's play."

Rudyard, the culprit, had the decency to look ashamed before puffing out his chest and attempting to defend himself. "Buuut she—"

"Nuh nuh nuh," Draven tutted. "I'll hear no excuses." From the corner of his eye, he saw Matilde, a dark-complected revenant, come to stand in the doorway, her body leaning against it as she watched him and the children. "I declare Abilyn honorary princess for the rest of the day, so she must be included in all of the games."

There was a general groan from a number of the boys, but the small spirit in his arms gave out a happy cheer. Around these parts, 'Drae's' word was law, and honored beyond all else.

"Now . . . I've brought a special guest with me today," he explained and glanced over at Eden, who was watching them all with a wide-eyed stare. He waved to her, encouraging her to come forward. "This is Eden—she is a little shy. It's her first time visiting Primis. Do you think you can show her around?" he asked them.

Always interested in a new playmate, the kids were soon converging around Eden, pestering her with even more questions than they had him. Abilyn pressed a soft kiss to his cheek, which surprised and pleased him, then she disappeared out of his arms to reappear next to Eden.

As he watched them together, Draven felt a presence at his side and turned to see Matilde beside him.

"So I see the rumors are true. A new mistress does reside at Aasha."

"She is a guest who has come to stay for a brief time," he murmured, his hands moving to clasp behind his back.

"One whom you thought to bring here to the children?" Matilde gave him a pointed look.

"I only wished for her to see that even in the dark sadness of this realm, there is light and happiness too," he argued.

"Mmmhmm," was Matilde's only response.

Draven didn't appreciate the insinuation that there was more to his actions today than what he had said. He was well aware that Eden was not long for this land. At the end of the six months, she *would* be going back to Lucem, no matter what anyone had to say on the matter. He had no intention of getting used to her presence in his halls. While the world may think Eden was his, Draven could not be more aware of the truth. Eden wanted no part of his life here and would be only too pleased to return home when the time came.

By this point, the children had dragged Eden down to the stream to show off the fire lizards that skimmed across its surface. Their excited voices and the ring of their laughter was a welcome break from the brutality earlier today. Being both judge and executioner was not a role that became any easier as time went on, but Draven had accepted it. Especially if it meant fewer children would wind up here, living out this unlife, even as happy as Matilde could make it.

"Eden," he called out. "It's time to head back."

There was a chorus of groans from the children, their disappointment obvious. He gave them all a patient look, hiding a smirk of amusement as Eden drew them all back his way, a child's hand in each of hers. There was a swell of emotion in his chest that Draven chose not to read too much into or even acknowledge.

"Do you have to go?"

"Please stay!"

"Can Eden come back??"

Draven found himself chuckling once more at the chorus of questions flung his way. His eyes lifted to take in Eden's expression. While she was not pulling away from the children, he didn't want to promise anything on her behalf.

"I must get Eden back to the castle in time for her evening meal, but I promise not to stay away so long next time." He nodded to Matilde, then waited for Eden to join him at his side before he returned to the street. The children followed, gliding along behind them until they reached the edge of the lawn, then they merely waved happily goodbye, calling out a series of farewells as the two of them walked away.

They didn't speak for some time, until Eden broke the silence between them. "Those lizards . . . I've never seen anything quite like them. Although they do remind me of the ones back home. My friend Aurelie's little brother Tamas liked to find them and put them in my hair."

An almost nervous laugh slipped out of her as she spoke, and Draven found himself looking over at her, uncertain of what to say in return. Small talk had never been his special gift. Fortunately, Eden continued.

"I'm sorry for what I said earlier. Truly sorry. I should not have lost my temper with you like I did . . . " She bit at her lip before continuing. "I believe I understand Andhera a little better now. Thank you for taking the time to bring me there."

Draven nodded a little, mulling over her words. "I understand your upset over what you saw, but thank you." He glanced at her, wondering if she truly meant it or if she were only trying to appease him. "Andhera is a place of much loss, and much death, but even in the darkest corners, there are rays of light if there are souls willing to feed it."

Silence fell between them again as they continued their walk back to the carriage. Ailith and the children were gone, as well as two of the wolves, and Draven could only assume they were already on their way back to Midniva. Channon and the remaining four wolves waited patiently for them.

"Let's be off," he told his wolf guard, helping Eden up into the carriage. They were soon heading back toward the capital city, and Draven tried not to notice the way Eden was plastered to her side of the carriage.

Blessedly, the return trip was uneventful, something Draven sent up a brief prayer of thanks to the moon for. He didn't think he had the patience for one more episode he had to explain away to Eden. It also left Draven with time to consider Eden's safety once more. While she seemed placated for the time being, he couldn't be certain something else wouldn't happen to cause her to flee. If there was even the slightest chance her fear and haste could land her on her own in the wilds of Andhera, she was going to need to know how to defend herself.

Perhaps some lessons from his wolf guard were in order. Eden should at least know how to handle an opponent in a fight, and while her life of luxury in Lucem had not called for it, in Andhera, even children knew how to properly hold a knife.

Their silence lasted until they were through the gates of the castle, and once a young were-panther had taken Rayvnin and the carriage from him, Draven led Eden inside.

"I was thinking that I would join you for your evening meal. If you will have me," Draven murmured to her. She could not be blamed entirely for her behavior today, not when he had distanced himself so much from her. After her words earlier, he had started to wonder if his absence had made things worse rather than better.

"I would li—"

"Draven! You're home!" a voice called out, cutting off Eden's response.

Draven's eyes narrowed, and he drew in a slow breath, watching the vampiress glide down the hall toward them.

Lady Mynata Perfidiae, the daughter of one of the founding families of Andhera, was a beautiful woman of caramel skin and dark brown hair. She possessed a face that could look as innocent as a kitten but hid the soul of a viper. Draven had witnessed far too many people fall into that trap to do so himself.

"Mynata," he said dryly.

Without hesitation, she stepped forward to drape her slender arms around his neck, leaning in for a hug that spoke of familiarity and comfort. Out of a sense of obligation, Draven gave her a single-armed hug before prying her figure off of his.

In the early years, when Mynata's family had first settled in Andhera and she had found herself making the transformation from fae to vampire, Draven had acted as a source of information and comfort, aiding the young woman and her family where he could. But what had come from a sense of patriarchal responsibility had been received in another manner by Mynata.

"Lady Mynata, this is Lady Eden of Lucem. She is my guest here in the castle," he stated.

Eden stood watching them with an uncertain look on her face. "Hello . . . " she murmured, eyeing the other woman.

"Lady Eden, such a pleasure," Mynata cooed in a sultry voice, her arm slipping through Draven's.

"You'll have to excuse us, I was just escorting Eden in for supper."

"Oh, I haven't fed either. Why don't I—"

"Not tonight," Draven cut her off. He was quick to detangle himself from Mynata's clutches. "Have a good evening, Mynata." With that, he moved up to Eden and, offering her his arm, took her down the corridor to the dining room.

The revenants had been expecting them, or perhaps it had been Seurat, for the dining table was already set with Eden's evening meal. Taking her to her seat, he drew the chair out for her and waited until she was upon it before pushing it back in.

"Bridine," he spoke out to the room at large. When the revenant who typically monitored the dungeons downstairs appeared, he requested his own meal. "Fetch me a goblet of blood, please."

Once Bridine disappeared, Draven took his seat at the other end of the dining table. Dropping down into the chair, he sighed wearily. Today had been more troublesome than he had anticipated, and he could only hope that things settled down for the foreseeable future.

"So . . . you truly do not eat then," Eden said, her own fork and knife in hand.

"No, I do not eat." Bridine appeared at his side once more, a silver goblet in her grasp. Taking it from her, he thanked the spirit before sipping from it, happy to find that the blood was fresh from the vein and still warm. "Those who come to Andhera find themselves transformed by the natural essence of the land. I was the first to find my hunger for food replaced by a thirst for blood. There have been other fae since who found the same transformation took them over. Others, such as Channon's human ancestors, became were-animals. Andhera affects everyone differently."

"So, even me?" Her words were soft, filled with apprehension, and perhaps fear.

"If you stay long enough, yes. Even you."

Eden

That evening, Eden tossed and turned, until finally, she huffed in frustration. It was no use. "Loriah," she called out and waited for the revenant to materialize.

When Loriah appeared, she bowed her head meekly. "My lady, how can I be of service?"

"It's far too quiet, even with the goblins arguing in the hallway." Eden ran her fingers over her face and frowned. "I just . . . I need someone to talk to. And I need to know a few things about D . . . about His Majesty."

Loriah's dark eyebrows lifted in uncertainty, but she waited patiently nonetheless.

"Today, I witnessed something I wish I never had. It was the very sight I'd heard whispers of in Lucem." Eden watched Loriah's expression carefully. The girl's lips thinned, as though she'd already heard the story a thousand times over in the castle. Perhaps she had. Who knew how many were currently chuckling over it? "I need to know if the fa—" Fae wasn't the right term. Draven was no longer a being of the sun. She frowned. "If the king I am to wed is just."

"Wed, my lady?" Loriah whispered the words, but her face brightened. "His Majesty is just in all ways."

The revenant may have answered the question, but she gave nothing else away. Eden arched a brow and leaned forward, bunching up her oversized blanket to hug it. "Did you not know about the betrothal?"

Loriah's expression reflected the bewilderment she must have felt. "No," she offered quietly, then added, "But most have guessed as much. Nearly everyone says you are but a guest in His Majesty's castle. However, servants talk, my lady." She looked down, smiling sheepishly.

"But what I saw today . . . and then the children . . . " Eden leaned her face into her palms and sighed. "Is he the ruthless beast or a generous king?"

Loriah remained quiet. In fact, Eden assumed she'd disappeared. Then, "Both, my lady." She moved from the end of the bed and to Eden's side. "Would you like a hot cup of tea to relax you?"

"No, just stay with me, please?" She let her body sag into the mound of pillows behind her, wishing sleep would claim her.

Loriah eventually relaxed enough to bend down to play with Alder. It was enough to fill the silence in Eden's room but still not enough to blot out her thoughts.

Lucem wasn't known for violence. Most of its citizens spent their days gossiping, entangled with a plethora of lovers, or sipping wine. Sometimes, it was all three at once. But this realm was full of shadows, and within them lurked dangerous possibilities.

Eventually, Eden's eyes drooped, and her body grew heavy, until she could no longer deny the pull of sleep.

When morning came, Eden roused to the sound of her bunny digging in the corner of the room. It took her a moment to brush away the fog of sleep, and when she did, her mind immediately focused on the vampiress she'd met. Perhaps she'd had a dream of her, or maybe it was just the instant dislike Eden had for her.

It was the way Mynata forced herself into Draven's space, claiming him, then glanced at Eden as if *she* were intruding. Delight had tickled Eden's lips as he declined to dine with Mynata. She had no reason to be pleased other than that she saw how the vampiress' face fell in disappointment.

Although it had been short-lived, for at dinner, and throughout the night, she had wondered what she would become over time. Perhaps Mynata had been a soft lady once, and maybe Andhera stripped that away from her. Who could say? Eden wouldn't mourn for a female she never knew, but it still terrified her to picture herself becoming just like Mynata.

After breakfast, Loriah dressed Eden in a gown similar to the sheer, draping fabrics of Lucem, but it consisted of a few more layers. The bodice was a deep black with silver vines crawling up the left side, and on the right shoulder, a silver clasp clipped to a gray fur shawl. But it was the melding of dark red, purple, and black in the skirt that stood out most, for as it spilled from the black bodice, it gave way to the same colors but in a bright pastel hue. A clash of Lucem and Andhera.

Eden pulled the shawl closer to her neck as she stepped

into the hallway. She was growing accustomed to the cooler air, but it still nipped at her skin.

As she walked through the corridor, the sound of wailing echoed in the courtyard. Startled, Eden peered through one of the windows nearest it. Below, harpy guards unloaded a caged wagon full of individuals who were bound at the wrists. She bent forward, squinting to make out the details of them, and noticed not one had fae features.

With curiosity fueling her steps, Eden quickly made her way into the courtyard. Rather than assume the worst, she opted to ask.

"Excuse me." Eden stiffened as several harpies looked her way with their intense black eyes. "What are you doing with them?" She motioned to the middle-aged human males chained together. Fear shone in their eyes, an emotion she knew too well. She swallowed, returning her gaze to the harpy, who set herself apart from the others.

"Let us out! Please!" one of the men pleaded, rattling the bars on the wagon.

The harpy snorted at the protest, then replied to Eden. "These are prisoners sent from Midniva. They are sent to us to serve their punishment before returning home, in hopes of deterring them from repeat offenses." The harpy cocked her head, watching Eden carefully.

Eden nodded. "I don't recall your name?" They'd not been introduced yet.

"Dhriti, my lady." A soft breeze ruffled her inky short-cropped feathery hair.

Eden didn't want to know what their punishment was, yet she had the sneaking suspicion that they fed Draven.

While she knew he needed sustenance, she didn't want to think of where it came from.

A curse rang out behind Dhriti, and two guards dove off toward the side while another slammed the wagon's door shut.

Eden blanched. She had been a momentary distraction for them, and all it took was a second for the humans to attempt escape.

"They went over the side wall!"

Dhriti shifted to block Eden. Her talons clicked on the cobblestone as she surveyed the immediate area for a threat.

"Run after them, or else they won't stand a chance," Dhriti hissed.

The sound of wolves barking at one another filled the air, and Eden peered over at Dhriti, who towered over her. The harpy guard returned her glance, then bowed her head. "I believe it is best if we relocate you."

So did Eden.

"I was on my way to the gardens . . . " *But* her curiosity had gotten the better of her. Now two humans were running amok, and more than likely to their deaths. She frowned, rubbing between her eyebrows with a finger. "I'll leave you to your task. I didn't mean to interrupt."

"They'll be punished for their impulsive decision." A grim smile tugged at Dhriti's full lips before she turned back to the wagon.

How? Eden wondered. Would their planned punishment increase, or did Dhriti simply mean that they'd meet their end, however Andhera saw fit? She didn't want to think about it. Instead, she wound her way down the path toward the gardens and submerged herself into something familiar.

When she had been in the garden before, Eden wasn't able to focus on the plant life and how different it was from home. But now, with the unique foliage surrounding her, she couldn't help but explore it.

There were deep purple flowers with strands of black or white spilling from their centers, making it look as if they had whiskers. On closer inspection, they looked much like bats in flight.

Eden couldn't keep her hands at her side. She reached forward, stroking the silken petals, the strands of whiskers, and out of curiosity, she allowed her magic to pulse outward. Much to her surprise, life greeted her. Warmth swelled within her chest, for even amidst the unforgiving landscape of Andhera, life as fragile as a flower could blossom. Why couldn't she do the same?

As she moved down the row of flowers, she was lost to their fragrance and her desire to coax them into growing or blooming a touch earlier than they ought to.

"Be careful of that one," a familiar female voice said.

Eden froze, then withdrew her hand and faced Mynata. "Is that so?"

"It has quite the appetite and prefers to eat its meals alive. Screaming, even." She strode toward Eden, folding her arms across her chest as her dark eyes dragged along Eden's figure.

Eden swallowed roughly. Not because she was nervous in her company but because the dislike she felt for Mynata seemed to evolve into something ugly. Rather than speak, she simply waited for the female to continue.

"I want you to know how out of place you are here,

Eden." Mynata plucked a white flower from its bush and drank in the scent of it. "Draven and I are meant to be together. Not you. So, whatever little game this is, know that it's only temporary." Mynata closed the distance between them, baring her teeth in a wicked smile. "He will tire of your *innocence* soon enough."

Eden, riled by her words, narrowed her eyes. "I am sorry to disappoint you, Mynata, but Draven and I are to be married. This isn't a game; it's politics, and it is our duty." She curled her fingers into her palms, biting her tongue to keep from letting the growing bitterness slip out, but the flap of wings brought her attention toward the sky. A harpy lighted on the stone path. Dhriti.

"Lady Eden, I've prepared a carriage for you as instructed." Dhriti's gaze locked with Eden's—the harpy nodded to her in silent understanding.

Mynata spun on her heel. "I will see you around, *Lady* Eden." The vampiress disappeared down the pathway.

When she was no longer in view, Eden's shoulders relaxed, and she approached the guard. "Thank you," she murmured. "I don't like her." Shame painted her freckled cheeks.

"You are not alone." Her long talons scraped across the stone pathway.

Eden laughed, covering her mouth with the back of her hand. "I shouldn't . . . " She paused, cocking her head in thought. "Is a carriage ready for me?" In truth, she hadn't asked for one and hadn't planned on going anywhere, but maybe that was what she needed.

"No, but that doesn't mean one can't be. I was on my way to better introduce myself, for His Majesty has assigned me as one of your guards." Dhriti's dark, feathered wings folded tightly against her back. "Should I have a carriage prepared?"

Eden hesitated, considering the news. Draven was assigning her guards? Initially, the thought rankled her—as if she needed constant supervision. But then Eden thought of how quickly terrible things unfolded in Andhera. And she didn't want to be alone in the dark realm. "Yes, I'd like to visit the . . . " Where? Having only passed outside of the village and through the capital, she had limited access to the city. "I want to experience Arcem. Whether that is visiting the shops or listening to scholars or tradespeople, I want to know more." Draven had left her a purse of currency, and while she didn't need a thing, she longed to do something *normal*.

Dhriti's lips twitched, and when she bowed, this time it was more genuine. "As you wish."

By the time Eden made it to the courtyard, she only had to wait a few more minutes for Dhriti to arrive with the carriage. Settling into the cushion, she fussed over the colorful skirt. It felt so odd to her, being free to go as she wished, without anyone to tell her where she could and couldn't go. The feeling induced a fraction of anxiety within her chest.

"If my lady truly does wish to learn more, then I will gladly show you the heart of Arcem. Those who create the beating life of the city." Dhriti leaped into the air, her great wingspan carrying her high enough above the carriage that she could survey any potential threats.

Eden gathered the reins in her hands, but the presence of someone by her side stilled her. A male of medium build, with sandalwood skin and bottomless eyes, smiled at her.

"I didn't mean to startle you. I'm Tulok, one of the many wolves you'll hear howling their days away—and also one of your assigned guards. Undoubtedly, I'll be your favorite guard."

Eden decided immediately that she quite liked his friendly demeanor, and something about him reminded her of Tamas, if he were older.

A pang of longing for home gripped her, but when Tulok clucked to the single kelpie, they began their journey down the winding path of the cliff, and the passing scenery served as a needed distraction.

It didn't remain quiet for long because Tulok knew how to fill the silence. "My lady, if I may say, you've caused quite the stir as of late." He paused, then placed a hand to his heart. "A personal favorite was watching you assault His Majesty with such enthusiasm. It isn't often we get to witness such a thing and not see the offender torn to shreds." Tulok's eyes closed as he laughed, clearly recollecting the moment.

He had been there? Eden hadn't realized. Not that she could differentiate between the wolves in their other forms, and she hadn't exactly taken note of them. She had been too busy running from the horrific sight of Draven tearing the lamia's heart out and lapping up her lifeblood.

"Will you just shut your mouth?" Dhriti hissed from above. "You'll make the lady ill."

Tulok sobered and glanced down at Eden. "You're not going to be sick, are you?"

She clenched her jaw, shaking her head. She couldn't help but laugh at the earnest expression in his eyes and the mounting horror on his face.

"I just got this uniform," Tulok mumbled, scooting a fraction away from Eden.

When the land evened out, Dhriti led the way. The wealthier, larger homes gave way to a familiar cluster of establishments. The citizens of Arcem carried on about their lives, painting the picture of normalcy to Eden. It didn't matter if they were were-creatures, vampires, or revenants; this was their home and their life.

Dhriti landed in front of a shop. Pots lined shelves outside, as did stone statues. Tulok pulled the carriage to a halt, then reclined in the seat.

"Enjoy your shopping, my lady." Tulok offered a sharp canine smile.

Eden hopped down from the carriage and approached Dhriti. The harpy motioned toward the side of the shop, which she hadn't seen yet. Between one building and the next, a glasshouse sat, and within it, Eden recognized the sweet smell of plants right away.

Unlike the outdoors, the glasshouse was warm, more like the nights at home, and the smell of churned soil and watered plants awakened her senses.

It dawned on her that perhaps Aasha's gardens could use a gift, a new addition to their growth. If Eden continued to foster it, perhaps it would feel more like a sanctuary to her. But what would fit amongst the exotic beauties? She searched through purple blossoms, midnight blue spires, and neon-colored lilies, but it was a succulent of sorts she was drawn to.

It was the shape of a starfish, but on each point were dozens upon dozens of beads. When tapped, they rolled and opened. *They were eyes.* The sight of it was both alarming and intriguing.

129

On her way out of the glasshouse, Eden spotted a small statue. It was a gargoyle with the face of a cat and body of a dragon, wings and all.

In her element, Eden felt more at ease, enough so to speak to the intimidating harpy soldier. "Dhriti," she started, biting her bottom lip. "What . . . exactly is a harpy? Are they born?" It was a question which had prodded at her since arriving, but it seemed as though she had endless questions and didn't want to sound like a child.

Dhriti didn't so much as flinch, and her gaze shifted from a stone fountain to Eden's face. "Harpies are not born but created by our prior life." The words were vague, but when she smiled, it was mirthless and a touch cruel. "We rise from a gruesome death inflicted by a man, fueled by our vengeance and wrath. I suppose you could say we refuse to truly die."

Eden's brow furrowed as the words settled in. Dhriti had been a victim of murder? It felt strange to feel sympathy for a creature who not only looked as if she could tear another in half but *would*, and yet here she was.

"If it saddens you, know that His Majesty allows us to hunt down our murderers. And when I found mine in Hillbride's tavern, pissing himself, I reveled in exacting my vengeance." Dhriti lifted her hand, black talons gleaming in the day moon's light. "First I took his legs, then his tongue, and then his c—"

Tulok burst in between them. "Well, that was a tragic story, Dhriti." His dark eyes flicked to Eden and made her wonder if she looked as mortified as she felt.

Her stomach tightened as she pictured Dhriti taking on the persona of fury and vengeance. With Eden's vivid imagination and what she'd seen of Andhera so far, it was enough to chill her blood.

Dhriti shrugged. "Apologies, my lady. It was only fifty years ago for me, still fresh in my mind."

"No, you shouldn't apologize. I am . . . glad that you were able to find him." It dawned on her that she actually was pleased Dhriti could bring him to justice.

At their side, several figurines tumbled to the ground, shattering. Tulok folded his arms, feigning innocence. "Are we done here?"

Eden laughed, despite the weight of the current mood, and eased into browsing the shop again.

When she was finished, she settled in next to Tulok, who perked up once again.

"Onward?" he questioned.

"Oh yes, we are not finished today." How peculiar was it that freedom came with an almost intoxicating feeling? There was no need for her at the castle, and she was fairly certain she would not only be in the way but would frustrate more than a handful of individuals. Now that she was away from the confines of the castle, she had no desire to return so promptly.

At least, not until her body yearned for food and rest.

Draven

Eden's safety had been much on Draven's mind since their visit to Primis. While he had already designated a harpy soldier and were-guard to accompany her into town and watch over her in the castle, he hadn't forgotten the notion of giving Eden some hand-to-hand training. After all of her escapades since arriving at Castle Aasha, he couldn't trust her not to find another mishap to tumble into.

The were-guard trained regularly. It was good for them to exhaust some energy if they had nothing to track and kill, and fighting each other not only kept them in ready shape, it burnt off the excess that would otherwise make them impossible to live with. Were-people in general seemed to possess more exuberance than the average being. Perhaps it had something to do with the energy required to shift between forms, but were-wolves especially could grate on one's nerves.

It was better they train, and often. For all their sakes, but most importantly for Draven's.

Glancing at the day moon outside, Draven called Loriah

to his side. The revenant appeared before his desk with her head bowed respectfully as she curtsied. "Your Grace?"

"Please see to it that Eden is clothed in garments befitting exercise. I am of the mind to have her train with the were-guard today. Do this at once, as I will be collecting her momentarily."

"Of course, sire." Loriah bowed, then disappeared.

"Training, Your Majesty?" Seurat asked, coming closer to the desk as Draven stood.

"Yes, training. Would you go and let Captain Channon know she and I will be joining him shortly?"

Seurat nodded. "At once." He turned on his heel and left the study in haste.

Gazing at his own garments, Draven moved across the hall to his private chambers that were used to dress and bathe. Stripping quickly out of his vest, shirt, and breeches, he pulled on a loose-fitting tunic, leaving the stays at the top unlaced. He then pulled on a pair of soft, broken-in leather trousers that would leave him more capable of moving freely than his everyday wear. Tugging on boots, Draven then left to retrieve Eden.

The goblins were in the hallway, excitedly chirping at him as he exited his chambers. Gruff launched himself at his ankle, sinking tiny claws into the leather and leg beneath so that he might hitch a ride.

"Damn it, tiny beast. Haven't you legs for a reason?" Draven growled at him but did not shake him off.

Gruff began to happily squawk about how the lady down the hall no longer screamed at the sight of them.

"Did I not say she was a friend?" He finally stopped to extract Gruff from his trouser leg and left him hanging off a wall torch nearby. "Now, do try to behave."

Making his way to Eden's room, Draven rapped lightly on the door. When the door opened, it was to reveal a confused looking Eden. Her hair had been braided off to one side, and Loriah had dressed her in a pair of her own leather trousers and a white linen shirt with a corset vest over top. It was a sight that nearly made Draven take a step back as it ignited a flash of heat within him. Instead, he schooled his features and fought for aloofness.

"Are you ready?"

"Yes, except that I'm not quite sure what it is I'm ready for."

"Come with me. You're going to learn to fight." Draven stepped back and motioned into the hall beside him.

"Excuse me?" Eden asked as she stepped out of her room and fell into step with him, her confused look only growing.

"After your escapade in Primis, I've decided that you need to learn how to defend yourself."

"But . . . I've never even held a toy sword before," she stammered.

"That's fine. Today you will begin to learn hand-to-hand combat. Swords won't come until later, when you're ready."

"Wh-what?" Eden continued to walk beside him, but Draven could tell she was feeling a little stunned.

"You're learning to defend yourself, Eden. I can't trust you not to get yourself killed otherwise," he responded curtly.

She fell silent as they made their way outside the castle and into the courtyard, where the were-guards were in the midst of training. Captain Channon stood off to the side watching them. Typically, he participated, but there was a pinched look to the captain's brows that told Draven he was waiting for them to arrive and was wondering how to take this latest request from his sovereign.

"Your Majesty! My Lady." Channon bowed his head as they arrived before him. "I don't believe we've been properly introduced. I am Captain Channon, captain of the Royal Wolf Guard." He bowed formally to her before lifting his head and shooting her a mischievous look through the fall of his blond hair. "You may not remember me, as I'm wearing far more clothing now than the first time we met."

"I remember you." Eden cleared her throat.

Channon shot her an ear-splitting grin, which made Draven's eyes narrow. "So happy to hear I made an impression." When Draven grunted lowly, Channon straightened up. "I've been told you're interested in training with our guards today, which I must say excites us all very much. Why don't you fall into ranks with my men, my lady?"

"Oh, I don't know—"

"Actually, I was thinking we could start with a demonstration for her, before we begin teaching her the moves. Lady Eden has never been trained in combat before," Draven interrupted.

Before Channon could respond, Tulok slipped up beside them. "Might I make a suggestion?"

Draven nodded to the guard.

"Perhaps His Majesty would like to take on Captain Channon? It has been a while since we've all had a chance to witness our king in a lighthearted battle."

Eden was peering up at him with wide eyes, and Draven decided that Channon could use a lesson for getting a tad too familiar with her. "I suppose I could be persuaded to do so."

Channon grinned, but there was a twitch in his jaw as he swept his hair back out of his eyes. "Splendid!" Turning from them, Channon wrapped his arm around Tulok's neck, hauling him in against himself as he growled threatening words into his ear and moved toward the middle of the group.

Draven watched the were-guards break apart, creating a clean space for the sparring match to take place. It had been a while since he had done something of this nature with his men. He supposed it would be good for morale as well.

"Watch what we do closely."

"What?" Eden blinked, then looked up at him once again.

"While Captain Channon and I spar, watch how we interact with each other. The way our hands and feet move to both block and attack. Be mindful of our stances, how far apart our legs are, how our hands come up to protect our faces. It may seem like a lot, but the more you watch others, the more familiar you will be with the movements when you begin practicing them yourself."

Draven turned from her then and moved into the center of the crowd, rolling his shoulders as he loosened his body for the inevitable impact of another body coming at him. Channon stepped up opposite him, shifting his head back and forth as his steel-gray eyes sized him up. His captain was a good fighter. He wouldn't have obtained his rank if Draven weren't fully confident in his abilities. However, he had no intention of letting him win this fight.

Moving up to Channon, Draven stuck his hands out in

fists, and Channon tapped his own fists on top of Draven's in acknowledgement of a friendly fight. The were-wolf then lost no time in swinging toward him with a surprise uppercut.

Draven just managed to dodge it, feeling the light graze of knuckles brush along his jaw. As he ducked, his hand came up to push Channon's arm away, and he easily blocked the next blow from the captain's left hand.

Growling, and eyes narrowing at the cheap shot, Draven threw a punch of his own, which Channon managed to block, though he stumbled back in the process. Having gained a little ground, Draven struck at him again. This time, however, he pressed on, sweeping out with his foot just shortly after.

Channon wasn't expecting the foot and tripped in the process of ducking the fist. However, as he fell, he hit the ground in a roll and popped back up several feet away. Spinning to face him once more, Draven found himself following Channon in a slow circle as they eyed each other up.

Draven could be patient, though, and he was fully willing to let the wolf come to him. When he did, the guard's eyes glowed, and he released a growl as he lunged. Prepared for it, Draven blocked his attack. Grabbing at the captain's side and bicep, he lifted him off the ground to toss him over his shoulder.

In the process of being tossed, Channon grabbed ahold of Draven's loose tunic and pulled him over along with him. Rolling on the ground, Draven pushed himself back onto his feet quickly, eyes narrowing on his captain once more. Swiftly, Draven grabbed his shirt and pulled it off, tossing it to the side. If Channon was going to use it to his advantage, Draven would be rid of it. Seeing this, Channon lifted a hand and waggled a finger at him.

"Worried, Your Majesty?"

"Denying you the ability to cheat."

Channon shot a smug grin his way. "Is it cheating, sire, if I use all that I have to my advantage?"

Draven smirked deeply. "Mmm, I suppose not." This time, it was Draven who lunged at Channon, and he used some of his preternatural speed to do so. The wolf yelped and leapt back, stumbling but keeping his balance. Channon managed to get a fist in, catching Draven on the jaw.

Shaking his head, Draven growled and swung at him. Channon blocked, but as the were-wolf swung at him in return, Draven brushed the fist away with a quick press of his wrist, then spun his hand and grasped his forearm, bending the arm back. Channon winced but turned on his heel to change the angle of his arm and pull free of the hold.

Draven didn't give him a break. With a growl, his fangs popping from his gums in the excitement of the fight, he grabbed at Channon's other arm. Pulling it, he kicked at the captain's ankle, knocking him off balance and forcing Channon to tumble to the ground.

This time, as the were-wolf rolled over onto his back and jumped to his feet, Draven used his abilities to go invisible. Channon spun, sniffing at the air.

"Now, now, Your Majesty, who's cheating?" Channon turned slowly in a circle, trying to catch a subtle shift in the air that might give his master away or a scent of him on the breeze.

Moving as silently as possible, Draven snuck up behind

Channon. When the wolf was looking in the opposite direction, he lunged and wrapped his arm around his neck, pulling him swiftly in against his chest, where he locked his captain in place. Dropping the invisibility, he opened his mouth and pressed the tips of his fangs to the edge of Channon's throat.

Draven felt Channon stiffen, and then he released a shaky laugh. "Cheater," he rasped, tapping his arm to indicate he was submitting.

"I was merely demonstrating an important fact to the lady," Draven stated, releasing him.

"And what fact was that, sire?" Channon asked, a shaky, nervous laugh leaving him. In the depths of his eyes, there was just a hint of latent fear.

"That your enemy will do anything to win, including cheat. So never hold back." His eyes left Channon's to search out Eden, who was looking at the both of them wide-eyed. Swiping the back of his hand across his forehead, Draven lifted a brow at her. "Now, would you like to begin learning the basics?"

Eden

Watching the brawl had been amusing to begin with, then difficult as Eden focused on each foot placement, hand strike, and twist. Frustration coursed through her because she couldn't keep up with their movements. It was too dark, and her eyes couldn't focus. Even with the day moon's brighter glow, each lightning-fast or subtle movement was nearly lost on her.

Or it would've been. The moment Draven's shirt was removed, his pale skin on display beneath the moonlight, she seemed to hyper-focus on him. How his muscles coiled, bunched, and flexed with each swipe or strike.

Eden's cheeks warmed.

"My papa was not a fighter, not with weapons," Eden offered to Tulok, who stood by her side. "He fought with his wisdom." But perhaps if he'd known how to fight with a weapon, he'd still be alive.

He drew in a breath, weighing her words. "Wit is certainly a sharp tool, but there is nothing wrong with learning to defend yourself. Wit and defense have a place together." Tulok gently nudged Eden with his elbow. "It looks like it's your turn."

Her turn. She lifted her hands to press her fingers to her mouth. Did Draven mean she was to spar with him? Eden glanced over her shoulder at Tulok, who took his fist and swung through the air. He winked at her, recalling how he'd enjoyed her flailing and swiping at Draven in Primis.

None of this boded well with her, but she had little choice.

Her shoulders lowered from her ears as she stepped forward, her hands dropping to her sides. "I suppose now is as good a time as any."

The soft chattering of voices around them silenced as she took her place in front of Draven. She'd seen her fair share of bare chests in her lifetime but none that had inspired conflicting feelings in her like his did. Eden yearned to run her hands along the hard planes and wondered what they felt like as they tensed.

And he stood there, an impassive look on his face, as if she were another of his subjects he was patiently dealing with. It could've been worse, she reminded herself.

That thought was like a much-needed douse of cold water.

Draven cocked an eyebrow. "It is best to begin with the foundation of combat. Always remember to keep your core engaged," he said as he brought a hand to his abdomen, then dragged it to his back. "Like with riding a horse. And you'll want to keep your stance wide enough so you'll not topple like a pine in the wind. Oaks are strong because their roots spread far, and it sturdies them." Draven's body, although lax, gave Eden the impression he could still pounce faster than she could blink. He moved gradually so she could watch how he placed his feet shoulder-width apart, knees bent, muscles engaged.

She followed his lead, finding that she enjoyed his comparisons to nature. Was it because he knew she was fond of it and understood them?

"Your arms, like the limbs of a tree, will bend and block. Refrain from growing too rigid."

"Because what doesn't bend will break," Eden finished.

Draven nodded, and for a moment, a faint sliver of surprise filtered into his gaze. "That is right." He stepped in front of her, guiding her arms with a light pull. "Now, we will shuffle through some basic drills."

Was Draven going to instruct her the entire time? It wasn't as though she were complaining. He was being more than patient, and was an adequate tutor, but didn't he have other matters to attend?

His fingers tapping on her elbow pulled Eden from her thoughts. And then, they began a slow start to a dance. At least, that was what it felt like. Slide forward, arm block, a duck, a squat, and move back into place.

It felt like they'd practiced for an eternity, but it finally became ingrained in Eden's mind. She was panting, and sweat trickled down her temples, her neck and back.

"Now, let's put it to use, shall we?" Draven's tone was just above a friendly growl, but no laughter shone in his blue eyes.

He made it difficult to forget, especially in this state, that he was as much a predator as one of the wolves, and this was his element. Not Eden's. But, with the building trust between them, she believed Draven wouldn't test her if he didn't think she was capable.

He stood in front of her this time, poised to advance,

and Eden mentally chided herself for standing limply. *I must look like a lost waif to him.* She squared her stance, lifting her arms. Then, rather than waiting for Draven to make the first move, Eden launched forward, taking a wide swipe with her fist. He shoved it aside, causing her to step off balance.

Draven hardly relented, but he was still going easy on her. He struck out with his arm, far slower than he normally would, but Eden shoved it away.

His earlier lessons jumbled in her mind, but she recalled him speaking about cheating. How could she cheat? She had no weapon. Just her bare hands and the . . . ground.

Eden was nothing if not clever. She had no choice but to be, not when her mother was so strict, and it had forced her to become creative in how she went about things. How to lie, and in a way, manipulate. She was naive, but she was not dimwitted.

While Draven had been showing her several defensive moves, all of which she'd committed to memory, she'd stumbled on a rock jutting out. If she could maneuver Draven closer, she could use it to catch him off balance, in theory.

"Don't give up. Continue as you were," Draven coaxed her and slid forward, but Eden dodged out of the way, then circled around, forcing him to turn his back to the stone.

There was no way she could outmaneuver him. He was faster, taller, and had centuries of training. But Tulok was right . . . Wit had its place.

When Draven struck out again, Eden blocked it, twisting as she did, and it knocked her off balance and onto the ground with a thud. Her hands dug into the gravel, scratching away tender flesh.

Eden glanced up at him. Concern rumpled his brow, but his expression hardened, and a warning blared in her head. She was bleeding. The game was over, and with every ounce of strength she possessed, she kicked out at his leg, causing him to stumble back and over the rock. It was enough time for her to scramble to her knees. Somewhere, she could hear the wolves clamoring, but it happened in a blur.

Draven descended on her, grabbing her shoulder, but Eden was in flight mode, and she jerked her elbow back hard enough that when it connected with his jaw, she heard and felt it in her marrow. She wouldn't be his meal.

He twisted her around, his fangs protruding as he shook his head, frowning—a truly pained look on his face. "Tulok!" he hissed, and already, the wolf was peeling his king away from Eden's prone form. "Finish this," Draven said, strained. Soon Captain Channon was by his side, too, escorting him away.

Tulok remained behind and he extended his hand to Eden, hauling her up. Although he wore a smile, tension oozed from him. "The elbow to the face may be my new favorite sight to see." He leaned in closer. "Are you all right?"

Her heart pounded violently, threatening to send her to the ground again. She was alive, and Draven was a few yards away. "I . . . I suppose."

"You got scratched, didn't you?" His dark eyes searched her body over. "Your blood is like nectar to him. Even trained warriors will lose themselves to adrenaline, but mix instinct in with it . . . " He shrugged. "The king will recover and be his cheerful self again in a moment. But you and I will finish what was started." Tulok clapped his hands together and took a step backward, rolling his shoulders. "I commend you on your use of the stone and your quick thinking." He wagged a finger in the air at her, grinning. "I don't care what the captain thinks, you don't have a penchant for death."

It took a moment for his words to register. "What?" Her tone was a little more shrill than she cared for. "I don't!" She glared off in the direction of Channon, who had, in fact, heard everything. He didn't look apologetic, and only arched a brow as if challenging her to prove him wrong.

"Fine. Show me what to do if it wasn't Draven and a pack of wolves watching me flounder." Eden huffed, thrusting her hand in the air in annoyance.

"You can get frustrated, but try not to get angry. It clouds your thinking. And I will show you what to do in case it *is* Draven again." Tulok didn't smile or laugh; it was a simple fact.

The notion chilled her, but somewhere in her marrow, she knew he wouldn't hurt her. Every creature had instincts, and what were Draven's telling him? That a lesser being lay beneath him, fighting, and that he should act, no doubt.

Even as the adrenaline slid from her body, leaving her knees shaking, she was willing to prove herself, wanting to learn.

"Only a little longer. There is no point training you until you collapse." Tulok demonstrated the same moves Draven had, motioning for her to repeat. He was facing her, so they mirrored one another, and it became a push and pull of movement.

145

For nearly an hour, Eden practiced, until she was entirely breathless and her sides ached. Somewhere amidst the tutoring, Draven had disappeared, only to return as she finished up.

He approached her wearing a clean shirt. "Eden." He inclined his head, his lips pressing into a thin line. "Forgive me for that. I didn't mean . . . "

Eden lifted her hand, shaking her head. "No. Don't apologize." She was exhausted, wanting nothing more than to sink into the depths of a steaming bath. But she'd gone over the scenario a multitude of times since it'd happened. It had frightened her, but she hadn't been disgusted, hadn't despised him for what he was in that moment.

Confusion knit his brows together. "Surely I must . . . "

Eden flexed her fingers at her side, glancing over his face. He didn't bear a mark where her elbow had connected with his face. "I would no sooner ask a lion to apologize for his urge to hunt. You frightened me, I won't lie about that, but I don't hold your actions against you."

He folded his arms, and his expression softened a fraction, a pensive look pinching his features. "Very well. Thank you." He subtly jerked his chin to the side. "You did well today. I suggest you venture inside and take advantage of the oversized tub. I'll ensure Loriah fetches you balms for your muscles." Draven inclined his head before he turned and walked away.

Eden released a breath and watched as the nightmare king disappeared from sight. Every time she was in his presence, a conflicting array of emotions rose, and it was growing difficult to sift through them all.

If she knew more of the king she was to spend her immortal life with, perhaps it would put an end to the questions, the uncertainty. Eden may not have known him well, but she knew enough of Draven to know he wasn't going to sit her in front of the fire and discuss his life with her.

Flicking a strand of hair from her eyes, Eden followed the same path Draven took. A bath sounded good. Her muscles ached, and the cooling fabric against her skin left her chilled.

Maybe the heat would chase away the frisson of fear threatening to crawl down her spine, but the more she considered the feeling, the more she realized it wasn't fear at all but excitement.

14

Draven

Life had certainly been eventful in Castle Aasha since Eden's arrival. In her first week alone, she had upset the goblins, aggravated the harpies, set the revenants all atwitter for fear she was starving to death, attempted to flee from him on foot, and been the main cause of distraction for a number of human prisoners to escape.

While explaining to Travion why two of his human subjects would not be returning had been unpleasant, in the days since their first visit to Primis, life seemed to have settled. If he were being honest, it had more than settled.

From his study window, Draven peered at the garden below. At the moment, Eden was nowhere to be seen, but the evidence of her presence still remained. Her attentiveness had somehow brought a vitality to the garden, and truly the castle as a whole, that had not been there before. A spark of life Draven had thought not possible for his dark realm.

He was seeing once again the innocent and curious

creature he had met the night of the ball, and it pleased Draven to know that at least he and his brothers hadn't taken that away from Eden.

Draven was pulled from his thoughts as a soft thrumming noise sounded from the other side of the room. Glancing over, he found the granite basin on the edge of his desk glowing. Crossing the room, he stepped up to it and waved a hand over the surface. Travion's face soon replaced the glowing light.

"Brother, I wasn't sure you would be there to answer. I thought perhaps you may be a little . . . distracted." Travion grinned up at him from the surface of the water.

"If by that you mean I have more important things to be doing than speaking to you, then you are correct." Draven simply eyed his brother's features. He could tell by how well-lit Travion's face was that the sun was shining brightly in Midniva today. While he hadn't felt sunshine on his skin in several millennia, he could still remember its warmth.

"How *are* things between you and the young one?"

"Well, she no longer looks at me as if I am the embodiment of death, so I suppose our nightly dinners are achieving some form of reconciliation."

"You dine with her?" Travion seemed surprised.

"Well, she dines, I sip."

"Not from her, surely . . . "

Draven glared at his brother through the rippling surface of the bowl. "Of course not. No matter what they whisper of me, I'm actually not a bestial tyrant, at least not entirely."

Travion was giving him a knowing grin.

"Is that all you wished to know, or was there a purpose

149

for your summons today?" Draven's tone was short, pushing Travion to get to his point. While conversation was easy between them, it wasn't his brother's tendency to use the basin for the sake of gossiping like two court widows.

Travion's features turned somber at once. "I'm afraid I haven't good news for you, Draven."

"What?"

"There have been signs of vampire attacks in Hilbride, as well as in Ordine."

Draven cursed loudly, a hand brushing over his face. This was not the first word he'd had of such tidings in the past week. "How many deaths?"

"Only two. But not from a lack of trying." Travion's face creased with further displeasure. "We haven't been able to locate the culprits. However, I don't believe they've crossed back through to Andhera yet. We placed patrol at the gates to the Veil, and there haven't been any attempts to go through."

"Do you wish for me to come?" he asked, hands gripping the edge of his desk as he leaned over the basin.

"No. There's no need for it. By all appearances, we're dealing with fledglings. My men should be equipped to deal with this situation. I simply wanted to make you aware."

Draven sighed and nodded. "I appreciate the warning. I'll bring my nobles before me and see if they know of one who could be producing fledglings in Midniva."

"I will let you know once we have caught them."

"Send word if you need my presence."

"I shall. Oh, and Draven?"

Draven lifted a brow, waiting.

"Do try to enjoy yourself a little. She may not be staying for long, but that doesn't mean you can't partake in the gift Zryan dropped into your lap." Leaving no time for a rebuttal, Travion was gone.

Grumbling beneath his breath, Draven called out for a revenant. When Stevron appeared, Draven requested the elderly man fetch General Ailith for him. The nobles would need to be contacted at once, brought before his people, and plundered for information until someone gave him an answer. He would not leave them to their peace while Midniva was threatened by careless fledglings.

No one made new vampires without his consent. Now there would be hell to pay.

When his door opened, it was not Ailith who entered but Mynata. She wore a gown of gold satin, which clung to her hips below her black corset, spilling down her long legs in a rippling wave of gleaming fabric.

"Now is not the time, Mynata."

"But it must be, Draven. You cannot simply ignore me and the rest of your subjects because you have a new pet."

Draven's eyes narrowed at her words, his lip curling back slightly in the beginnings of a snarl. "Excuse me?" He didn't know what she was alluding to, but he definitely did not like the direction she was taking. Nor her tone. There was only so much familiarity Draven would accept.

The vampiress took this as a sign to enter, for she stepped farther into the room and nearer to him.

"Why is she truly here, Draven?"

"I do not believe that is any of your business," he replied in a soft but dangerous tone. His ire was rising, and if she was not careful, he would not control his temper.

Mynata did not seem concerned and pressed on. "It was assumed she was meant to be your queen . . . but there has been no talk of a wedding. I know you, Draven! You've always said you would not take a bride, and if you did . . . I know it would not be some naive, simple fae maiden from Lucem."

Draven was moving before he was aware, standing over Mynata. His hand went to her throat, and he thrust her back against the nearest wall, pinning her there. Forcing her head up with the hand still around her neck, he made certain she was looking into the depths of his cold eyes.

"Simple?" His voice was low, barely above a whisper. "Do not disparage someone simply because they possess qualities you never will." He leaned in closer, his fangs protruding from his upper lip. "Eden holds a goodness and innocence to her that is a beacon of light in this dark hell, and I will keep her here for as long as it pleases me. The hows and whys are no concern of yours."

Mynata's eyes darkened with anger, and she wrenched away, stepping to the side and several feet from him.

"Say what you will of it . . . Your Majesty." His title rolled off her tongue like venom. "But the nobles are talking."

Draven's eyes narrowed on her once more. "They will always talk."

"They know you have a fae tucked away in the castle that you have introduced to no one. They find it terribly unfair that you keep a toy from Lucem to feed off of whenever you please, yet they are barely able to cross into Midniva for a human."

Draven stilled, his rage now a low simmer. So, this was the gossip amongst his people.

"You're feeding into their agitation. After all, what is good for the king . . . is good for his people, is it not?" she finished with a hiss.

Draven took a step toward her, which caused Mynata to retreat, some self-preservation breaking through her recklessness.

"Thank you, Mynata." She looked surprised at his words. "You are right, my people have not met her. It is time I introduced my future queen to my kingdom."

She looked startled, and it pleased him to find her finally at a loss for words. Without anything further to say, Draven left her standing there in his study. He found Seurat in the hallway, looking apologetic for not being able to stop the noble. Beside him was General Ailith, a look of annoyance on her features as she gazed into his study at the vampiress behind him.

"General, schedule interviews with all of the noble families. You must question them at length. Fledglings are being made in Midniva. Travion has found them in the villages just beyond the Veil."

Ailith's features hardened, and the harpy nodded. "Of course, Your Majesty. My soldiers and I will not rest until we have helped you unearth the culprit."

Nodding, Draven turned his attention to Seurat. "And you must prepare them for a ball."

"A ball? Sire?" Seurat sputtered.

"Five days hence." He left them both then, striding purposefully down the hall.

Mynata's words had the opposite effect on him than he was sure she had intended. Rather than making Draven rethink having Eden here, she had only made him realize that while she was here, she must be seen in every way to be his future bride. It was the best way to keep her protected in his kingdom, as well as to not leave any questions of what Draven was doing with a fae in his castle.

If the recent proceedings in Midniva were any sign of the times, he could not afford to lead the vampire nobility into thoughts of kidnapping fae to fill their blood coffers. That was not a battle he wished to partake in.

So, he would throw this ball, introduce Eden as his bride-to-be, and make certain all of his people knew she would be the only fae crossing over into Andhera.

Eden was in her room, and as he rapped on the door and stepped in, he found her down on her knees, peering beneath her bed. Draven took a moment simply to observe, puzzling over the positions he continued to find her in.

"What are you doing now?" he asked. "Is there a little man under your bed?"

Unlike in the garden, Eden did not startle at the sudden sound of his voice. Perhaps she was growing more used to his silent step.

"Actually, there is a bunny . . . Something appears to be wrong with Alder." She turned to peer over her shoulder at him.

"Oh," he murmured and took another step into her room, realization dawning on him. "He is transforming."

Draven found himself down on his knees beside her, taking a look beneath the bed to see only a pair of glowing eyes staring back at him through fits of sneezing and growls.

"I had not thought it would be so soon."

Draven peered over at her, pleased to see that she did

not seem distraught at this news, merely puzzled as she thought it over.

"Andhera affects us all differently. Animals the quickest, especially those that are young. Humans also react quickly. It is why Midniva's prisoners are only kept here for one month before being sent back, so that they do not begin the change."

"And fae?"

"For fae, it is longer. Months, typically, before there are any signs it has begun."

Alder released a low hissing noise that interrupted their conversation. Seeing the pained look on Eden's face, Draven stooped low once more and locked eyes with the rabbit. Murmuring softly, he used his summoning charm to glamour the creature into slowly crawling out from under the bed.

When he had, the two of them stared down at the ashen bunny, who had sprouted a pair of black leathery wings on its back, and where he had once had a ball of fluff for a tail, it was now long and sparsely furred. From its tiny paws, razor-sharp claws glinted, and if Draven was not mistaken, the overhanging teeth had become sharp fangs.

Draven glanced from the critter up to Eden, expecting to see the worst, only to find himself shocked. Eden let out a soft coo at the sight of her pet and reached out to pick it up without a hint of fear. With the creature curled up on its back, tucked into the crook of her arm, she rocked it back and forth.

"I knew he would change . . . but what sort of creature is he now?" Her brow slightly furrowed, Eden looked from Alder over to Draven.

"Well . . . I don't believe anyone has ever brought a rabbit here before. So I am not certain what he is." Besides another rodent-like creature to scurry around his castle tripping him up.

"It's silly to think, but he is a rabat." Eden laughed and gave his wiry whiskers a tug. "You've lost your fluffy tail, but you have the most darling wings."

Draven found himself, yet again, surprised at Eden's versatility in accepting the oddities of Andhera. In her first days here, he had been certain he had brought her into a living hell that she could not wish to leave fast enough. Yet she seemed to have found a way of life here, or at least he saw that she was trying. Draven felt the surge of that foreign feeling once more.

"I'm throwing a ball," he announced suddenly. While balls were some of his least favorite things, and thus were not terribly common at Aasha, he couldn't help but wonder what Eden would think. Would it please her to attend one here? Or would it be a brutal reminder of the last one she had attended and her life being turned upside down?

Eden lifted her eyes from Alder to glance at him, her face showing more surprise over this than she had over the transformation of her bunny. "A ball?"

"Yes. You've been here a month, it is time you were introduced to the noble families. Seurat will be helping to plan it, so let him know anything special you would like brought through the Veil. Foods, jewels, fabrics . . . "

Eden was studying him as if he were some peculiar thing she had just stumbled upon in the garden. A new species of flora that had not been identified yet and may turn out to be nothing but a weed.

"This ball . . . Will you be attending?" she asked.

"Yes, I will be attending."

She nodded. "Very well." A smile slowly slid over her lips. "Then I shall as well!"

Alder growled softly from the nook of her arm, his tail thumping lightly against her chest.

Eden

E den hadn't believed her ears at first. Draven wanted to throw a ball? She had, in fact, been far more surprised at that than at the change Alder had endured. At first, she'd felt sorry for her pet, but as he grew used to his wings and discovered how he could both hide beneath the bed and fly away from grasping fingers, he delighted in it.

Still, a ball? When she summoned Loriah to rake over the details of what she wanted for her gown, Eden opted for something Andherian. If she were to be their queen, she wanted to look the part but also still hold true to herself.

In the end, she'd settled on a deep plum dress with a plunging neckline and, unfortunately, a corset. Eden was still growing used to the confining nature of the blasted things. Silver petal buttons adorned the front of the bodice, staying true to her love for the flora.

How had it already been a month in Andhera? The first week had been atrocious. She'd created her fair share of trouble without meaning to, but she'd like to think she'd settled in and that everyone else had grown used to her.

Loriah placed one more pin in Eden's hair. Her waist-length strands were, for once, pulled up, styled into an intricate chignon. It looked as if it were a blooming rose.

Silver teardrops swung from her earlobes and settled at the hollow of her neck, with a vine of silver and amethyst nestled just above her breasts.

"There. You are a vision, and if His Majesty doesn't find himself lost for words, he's blind. Now, go to him and enjoy your time." Loriah didn't often speak so boldly, but there was a glint in her eyes this evening, and it sent Eden's heart into a frenzy. Did she know something Eden didn't, or was it simply due to the official announcement that she would be their queen?

With a steadying breath, Eden stepped out into the hall. Nerves coiled within her, and she was uncertain why. Her days had acquired a new routine, and instead of Draven purposely avoiding her, they met at meals occasionally. He was careful not to dip into heavier conversations, which meant it was mostly Eden discussing her additions to the garden or what trouble she'd managed to stay out of in Primis while visiting the children.

Eden was so lost in thought that as she rounded the corner in the hall, she bumped into Draven. He steadied her by clutching her elbows, and she didn't miss the way he cocked an eyebrow down at her.

Draven's mouth quirked at the same time he opened it, but he stopped himself, his eyes drinking in Eden's appearance. "I was wondering if you'd run away. It turns out that it's bad form to not show up at a ball which is held in your honor."

Eden's eyes widened at his words, but then she laughed. "Yes, well, it turns out that I wouldn't get very far." She blinked, taking in his dress coat, which was the same purple as her gown, with a silver vine embroidered up one side and over his shoulder. She hadn't known he'd planned to match her, but the gesture warmed her. Even the silver buttons on his vest matched the adornments of her bodice.

As they teased one another, Eden saw the change within his eyes. The shift of color and the lightening of his irises. She'd grown used to watching them carefully, because while his body said otherwise, his eyes appeared to have a harder time pulling up a barrier, at least in her presence.

"No. You wouldn't." Draven offered his arm to her. "But we are working on that."

Without another word, Eden looped her arm through his, and the pair were soon entering a ballroom full of Andhera's nobility, both vampire and were-people.

"Announcing His Royal Majesty, King Draven, and Lady Eden Damaris of Lucem," the herald proclaimed loudly to the room. The middle-aged were-panther bore the insignia of the dark realm upon his breast: a black papaver with a golden center that declared him a part of the House of Draven.

A month ago, when Eden had been the center of attention at a ball, it was within Draven's arms and she'd felt so different. She'd been full of hurt, fright, and confusion, but now . . . She couldn't exactly put words to what it was, but she was no longer feeling those things.

As they were announced, Draven led her toward the center of the room. His hand resting on the small of her back was enough to paint her cheeks red. She wasn't embarrassed. It was more that a part of her yearned for that searing heat his touch left in its wake.

Eden swallowed roughly, turning her eyes to his, and she found a silent question in them: *Are you all right?* She nodded. As the music played, Draven led her across the dance floor with an easy grace. Eden felt as though she were walking amongst the clouds, and when he slanted her in a dip, she laughed.

Draven slid his hand along her back, righting her once more, but heat flared in the wake of his fingers, burning inside Eden. She was breathless halfway through the dance, which had little to do with the physical exertion and everything to do with what she anticipated—*wanted*, even.

By the sun, Eden had tried to ignore the mounting feeling inside and stop herself from following Draven wherever he may go, but she couldn't help herself. It was good, wasn't it? If he was to be her husband, she might as well find him attractive. *But how does he feel?*

His touches were bolder than usual, lingering, so she let her fingers trail from his shoulders to the back of his head. A small, innocent gesture that had his blue eyes darkening on her. Instead of cool depths, there was a simmering heat that threatened to turn Eden limp.

However, the first dance ended, and it wasn't time for them to partake in the festivities. There was still the announcement to make, which sent her stomach into a fit of flapping butterfly wings.

Eden wasn't daft. She knew rumors flew wildly, and she could only assume or hear secondhand what Andhera thought of her as their soon-to-be-queen—if they even saw her as that. After tonight, they'd have no choice but to.

With his arm firmly snaked around her waist, Draven

led Eden toward a dais in the back of the ballroom. On it sat two thrones of carved black wood. The back of each was a pair of bat wings, clasped at the top, and the cushions were of a deep blood red. Between them sat a small ruby-clothed table. As they ascended the two steps, a servant rushed up with a tray of drinks.

Eden plucked a glass, and Draven took up a goblet. Even her flute, though the drink sparkled within the glass, was crimson. She knew it was the pomegranate wine she'd had with dinner before. It was her favorite.

Draven's fingers flexed against Eden's hip, but his eyes never met hers as he scanned the faces in attendance.

"My friends, my family, it has been far too long since we were all last gathered here together in a festive manner, and I want to thank you for your presence. However, you have been called here tonight not just for idle amusements but for a greater purpose. For almost three thousand years, I have ruled over this land both proudly and fiercely, never regretting my initial journey into the darkness. But it is time that I no longer ruled alone. Tonight, I wish to introduce to you Lady Eden Damaris, my betrothed and the future queen of Andhera. Just as you have offered loyalty and respect to me, you shall show the same to her." Draven lifted his goblet in the air, ruby blood glistening in the candlelight. "Raise your glasses in celebration, and tonight, let us welcome her in true Andherian fashion. Eat, drink, and dance with hearty abandon. To our queen!" Draven brought his goblet to his lips and took a sip.

Eden's fingers clenched the stem of her wineglass at his words. Even though she knew the truth, not once had Draven mentioned their union or what would be expected of her. She took a greedy sip from her glass and set it down

162

on the table as she claimed her throne for the first time. If she wasn't careful, she'd drink more than she was capable of.

Luckily, beneath the table, goblins fretted over the skirt of Eden's gown, distracting her from the raging storm of mixed emotions. A few times, she gifted the goblins morsels from her plate as the food was served. It was too much for Eden, and they cooed their appreciation.

"Well, now you're only spoiling them," Draven drawled, sighing as if he were displeased, but the subtle tilt of his lip said otherwise.

Eden continued feeding them even as he spoke. "This is how I'll win them over. I can't offer my jewelry to them continuously."

He turned to face her, lifting a brow. "Why would you offer them anything?"

Eden's brow furrowed, and she studied his face, wondering if he were only toying with her again. "It's what friends do."

After that, he said nothing else, only nursed his goblet.

Eventually, the food ceased, and the music took on a lively beat. Eden watched as the guests filled the dance floor, smiling to herself. They were enjoying themselves, vampires, were-creatures, and otherwise. A melding of species, and Eden thought it was no different from home.

The shift of Draven's body caught her attention, and much to her surprise, he offered his hand. "Shall we?"

She nodded and took his outstretched hand. His arm slipped around her waist as he led her to the center of the throng, then drew her against him until their bodies were flush.

His form-fitting clothing didn't leave much to Eden's

imagination as far as what his muscles felt like. Every angle of him was hard, like he'd been crafted of stone. She knew what lay beneath, had seen his well-toned torso on display, hovering above her as they sparred.

Eden's breath quickened as he invaded all of her senses. He smelled of woods and lavender, with a hint of a metallic tinge. It was the latter scent she could nearly taste as he leaned into her. Draven was overwhelming her, even more so as he spun her around so her backside was flush with his front.

Eden wouldn't complain, for it was thrilling and she yearned to experience more of his touches.

Draven dragged the back of his hand down her side, which brought forth an involuntary gasp. Heat bloomed from the trail, and Eden wondered what he was doing. Was this a show for his people? He spun her around to face him again, and she decided she didn't care whether it was a ploy or not. Not in that moment, as the music played and their bodies were so close to one another.

When Eden's feet grew sore, her legs too tired to keep her upright, and her lungs burned for air, she reclaimed her place on the dais and drank down the rest of her wine.

"Are you enjoying yourself?" Draven leaned to the side, slipping his arm around the back of her throne. He cocked his head, far more attentive than he typically was.

Eden's cheeks reddened, but she was thankful for the distraction of a goblin scurrying up the back of Draven's throne. The creature perched there for a time.

"I am. I can't remember the last time I've had as much fun." She leaned on the arm of her throne, which brought her face mere inches from Draven's. Maybe it was the rush of the evening, but something sprouted within

Eden's chest. A warmth that hadn't been there before, and it filled her with glee. What it was, she wasn't certain, but it was far more intoxicating than the pomegranate wine.

He yanked back, cursing as he slapped a hand against his neck. "Damn you." It sounded like both a question and statement. Confusion and anger blossomed on his features. "You bit me. What has gotten into you, Gruff?"

Eden grabbed her napkin from the table, then stood so she could get a closer look at the wound. "Let me see it."

Draven lowered his hand. Blood drizzled down his skin, running beneath the fabric of his collar.

"That is a decent bite," Eden murmured as she hovered over him, dabbing at the blood. "Just a moment." She brushed her fingers down his throat, then slid toward the back of his neck so her palm lay against the wound. Eden didn't chance a look into his eyes, not trusting herself with as much wine as she'd had.

A familiar thrum of magic passed from her into Draven. She bit her bottom lip and withdrew her hand as his skin wove together again as if nothing had been there moments ago.

"Thank you," Draven murmured, looking surprised but pleased. "I would have healed by tomorrow."

Eden only nodded and pressed against the side of her throne. She was immediately met by a familiar face. Mynata.

"I've come to toast the both of you." Mynata brought forth a goblet of blood for Draven and a glass of wine for Eden. "To King Draven and his lovely bride, Lady Eden. May your lives be full of delicious moments." Mynata shimmied her hips, laughing. "And may you shower one another with equal respect." She bowed her head, taking her own goblet and downing it.

Eden didn't trust Mynata, but in a room full of people, what else could she do but smile and act as though her words touched her. She took a long sip of the wine, which she thought tasted far sweeter than the other glasses she had already consumed, but perhaps she was tumbling into her cups a little too quickly.

Mynata nodded to them, then slid off into the crowd.

"Would you care to dance more?"

The sound of Draven's voice snapped her from the mounting desire to seek Mynata out and have words with her.

"No, I can't possibly dance any more. If I do, my feet will fall off, and you'll be forced to carry me out."

Draven tipped his head toward the door. "I can think of worse ways to end an evening."

Eden's face contorted into a mixture of amusement and horror. "What?"

"Mm-hmm. I'll tell you a story."

It was a tale of one of the banquets in Castle Aasha. A member of the noble court had decided to test Draven, and it ended in a brawl. The young were-wolf who'd thought to make a stand against his king soon found himself without an arm—the very arm he had raised against Draven.

By the end of the tale, Eden had grown quiet but not horrified as she once would have been. None should have raised an arm to a king without expecting a fight.

"So that was how the night ended?" Eden pressed.

"No, the night ended with a head rolling out that door." He motioned toward where they'd entered from. "So, me carrying you out that door without your feet wouldn't be the worst thing to have transpired here."

A laugh bubbled in her throat until she couldn't contain it. She slapped a hand over her mouth, but her shoulders still shook.

Soon, members of the room began to approach the dais, congratulating them and welcoming Eden to Andhera. The minutes passed into a blur, and she wasn't certain if it had actually been hours instead. But as time ticked on, she began to hear the thrumming of her heart in her ears.

Eden eyed her full wine glass. Clearly she had been partaking in too much of the sweet drink.

Just as she mentally berated herself, Draven's hand moved into her peripheral, and he tucked a few loose strands of hair back into place.

Eden clenched her jaw and closed her eyes. A flood of heat entered her body, but it stemmed from her center. It only intensified as Draven's fingers brushed the inside of her wrist.

What is wrong with me? Eden lifted her hand, pressing the necklace into her skin. The coolness bit into her flesh, but it kept her from focusing on where she yearned to have Draven's hands.

The music paused, which brought the noise of the ballroom to a soft hum. But as the slow whine of a violin filled the room, it was too much. Eden pulled her hand away from Draven, then without a word, she bolted from the room. She couldn't endure it any longer, the mounting need to know what his lips would feel like against hers or on her skin.

"Eden!" Draven hissed her name.

It didn't stop her from walking away briskly. If she spoke right now, who knew what would come out?

"Why are you always running away?" he called to her, teasing, but uncertainty had crept into his voice. He followed her into an alcove not far from the ballroom.

Eden spun to face him just as he grabbed her by the elbow to turn her around. Her chest rose and fell quickly as she drank in his features. The beautiful sharp angles, the tilt of his lips, and the light within his gaze. The last glimmer of Lucem shone within them.

She lifted her hands, at first placing them against his chest. "I don't know," she murmured.

"Are you all right?" Draven breathed, slipping his hands to rest on either side of her waist.

The simple gesture was enough to undo her. Eden leaned forward, pressed her lips against his, and discovered what the king of Andhera tasted like.

She inhaled the metallic sweetness of him, and encouraged by his arms wrapping around her, she pressed on, allowing her tongue to slip into his mouth.

Draven groaned as Eden wound her arms around his neck, threading her fingers through his hair as their bodies pressed closer than they had been on the dance floor. She moaned into his mouth as he pulled her hips flush against his and his hardened length pressed into her.

In all her life in Lucem, she had never been so heated. It spread from within, awakening a piece of her that had been asleep for far too long.

"Eden," Draven rasped into her mouth, his grip tightening on her, which only brought forth moans of excitement.

Her name lingered on his lips, causing an ache to form

in her body. "Draven, please," she panted, uncertain of what she meant by it. But her body knew exactly what she meant. She wanted him to peel the layers of her clothing off and show her a world of pleasure as their skin melded with one another. Knotting her fingers in his hair, she lost herself in the feeling of his mouth on hers.

16

Draven

Her soft voice panting out his name stripped any hesitation from Draven's mind, leaving him with a well of desire he hadn't realized had grown so deep. With her fingers in his hair, causing pleasurable tingles at every light tug, Draven allowed one of his hands to drop to the swell of her bottom, sliding down to curve around the back of her thigh so that he could pull her leg up his hip a little. Pressing in against her core, he cursed the heavy skirts in his way, preventing him from making a true connection with her.

She tasted of wine and innocence, unsure kisses slowly shifting into heated drags of exploration and need. A moan tore from his throat as he parted her lips, dragging his tongue along her tentatively seeking one. Eden was honey and sweetness, coating him with a need that burned deep into his bones.

Shifting quickly, Draven pressed Eden back into the wall. It wasn't enough. Too much space remained between them still. Draven dropped his hands to her full skirts and quickly pulled them up so that his fingers could slip beneath, gliding over the silken feel of her bare thighs. Wrapping around the backs of them just beneath her bottom, Draven hoisted her up onto his hips.

Fitting himself between her thighs as if they were a cradle crafted for him alone, Draven's hips rocked against that tender place between them, and he felt a thrill go through him at her ragged whimper in response. The desire in his own blood seemed to triple with the action, as the heat of her liquid center pressed back against his aching shaft. The pleasure coursing through him at just this simple act was unnaturally good.

"By the moon." Draven's voice was harsh against his own ears, throat tight with need. "Eden . . . " It was overwhelming.

"Touch me," she pleaded, her lids heavy over her eyes, chest heaving with each breath she took.

It was a plea he could not ignore.

His head dipped toward the silky breasts that had been torturing him all evening, lips brushing over the rounded curve of first one, then the other. Eden's fingers tightened in his hair, pulling on the auburn strands as she released a breathy moan of pleasure. In response, his lips parted, gently sucking some of the flesh between them for his tongue to glide over. He wanted to go deeper, to pull her free of the tight corset and tease the tiny beads of her nipples to hard peaks. To feel her squirm against him as her breath hitched.

And so, he did. Hips pressing her back into the wall, Draven's hands lifted to grasp at the corset that bound her and, with an easy motion, ripped it down the middle. Gasping, Eden stared at him with desire-laced eyes and kiss-swollen lips.

"By the sun, thank you. I hated that thing."

Smirking, Draven dropped his gaze to her heaving chest, which was now left free beneath the neckline of her gown. Pulling the dark plum fabric down, he was greeted with the hard peaks of her nipples. Answering their call, Draven dipped his head to capture one between his lips, pinching the tiny bead between his teeth. The action wrenched a cry of pleasure from Eden in response, and her nails clawed at the back of his neck, scraping at flesh that wanted her abuse.

Draven kissed his way over the swell of the first breast, across the valley between and made his way to the second. Eden's back arched, pushing her flesh into his mouth, and she whined in delight as his lips fastened on the next nipple, sucking firmly until she wriggled against him.

His name was a harsh moan on her tongue that left Draven groaning and straining unbearably against the tight cloth of his trousers. He was dizzy with desire, each gasp and moan of pleasure from Eden setting his body on fire.

Reaching back, he drew her hands from his hair, lifting them up to pin against the stone wall above her head. His lips then began a heated course up her chest, tasting every inch of flesh now bared to his needy mouth.

Draven kissed over her collarbone, to the tender hollow of her throat and then up the pale expanse of it. Fighting a moan, his fangs gently scraped over the soft flesh at her pulse, the quickened beat of her heart sounding in his ears and her tantalizing scent overriding his senses. Draven wanted to sink into her, in every sense of the word. Feel her needy body welcome him in while her blood coursed over his tongue.

He was seconds from tearing open his trousers and

thrusting into her, Eden's breathy moans sounding in his ears as his mouth worked its way up her neck, when a thrill of pleasure coursed through him that he realized was not his own.

Freezing, Draven inhaled Eden's scent once more and groaned. She rocked against him needily, her chest still rising quickly with her excitement.

"Draven . . . " Confusion laced her words, her hips pressing to his in a silent plea for relief.

"You smell of me . . . " he rasped.

Quickly he slid her back down to the floor and stepped back, separating them as his mind reeled. A hand tore through his hair, his body protesting at being drawn from its source of pleasure.

"What?" Eden, still leaning against the wall, let her hands drop down to her sides. Her lips bruised from his kisses.

"You've had my blood." His words didn't make sense, even as he said them, but he knew that they were true.

"No." Eden was shaking her head, brow furrowed. "No, I haven't."

"You have. I can smell it on you . . . " He took a further step back, needing to separate himself from the call of her body to his, the thrum of her desire mixing with his own. *By the moon . . . I want her.* But he couldn't trust that her desire was real, not with the influence of vampire blood coursing through her body.

"I don't understand." She was flushed, the heat in her cheeks melding with the marks his lips had left over her skin.

Draven turned away from Eden, needing to put more

distance between them, needing to clear his mind enough of the fog of lust so that he could think.

"Somehow, you've been laced with my blood. It's in your veins, and I can feel your emotions in my mind." He growled, anger rising up to take over the desire. How had it happened, and who had dared do it?

"You can . . . feel me?" There was embarrassment in her voice.

Draven shut his eyes, a hand drawing over his face as he seethed. "Yes. And what you're feeling isn't real, it's an effect of the blood bond."

She hadn't been given much, just enough to increase her desire and leave her turning toward the vampire whose blood she had tasted. A handy trick of nature to aid a vampire in hunting and breeding. It was much easier to feed or to turn another if they were a panting mess instead of a screaming one.

"Yes, it is," Eden insisted softly.

Turning back, Draven studied her, confused.

"It is what?"

"It's real." Her green eyes peered at him, wide and full of honesty, before her hands rose to hide her face, perhaps out of embarrassment or shame.

"Eden—" he began but was cut off by her escape.

Quickly, she turned and fled down the hall, leaving only a trail of her heated scent and the matching desire still humming through his own body.

Cursing, Draven struck the wall where she had been pressed, cracking the stone and causing pieces to crumble to the floor.

She had eaten and drank only what had been offered to her at the ball, items prepared by his own household.

Everything she had consumed had been at his side. How had this been done to her? And a better question was, how had they managed to get some of his blood without his knowledge?

Draven's body straightened as his mind cleared.

"Gruff!!" he roared, his voice echoing off the arched ceilings above him.

With quick, angry strides, he made his way back to the ballroom, shoving the doors open so harshly they banged against the inside walls. It was enough commotion to have everyone turning to look at him. Draven ignored them, heading straight for the long buffet table where the goblins had spent most of the night. In one swift motion he upturned the table, sending it flying across the room to crash into the wall, silver dishes rolling across the floor.

There were five goblins beneath the table. Not a one of them was the little vermin who had bit him. Grabbing up the goblin nearest him while the others scattered, Draven brought it close to his face.

"Who made him do it?" he growled low, blue eyes gleaming as he squeezed it tight.

The goblin let out a high-pitched squeal, wriggling against his fingers, small nails digging into him as it fought.

Knowing he would get nothing from it, he tossed it aside, his eyes narrowing on the crowd of people, who stared at him in shocked silence.

"Tonight, someone committed an act of treason against my soon-to-be queen. When I find out who it was, they will be killed on sight without question. Anyone found to have helped them will also meet the final death."

Shocked gasps rang out around him, eyes shifting back

and forth as guests questioned who could possibly be the guilty party.

"Enjoy the rest of your evening." The smile he gave them was slow and deadly. With a sharp turn on his toe, Draven left the ballroom.

Something was going on in Andhera, and it didn't sit well with him. Fledglings being made without his consent. Someone using goblins to steal his blood, only to then turn around and use it on Eden.

Draven had struggled too hard for peace and control here in the dark realm to see it all come undone again. He would get to the bottom of this.

His emotions and hunger still far too riotous within him to control, Draven made his way down into the bowels of the castle, where the human captives were kept chained up in the dungeons. Gliding past the were-wolves on guard, Draven stepped up to the first cell. With the glide of one hand over the lock, it unlatched, and the door swung open before him.

Inside, two humans cowered in fear, their eyes bright in pale faces.

"P-please . . . no . . . " one stammered, his chains rattling as he pressed back into the wall behind him.

"Unfortunately for you, the entire reason you're here is for this." Crossing the dungeon, Draven clutched the back of his head with one hand and the front of his shirt with the other.

Pulling the man's head back sharply, he lashed out, sinking his fangs into the column of the man's throat.

The blood exploded into his mouth like a fountain. While his body raged, the anger and need were soothed by those first drags of coppery liquid, coating his tongue and streaming down his throat. Drinking greedily, he tasted the fear and fight in the prisoner, who pushed against his chest, moaning in pain until at last succumbing to the venom of his bite and stilling.

They weren't the moans Draven wanted to hear, but they were the moans he would accept tonight. He fed until the need in him was sated enough that he could feel rational thought returning. Pulling from the man, he released him and watched as he dropped weakly to his knees.

Stepping back, Draven wiped a drop of blood from the corner of his lips with the tip of his middle finger, then slowly licked it off. "You can be sent home tomorrow," he stated softly. "But remember what actions brought you here."

Eden

Her heart pounded in her ears, drowning out the questions tumbling in her mind. Except for one: *How did his blood wind up inside of me?*

Each stride Eden took back to her room was trying. She frowned, pulling at the bodice of her dress, which had been reduced to scraps. Every time the fabric shifted against her skin, it sent a thrill through her, and she recalled the feel of Draven's kisses against her breasts. By the sun, she wanted him so desperately, and to have him pull away, to end it, left a void in her. Eden ached in her core and longed for him to soothe her with his deft fingers.

Inside the warmth of her bedroom, Eden stripped free of her gown, then hurled herself onto her bed. She closed her eyes and traced where Draven's mouth had been, where she wished it had been.

None had touched her before save for her own fingers, but by the sun, she wished Draven would. She traced her fingers over her hardened nipples, then downward until she met a pool of warmth. Eden ran the pad of her finger along the bead of pleasure, moaning as a new thrill ran through her veins. This wasn't her first time exploring herself—she was a virgin, but that didn't mean she lacked knowledge in how to pleasure herself.

She panted, writhing as she quickened the motion against the knot of nerves. Eden had been so wound up in the hall, with Draven against her, it wouldn't be long. She rasped, dipping her fingers into her warmth, wanting, so wanting more.

"Draven," she whispered, shuddering as pleasure burst within, releasing a fraction of her frustration. Her body relaxed against the mattress as she panted and stared up at the ceiling.

Even the languid feel of her body could not keep thoughts of tonight from filtering back in. Eden frowned. How *did* Draven's blood wind up inside her? She lifted a hand to her forehead as she stared up at the ceiling, trying to dissect the evening. There had only been one moment she felt uneasy, and that was with Mynata's toast. But there was no way she could have obtained his blood. Unless they'd been entangled . . .

Eden growled in frustration. The image of Mynata with Draven was enough to raise her hackles. She didn't trust the vampiress as far as she could throw her, and the way she cooed at Draven maddened Eden. *Mine*, a not so quiet voice said in the back of her mind. But he wasn't. Not yet.

"Loriah," Eden eventually summoned her handmaiden. She sat up in bed, beginning the laborious process of undoing her hair.

The pale revenant assessed her with one look. "Well, did it work?" Loriah softly pressed as she approached the bed. She began plucking the pins out of Eden's hair, carefully placing them in a pile beside her.

"Did wh . . . oh." She lifted a hand to her swollen lips, closed her eyes, and swore she could feel Draven between her legs, pressing into her core as she ground into him. "Yes. But it ended quickly. Someone fed me his blood." Eden could scarcely speak, her throat tight with a mix of emotions.

Loriah, amidst her careful plucking of the pins, froze. "What? That is no minor offense, my lady. It is bad enough to use another vampire's blood in such a way, but the king's? And to toy with his future queen?" She froze again, but this time she stared into the distance.

Eden had grown used to Loriah's absent moments. It was her listening to the chatter of the castle. But what did she hear or see?

"The king has just declared that anyone found guilty of this crime will be sentenced to death." Loriah glanced down at Eden as she shivered, and as if noticing for the first time her mistress was naked, she turned to fetch the robe hanging up in the corner of the room. When she returned to Eden's side, she draped it over her shoulders.

Eden blanched. She lifted her hands to cup her cheeks. "Death? Surely it . . . " But then she recalled the story Draven had told her, of the were-wolf lifting his arm to strike him. Was this not similar? Only this time, it was Draven *and* Eden. Anger bled into her desire. How dare someone insult him on their night of celebration!

"Loriah, I'll need some tea to help me sleep."

The handmaiden nodded and promptly discarded the last of the pins in Eden's hair. A far-off look entered her gaze for a moment, then she was back to tending Eden.

"I don't think I could bear anything more than my own skin tonight." Her skin still felt far too hot, and to consider the weight of her blankets, as well as a heavy nightdress— it was too much.

Loriah, spirits love her, only smiled as Eden suffered in silence. But the tell-tale shredded dress, kiss-swollen lips, and marks from where Draven's mouth had been along her neck said enough, Eden surmised.

Eden opened the trunk and pulled free one of the sheer articles, then slid it over her head. The friction against her nipples was torture; all she longed for was Draven's teeth to graze the tender flesh of her breasts once more. Even his fangs were welcome to prick her skin.

Loriah vanished from the room, only to appear minutes later, this time with a cup of tea in her grasp.

Eden growled in frustration, and she quickly climbed into the bed. She didn't drink the cup down delicately, she sucked it in and prayed it would send her into a deep sleep fast.

It did not, but eventually, she fell into a sleep full of tantalizing dreams.

The next morning, Eden wished to speak with Draven about the previous night. She didn't need or want to explain herself, but she felt as though he needed to know it wasn't just his blood coursing through her that had drawn those feelings out. It amplified what had been building the entire evening.

As she approached his study, she rapped her knuckles

on the door frame before walking in. Seurat stood in the corner, his lips twitching—the faintest of smiles—and he nodded to the chair where Draven sat.

"My lord, I—" Eden's eyes widened as she caught him amidst his breakfast. His fangs were buried deep in the wrist of a human. Not one trickle of blood escaped his mouth. A few weeks ago, Eden would have screamed, but she had grown accustomed to this being his way of living. If he did not feed, he would suffer, and the thought of him suffering sent a pang of sorrow through her.

Eden approached as Draven lowered the human's arm, his eyes following her as she walked forward. "Yes?"

"I wish to have breakfast with you."

"Breakfast?" Before him, a goblet sat on the desk. He grabbed it and looked rather lost, awkward, as he drained his meal into the cup. Once he was done, he motioned to Seurat. "Send this one down with a harpy, and we will be in the dining hall."

Eden slid out of the study, unsure of what to say now that it was just them. She opted to say nothing for now as she recited the words in her head. But once they were at the dining table, Eden chose to sit in the chair next to him instead of farther down the king's table.

"Last night—"

"Eden—"

Color rushed into her cheeks as she searched his gaze, wondering what was going on inside his mind. If only she could be privy to it.

"Eden, I want to apologize first and foremost. No one should have tampered with your drink. Also, what you felt or what you . . . " He was clearly grasping for what to say next, or how to say it in a way that wouldn't offend her.

Eden stared down at the table, feeling her entire body flush with a mixture of desire and embarrassment. "I did exactly what I wanted to. Long before your blood ever coursed through me, I wanted to kiss you." She turned her gaze to him and studied his expression, which had formed into a look of surprise.

"When I cleaned your wound, and when you held me against you during the dances, I wanted to know what it felt like then. Only, with my inexperience, I didn't know how to go about it, or even if you wanted it."

Draven ran his finger along the rim of his goblet, his eyes trained on hers. "How . . . inexperienced are you?"

Eden flushed, but she didn't look away from him. In Lucem, it wasn't abnormal to see lovers rutting in the shadows or even in the streets. It was an open kingdom, where one didn't hold innocence on a pedestal unless it was for political gain. But Eden had never partaken in one of the parties of pleasure or tasted another's lips until last night.

"As far as first kisses go, I think that was adequate," Eden lightly teased him, but it was the truth, and she only wanted to lift the weight of the situation.

"By the moon . . . Eden, I shouldn't have been so—"

Eden extended her hand, letting a finger graze his. "No. None of that." She turned as servants entered with her meal, and when they left, Seurat promptly shut the door as he, too, disappeared.

Draven's fingers caught her hand and gave it a gentle squeeze, but he said nothing more on the matter.

Eden turned to her plate, which consisted of an array of fruits. She jabbed one with her fork and broke the silence that threatened to spread between them.

"What do you do when you're not busy with kingdom affairs?" It was a question that had been niggling her. What did he do for fun?

Amidst a gulp of blood, Draven's eyebrows raised. "Well, I sometimes take Rayvnin for a ride through the fields, and there is a lake near the mountains that I enjoy swimming in."

She smiled as she listened. What would Draven look like, unburdened by responsibilities and duty? Eden knew the deep history of the brothers and what they'd suffered through, but still, she wondered what it would take for Draven to let himself enjoy a moment instead of rushing through it.

She sighed. "I used to do the same. I'd take Aiya, the mare my father gifted me, for rides in the meadow by the manor. My mother loathed it, but I'd never felt so free in my life." Eden ate another mouthful of berries and shrugged a shoulder. "When we were both lathered in sweat, we'd go to the lake and cool off, then the sun would dry us on the bank."

The sun's strength would only produce more freckles against her pale skin and redden her complexion. There was no way to avoid being caught by her mother, but it was worth it in the end.

"Usually, my friend Aurelie would be with me." She lifted her lashes and chanced a look in his direction. "Believe it or not, at home, I wasn't the troublemaker. Aurelie was."

Draven chuckled then shook his head. "Oh, you're right. I don't believe it."

As he laughed, Eden decided she much liked the sound

and wanted to hear it more often. She quieted herself, only so that he had the chance to speak and she could actually finish her morning meal.

18

Draven

While Eden ate, Draven's mind reeled. Last night he had allowed his own actions to get away from him. Throughout the ball, he'd made a show of touching Eden, drawing her close, dancing with her, and paying her more attention than he had ever paid another. He had wanted his people to realize that Eden was here as a mate for him, not as a plaything, and she was not to be touched by any other.

The ruse hadn't only fooled the nobility, it had gotten into Draven's head as well. Her scent was intoxicating, increasing his hunger and his desire equally. He had wanted to taste her lips long before she had faced off with him in the hallway. When Eden had kissed him, a part of Draven had wondered if he'd unknowingly glamoured her into action.

While he was still aware of the fluctuations in her body this morning, due to the connection formed from her drinking his blood, Draven had convinced himself that was all it was. That it was only the powerful force of vampire blood coursing through her, stimulating her sexual drive and leaving her wanting. It was easier that way. The temptation to finish what they had started was easier to ignore if it wasn't based on something real.

But had Eden truly changed her mind about him? She claimed to have felt a stirring of desire for him before she'd been given his blood. What would be her purpose for lying?

Draven studied her face, taking pleasure in the fact that she no longer shied away from his touch, that her eyes continually sought his own, and that she had chosen to be closer to him. Did he dare let himself follow whatever pull was bringing them closer together? Or did he let common sense overrule?

She was only allowing herself to think better of him because she thought she was to wed him . . . If she knew she would shortly be returning home . . .

Draven didn't want to let himself believe that her changing opinion had any true value. Eden was making the best of a terrible situation. She wasn't going to remain here and be the one bright spot of sunshine in a dark world just for him. Draven wouldn't allow her to, even if it were something she could possibly fathom wanting.

Andhera was no place for someone as pure as Eden. And he would be the monster she had first named him if he allowed this dark realm to transform her for his own selfish desires.

"Would you like to go for a ride today?" he asked suddenly, ignoring every ounce of reality telling him this was a terrible idea. Perhaps Travion had been right: he should enjoy what little time he had with her.

Eden glanced at him, a smile forming on her lips that he

would do most anything to keep there. "Truly? No matters to attend to?"

"Oh . . . there are always matters that require attending. However, this morning I find I would much rather ride out to the lake with you." He had most certainly gone insane if he thought humoring this situation would bring anything but grief. But Draven couldn't seem to stop himself. "Would you care to see a little more of my land?"

"I would like that very much," Eden said, the smile still upon her lips.

They had parted ways to change into proper riding attire, and once he was ready, Draven called Hannelore and Channon to him, letting them know he would be leaving the castle and heading out over the fields.

"Keep your distance as best you can. I don't think anyone will interfere, but after last night, I don't care to chance it."

Channon nodded. "Of course, sire." The were-wolf then transformed and headed outside. Hannelore went along with him.

It may have been excessive to bring a guard with him for a simple outing, but with Eden coming with him, Draven would not risk being taken by surprise. Not again.

He went to fetch her at her bedroom door, casting an appreciative glance over the black leather riding breeches, white blouse, and black vest with thick brass buttons down the front that Loriah had dressed her in. Draven did his best not to allow his mind to wander, but the thought of her shivering body pressed against his the night before seemed a constant thought in the corners of his mind. It felt as if this outfit had been chosen specifically to torment him. To remind him of the taste of her tender flesh upon his tongue and the sound of her needy moans breathed into his ear. The memory stirred his blood, and Draven had to grit his teeth and physically will his fangs not to extend.

"Ready?" he asked.

"Quite. Lead the way, Your Majesty." She tilted her head back, a twinkle of mischief in her eyes.

Eden was smiling at him once more. Draven offered his arm to her. Once her hand rested on his forearm, Draven moved them through the firelit corridors.

"I've had one of our kindest kelpies saddled for you. She will be yours to use whenever you choose to ride."

Eden glanced up at him, curiosity on her face.

"Is it safe? I thought kelpies had a murderous streak and were likely to drown anyone who rode them?"

"That is a common misconception," he stated, leading her outside and over to where two black kelpies stood saddled and waiting, the sharp black horn centered on their foreheads glinting proudly in the bright moonlight.

Draven led Eden up to her mount. Taking the reins, he gently brought Karistand's head down toward her. The kelpie's braided mane dripped with black ichor, the true sign of her dark nature.

"This lovely filly is Karistand. She is patient, the mount we use to teach the young were-pups to ride."

Eden reached out to stroke the filly's nose, peering up at the horn protruding from her forehead.

"Where do kelpies come from?" she questioned softly.

"When a unicorn is slaughtered, if they die before their

horn is severed, then their spirit arrives here on the shores of Andhera."

"And if they don't?"

"Then they are lost forever, as if they never were."

Draven drew her over to the side of the kelpie and helped her up into the saddle. Offering what he hoped was a comforting smile, he moved to Rayvnin and mounted the stallion. Checking to be sure Eden was settled, he kicked back with his heels and directed his steed away from the castle and through the city walls, heading over the silvery fields ripe with darkly sweet scents.

Behind them, Seurat followed with supplies, while Channon ran alongside him, and Hannelore flew overhead. It didn't give Draven and Eden complete privacy, but they remained far enough back that there was a semblance of it.

He didn't try to speak as they raced freely over the field. Instead he took the moment to appreciate the freedom of being away from the castle and the heavy weight of responsibility that trailed him there.

"Just follow me," Draven shouted to Eden as they drew farther away from the city and its lights. While the day moon was bright in the sky, the land was still darker than what Eden was accustomed to, and without eyesight especially adapted to the darkness, he knew that she and her mount could end up in danger.

He took them along the easiest path, passing through a small wooded area to come out on the other side near the lake. It was a dark body of water, flanked by a large mountain on either side. Above, the moon shone down, its light reflecting off the lake's smooth surface. Between the two mountains, a rainbow arched over the lake, offering a soft glow on the waters. Draven had grown to love the subtle beauties of Andhera, but he was a creature formed in the darkness; Eden was not.

Draven drew them to a stop just shy of the shore, on a small hill that overlooked the full body of water. Eden pulled up beside him, and he glanced over as he heard a soft gasp leave her.

"It's beautiful." She looked up at the sky, the glittering stars a stark contrast against the dark blue. "Before Midniva, I'd never seen the moon, let alone stars. I'd wondered why poets wrote about them incessantly." Eden turned to look at him. "I now know why."

He gazed at her and found that her words did not lie, for upon her face was a look of wonderment.

"It is," he murmured softly. Draven had never had someone to share the wonders of Andhera with before. While his brothers appreciated what he had built here, from the ground up, neither were interested in spending enough time in the dark realm to become acquainted with her delights. It did something for his soul, to see the appreciation in Eden's eyes as she beheld his land. Her hatred of it slowly melting away to make way for something new.

"How cold is it?"

"Excuse me?"

"The water . . . is it very cold?" she asked.

"I don't find it unpleasant. But then, I'm not—"

"A warm blooded Lucemite?" A defiant look filled her green eyes.

"I did not say those words."

A smile tugged at Draven's lips as Eden slid from her kelpie and raced toward the rocky shoreline surrounding the beach. With a shake of his head, he also climbed down from Rayvnin and released him and Karistand to wander along the water.

Following Eden down to the shore, he was surprised to see her already in the process of disrobing.

"What are you doing?" he asked as he stopped a few feet away from her.

"What does it look like, Your Majesty?" She shot him a shy, playful look. "I am proving that I can handle the water just as well as you can."

"I don't believe I ever said you couldn't," he responded in his standard dry tone.

"Perhaps not, but it was implied." With that, Eden cast aside her black vest, and soon her blouse followed.

Draven knew it was improper to stare, yet he found his eyes glued to her sun-kissed skin as quickly more and more of it became bare to his discerning look. Once her garments were gone, Eden twisted her hair up on top of her head in a quick knot and then began to wade into the water.

He felt a breath of air rush out of him, watching the dark water swirl around her slender legs as she walked in, unhindered by cold or concern. Once she was up to her chest, she turned to face him once more, that sweet smile playing over her lips, and beneath his breath, he cursed her brazen, Lucemite ways. She truly did wish to torment him today.

Channon and Hannelore had moved much farther down the shoreline, enjoying the water themselves where they were out of earshot. Seurat, for the moment, had also disappeared. Draven stared down at Eden in the water, wondering what was holding him back. Should he succumb to his desire, would she hate him once she learned why she was truly here? Was it worth the risk?

Eden was an independent female. If she wished to interact with him in this manner, it was her choice to do so. Would he be yet another controlling force in her life attempting to curb her behavior?

His fingers were working at the stays of his clothing before he could rethink his decision. As he undressed, he felt Eden's unblinking eyes on him. Even in the darkness he could see the faint flush of desire rising up her neck into her cheeks as his slacks joined hers on the rocky beach.

Naked, he headed into the water, wading directly towards her. Seeing his narrowed look, Eden pushed off from the sand below her to swim backward, trying to move out of his reach.

"Why do you flee from me?" he drawled. "You called for me to join you." Lowering fully into the water, Draven swam in her direction.

"I called for you to join me, not to devour me." Eden's voice lowered, and because of their remaining bond, Draven could feel that was exactly what she wanted him to do.

"Something tells me that perhaps that is a lie." The timber of his own voice lowered to match Eden's, and his eyes dropped to her lips. Draven caught the quick dart of her tongue out to moisten her upper lip. He pushed off from the bottom, moving closer toward her.

Eden continued swimming backward as Draven progressed closer to her. When he was close enough, he reached out to try and grab at one of her ankles, but before he could, she had sent a wave of water his way.

Sputtering as it streamed over his face and splashed up his nose, Draven blinked droplets of water out of his eyes and glared at her. Was she *playing* with him? His blood heated even more. "That . . . was terribly unkind," he growled.

Eden released a nervous laugh and turned to swim away. This time, Draven lunged with enough speed to grasp onto her ankle, and with a jerk, he drew her quickly under the water pulling her toward him. He kept her below the water for only a moment before releasing her ankle. As she surfaced, she let out a soft cough, then shot him a fierce glare.

"That, Your Majesty, was very ungentlemanlike."

"I am only a gentleman when the lady deserves it."

Gasping, Eden swam to him so that she could lift a hand and flick a drop of water into his face. Draven grabbed her wrist quickly, and pulled her in against him, their bodies grazing in the water as they kept afloat. Releasing her wrist, his hand dropped below the surface of the water to rest on her waist. Gone was the playfulness of a moment before. There was no denying the heat rising between them.

"Also . . . I thought by now we were on a first name basis?"

"Are we? You never said . . . " Her whisper was on the edge of breathy, just enough to make his length stir.

"Well, now I am."

She was close enough to him that he could count the freckles over her nose and cheeks, and Draven found he much preferred those to all the stars in his sky. If he should follow their trail over her body, would they lead him to a treasure more heavenly than the sweet afterlife?

"Draven." Though not the first time she had uttered it, it was perhaps the first time she had done so intentionally.

"Why did you come to Andhera, and neither of your brothers?"

He was taken aback at first by the sudden inquiry. It had been a very long time since anyone had questioned his presence in the dark realm. And this was not at all where his mind had been taking him at their present nearness.

"It was dark, unruly, and filled with chaotic creatures that needed to be contained and ruled before they destroyed the other realms. I came so my brothers did not have to."

Eden's eyes were studying him in a way that left Draven feeling rather exposed, a sensation that he was neither used to nor did he like. What did she see, this innocent fae of the light realm?

Her arms slipped around his neck, forearms resting lightly on his shoulders as she relied on his frame to keep her afloat. Her nearness was like a dose of belladonna, leaving his senses reeling and his nerves on fire. Since their moment in the hallway the night before, he had been able to think of little else other than kissing her once again.

"Did you know you would change once you got here?" Her fingers played with strands of his hair, which both ignited his nerves and relaxed him at once.

"We assumed."

His hand slid around to rest at the middle of her back and pulled her a little nearer. Though space remained between them, they were close enough that the occasional kick of a leg or shift in the water allowed for satiny curves to brush against firm muscle. It was a test in endurance, one that Draven was intent on winning.

"But you didn't know what you would become." It was not a question.

"No."

"And yet you did it, so that neither of your brothers would have to face it." Once again, she seemed sure of her statement.

"Yes," he replied honestly.

No matter what had become of him, the years of torment and horror that had awaited him when he first arrived, Draven would never have allowed either Travion or Zryan to be the ones to face Andhera's darkness. Zryan had not been cut out for such a trial as this, and the last thing Draven would allow Travion to face was more torture. Now that he had gone through the madness of claiming this land, he only felt more secure in his decision all those millennia ago. It had been his duty. It was what Ludari's dungeon had earned him.

For a moment, Draven was transported back to the dank, musty depths of his father's castle. The feel of iron around his wrists and the cold stone below his bare feet. A sweet, young face stared up at him from the cell beside his own, begging for his comfort and reassurance. A young face he would watch age into a young man's, and later be required to bloody, if only to spare him a worse fate from another.

He was surprised when Eden pulled him in closer, pulling him from the dark memories his mind had transported him to. The soft swell of her breasts pressing against the bare expanse of his chest brought him firmly back to the present. His head dipped, and his lips met hers without hesitation, forcing them open to taste the sweet berries of her breakfast still there upon her tongue. This time there was a heat to their kiss that was not fueled by vampire blood or confusion.

While it did not burn as quickly or as hot as it had in the corridor, there was an underlying current of promise. Both arms around her form, Draven drew her nearer still, body thrumming with desire as he felt the silken glide of her naked body against his own in the water. Eden's hands traced over his shoulders, exploring the skin at her disposal.

Though he could still feel the subtle hum of Eden in the back of his mind, he was not overwhelmed by her emotions and was instead able to feel the way she moved in his arms, pressing against him, willing, if unpracticed. A deep desire flared up inside of Draven to be the one to make her body come alive with new and fantastical pleasures. To watch her blossom from inexperienced need into knowledgeable desire that she could control and seek for herself.

Draven pulled his lips from her mouth to trail kisses over her jaw and down the side of her neck. The thrum of her rising pulse sent wafts of her fragrant fae blood into his nostrils, causing his incisors to extend as headily as his own rising desire. But he ignored his physical hunger and focused instead on Eden's need.

His hand moved between them to cup her breast, feeling the bead of her hardened nipple against his palm. Eden's welcoming moan spurred on his actions, and Draven grunted as her fingers twined tightly in his hair. Massaging her lightly, he nipped gently at her throat, growling as she gasped happily into his ear. Shifting his hand, Draven brushed the pad of his thumb over her nipple, then pinched at it lightly.

"More," Eden rasped softly, her chest rising faster.

Spurred on by her demand, Draven dropped both hands to wrap around her thighs, lifting her up so that she could wrap her legs around his waist and secure herself. He then laid her back on the water's surface and dipped his head to capture that same nipple between his lips. Sucking, he laved at it with his tongue and felt her body arch and her hips grind against him in response. He hardened further, feeling the way her body reacted to him.

He wanted to witness her come undone. To know that he had brought that pleasure to her.

Pinching the nipple lightly between his teeth, Draven slid a hand between them, parting her soft folds to find the small bud waiting for him there. Eden's soft moan of pleasure was all he needed to press on, and he rolled his fingertips over her clit, watching as she began to wriggle in pleasure.

Draven's eyes drifted up to Eden's face as he tugged at her nipple, letting it pop from his grasp while his fingers toyed with her. Eden's hands dropped to clutch his shoulders so that she could lean back farther into the water, her eyes falling shut as she gave in to the sensations he was creating in her. He felt her heels digging into his thighs as Eden rocked her hips up into his hand, helping to drive her own pleasure forward.

He murmured in delight. The moonshine glinted off her glistening skin and highlighted the beautiful peaks of her breasts. He dipped his head to capture her other breast, sucking firmly on the nub while his fingers parted her so that he could slowly press two into her depths, feeling the way her wet heat welcomed him greedily.

"Yes . . . " It was a soft breath, one of acceptance but also encouragement. The way her hips arched into him, Draven could tell Eden wanted more. Needed more.

He began to stroke her, fingers gliding over that spot

within her, which elicited moans of pleasure that carried over the waters. Eden's lips parted for more air, and her nails bit into his shoulders as she held more tightly to him.

"That's it, lovely," he whispered encouragingly, adding his thumb into the fray, rolling over her nub as his fingers worked faster within her. Nipping at her breast, he lifted his head to watch Eden's features as her body started to tremble. She rolled her hips into his fingers more rapidly, her breath coming more harshly.

"Draven . . . " His name was a moan on her lips, and it caused a shudder of desire to course through him.

Working his thumb over her harder, he growled, fangs biting into his bottom lip as Eden arched into her pleasure, her breath halting as it took her over. He wished for the deeper link of blood then, to be able to truly feel how it took her away, wiping out all thoughts in that white hot moment of release.

Her cry sounded out over the lake, making his member stiffen painfully and increasing his need to plunge into her. Draven wished to ring more of those cries from her, to physically feel her body clamp around him as she lost herself to the orgasm. To bring her to that point and push her over it time and time again.

He was also panting as Eden's body stilled, and he gently withdrew his hand so that he could press it between her shoulders and carefully lift her up against his chest once more. Eden rested against him, slack and breathless, a murmur of contentment slipping from her lips.

"That was so much better than anything I've done myself," she said.

Draven chuckled softly, then turned his head to capture

her lips, kissing her deeply. His body thrummed with need, skin almost burning with the desire to touch her further. Instead, he kept his arm securely around her languid form and enjoyed the taste of her on his tongue. A shiver coursed through him as her tongue grazed over one of his fangs. She had no idea what she did to him.

His hand tightened on her bottom, fingers pressing into the fleshy cheek. It would take nothing to hoist her up so that he could lower her down onto him, piercing her tender flesh. Seconds from asking her if she wished to experience more, Draven grumbled as Eden pulled away from him suddenly. He felt her stiffen in fear, and the clinging turned from a gentle embrace to one of shock and concern.

"Draven, is something in the water with us?" she hissed, arms tightening around his neck.

His eyes fell to the water, and beneath the surface, he could see the end of a tail sweeping away, likely fleeing in shock of its own. The lake was not the place for such pleasurable antics, as delightful as they may be, and he sighed, the heated spell between them now truly broken.

"Of course there is," he stated matter-of-factly, fighting to keep the irritation from his voice. He could only blame himself for this current predicament.

"This is Andhera," she finished for him.

With a sharp whistle, Draven called forth the creature he had seen below the surface. As it rose from the water, two large serpent heads with blinking bottomless eyes appeared. There was embarrassment within their depths, for having caught and disturbed this very private moment of the king's.

Draven couldn't help but chuckle as Eden wailed her

distress and half crawled, half swam her way around to his back, placing him between herself and the water beast.

"What is it?!" Her arms clung tightly enough around his neck that Draven found himself choking slightly.

Pulling on a forearm, he loosened her hold just a fraction.

"Not what is it, but *who* is it." Smirking, he reached out to graze fingers over one of the serpent heads that joined together at the same set of shoulders. "Eden, no need to be afraid, it is only Seurat."

"What?" she whispered.

Draven drew them inland a little more so that her feet could touch ground once again. Reaching behind him, he pulled Eden back to his front. Holding her securely within his arms, Draven made her face the large water beast, which dipped below the water to swim nearer to them, only so that he could rise farther out of the water this time, showing off the dark scales.

"This . . . is Seurat?"

She seemed surprised. Draven was further amused, since all of them in this land were a monster of some sort. Hearing her uncertainty, the body before them wriggled in the water until it shriveled down in size, two heads became one, and the serpent body became that of Draven's manservant.

"M'lady." He bowed his head to her. "I apologize if I frightened you." His eyes met Draven's. "And for interrupting."

Bowing his head once more, Seurat waded away from them, off to another portion of land where his own clothing awaited him.

"What . . . is he?" she asked.

"That is Seurat's story to tell. Come, let's dry off, and then you can have your fill of questions." Keeping his arm around her waist, Draven drew Eden back to the shoreline and up over the rocky beach.

On a rock sat a pile of towels Seurat had brought with him. Handing one to Eden, Draven unfolded his own and began to dry off as best he could. Then, with some difficulty, they both redressed, Draven tucking his still aching length into the confines of his breeches with a hiss. The intimacy of the moment before was gone, but Draven was still highly aware of every shift of Eden's naked form. While Seurat's sudden appearance had interrupted their moment, it did not change Draven's need of her. Though it had not been his intent to seduce her at the lake, he could not say he regretted what had transpired between them. So long as she did not either.

Once clothed, Draven turned to find Eden staring at him, a faint flush to her cheeks and a soft smile on her lips.

"Thank you for the swim," she stated, her words inferring more than just their dip.

Draven stepped closer so that he was towering over her once more. "It was my pleasure."

He felt the pulse of desire between them once again and would have dipped his head to kiss her had the approach of Seurat not once more drawn them apart.

Starting to rethink the presence of the other man in his life, Draven eyed his manservant's approach.

Seurat led his kelpie over to them, looking uncharacteristically sheepish. An odd look for a man that always seemed so composed. However, it wasn't often he swam upon his lord pleasuring a maiden in the lake. "I wanted to make certain the lady was okay. It was not my intent to scare her."

"I am quite all right, Seurat. I suppose I should have asked you when we met what you were. I simply wasn't sure how to go about it. That being said, what . . . are you?"

"I am a hydra, m'lady."

"A hydra?"

"Mmm, we thought he was simply a water beast when he first arrived. At least until someone cut off his head," Draven supplied.

"Someone cut off his head?" Eden gasped, looking between him and Seurat quickly. "Someone cut off your head?" She stared at the other man. "Why!?"

"It was the early days, madam, and His Grace was not yet welcomed here. The creatures and men that had come to live in Andhera did not want to be ruled by a king who would enforce laws and govern with an iron grasp. They wished for chaos and death. I was simply one more thing between them and King Draven. However, when they cut off my head . . . "

"Another grew back," Eden supplied.

"Well, technically two grew back," Draven corrected.

"Did it hurt?"

"It did. Fortunately, it has only happened the once."

"Why did you come here to Andhera?" Now that her curiosity had been freed, it would seem there was no stopping it.

"I was a man running from his mistakes, and this seemed like a better opportunity for a free life of some kind. However, I was not expecting the change to come over me as violently as it did. Fortunately, His Grace found me and nursed me through it."

"You did?"

Eden was looking at Draven in such admiration that it made him turn from them.

"Come, we should be getting back. I've been gone long enough."

She was still studying him as they mounted their kelpies once again, and while he wanted to ask her what was on her mind, Draven was also rather glad that he wasn't aware of her thoughts. He was beginning to think that perhaps he couldn't measure up to the person Eden was forming in her mind, and the disappointment of that coming to light was not something he was yet ready to face.

Their ride back was a silent one, though Eden rode along beside him rather than behind. Shared glances were passed between the both of them, and Draven could tell she was wondering the same thing as he. Would what had happened in the water be something that they picked back up once they were in the privacy of a castle chamber?

Such thoughts died away once they rode into the courtyard of the castle. General Ailith was waiting for him, along with a messenger from Midniva. Jumping down off Rayvnin, Draven met Ailith on her way to him.

"What is it?"

"Your Majesty, there have been more attacks in Midniva. This time villages farther to the east, and it doesn't look to be just vampires. Hearts were missing from three children in a small village outside of the Veil, and several travelers have been left charred and mangled on the road leading toward Hiregarde."

Draven growled low, his shoulders tensing in frustration. "What in damnation is happening?" he shouted, snatching the letter from the messenger. It was a missive from Travion, and a map of the areas where all of the attacks had happened. "I will need to go to Midniva at once."

Ailith's questioning of the nobility had so far presented no clues as to who the guilty party may be. They needed to uncover the truth before it was too late.

"Draven?" Eden was at his side, a concerned look on her features. "What is it?"

Sighing, he turned to her. "There have been attacks in Midniva . . . more deaths than have happened in centuries. Something . . . or someone is rampaging through the middle realm. I must go and help Travion hunt them down."

Eden

E den's body still hummed with desire. Between last night in the hallway, enduring Draven's heated kisses, and wanting nothing more than to experience the delicious taste of pleasure, the lake had been her undoing. She'd seen him without his shirt once, had felt the muscles shift beneath her fingers while they danced, but knowing what his mouth tasted like, knowing and wanting his rough fingers against her trembling form . . .

She had wanted to explore every inch of Draven's exposed skin, but he'd taken it upon himself to bring her to the edge of pleasure, let her erupt in his arms, and even Seurat's abrupt appearance couldn't quell the thirst growing in her.

As Draven stormed off, preparing to leave for Midniva, Eden watched him retreat. The mood had shifted dramatically. Not that she blamed him, but his relatively lighthearted air crumbled to dust with every stride the kelpies took back to the castle.

Eden sighed, then disappeared into the castle, opting to

fetch Alder and play with him in the garden. He enjoyed nibbling on the vegetation and, much to Eden's surprise, feasting on the small sprites that hid within the flowers.

Still mulling over the news which had upset Draven, and even herself, she rounded the corner in the hall only to discover Mynata strolling toward her. The shorter female wore a smirk that Eden longed to swipe right off her face. Of all the times, now?

"Eden, it's so good to see you. You ran off from the party far too early. Were you feeling all right?" She tilted her head, clearly baiting Eden.

The ball had been wonderful, and she had left early not because she hadn't been feeling well but because she had felt too good. The mounting want in her, the need to feel Draven explore every twist and turn of her body, had grown too much.

Eden's cheeks filled with warmth. "I'm touched by your concern for my wellbeing, Mynata, but I felt fine." She flexed her fingers by her side, trying to will her flaring temper down. Draven didn't need another dilemma on his hands, especially something so petty as a dispute between the two of them.

Mynata's black skirt rustled against the floor as she stepped forward, then tilted her head up to look at Eden. "Are you certain? Draven seemed put out when he came back in to dance with me. Perhaps he was a little upset because your actions were not as pure as he had been expecting."

Inwardly, Eden hissed. *That's a lie,* she told herself. A lie because Loriah had told her that he'd been infuriated enough to order the culprit put to death when he found out who drugged Eden. So why would he take the time to dance with the vampiress? But it was what Mynata had said about her actions that truly struck Eden as odd. Was it her? Had Mynata dared to dose Eden with the blood?

"You speak boldly, Mynata. I would watch your tongue if I were you." Eden cast a glance to the side. Shadows of an approaching individual played on the wall. She turned back to glare down at Mynata. "I am Andhera's future queen, which means I belong to Draven as much as he belongs to me. We will be husband and wife, so keep your petty remarks and games to yourself." Eden shoved past her, and once inside her room, she slammed the door.

Mynata knew how to creep beneath her skin, with her prodding words and knowing glances. Eden shouldn't have let her rile her so, but she couldn't help it.

Inside her room, Alder flew from his perch near the window and lighted on her shoulder.

"We can go to the garden in a moment," she murmured, striding toward her desk, which had a letter on it. Eden's name was scrawled on it in a familiar hand. She lifted the letter from her mother. They'd sent letters back and forth in the past few weeks. They were always mournful on her mother's end, but Eden made sure to keep each one she penned light.

My dearest one,

I haven't experienced such heartache since your father was taken from us too soon. You share so much of him in you, it's as if I've lost him twice now.

I know you mentioned in your previous letter you're doing well, but are you truly? Andhera is cruel, and Draven isn't a kind king.

Eden, please don't trust him. You're young and don't know all of what he is capable of, or what he is.

I promised I would make things right, and I will. I will.

Eternally,

Your loving mother

"Does no one know Draven?" Eden murmured out loud as she stared down at the letter.

Or was it she who didn't know him? She had witnessed the beast who lay beneath the surface, had tasted the fierceness on his tongue, and felt his hands sweep over her in adoration. She had seen several layers to the dark king, and he spoke nothing but the truth to her. A truth so bare that it cut without effort.

It dawned on her how quickly her view of him had changed. Just one month with him and she saw how loyal his subjects were, and how he took time to visit the children in the village. A monster wouldn't seek out the spirits of children to ensure they were at peace and as happy as they could be.

Draven allowed Eden to see these different sides of him, and there was something to be said about that. So, no matter her mother's warnings or Mynata's poking, Eden would judge him for herself, from what she saw and heard.

Plucking a quill from its inkwell, Eden lowered herself into the desk's cushioned chair. How did she begin to tell her mother the truth? How the beginning of what she feared to be love stirred within her?

With a frustrated sigh, she pulled at a piece of parchment and at least tried.

Mama,

It pains me to know that you worry so, but I am well taken care of in Castle Aasha. Draven has afforded me so many luxuries that I had never dreamed of, and I've witnessed such beauty here in Andhera that's left me breathless. Who would have thought?

I must disagree that Draven isn't kind. Coarse, yes, but he is honest and generous. Mama, please don't prod King Zryan. I have accepted this as my fate, despite the abruptness of my departure, which was upsetting for us all. However, Andhera is a realm of enchantment and mystery, which only feeds my endless curiosity.

Have heart. Perhaps I can convince Draven to allow me into Lucem soon.

With love,

Eden

After penning the letter, Eden scooped Alder up off the desk he was now scurrying across and placed him onto her shoulder so they could escape into a place that made her feel at peace.

Outside in the gardens, Eden knelt in the soil. Her hands coaxed small shoots of new growth into fully formed flowers. Just beyond where she knelt, Alder scooted around the back of the carnivorous plant. It had grown beneath her care, sprouting long vines with snapping mouths. But it was nothing in comparison to the large head of the venandi flower that twisted with every vibration in the garden.

Eden had discovered that it would not snap at her as long as she soothed it with energy first. In a way, the carnivorous flower had grown fond of her, and it always seemed to search for her nourishment. The venandi was a temperamental and sensitive plant; even Alder was enough to send the plant into a frenzy.

Whistling echoed off the pathway, and moments later, Alder darted out from the bushes, then soared through the air down the bend.

"By the moon! Get off!" a familiar voice growled.

Eden stirred from her kneeling position and ran down the path, only to discover Alder lunging for Tulok. Who, much to Eden's surprise, wasn't trying to squash the hybrid creature but swatting him away instead. She quickly grabbed Alder from the air and pressed him to her chest.

"I'm sorry, he can be touchy when I'm in the garden." Eden quickly assessed the were-wolf, wondering if any harm had been done.

Tulok wiped away blood from a scratch on his cheek. He frowned at it, then brushed it off on his chest. "That was my good side."

"Your good side?" Eden puzzled over what he meant.

Tulok strode forward, his lips twisting into a crooked grin. "Yes, the one that catches the attention of . . ." He caught himself, cleared his throat, and smoothed back his chin-length inky hair. Tulok may have been trying to brush off his almost-slip-up, but she'd seen him in the shadows when he thought no one was looking. Sharing kisses, laughs, and hungry looks with a fellow male wolf in the guard.

"I came to check on you, but considering your little beastie is on guard, I think you'll do fine without me," Tulok huffed.

"No." Eden bit her bottom lip. "I mean, yes, I would be,

but I'd like some company while I garden." She motioned toward the bench close to where they stood. "I don't like being surrounded by silence. Stay with me." She turned from him, her fingers coiling around a rose.

Without a word, Tulok handed Eden a small dagger. It was small enough that she could easily maneuver it in her grasp if she knew how to properly wield it. She cut a bouquet of roses, lilies, and sprigs of sweet alyssum.

"To be fair, I'm here because I heard Mynata in the hall with you." He cast a glance to the side, nose twitching. "I don't care for her."

Surprise lifted Eden's eyebrows. "You heard her?"

Tulok said nothing, but his dark eyes met hers.

"She is mean, and I don't trust her," she whispered as she cut several more flowers. It wasn't just the jealousy Eden had felt take root in her being. It was the way Mynata looked at Draven, as if he were a possession that belonged to her and her alone. Then the way she glanced at Eden as if she were a bug to be squashed.

"She is ruthless and determined." Tulok waved Eden off as she offered the dagger back to him. "Keep it. I don't know if His Majesty has given you anything, but keep it on you. Andhera is a harsh land and not one you should be caught unawares in. You've had your tutoring with me, and you know Dhriti and I will do what we can, but if . . . if we are not around in your moment of need, I think you should have a blade."

At first, she nearly brushed off his words, but his earnest expression and the soft tone made her reconsider. Eden took the dagger and placed it down beside the flowers. "I'm realizing that, thank you." Eden pulled on long, dried blades of grass and used them to secure the bundles of flowers.

If Eden had been foolish enough to run into the woods a few weeks back, she would have died within the hour, she suspected.

"Will you tell me about growing up in Andhera?" Eden bit her bottom lip, thankful her back was to him. Had she only assumed he'd grown up here? She bent to tie another bundle up and hoped she didn't offend him.

Tulok grunted. "Well, I actually grew up in the orphanage. My parents passed away during a brutal attack on our home in the middle of the night. I was only a pup then, and I'd hidden away when the assailant crashed into the house. By the time our neighbors were alerted, it was too late. They found me crying in my closet and whisked me away."

Eden turned around halfway through his story, and she watched as he picked away at his sleeves. "I'm so sorry."

"Don't be. I grew up in the care of a wonderful woman who snagged the ever-so-busy King Draven's attention so that I could work my way up amongst his ranks." Tulok smiled. "That was ten years ago. And here I am."

"Thank you for sharing that with me." Eden offered him a bouquet and smiled. "It matches the scratch on your cheek," she teased him, then turned away to continue her work.

By the end of her time in the garden, she knew the wolf and where he came from a little more, and she'd discovered another reason why her mother was so wrong. And why she had been as well.

Andhera was full of far more life than people knew.

Draven

Travion was waiting for him on the other side of the archway as Draven passed through the Veil into Midniva. Rayvnin tossed his head in protest at the sudden appearance of another stallion and rider before them. As Draven reined him to a halt, the kelpie reared before settling, letting out a snort of displeasure. His black horn glinted in the moonlight, piercing the air as strikingly as a blade drawn in the night. Travion eyed the creature with disdain before looking to Draven.

"Still riding that beast, are you? A simple horse won't do?"

"Do you remember what happened to the horses we brought to Andhera? You call Rayvnin a beast . . ." Draven merely shook his head.

The horses had sprouted giant black wings and spikes along their necks, which hadn't even been the worst of it. They'd become ferocious and bloodthirsty. Their teeth grew razor-sharp and their saliva acidic, so any who survived their bite did so only to lose the limb that had been bitten. Training them had been nearly as difficult as attempting to ride a manticore. After the first were-tiger had lost his life, Draven had decided horses were not worth the risk. They'd put them all down, not trusting them to not head into the nearest village on a hungry rampage.

"Bloody Andhera," Travion muttered bitterly.

Draven would have fought against that curse had he not been presently in Midniva due to *bloody Andherian* actions. Drawing his kelpie up alongside Travion, Draven pulled out the map from inside his black velvet waistcoat and opened it before him.

"While we have plenty to tackle tonight, you and I will head after the chimera that seems to be guarding the roads leading into Hiregarde. Channon and his pack will sniff out the lamia in the village just a few miles from here. If three bodies are all that have been found, it should only be one creature, but they will make certain of it." Draven looked to the wolf, who currently stood naked in his human form, blond hair shaggy and ruffled from the wind.

He stepped up to the kelpie and allowed Draven to point out where they were currently situated on the map and where the wolves were likely to find the guilty lamia. When Channon had oriented himself with their position, he let out a grunt of acknowledgement.

"Shall we leave at once, sire?"

Draven nodded and watched as Channon returned to wolf form. While he was often a lighthearted individual, his Captain of the Guard could always be counted on to accomplish whatever mission Draven set before him. With a loud, eerie howl, Channon signaled his pack, and the were-wolves left, kicking up a small cloud of dust in their wake.

"What of the vampires? We haven't confirmed their

location. Are we not better suited to following them?" Travion questioned.

"No. General Ailith and the harpies will track them. They know all the signs of a vampire and will hunt them down and secure them. Meanwhile—"

"Meanwhile, we shall take on the fire breathing hellspawn," Travion muttered. "I sorely regret not polishing off that bottle of mead in my study."

Draven looked at his brother and sighed. "I am one of the few able to glamour a chimera. Just don't get in its way and you should be fine."

Travion was giving him a look of mild irritation, like one unsure if he should argue a point or simply smack the offender.

"Your Majesty, we'll be heading out now." General Ailith stood beside him, her tall form clothed in leather and chainmail, a sword strapped to either hip, and several blades around both thighs.

The other harpies stood off to his left, having landed and stayed in formation. They were prepared to embark on their own hunt, a glint of hunger and determination in their eyes.

"Go. And, general? When the culprits are found, notify me at once. I wish to be there when the final questioning takes place."

"Of course, Your Majesty." Ailith bowed her head and then turned back to her squadron.

With a loud beat of wings, the harpies took to the air once more, leaving Draven and Travion with the small infantry of men who had come with their king from Midniva.

Turning his mount to face Travion's men, he eyed their

steady gazes. "It is unlikely that the chimera has wandered too far from where the first bodies were found. When they find a location ripe with food, they seldom leave it. Once we have located its burrow, you will surround the space and allow for myself and King Travion to approach it on foot. It is imperative that you remember: no sudden movements. Their fire isn't the only part to be concerned about. The serpent head on their back end has a paralyzing bite."

With those words of warning issued, Travion called for his men to steel themselves, and the troop moved as one unit down the lone road.

"Have you any notion as to what is happening?" Travion kept his voice low so that it was only Draven who would hear.

"I haven't. It is not uncommon for one creature to attempt sneaking past our watches . . . but this is something I haven't seen in many a century. This feels larger than mere coincidence."

"I didn't want to say it out loud, but that has crossed my mind too."

They fell silent, each brother falling into his own thoughts on what this could mean for their kingdoms. The creatures of Andhera were well aware of what fate awaited them if they broke the laws and traveled into Midniva to feast on humans. What could possibly be provoking them to ignore all common sense and risk King Draven's wrath?

Their journey took them just under an hour. As they approached the area where the first bodies had been found, Draven stopped the men and slid off Rayvnin's back. He could smell it in the air: charred flesh and wild animal.

Raising his arm, Draven motioned for the men to circle out.

"Keep your eyes open for a large hole in the ground. It will have dug itself a burrow to sleep the day away. Now that the sun is down, be cautious. It will be hungry."

Beside him, Travion shifted a shield onto his forearm and drew his sword from its sheath. Draven met his familiar blue gaze, and silently they acknowledged they were ready to proceed. Unspoken words had always been easy with Travion. After centuries bound together in the depths of their father's castle, they had learned the innermost crevices of each other's minds.

Not even several millennia in Andhera had been able to steal that away from him.

With the soldiers fanning out into the woods, Draven followed the smell in the air, his footsteps cautious as he moved deeper into the shroud of trees. All around them was silence, the forest too quiet. A sure sign that there was a predator lurking in the darkness.

"Be cautious," he whispered. "I believe it is—"

A shriek of pain and terror cut him off, followed by several shouts and a flash of fire that lit up the woods to the left of them. In the flash, Draven could make out several soldiers converging on the large, three-headed beast. Cursing, he ran toward them.

"Back away!" he shouted.

They didn't listen. One of their own was pinned beneath the front claws of the monster, its lion paws heavy upon his chest, crushing the air out of him. The fierce lion head roared a warning cry at a soldier, who sliced at it with a sword. In retaliation, the goat head that rose from its back opened and shot a stream of flame into the soldier's face.

Another scream of pain filled the air as the man dropped to the ground, hands beating at his face and chest as the fire melted them away.

The goat head blended into the creature's lower half, which consisted of sturdy black fur-covered legs and hooved feet. If that wasn't monstrous enough, the large, scaly tail that completed the chimera ended in a serpent's head, a bite from which could kill a mortal man almost instantly.

"Back up!" Draven yelled as he came nearer. "Keep your distance, but surround it, so that it is trapped here. Do not get close enough to be hit by its flame!" Draven pressed a hand to Travion's chest. "That means you as well."

His brother slapped his hand away. "I'll be pissed if I'm to leave you to battle that thing on your own. Do what you must, but I am going in with you."

Draven shot him an irritated look—his brother never seemed keen on doing the things that were best for him. But, knowing there was no arguing with Travion, he simply growled. "Watch yourself."

Together, they approached the chimera. Draven drew his magic about him and slid into his invisibility glamour. Raising his hand up before him, he sought to find the dregs of the creature's mind. Travion stepped away from him, moving in the direction of the serpent head.

While his own footsteps were silent, the beast was not so distracted by the feast at his feet as to ignore the dark force approaching its side. Invisible or not, its many heads could scent him on the wind. Draven ducked just in time to miss the blaze of flame shot in his general direction. Rolling, he came up near the chimera's lion head, and instead of flames felt sharp claws tear down through his side, shredding his velvet waistcoat and flesh all in one go as the chimera sought to find the unseen force bent on attacking it.

Groaning as pain lanced through his side, Draven grabbed handfuls of lion's mane as his invisibility glamour slid away from him and a wide jaw spread and darted for him. Clenching onto it, he steadied the creature, forearms flexing as it struggled against his hold.

Behind him, Travion blocked a burst of flame with his shield, swinging out at the serpent's head attempting to lash at him. There was a sharp hiss as the tip of his blade cut through part of its neck.

Pulling his attention away from his brother, Draven looked into the eyes of the chimera, predator staring down predator. With his mind, he reached out to the essence of its thoughts, struggling against the pull of all three heads. At the connection, he felt the overwhelming desire to kill rather than be killed coming from the creature.

Furious at the attack, the chimera rolled, taking Draven with it. As his form hit the damp earth of the forest, he steeled his body to move where the animal took him, keeping his eyes locked with those of the lion. He reached out mentally, pushing against its resistance, fighting to take control of its mind to lull it into gentle submission.

It bucked violently, causing his form to whip into the air. Draven lost the hold of one hand and found sharp fangs latching onto his shoulder. With a roar of frustration and agony, Draven swung his legs up to wrap around the beast's neck, and with a burst of telepathy, at last pushed through the monster's inner barriers.

When he felt it staggering, he pushed further, and the jaws unclenched from around his shoulder.

"Kill it now!" he shouted. Eyes remaining locked with the chimera's, lulling it into a false sense of safety, he saw Travion slice off the serpent's head while two other soldiers bore down on the beast, piercing its side and attacking the goat head.

The chimera released a low keen of pain. For a moment, its dazed eyes cleared to pin Draven with an accusatory stare before it collapsed to the ground.

Releasing his hold on the large lion head, Draven fell back against the ground, panting a little as his side and shoulder protested the sudden movement. Travion, looking a little singed, shoulders steaming, came to stand over him.

"I don't remember you being nearly eaten as a part of the plan." He squinted down at him.

"I wasn't nearly eaten," Draven bit back.

"Your body would say otherwise." Travion extended a hand to him, and Draven allowed himself to be pulled back up to his feet.

"Chop it up and burn it," he told the nearest soldier. "These bloody things have a tendency to remain alive, too many hearts and heads." The soldier just stared at him for a moment before looking to the chimera a little apprehensively.

Swiping his forearm over his forehead, Draven moved back toward the road, his hand dropping to gingerly feel out the wound in his side.

"How bad is it?" Travion frowned.

"Better than your beard." Draven pointed to a patch on his cheek that had clearly caught some of the flames.

Travion chuckled a little. "Damn, there goes my beauty award."

"Are your men fine to be left here? We should head back to the gateway. Hopefully there will be word from Ailith once we get back."

"They're big boys. They'll be fine."

There was little time for talk after that, only the sound of their mounts' hooves thundering on the road back to the Veil. When they arrived, word had come in the form of one of their trained owls. The bird, with three wide eyes and one long sweeping tail coiled around its legs, stared down at them from atop a tall tree near the gateway into the Veil. Whistling for it, Draven held out his arm and allowed the bird to land on his forearm. He untied the note from its leg, then threw it back up into the air.

He skimmed the piece of parchment, and his face became pinched with fury. "Ailith has discovered a small hive of vampires. They're making their way here with them now."

"A hive? They had established a dwelling?" Travion eyed him cautiously.

"Yes, which means these attacks weren't carried out by a fledgling. This wasn't a lack of control; this was on purpose."

Draven's rage only worsened as Channon and his pack returned.

"Your Grace, we found the lamia, as well as a nest," Captain Channon announced as soon as he had shifted back into his human form.

Draven's features darkened. "Were all the eggs destroyed?"

"Yes, sire. We made certain she was the only one in the

area." Channon fell silent, but Draven could tell he had more to say. After a moment, he spoke. "She had built her nest beneath an orphanage."

Draven's hands tightened on Rayvnin's reins. Where had all the discipline he had fought so hard to establish suddenly disappeared to? These things were no longer supposed to happen because he had stomped down any and all insurrection. Or so he'd thought.

"Burrows, hives, and nests? By the sea, Draven, what is going on?" Travion growled his displeasure.

"Someone is breaking rules."

When General Ailith and her harpies landed around them, there were five vampires in their grasp. As they tossed them down to the ground, Draven found that the harpies had bound the vampires' hands and feet so there was no escape.

Dismounting, he strode up to them and peered at the upturned faces of the beings kneeling before him. From their scent, he could tell some were obviously young and one brand new. He didn't feel an ounce of regret as he stepped up to the fledgling, placed a hand on either side of his head, and tore it off his shoulders with one violent tug. Tossing the head with its frozen features at the knees of the older vampire, Draven only growled as cries of protest and rage filled the surrounding air.

Channon, once again in wolf form, came to stand on his left side, while Ailith, her hands on her hips and wings partially unfurled, remained behind the group of vampires.

"Braevl was only a fledgling! You didn't have to kill him!" the elder vampire spat out, tears of fury blurring her eyes.

Draven stooped down enough that his face was inches

from hers. "Everyone knows the rules. The penalty for breaking my law is death."

Draven motioned to the other vampires, looking up to Ailith and nodding. Without a word, she drew her blades and, crossing them over each other, swiftly cut off the head of the vampire before her. Two other harpies stepped up to do the same.

When it was over, only the elder vampire remained, her chest heaving with quiet sobs as her hive lay dead around her.

"You have one chance and only one chance. Tell me why," he demanded, voice soft and laced with a fury that only mounted the longer he waited.

"Why should I? You will kill me no matter what I say," she spat out, cheeks damp.

"Yes, I will. But you can choose how slow a death it is." Draven reached out to grasp one arm and began to pull, fully intending to rip it from the socket.

"I'd tell him what he wishes to hear, if I were you," Travion grunted off to the side.

Sensing his intentions, the vampiress shrunk back. "It was Lord Capala!" she shouted. "He sent us here to form a hive, to hunt humans and send them back through the Veil for his family!"

Draven paused. "What?" Lord Capala was the head of one of his founding families. While he had protested the implementation of Draven's feeding laws, which forbade human deaths, his family had always abided by them. "Will you stand by this in the judgment chamber?"

"Yes."

Draven straightened up, his eyes finding Travion's. "I must leave at once. It would seem there is treason in my kingdom, and I must flush out those guilty of it before this continues." At least now he had a name.

Travion nodded. "Should you need aid with anything . . ."

"I won't. This is an Andherian issue; Andhera will deal with it. Be well, brother. The threats in your kingdom have been slain."

Without further words, Draven moved to climb back atop Rayvnin. Sensing their king was ready to be on his way, two of General Ailith's harpies grasped the vampiress beneath her arms and lifted her into the air with them. Draven led his people back through the Veil and off to deal with the remaining threat.

Lord Capala and his family were pulled from their homes beneath the blue night moon and ushered into the judgment chamber of Castle Aasha. Draven hadn't bothered to change from his time in Midniva. Instead, he had paced the dark chamber, its midnight-black floor and walls only a reflection of the storm brewing in his mind. Blood seeped steadily from the wound on his side, dampening his pantleg and leaving the scent of him in the air.

The door in the chamber's side sat open, the threat of the pit a looming presence below. Tonight, people would die. It wasn't a punishment Draven enjoyed enacting, but if his noble families sought to undermine his rule, it would only be so long before others followed suit. This must be stopped before it could spread.

As the vampire lord and his family were brought into the chamber, General Ailith at their backs and the wolves flanking their sides, Draven could see the uncertainty and confusion on their faces.

"Your Majesty, while my family appreciates any audience with yourself . . . might I ask what this is about?" Lord Capala stood, hands clasped in front of him. His wife, a stern looking woman with silver-blonde hair, stayed close.

They had two children: a son who had been an adult when they had made the journey into Andhera and a daughter who'd been just on the cusp of maidenhood. She was now frozen in time, ever a lovely blossom set to bloom.

Draven pointed to the vampiress he'd pulled from Midniva. "Lady Aamanee was found forming a hive in Midniva. A hive which was feeding willfully on humans and bringing others back here to find their deaths at your hands."

Lord Capala looked startled, and Draven watched him, attempting to read his features.

"You can't honestly believe—" Capala looked between Draven and Aamanee.

"I confessed to everything," Aamanee announced. "He killed our entire hive and threatened to tear me to pieces if I didn't!"

"Told him everything what?" Capala's features grew dark as anger filled him.

"He is the one, Your Majesty." Aamanee looked at Draven. "He told me to go into Midniva and feed on humans . . . to make a place for our vampires there, so that we could finally live as we were meant to. It was his plan to form an entire chain . . . Vampires who captured humans in Midniva, others who carted them across the Veil, and then he would sell them to the highest bidders once here."

"You can't honestly believe this wench," Capala protested, distress beginning to form on his face.

"The unfortunate thing, Lord Capala, is that I do." Draven paced, a hand going through his short-cropped hair. "You have never hidden your distaste for my laws."

"This is absurd! We have lived for millennia under your rule! Why would we fight against it now?"

Draven was across the room before the other man could move, his hand around his throat as he lifted him into the air. "That is what I would like to know." His words were a low growl of fury, body seething with it.

"You have no place here!" It was Forstuss, Capala's son, red faced and hands fisted at his sides. "You rule for the good of Midniva, not for the good of your people. This proves it now! You wish to punish us for what? Longing to feed true to our natures?"

With a snarl, Draven tossed Capala aside, his body sliding across the room. Moving to Forstuss, Draven grabbed the front of his shirt and pulled him forward. He had to give it to the vampire: he held his own beneath the king's glare.

"Were you a part of this? Plotting against me?"

Forstuss remained silent, the muscles in his jaw ticking but the hatred in his eyes obvious.

Leaving no time to second guess himself, Draven pulled Forstuss across the judgment chamber to the wide opening. Capala and his wife both shouted, realization dawning on them.

"For treason, you are hereby sentenced to death."

Forstuss showed his first flicker of fear and uncertainty as they reached the edge of the chamber, the cool winds from outside reaching in to coil around both their forms. Forstuss' lips parted, about to say something. Instead of listening, Draven pushed him past the edge, and watched him tumble down through the empty space toward the pit below.

As Draven turned back to the room, Capala was on his feet, surging toward him. General Ailith, however, was faster, and grasped Capala by the arms, pinning them behind his back.

"Lord Capala, you, too, are sentenced to death for plotting human slaughter." Draven nodded his head to Ailith, who pushed the struggling man forward.

"You will regret this, Draven! Do you hear me?! You will regret this!"

Those were his last words, as the harpy general shoved him out into the air, and Lord Capala followed the same path his son had, down into the afterlife.

Meioral Capala clasped onto her daughter, holding her tightly as they both cried silent tears. Draven eyed them with pity but said nothing as he stepped toward them. Both shrank back from him in fear, which he bore with as much tolerance as possible. He took hold of Meioral's wrist and forced it up to his mouth. She struggled but didn't possess the strength to resist his actions.

Draven sunk his teeth into her flesh, drinking deeply of the blood that flowed there. He searched her memories, and when he saw that she had no knowledge of either her husband or son's activities, he released her and turned away.

Sensing that he was finished, two harpies stepped

forward to usher mother and daughter back out of the chamber.

"And her, sire?" Ailith asked, motioning to Aamanee.

"Make it quick."

Leaving his general to handle the final execution, Draven left the judgment chamber and headed for his study. Tonight would be a night to dive deep into his cups, and laced heavily with belladonna, perhaps he could find some solace.

Eden

The hearth crackled in Eden's room, tempting her to crawl into bed and fall asleep. It'd been a long day, one that left a smile on her face. The time at the lake with Draven had left her wanting more. By the sun, despite the heated moment in the hallway, she never thought he'd indulge her in such a tantalizing way. Still, Eden yearned to explore every inch of Draven and learn the ways of pleasuring him.

Unfortunately, he'd been called away to Midniva. For what, she didn't know. But Eden wished she did, that she wasn't viewed as some trinket to be set away or pulled out for guests. If she were to truly be the queen of Andhera, she'd want to aid in ruling it too.

With a sigh, she sat at her desk and penned a letter to Aurelie. She missed her friend deeply, and there was much to tell her. For all her friend knew, she'd been consumed by the nightmare king. The thought gave Eden pause, and a dark laugh erupted from her. *If only*, she thought.

Regardless, Aurelie deserved to know the truth of who she'd been betrothed to.

As she finished the letter, movement caught her eye. Eden spun in her chair to see Loriah moving toward her. If blood could have drained from a revenant's face, that's what had happened to her handmaiden.

"Loriah, what is it?" Eden stood and crossed the space between them. She searched the woman's gaze and lifted a brow in question.

She hesitated for a moment. "His Majesty has returned . . . "

Eden's eyes widened. He had? Was he all right? Her thoughts jumbled together. "Is . . . he well?" Everything in her wished to see for herself, but Draven was likely weary from his efforts, and the last thing he needed was Eden hovering, surely.

"Well, he is and he isn't." Loriah's slight frame plopped onto the bed, then she fidgeted with her blouse. "He's been drinking, which is a rarity, but it's a telltale sign of how dour his mood is. His Majesty has been physically wounded too. Those marks will fade, but I'm not so certain his emotional ones will."

It was a bold remark coming from Loriah.

"I will go to him."

Loriah shook her head. "I don't think it's best to see him like this."

"Perhaps, but I will need to at some point. It may as well be now." Eden grabbed her black velvet robe and secured it over her sheer nightdress. She left the room and ventured down the hall, only to find a cluster of goblins outside of Draven's study.

Drizz sat closest to the door, one of his clawed fingers rubbing his ear in a soothing gesture. Whatever state Draven was in had upset the goblins too.

Eden bent down to scratch beneath his chin, then prepared for whatever lay beyond the door.

She caught Seurat's eyes as she walked into the room, but her gaze didn't linger long on him. Draven sat at his desk, grimacing at his goblet, and didn't look her way.

By now she should be used to how quickly things could change, but it still surprised her.

Inwardly, she assessed him as she drew closer. She saw a wound on his shoulder, but it wasn't as bad as the one on his side. This one still bled actively, and judging by the cloth's current stage, had already bled quite a bit.

"Not now, Eden," he muttered.

She stood before him, leaning against his table. "I'm glad to see you've returned alive." Eden paused, her brow furrowing. "Barely."

Draven lifted his darkened eyes to her. "Is there a reason you're here?"

There were a thousand excuses she could have made for him, all of which were valid, but they didn't excuse his dismissal of how she may have felt about his current state. Eden had endured a lifetime of being dismissed, and it had taken moving to Andhera to realize she had a voice and that it was valid. So for Draven to now make her feel as though she didn't, it grated on her, and it hurt too.

Eden struggled to keep her eyes from narrowing on him. "I wanted to see you. I heard you had returned and weren't well."

"I'm fine. You've seen me, now you can leave." Draven slurred his words, but even that didn't take the edge from them.

"By the sun," she huffed in annoyance. "Let me see your wound." When he didn't move the rag, she took it upon herself to tug it out of his grasp. Eden's gaze met his stony blues, and she glowered right back. "It looks as if your entrails are still where they ought to be." A new trail of blood formed once the cloth was gone, and Eden carefully dabbed at it.

Draven grunted his response.

The fact that he was bleeding was the only thing keeping her temper in check.

Eden discovered she was not only annoyed with him but angry at whatever had done this to him. In the end, the two melding together lent her a boldness she didn't typically possess.

"I'm sorry," Eden murmured.

"For what?"

Without another word, Eden lowered herself to kneel before him and gently pinched the torn flesh together as best as she could. Magic pulsed from her fingers, surging into him, weaving his skin and muscles back together. She was rewarded with a colorful array of curses, including some words she didn't even know.

Draven's blood coated her fingers, which she ignored as she continued to heal the wound beneath the newly formed flesh.

His breath came in ragged draws, and when Eden chanced looking up at him, she spied his jaw muscles leaping violently. "You could have warned me."

"I could have." She drew her fingers away from his abdomen and stood to inspect the mark on his shoulder. It was less severe than his other injury but still looked angry. "And you could have been kinder before, but here we are."

His eyes shifted to watch her, but Eden didn't return the glance. She focused on the wound, pouring a warmth over his skin, which in turn started to heal it. Soon, the holes and redness faded, and all that remained was a deep bruising.

When Eden pulled away, Draven's eyes darted to the discarded article of clothing. From what she could see, it was splattered in blood and shredded.

"Will you tell me what happened?" Eden hoped that he would respond more kindly, but judging by his pinched expression, that wasn't going to happen.

"That was my favorite waistcoat." He evaded the question, which didn't surprise Eden in the least.

She slowly turned to take in the waistcoat. His blood still coated her fingers, and the rag was growing stiff from the blood drying on it. Yet, Draven was fussing over a piece of clothing?

"You can get another one."

"I don't want another one. I want that one."

Was he pouting? Eden bit her bottom lip and shifted so that she blocked his view of the clothing. "You should rest. I know you can't sleep, but you can at least lay down in my bed. I'm writing, so you won't be keeping me awake."

"No."

It was a simple answer but one that colored Eden's cheeks with annoyance.

"Draven, I won't press you to talk, but I'd rather not leave you alone right now—"

He arched a brow. "Why do you even care?"

In her time in Andhera, Eden had learned that Draven spoke very little, but the words he chose to use were impactful. It was no less true now, and he was clearly unaware of how they stung. Wasn't it obvious that she'd grown to care for him?

"I find myself wondering the same thing," Eden bit out.

The barbed comment seemed to rouse him, because Draven stood from his chair and leaned heavily on the desk. Eden idly wondered how much he'd actually had to drink, or what it was exactly that had such an effect on him.

A mixture of dwindling patience and something else, some softer emotion, melded into one expression before he turned on her.

"Leave, now."

"Draven, please." Eden stood her ground until he took one step in her direction. His lips pressed into a firm, thin line as he grabbed her by the elbow. It was rough enough that she couldn't pull away.

"No, I wish to be left alone."

Then why did his voice betray him? Why did the raw quality of it, even with his slurred speech, claw at her heart? Every quick step Draven took toward the door, Eden fought to slow.

The goblins, smartly, had vanished into the darkest part of the shadows as Draven pulled her into the hallway, and she only assumed they were watching, shaking their heads or trembling in fear.

"I am not a child!" Eden finally ground out only a few doors away from her own.

Draven relinquished his grip on her and motioned toward her door. He laughed darkly as he sauntered forward. "Then I suggest you stop acting like one."

"Me? Says the one who was mourning for his waistcoat while his entrails fought to break free."

"I told you it was my favorite one!"

Eden slowly continued toward her room, folding her

arms across her chest as he stalked after her. "I don't think for one moment that me showing you that I care, or not wanting you to be alone when you're clearly not well, is me being childish in any form."

Draven lifted a brow as he drew closer, his body trapping her against her door. Eden had seen many expressions on his face during her stay, but none like this, and all she knew was that she wasn't keen on it. If she could read his mind, if she could feel what he felt, perhaps she'd better understand what he was going through. But when he spoke so few words on a good day, trying to pull anything from him when he was having a foul one was nigh impossible.

Draven shifted his arm behind her, then twisted the doorknob to push the door open.

Eden stumbled back, but he didn't attempt to catch her. Draven only watched her with his cool blue eyes. It was maddening to think that just that morning they'd been tangled with one another and on the verge of so much more. Confusion bled into hurt, and Eden shook her head as she frowned at him.

"Stop this!" Eden took a step forward and froze as Draven's hand caught her chin. His thumb brushed along her jawline, which ignited another feeling she didn't want.

"Why?" he murmured as he moved his fingers into her hair, winding them in the thick strands. "Why now of all times?" Again, his voice sounded hollow, broken, and it twisted Eden's heart.

Whatever it was that festered within, she wanted to heal it as she had healed his other wounds. Eden leaned forward, her lips touching the bare skin of his chest in a featherlight kiss. He sucked in a breath but didn't pull away, his fingers combing through her hair as she continued to kiss along his neck.

She didn't have an answer to his question, but Eden hoped that in some form, her actions were one.

"Eden," he murmured as he leaned in to drag his nose along her ear. His breath grazed her skin, and rather than cool her flesh, it heated it.

Draven moved farther into the room, using his foot to close the door behind them. As he did, his fingers slid the velvet robe from her figure, and it pooled around her feet in an inky heap.

"By the moon." His gaze raked along her form, and Eden felt it linger. "I didn't mean . . . "

She turned her head and caught his lips before he could finish. Then his hands slid down her backside and toward her thighs. With ease, he hoisted her onto his slender hips. Not entirely lost to her desire, she recalled his wounds.

"Draven, your injuries," she murmured in between kisses.

"I don't bloody care." Draven crossed the room and carefully laid Eden down on the bed, his hands slipping up her bare legs to her bottom. A hunger filled his gaze, one that she'd seen in the hall and in the lake. One that she felt deep within her being too.

At the lake, Eden hadn't thought anything of her bare skin before him, thought nothing of how he watched her come undone before him. But now, as his eyes drank her in, she felt far more bare than she had then. More vulnerable.

Draven leaned down, his lips covering hers in a slow, heated kiss that drew out Eden's mounting desire. She groaned, shifting her legs so he could settle between them, and when he did, he slid his hand up her thigh, his thumb grazing over her heated mound.

Every nerve came alive the moment his fingers touched her, and she wanted more. She wanted to feel him everywhere.

Eden looped her arms around his neck, drawing him closer toward her as she deepened the kiss. His fangs protruded, which she discovered when her tongue slid along the tip of one.

Draven moaned as the kiss intensified. He lifted a hand to her breast, using the sheer gown to his advantage. His thumb and forefinger rolled the stiffened peak until she squirmed beneath him.

Eden could barely stand it. She pressed her head against the bunched-up blankets and arched her hips up into his. She felt him there, stiff against her core. Her breath hitched as her skin ground against his restrained length.

"Draven, I want you." She wanted him inside of her, against her, until they were a mess of tangled limbs, gasping and writhing against one another.

Her plea fell on deafened ears. Draven dipped his head to take her other nipple in his mouth, flicking his tongue over the hardened nub until she cried out again.

He pulled back, but Eden was through being timid. She followed him with her lips even as he sat back. She took the cue to crawl onto his lap, her hands peeling the straps of her gown down so that her breasts could press against his chest.

Draven's fingers pulled at her hair, twisting her neck so that he could kiss a trail along her pulse and down to the valley between her breasts. His tongue followed the path back upward, then his mouth hovered as she ground into him.

"Eden." His voice was hoarse with desire. "Eden," he repeated her name, then gripped her by the shoulders. Draven lifted his head; his eyes had blackened considerably with desire. "Not like this," he mumbled against her lips.

Eden leaned forward to capture his lips again, but he halted her. Inwardly, she whined, but it gave her a chance to clear her head and to respect his wishes.

"I'm not myself still. You deserve more than a rushed moment, and believe me, when I'm of the right mind again, I'll make sure I fulfill every one of your wishes." Draven's hand cupped her cheek, his thumb brushing beneath her eye tenderly. He then brushed a warm kiss against her brow and lifted the straps of her gown back into place.

Eden's entire body was still flushed, but she didn't retract in embarrassment. Her body still hummed with a deep need. She couldn't help but sigh in disappointment as she withdrew from him. Physically, she needed him. But emotionally, Draven needed her more. Patting the spot beside her on the bed, she tilted her head. This had been what she wanted in the first place. It wasn't the shared heated moment but something more intimate than that. She wanted to share his space, absorb his company, and just lay next to him.

She glanced down at her hands and realized his blood still stained them. She slid from the bed and to the water basin, washing herself and using the moment to calm herself. Every nerve ending was alive, waiting and yearning for release. But it would have to wait.

Draven crawled up the bed and laid on his side, head

239

propped up with his hand. He watched Eden as she slid back into bed.

"Come here." Eden pulled the blankets down and slid her feet beneath them. "Just stay until you're feeling well again. We don't have to talk. I just don't want you to be alone right now."

She half expected Draven to decline the offer, but he surprised her by resting his head against her chest, and she felt a pang of empathy for him. Eden's heart still galloped steadily, and there his head rested, listening to it.

Draven tugged at her free hand, then drew her knuckles to his mouth where he kissed them tenderly.

Eden pushed down her desire and lifted her hand, stroking her fingers through his hair lazily.

In a thousand years, she'd never have expected to find herself in this situation, much less feeling as she did. It wasn't the heat of the moment but something far more powerful and terrifying.

It couldn't be. But it was, wasn't it? She loved him.

It took her far too long to unwind, but Draven kept her hand within his, and the steady back and forth of his thumb along her skin soon lulled her into a deep slumber.

Draven

Draven lay there for a long time, lamenting his choice of a pillow. The sheer quality of Eden's nightgown left nothing to the imagination, and the memory of her skin beneath his lips and tongue was a torment. In the end, he shut his eyes against the beauty beneath him and concentrated instead on the steady decline of her heart rate as she began to fall asleep.

When he was certain Eden was lost to her dreams, Draven contemplated getting up and leaving. But the belladonna still swam heavily in his veins, and he found himself inclined to remain where he was. There was a comfort to laying there beside Eden, his head nestled on the soft mound of her breast and the steady rise and fall of each breath taking him with her.

Her fingers had played gently in his hair until she had fallen asleep, and the soft tingle of pleasure they had sent coursing through him went beyond desire to something wholesome and filling. Bringing to light a sensation Draven wasn't sure he had ever truly experienced in his life.

Peace.

Having found it, even for this short moment, Draven was wholly unwilling to abandon it. Beyond her bedroom door lay a tumult of questions, worries, and battles that he did not wish to deal with, not yet. So he allowed himself to lie there beneath the blankets of Eden's bed, one hand having fallen to rest at the base of his neck and her other hand still gently held in his own.

Though his lovers over the centuries had lain in bed with him after the completion of their passion, none had looked at him as truly and deeply as Eden. In Lucem, he'd been a king to be bedded and won over. In Andhera, gentleness was often seen as a weakness.

The last person to hold him in such a tender, comforting manner would have been his own mother. Draven could faintly remember being held as a child against her bosom and rocked until he fell asleep. Caring fingers brushing dark auburn hair out of his eyes as he allowed himself to drift off. But that had only lasted while he was very young. Once he began to age, and his abilities began to present themselves, his father had feared what it could mean for Draven to reach adulthood.

Ludari, king of all three realms and a tyrannical beast of a fae, had not been willing to risk his son aging into an adult, free to overtake him and steal away his throne. Convinced by his wife not to kill their firstborn, Ludari had placed Draven in a locked cell in the dungeons of their castle, where he had remained, imprisoned in the dank darkness of the earth. Alone, with nothing but the grunt of a guard or the occasional scurry of a rat to entertain him. A male grown, quiet and bitter, until Travion, the second born, had arrived.

A young child, scared and uncertain. Unsure of his future and not understanding what he had done to deserve his new fate.

"Father said I had a brother here in the darkness . . ."

"You have. I will not abandon you as she did."

Madryall, beloved wife of Ludari, was weak. Incapable of protecting her children from the man she inexplicably loved.

There, in the darkness of the dungeons, with only iron bars separating them, Draven had watched Travion grow into adulthood. Believing they would spend their lives in the bowels of the kingdom, there had been no coddling, no comfort, just the quiet conversation between the two of them. Later had come the added agony of Ludari's competitions as he pitted them against each other. Better to dole out the pain and affliction himself than watch Ludari do worse to his younger brother because he had refused.

While his body had healed from the wounds, there were some scars that cut too deeply into the soul to ever be free of. Scars that had only deepened as he'd entered the fresh hell of Andhera and fought a constant battle to restrain the chaos that had reigned here.

Draven's eyes opened, and he gazed at Eden, red lashes resting against pale cheeks dusted with freckles. She looked so at peace, which surprised him, considering the realm she found herself in. Tonight, she had wanted only to soothe him. To offer comfort in whatever way that she could.

He had pushed her away, harshly. Trying to bury himself in the darkness of that dungeon once more, tucking himself away where no one could see or hear him. Where he could be alone with the misery rising inside. But she hadn't allowed that. No matter how much he had pushed, she had simply planted herself before him. Insisting that he allow her in.

Draven wasn't certain why this beautiful creature wished to console him, to hold him in her arms and show him a world of mercy no one else ever had . . . but he found himself not wanting to let it go. It worried him. Eden was burrowing her way into his life in a manner that may leave him more shaken when she finally departed than anything in that dungeon ever had.

The yellow moon had crested in the sky and begun to lighten the bedchamber when Draven finally realized he had spent the remainder of the night in her room, laying there listening to the gentle beating of her heart. The thought of silently slipping out crossed his mind, but he found a desire within him to see her wake for the day. To know what Eden looked like as she became aware of the world once more.

"Oh, you stayed the whole night," were the soft, sleep-roughened words that announced Eden had woken finally.

Lifting his head, Draven peered down at green eyes blinking to adjust to the dim lighting in the room. "I did."

"I'm glad that you did." She seemed to sigh the words, her arms drawing up over her head as she arched her back, stretching.

Draven felt his heart do a strange flip in his chest at that simple statement. So accepting and happy for his continued presence here. Unable to hold himself back, he dipped his head to press a soft kiss to her bare shoulder, and was pleased when her hand moved to slide through his hair.

"Do you feel better now?" Eden asked.

When he lifted his head, Draven found her eyes more alert and peering into his own. "I do."

"What about in here?" The tips of her fingers tapped lightly against his temple, then slid down to cup his face.

Draven turned his head to press a kiss to her palm, then looked to her once more. "I find in the confines of this room, it is easier to block out the rest of the world."

Eden looked a little surprised at this confession, then smiled happily up at him. "Good." Her thumb brushed along his chin, tracing just beneath his lip.

"I must apologize for my behavior last night."

"Yes," she agreed simply.

Draven gave Eden a dry look, then reached out with his hand toward the sconces on the wall and forced them to light once more, illuminating her bedroom in a bright, cheerful flame. He raised himself up on an elbow, his free hand coming to rest on her abdomen.

"I should not have taken my ill humor out on you."

"I didn't think it was possible for vampires to become drunk . . ."

"Not on alcohol," he stated. "Belladonna. While the poison won't harm us, it impairs us enough to produce drunk-like symptoms."

"What happened in Midniva that you felt the need to sink into your cups?" Her hand was on his bicep, fingertips lightly tracing the muscle there. "You needn't tell me . . . if you don't wish to."

Draven sighed and let his head fall. Having someone who wished to hear his woes was a foreign concept, but he supposed that after last night she deserved some explanation for his behavior.

"I believe some of my nobles are scheming behind my back . . . attempting to infiltrate Midniva and perhaps even usurp my rule here. Last night, I had to execute one of my noblemen and his son. A man who has been here since the founding of Aasha. I don't know if he was the only one."

Eden frowned deeply, but to her credit remained silent for him to continue.

"The first hundred years I spent here in Andhera were bloody years . . . Every moment was a battle to keep the beasts from killing each other and me. Guarding the entrance to the Veil was a never-ending duty, and I thought peace would never come. That there could be no reining in their hunger for death." Draven ran a hand over his face, the weariness of those years returning. He had thought he had thrown himself into hell. A hell that would be eternal and would drive him mad in the end. "Once that was over and the first families arrived to help found Andherian society, there was more madness as their transformations took place and new species were born. I had to reinstate my will and reign all over again. Bend newly formed beasts and bloodthirsty monsters to the laws I had created. Infuse each with the understanding that humans would not die here or in Midniva without my say-so." It had taken so very long to achieve that goal. To find a semblance of peace here. "I cannot go through that again."

It was the first time he had uttered his concerns out loud, and it made them all the more real.

"Oh, Draven . . ." Her hand raised to cup his cheek once more, and he found himself leaning into it again. Soaking up the gentle comfort that came from Eden's touch.

"There were many executions last night."

Eden merely nodded, her face soft and understanding. He hadn't expected it. To find that the innocent creature he had met in the gardens of Midniva could accept the ways of Andhera so quickly. Yet here she lay, taking in all he had to say and not balking.

She looked so beautiful that he could not contain himself. He dipped his head to press a soft kiss to her lips, exploring the eager response that greeted him. His hand slid beneath her head, tilting it back slightly so their lips fit better together. Eden's hands rose to his shoulders, no hesitation in returning his kisses.

With a swift motion, Draven rolled them, so that he lay on his back on the mattress with Eden half sprawled on top of him. Her light-red hair spilled down around her face as her head lifted, lips pink and parted. He brushed his knuckles gently over her cheek, then tucked a few strands of the silken hair behind a delicately pointed ear.

Eden was the very essence of Lucem. Vibrant and full of life, innocent yet looking to bloom into a delicately beautiful flower that could not be replicated. She did not belong here in Andhera, the land of eternal darkness, yet she believed herself to be trapped here. Tied to him. Would she have welcomed Draven into her bed so readily if she knew the truth?

Draven sighed, twining his fingers in her hair. "Eden . . . I have something I must tell you."

She stilled, fine red brows lifting in question. "What is it?" Her arms folded on his chest, her chin coming to rest on the backs of her hands. But despite her display of calmness, he could hear her heartbeat quicken.

"Zryan did not send you here to be my bride." Her

forehead creased with confusion. "He was upset with your mother because she's been telling Alessia of his indiscretions. He only meant to punish your mother, and her punishment was losing you."

"What?" She rose up a little, fully frowning now.

"Announcing our betrothal was only a disguise for the truth."

"But . . . you took me," Eden whispered and withdrew herself from him. She stared down at him, visibly trying to make sense of the news.

"Only for six months." Draven studied her features, uncertain what was going on in her mind. "I insisted you be returned before Andhera had a chance to change you."

Eden sat up, her arms wrapping around her form, eyes on her lap rather than on him.

"So, did you know at the ball then?" Slowly, her head lifted so that she could look at him. Pinning him with her eyes. "Did you have any part in it?"

"No. Zryan sprung it on me the same moment he sprung it on you." Draven frowned in remembrance of Zryan's announcement and how close to tearing a hole into him he'd been.

She only nodded a little, her eyes falling to her lap once more. She remained on her heels, and it left him feeling cold. "You'll be sending me away."

"Eden." He said her name softly but firmly, causing her to meet his eyes once more. "I would never force you to be my bride when you did not want to be. I would not force that on anyone."

Draven shifted so that he could sit up, his back leaning against the dark headboard.

Eden let out a soft laugh that sounded on the verge of tears, but then she took a deep breath, hands combing her hair back from her features. He saw the strength once again that he had seen the night they had left Midniva. The firm set to her shoulders as she squared herself to face whatever it was she found herself facing.

"That is why you ignored me," she murmured. "For that whole first week."

"Why burden you with the dark king if you could be spared." Draven found himself missing the connection they'd shared just moments before.

Tentatively, he reached out with his hand to take one of hers, his thumb brushing lightly over the back of it. To his surprise, Eden didn't pull away. Instead, her fingers curled more tightly around his.

"You are many things, Draven, but a burden isn't one of them." Eden's voice was soft, nearly breaking as she spoke. "I wanted to know more about the man who'd taken a moment to humor an oddity like myself." She squeezed his hand lightly. "I had hoped he was here," she said, lifting her free hand to touch her heart. "And I wasn't wrong."

They sat like that for some time, until Eden came to some decision in her mind. Moving up onto her knees, she shifted her position to straddle his lap, settling down on his thighs. Her hands lifted to rest on his chest as her green eyes peered back into his blue.

"Let's not waste our time arguing," she whispered, dipping her head to brush a tender kiss to the corner of his mouth, then trailed her lips along his jaw. Draven felt something inside him shift at her words, and relief filled him. He knew that he did not deserve these quiet, tender moments with such a beautiful being as Eden, but if she were willing to sully herself with the king of nightmares, then he would take what was being freely offered.

Her next words had him pausing and considering her response.

"But if I asked you to keep me, would you?"

His hands lifted to cup her cheeks, and he leaned in to kiss her, taking a moment to enjoy the tender sweetness of her willing response. Soft lips parting to the slow exploration of his tongue. Pulling back, he rested his forehead against hers.

"If I could?" His sigh spoke volumes. He wanted to tell her he would keep her and her sunshine here with him always, to brighten his halls and bring to him that peace he had found by her side in the night. Draven shook his head, forcing away what ifs. "I cannot destroy you for my own selfish desires. I will not suffer you to lose your family and home as I have," he whispered.

Draven slid his hands around her, pulling her in against his chest, and simply held her for a time, allowing that intoxicating scent to waft over him, making his senses come alive. A part of him wanted to sink his teeth into her throat as greatly as his manhood wanted to delve into her depths.

He wanted to possess her. To claim her as his as surely as Andhera had stamped her ownership upon his soul. But if he hoped to control the monsters in his realm, the first one he needed to control was himself.

Eden had said nothing to his response, and so he broke the silence between them. "We should see to your breakfast. The servants will be distressed if I keep you too long."

Eden smiled a little, perhaps with a twinge of sadness behind it. "They fret far too much for people who are no longer alive."

Draven chuckled softly and pressed another kiss to her lips.

Eden

I t was difficult, not showing how Draven's admission shocked her. To Eden's surprise, the news formed an ache inside of her chest. She'd be leaving in four months' time, which was not long at all. And Draven, in his own words, had assured her she couldn't stay, even if she wanted to.

Did her opinion or her choices matter to anyone?

How she'd managed withholding a flood of tears was beyond her. Eden wanted to stay. If it meant ruling Andhera with him, she would learn how. But more than anything, she wanted to be there when Draven needed to bow his head, allow his shoulders to sag, and give in to a moment of vulnerability.

It is love, Eden thought almost miserably.

In nearly two months, Eden had settled into Andhera as much as she could. She'd come to terms with the idea that in the not-so-distant future, she would take on the mantle of queen. And now she learned it had only been a farce to get back at her mother. Once more, she was only a pawn in the realms.

As much as Eden wanted to make the most of the time they had left, she couldn't dismiss her mounting feelings, either. She'd come to enjoy Draven's company, even when he was in his dark moods, and she found that she could typically pull him from them.

Why was it every moment she truly felt as though something was finally going right, it shattered into oblivion?

Eden didn't want to eat breakfast, but the revenants always feared her mood was spiraling into a similar one as when she first arrived if she didn't. So she opted for a slice of sweet bread and a cup of berries.

Draven sat by her side, nursing a goblet of blood. Even that had become a part of her new normal. It wasn't something she even thought about, outside of how it nourished him and was needed.

"Are you certain you're all right?" Draven frowned as he glanced down at her barely touched food. "I only wanted to be honest."

"Which I appreciate." Eden sighed, then took up a piece of the bread. "And I'm fine. It's just one more thing to process."

Draven nodded and said no more. Eden couldn't blame him. What else was there to say on the matter?

She pulled the bread apart and shoved a piece in her mouth. A moment later, Seurat intruded, looking remorseful as he did so.

"Apologies, sire, but you're needed in the throne room."

Draven downed the rest of his goblet and stood. He paused by Eden's chair, and she glanced up at him, trying to read his expression, but there was far too much clouding his gaze.

"I'll be fine. What trouble could I possibly get into?" Eden lifted an eyebrow and turned her head back to her plate.

Draven grunted. He slid his fingers beneath her chin as he lowered himself a fraction. "Try not to say such things and tempt fate." His lips twitched into a small smile, then he pulled away and strode out of the room.

Eden could have laughed at his small tease, but the weight of the news still bore down on her. As soon as he left, she abandoned her food and opted to seek out Tulok or Dhriti so she could escape for a few hours into the city below the castle.

A few days later, Eden received a letter from her mother that left her puzzled. She pored over the words a handful of times, hoping that she'd missed something, but she hadn't. The words she said tempted Eden to write back and let her know that she'd be home soon, but she thought better of it.

My darling daughter,

I believe there is a way I can ensure your safe return home. My heart breaks every day that you're gone. Trust me when I say that no good comes from dabbling with the royals of the realms. Draven is not to be trusted, no matter what he entices you with, my darling.

Be strong. We will be reunited soon.

"Loriah," she called.

The handmaiden materialized, her hands folded in front of her. "Yes, my lady?"

"Where is His Majesty right now?" Eden folded the letter in half.

Before Loriah could answer, the sound of hissing and squawking filled the room. It startled Eden, but she knew exactly the source of the sound. Charging toward her bed, she slapped her hand down on the floor.

"Alder! Drizz!" Eden half crawled under her bed and pulled her pet out. His whiskers jumped quickly as his nose wrinkled and twitched. "You cannot be terrorizing the goblins."

Drizz slowly made his way out from under the bed, his large yellow eyes full of remorse as he rattled off about something. But in the next moment, he was producing one of Eden's cuffs.

"Oh, I see." Eden placed Alder onto her mattress, then grabbed the cuff from Drizz. "You can't steal things. I've given you and your friends trinkets. Why steal?" She clucked her tongue and motioned for him to leave. "If you asked, maybe then I would have given it to you. But not now." She motioned for him to leave and looked to Loriah, who was trying not to laugh.

Finally able to respond, Loriah inclined her head toward the door. "His Majesty is in his study."

Eden stood, the letter still in her hand. "Thank you." She crossed the room and paused at the door. When she turned around, Loriah cocked her head in question. She wanted to tell her that in a few months she'd be leaving, but if she said it out loud, would that make it true? Would it speed up the remainder of her time that much more?

Saying nothing, Eden left her room and ventured down the hall toward Draven's study. As usual, Seurat stood close to the door, and when she caught his eye, she asked without speaking if now was a good time. When he gave a curt nod, Eden pressed into the room.

"Did you happen to find trouble after all?" Seated in his high-backed chair, Draven's eyes were trained on the desk, but he slowly lifted his gaze as he waited for a reply.

Eden huffed. "No." She glanced out the window, the golden moon at its strongest, hinting as to what time it was. "Although it is only noontime."

Draven loosed a breath. His shoulders shook with silent laughter. "Spare us all."

A bright toothy smile didn't break out on his face, but it was there in his gaze and in his voice. It was enough to set butterflies off in Eden's belly as she approached him.

"I received a strange letter from my mother." She placed it down in front of him as she leaned closer. One of his arms snaked around her midsection.

"What of it?" He picked it up, and his eyebrows lifted in question.

"I just found it strange that *she* found a way to bring me home." Eden shrugged, frowning. "Do you think she'll blackmail Zryan?"

He sighed. "With what? The truth? I'm sure she is only trying to soothe you whilst you stay in the land of nightmares." Draven spoke dryly and pushed the letter away, his other arm slipping around Eden's waist as he turned in his chair to face her, drawing her between his thighs.

"I don't know. I'll be in Lucem before long." She swallowed roughly and lifted her arm as Draven's forehead pressed against her abdomen. An ache spread in her chest, knowing that she'd be gone soon. It frustrated Eden every time Draven leaned into one of her touches, because she felt the desperation in them too. He didn't want to let go, and yet he'd return her home, unwilling to keep her in Andhera.

A moment ticked by, and Draven didn't move.

"Are you all right?" Eden whispered as she dragged her fingertips through his hair and down his nape.

"No," came his curt reply as he pulled back, his arms still around her. "Andhera grows restless as news spreads that half a noble family was slaughtered and a hive destroyed in Midniva." His fingers bunched the maroon fabric of her waistcoat as he shook his head. "It'll only get worse."

Eden didn't know how to soothe his fears. She couldn't tell him that he worried for nothing when even in her heart she knew that wasn't right. Andhera was an unforgiving land, and one misstep could mean death or betrayal.

"We will see it through." The words had barely left her lips when the sound of talons clacking on the floor disrupted them.

"My lord, apologies for the intrusion," Captain Hannelore began. "But you're needed." She turned her keen gaze to Eden and inclined her head. "My lady."

Eden felt every muscle in Draven tense up, and although she didn't see his face, she imagined the walls were in place in his expression. He stood a moment later, and Eden placed a hand against his chest to stop him from moving.

257

ELLE BEAUMONT & CHRISTIS CHRISTIE

"Come find me when you're tired of chasing shadows."

Draven brushed past her, and once again, she was left alone.

One emotion bled into the next. It felt like a knife twisting in her chest. Eden pressed her fingers against her closed eyes as she willed them all to still. She refused to give in to the prick behind her eyelids and instead strode out of the room and down the hall.

She could hear shouting coupled with cheering, which, given how still the castle was, seemed as if it were coming from close by, but it wasn't. As she approached a window, she peered down below to see what the commotion was.

A group of harpies stood in a row, and opposing them stood were-wolves. They saluted one another and launched toward each other in a fierce dance. It reminded Eden of the line dances she'd seen at the Blossom Festival, but this wasn't lighthearted. As a fist connected with a jaw, a wolf collapsed to the ground, and he laughed.

Eden pulled away from the window and ventured outside to where she'd seen the group. At first, she wasn't certain why she was there watching them. She'd trained with them before, but it had been with an invitation. This time, she'd join because she wanted to.

"My lady, had I known you would be watching, I'd have instructed Dhriti to strike harder." Tulok grunted as a fist connected with his ribs, and then Channon's hands swept him aside.

A roguish grin pulled at the other were-wolf's lips, unruly light hair spilling into his eyes. "Tulok tells me he loaned you a butter knife?"

Eden slid her hand along the smooth leather of her

breeches and pulled the dagger from its sheath. "This isn't a butter knife."

Channon folded his arms across his chest. "It may as well be if you don't know how to use it."

Tulok shoved past him and knocked him in the back of the head, which made Eden laugh. "I think what my captain means is, if you'd like to watch us and perhaps learn how to use the dagger for more than pruning, we'd be happy to show you."

The tutoring with Tulok had, thus far, been hand to hand, and although he promised eventually it'd include a weapon, they hadn't gotten that far yet.

Eden twisted the hilt of the dagger in her grasp. It still felt awkward to her, and they were right, the dagger may as well have been a butter knife. She tilted her head, still laughing at their antics.

"Very well. I'm ready to use a weapon in our training now." Eden chewed on her bottom lip and searched the eyes peering at her. It seemed to be the answer they were hoping for.

"Don't bruise her," Dhriti ground out.

"Do you think I want to die?" Tulok barked, then he laughed.

24

Draven

The air was cold, the scent of rain blowing in off the ocean. The corpse lay crumpled at the bottom of the cliffs. From the lack of splatter, Draven could tell the body had been drained of all blood before being dumped below.

"You couldn't bother to collect it?" Draven peered over at Travion, who stood beside him, hands on his hips as he looked down at the shore below.

Travion offered him a dry look. "Yes, because I have nothing better to do than fetch bodies myself."

Pointing to Hannelore, Draven motioned down at the lifeless form. "Send two of your soldiers down to retrieve the body." He stepped back from the edge and drew a hand through his hair.

"I thought we dealt with this at the border villages," Travion growled.

"As did I." But the vampires were upset, and it was an issue that clearly ran deeper than simply being unhappy feeding in the ways he had stipulated. He wasn't certain what it was going to take to right the problems.

Draven watched Captain Hannelore and another harpy land before him, the limp body in their arms. Carefully, and with a reverence for the dead that only those who were already dead could have, they laid the man at their feet.

At the sight of the puncture holes in the man's throat, he sighed. Draven had hoped perhaps this was something else.

"The child didn't lie. Vampire," Travion muttered at his side.

"It would appear so." Draven found himself caught by something strange about the sight of the puncture holes. Uncertain what it was, he knelt, a hand slipping beneath the corpse's head to angle it back, exposing the throat more plainly. Draven frowned. His thumb traced the outside of one hole, gently tugging on it to look at the edging of the wound.

"Do these holes look too clean to you?" he asked Hannelore, who unfurled her wings a little so that she could stoop down beside him.

"That's odd . . . " Her words trailed off in her own confusion.

"Too clean?" Travion asked from above him.

"Vampire teeth, while sharp, still tear the flesh when they pierce it. There is no tearing on these holes. Brushing his thumb over the holes, Draven sent a thrum of magic into them, and hissed when residual magic bit back. "This wasn't a vampire."

Draven dropped the head back to the ground and stood.

"Then what the hell—" Travion began.

"It was done through magic." He studied his brother. "Do you have someone who opposes your rule? That might look to cause trouble here?"

Travion's fingers ran along his short-cropped beard—which still showed signs of singeing from their battle with the chimera—as he glared down at the dead body as if it were to blame for all of his troubles. "Don't we all?" He sighed. "And here I had hoped this was just further proof you were doing a terrible job in Andhera."

Draven shot him a glower of his own, only to receive a shrug and a clap on the back in response.

"All hell is breaking loose, isn't it, brother?"

"This one was left at the base of your castle, Travion. They wanted it to appear as if my people were attacking yours right beneath your nose. They are either looking to stir up issues between us or make one or both of us look incompetent." Draven knew that his brother would never believe it was something Draven was doing on purpose. A bond had been forged between them in the pits of Ludari's hell that could never be broken. Just as Draven would never willingly allow harm to come to Travion ever again, his younger brother could be just as fiercely protective of him.

"If I didn't know Zryan was too busy with his head buried between another conquest's thighs, I'd think he were trying to discredit us," Travion muttered, mostly joking.

Draven snorted. "Too busy and too disinterested. He barely has a desire to rule his own kingdom, let alone the middle and dark realms as well."

"If only it were so easy an answer."

"You said there were more bodies along the coast?"

"Six in total." Travion knelt, brushing his thumb along the wound to discover the bite of magic that resided within the flesh. "I will check the remainder and let you know what I find. Head back before the sun catches you."

Draven nodded. "Inform me if you come across the culprit."

"You'll be the first to know."

Leaving his brother, Draven returned to his soldiers. While he didn't wish trouble on his brother's head, he was pleased that for once, this hadn't stemmed from his people.

Mynata was there in the hallway when Draven returned to Aasha, like a spider waiting expectantly on her web.

"Draven." She paused as he shot her a look. "Your Grace," she corrected herself, "welcome home."

"Mynata." Draven continued walking down the hall, the gray velvet cape clipped to his right shoulder flapping as he went.

"Speak with me? Please?" Her hand reached for his wrist to stop him.

Restraining a growl, Draven paused and turned his head to look down at her. "Now is not the time."

"Please," she pleaded.

He sighed but nodded, turning to look at her. "What?"

"Why?" she asked. "Why her?"

"Why who, Mynata?" Draven asked, irritated.

"Eden. You've always said that you would never take a bride. That you didn't need a queen. Yet you've chosen someone from outside of Andhera. A mere youngling from Lucem . . . of all places."

"Of all places?" Draven's brow lifted. "It is where I came from myself."

Mynata stepped closer to him. "But it's not who you *are*. Not anymore." Her dark brown eyes moved over his face, sizing up his lack of reaction.

"And it won't always be who she is either." He looked Mynata over, his gaze sweeping her from head to toe. "You were once a child of light. But look at you now."

Mynata tossed her hair over her shoulder. "I also chose this land, as did my parents. Draven, she's not what you need." Her hand closed around his wrist once more, and he growled in warning at the touch.

"You know nothing of me."

"But I do. I do know you. I've known you for centuries." She stepped closer still, her hand sliding up his arm to rest on his elbow.

"Let me correct myself. You know nothing of what I need."

"I do!" The volume of her voice rose, frustration lighting her eyes. "I am Andherian . . . I know this land, and I know its people."

Draven pulled himself from her clutches and leaned down. "Let me be perfectly clear with you. Even if Eden were not here, you would still not be my choice of wife. We are not suited."

Mynata took a step back, upset and hurt visible in her eyes.

"There is darkness in both of us, Mynata. I need someone to pull me out of the pits of this hell. Eden can do that. You cannot."

"I can!" This time her voice was almost a shout. "I will

do whatever it takes to prove that I am fit to be your queen!"

Draven's head tipped slightly to the side, his eyes growing more intense as he studied her. "Mynata," he rasped. "Did you have something to do with my blood ending up in Eden?" This time, it was Draven closing the distance between them.

Mynata stood firm, but her body trembled lightly. "Of course not," she whispered.

Draven invaded her space, his form towering over her petite one. "Gruff would only have done what he did on the behest of someone familiar to him."

The vampiress shook her head. "I would never overstep in that way. Surely you know that."

"Once, I would have thought so. Yet now, everywhere I turn, you seem to be here in the halls. What prey are you hoping to catch in that web of yours, Mynata?"

Her dark eyes sparked. "I thought I had already made myself clear on that?"

Draven shook his head. "Go home, Mynata. I haven't time to deal with this right now. I have also made myself clear on the matter." He left her then, heading toward his study.

He hadn't lied. He had far too much to deal with to be bothered with the petty idea of love that Mynata clung to with no encouragement on his part.

Seurat, wonderful at anticipating his master's needs, was there waiting for him at the study door, a goblet of fresh blood in his hand. Taking it, Draven nodded his thanks and stepped into the room. With a swipe of his hand, the torches were lit on the walls and flames lit in the fireplace; he didn't need the heat, but the crackle was a pleasant and comforting background noise.

"How did Midniva go, sire?"

"Not well."

"I'm sorry to hear that."

Draven sunk down into his seat, settling into the wingback chair with an appearance of exhaustion. Some days, he truly missed sleep.

"Seurat . . . Mynata has been in the castle a lot lately." His eyes drifted up to the other man as he took a sip of blood.

"Yes, she has been. Ever since Lady Eden arrived."

"She feels threatened." Draven's hand brushed over his face. "Keep an eye on her please. I think there is a chance she had something to do with my blood ending up in Eden, and I don't trust that we've seen the end of it."

"Of course, sire." There was a worried look on Seurat's face.

"What is it, Seurat?" Draven pressed.

"Nothing, sire . . . I just thought you should be aware that Captain Channon and Sir Tulok provided Lady Eden with a knife . . . "

"A knife?" he asked.

"A small one."

"A knife," he repeated blandly. Draven wasn't certain if it was a relief to know that she was armed or if he should fear the likelihood she would stab herself—or someone else —accidentally with it. "Are they teaching her how to use it?"

"It appears Sir Tulok thought it suitable, and Captain Channon did not dispute it."

"Well . . . perhaps this means she will at least know how to hold it."

The last thing he needed was to have to inform Zryan that Eden had lost several fingers in an attempt to wield a small blade.

Eden

I t was a dance, Eden told herself. A dance that her life could depend on. Tulok had shown her the moves repeatedly, and all she had to do was copy them as he advanced on her. Eden slid her foot forward, thrusting one of her arms out at Tulok, but he swept her arm to the side and used her momentum to pull her past him. In one swift move, he twisted and kicked her leg out from under her. She was falling one moment, and the next, she was in his arms and facing him.

Eden grinned up at him. "Thank you for not letting me fall on my face."

Tulok leaned back and lifted Eden to her feet with ease. "I have no desire to meet my end." He bowed his head.

"You still might." Dhriti jabbed him in the side with her elbow, but it was followed by a laugh.

"No one is dying." Eden swept hair out of her face. Rebellious strands of red blew into her eyes and mouth. "Although, that isn't what you showed me yesterday, Tulok." Eden frowned. She had been anticipating the same routine, but he had improvised instead.

Tulok shrugged and grinned sheepishly. "Always expect the unexpected?"

Eden arched a brow and laughed. "Okay. Noted for next time."

Tulok bowed. "Always a pleasure, my lady. You did well."

Eden turned to leave, but Channon approached, his arms folded across his chest. He glanced toward Tulok, then to Eden before he leaned in toward her. "All right. The next hit you get on Tulok, I'll personally give you more than a little butter knife, my lady."

She eyed her hip, where the dagger was hidden beneath the tailed waistcoat. "All for landing a hit on him?"

Channon only lifted an eyebrow in response.

Eden had sparred with Tulok, had even successfully connected blows to him, but she wasn't certain she wanted to hit Tulok, or even if she wanted a weapon larger than the dagger. But it felt like a challenge, and she wasn't one to balk.

Channon nodded. "You know what to do."

Eden was already exhausted from their morning routines. Sweat collected at her hairline and trickled down her neck. Her muscles ached from pulling, pushing, tumbling, and repeating the process.

She flexed her fingers at her side. "Fine."

Channon grinned and lowered his arms. "Tulok, Her Grace would like one more match with you."

Tulok turned on his heel. Delight warmed his tanned features. "Of course." The warm friendly smile remained on his face even as he readied to launch into action.

Eden was at a great disadvantage in the first place. She wasn't a wolf or a creature of the night, and even in the golden moon's brighter rays, it wasn't like the light of the sun or even a well-lit room. Shadows played tricks on her eyes, made movements seem sluggish. She simply had to focus and trust her instincts. At least that's what she told herself.

And so, she struck out with a fist, which was blocked by Tulok. But this time, Eden took notice of *how* he blocked. When she struck out with her other hand, he did the same. If she lifted a foot, he could unbalance her, so she kept her feet planted firmly.

Tulok lashed out in a controlled movement, which Eden pushed aside. If he was pulling his punches, there was no way she stood a chance against him. But what he had said before . . . it resonated in her mind.

Wit and defense have a place together.

The wind picked up, and the sound of nearby trees creaking cut through her thoughts as she circled him. Eden possessed a measly amount of combat skills, but what she did know was nature, specifically that of flora. Prior to beginning, there had been no rules stating she couldn't use her magic. She simply hadn't because she wanted to learn hand-to-hand.

"Are you done already?" Tulok teased.

Eden wasn't finished. She held up her hands and rushed forward. Tulok pulled her forward, but as Channon suggested, she found her center again and crouched low. She tapped into her well of magic, the warm heat of it flooding her body as the ground beneath Tulok shifted and bucked. It was enough to offset his balance, but it didn't stop there. Vines from the ground slithered toward his feet, and as he shook them off, Eden launched forward and struck out with her palm, clipping his chin.

The moment she did, she gasped and recoiled. "I'm sorry!"

Tulok stumbled back, surprised, but then laughed.

Eden's cheeks warmed. "Expect the unexpected?" It hadn't occurred to her before that she could, in fact, use her ability to call on the flora as a weapon.

"That is exactly right." Tulok shook his finger at her and stepped away from the vines. "If anyone ever attacks you, do that." He motioned toward the retreating vines.

"Well done," Channon said from behind Eden. "You've earned yourself a new weapon."

Tulok glanced between Eden and Channon. "What?"

"I will fill you in. I'm sure Her Grace has other matters to attend to?"

Eden nodded and took it as her chance to escape before she was dragged into another match. Truth be told, her lungs burned from gulping too much air, and her muscles were in need of a hot soak in the tub.

Even the walk up the stairs felt as though her feet were weighted. She paused when she heard what sounded like sniffling, then mumbling.

Ever the curious one, Eden finished climbing the stairs and listened for the sound again. Every sniffle, every whine, drew her closer, until she spotted the flickering figure of a child. She had grown accustomed to the way certain humans' figures flickered in and out of a tangible state. The poor child was a revenant. But where had it come from?

Eden approached slowly, until she turned a corner and saw the little girl's features in the brightly lit hall. "Are you lost?" Eden called to her. "I can help you."

"I don't know." The girl sucked in a sob. "I'm scared,

and it won't stop pulling me." She twisted, but her body continued to move down the hall.

What was going on? Eden didn't want to worry the child any more, so she followed along. "It's okay. We will go together. My name is Eden. What is yours?"

"Niamh."

"I like that name. Where do you live?"

"Mointeach."

Eden blinked. She wasn't familiar with the name, but since it was neither from Lucem nor, as far as she knew, Andhera, that left Midniva. She frowned. Draven had mentioned how bad it was in Midniva, and Niamh was potentially a victim of whatever tragedies were unfolding there.

"Tell me of Mointeach, I've never been. I'm from Lucem, and I don't get out very much." The small chatter was enough to soothe the girl, and before long, they were entering the throne room.

Eden stopped in her tracks as they entered. To her surprise, as well as amazement, a sea of individuals filled the room, and they flickered just as Niamh did.

"Can you hold my hand?" Niamh pushed closer to Eden's thigh, and when she solidified enough, her sleek blond hair tumbled into her face as she pressed her cheek against Eden's leg.

"I'll hold your hand, just make sure to squeeze really tightly."

Eden reached for the girl's hand as she walked into the room and slid between the revenants. If it weren't for Niamh asking questions at her side, she would have focused more on what was being said. Draven's voice carried in the room rather coolly.

When she emerged from the throng, Draven finished his dialogue and met her gaze, then peered down at the child. He motioned toward a section of the room, and Eden lowered herself.

"There are more children over there. Why don't you go make friends? I'll be right over." Eden nodded and smiled encouragingly.

"This is how the revenants come to Andhera," Draven supplied before Eden even had the chance to ask. "They're spelled to come here, and when they arrive, they learn the laws, and Pendentes"—he paused, turning to motion to the drawn man behind him—"escorts them to their new life, and the children to whichever orphanage has room. You may remain here, but I can't be delayed."

Eden nodded and swiftly made her way to the handful of children, who she distracted with games. But even as she played, she listened to the process of deciding where the revenants would end up, and what their new life would become. It struck Eden as chilly, withdrawn, and so impersonal. This was their second chance at a life, or as close to one as they would get. Not everyone needed to be coddled, but there were more refined ways of dealing with delicate matters.

Eventually, the room emptied, and all that were left were the children. Draven had long since disappeared from the room, but Eden had wanted to wish the group of children farewell.

Eden embraced Niamh and a little boy who had attached himself to her. "I will see you soon. I always visit the orphanage." She released them into Pendentes' care.

She combed her fingers along the ends of her hair and toyed with it as she left the throne room. As tired as she felt, she was now fueled by a new wave of adrenaline that came with ideas. If she were to leave in a few months, she could at least make herself useful and perhaps relieve Draven of some of his burdens.

In the corridor, she saw Seurat ahead and rushed up to him. "Is Draven in his study?"

"No, my lady, he's actually in the room adjacent to it, the door to the left." Seurat bowed his head, but not before Eden caught the quirk of a smile on his lips.

There was little time to wonder about the expression. Eden opened the door left of his study. "Draven, I was thinking. After witnessing . . . She dragged her eyes up to his form, which was situated in a steaming hot bath. Whatever speech she'd had planned withered in her throat as she took in his glistening bare chest, one she remembered the feel of all too well.

Draven shifted in the tub; his head fell backward as he stared up at the ceiling. "As you were saying, Eden?" He sat upright, inclining his head.

"It can wait. I didn't realize you were bathing I . . . Seurat told me you were in here and I . . . "

Draven pinched the bridge of his nose and muttered, "I'll deal with him later. But please continue, Eden."

With her thoughts still buzzing, Eden moved closer to Draven. "After spending the majority of the day with the revenants, I think I know what I can do to help while I'm here." She told him of what she thought of the process and what she had seen. "It should be more welcoming . . . and I don't mean crafting flower crowns for everyone. This isn't an easy process. So why not be warmer, softer, and be a guide, not a dictator?"

Draven dragged his hand along his jaw and rested his

chin in his palm. "If that's something that interests you, and could potentially keep you out of trouble, I can arrange for you and Pendentes to discuss changes and allow for you to oversee the process."

Now that the words had tumbled free, Eden felt her exhaustion creeping back in. And she wondered if she'd heard him right, but he had mentioned her knack for finding trouble.

Eden stepped forward, her brow furrowing. "Really?"

26

Draven

D raven could see the surprise in her eyes as he agreed so readily to the idea of her changing the long-standing process by which they greeted and sorted arriving revenants. Was he that much of a disagreeable tyrant that she should assume he would say no? Perhaps he had not yet dispelled all the Lucem-fueled rumors that were whispered about him.

"Truly. Why should you not? You are the one most closely linked to the lives which they have just vacated. I have long since forgotten what it was like to walk alive in the sun." Draven looked away as he saw something filter into Eden's gaze. He did not wish to see pity there, if that was the emotion coming to her eyes.

"Thank you. I will take this task seriously, I vow it. And do you proud."

Draven stood, deciding that what peace he was seeking in the steaming waters of his tub had now flitted away, and he might as well be about the rest of his day. Turning unabashedly toward Eden, he found her eyes locked on his water-slick form, a light in their depths that stirred the heat within his own body.

There was a blush spreading over her cheeks and down her throat. From across the room, he could hear the quickened pace of her heartbeat, and his own body responded, beginning to stir.

Draven heard Eden's breath hitch, and without hesitation found himself saying, "You were training with the troops this morning . . . Did you have time to bathe?"

Eden swallowed. A question bloomed within her gaze. "No, not yet."

Draven extended his hand out toward her. "Then come. Join me."

The red in Eden's cheeks deepened, but not from embarrassment, surely. Not when they'd been twined together in the lake, and close to so much more in her bed. Her eyes, which had risen to meet his gaze, dropped suddenly and landed on his member. Uncertainty flickered in her gaze, and as Draven waited, he wondered if he'd perhaps overstepped his boundaries.

Without a word, Eden lifted her gaze again. While there was an air of timidness about her, which Draven could only guess was due to her inexperience, there was also a glint of determination.

Draven watched as Eden quickly disrobed, an impressive act considering the layers Loriah had a habit of clothing her in. Each piece of fabric that was shed revealed another flash of pale, luminescent skin that intrigued and beguiled him.

"Come," he said softly.

Eden crossed the floor without hesitation, her hand rising to slip into his own. He could feel the subtle tremble as his fingers closed around hers. Draven offered her a gentle squeeze, then helped her into the tub.

A surprised hiss escaped her as she stepped into the water to stand before him. "Oh, that feels good," she murmured.

"Mmm . . . I like my water hot." Draven lifted his hands to pull the pins from her hair, letting them drop to the floor. When her hair tumbled free, he fanned his fingers through the heavy length, watching as Eden's eyes fluttered closed at his ministrations.

Draven leaned forward and pressed a kiss to her slightly parted lips, allowing his tongue to open them further. She tasted of honey and sunshine, the closest he would come to either ever again.

Eden, overcoming whatever hesitation she'd held before, leaned against his form, her hands resting against his waist. She murmured low in her throat, a sound of appreciation. Draven, encouraged by this, wrapped an arm around her waist and drew her more snuggly against him. His desire for her mounted, and he felt his hardening length press against her warm flesh.

He did not think there would be any stopping them this time.

Draven broke the kiss, peppering light ones over her cheeks and forehead. Eden sighed happily, her lids remaining shut. Draven smoothed a hand down the length of her back to curve around her buttocks, cupping the flesh lightly as he held her against him.

"Let's get you washed, shall we?"

Eden's eyes fluttered open, a soft smolder of desire in their depths. "I'd like that."

Smiling gently, Draven edged back, and prompted her to

sit down. Once she had settled in the water, he did so as well, his legs spread wide on either side of her. Eden sat facing him, her feet tucked beneath his thighs.

Reaching over the tub, Draven picked up the forgotten pitcher. Filling it with water, he leaned forward. "Tip your head back."

Once Eden had obeyed, Draven carefully poured the bathwater over her beautiful red locks, his free hand protecting her eyes from the droplets. It required not only a second but a third pitcher to ensure that the thick tresses were thoroughly drenched. Eden's eyes stayed on his features the entire time.

Setting aside the pitcher, Draven unstopped the vial filled with the fragrant soap he used for his own hair. He poured the liquid into his palm and set the vial aside. Gently, Draven began working the soap through Eden's hair.

"You needn't do this," she whispered, her skin red from both the heat of the water and from whatever emotions coursed through her.

"I've denied you your lady's maid. The least I can do is assist, is it not?" Draven said, a smirk lighting upon his lips.

"I suppose so," she agreed. Smiling back at him, Eden then shut her eyes and leaned into the action, seeming to decide to enjoy the moment.

Once he had thoroughly washed her hair and offered a light massage to her scalp, Draven began to rinse the red tresses free of suds, the bathwater filling with bubbles. The fresh scent of lavender and mint was welcomed by his nose, along with the natural scent of Eden, flushed with life and desire before him.

"Thank you," she whispered when he was finished.

"You are welcome." Settling back against the end of the tub, Draven allowed his arms to rest on the rim.

Eden reached for the bar of soap that sat on the top of the tub, and wetting it, washed herself. Draven found his eyes following every dip and glide of her hand over the soft curves of her body. Each teasing brush of her fingertips over a sensitive area brought a growl, just to the surface without spilling out. He wanted his hands on her. His fingers teasing her flesh to a quivering mess beneath him.

When the bar of soap dipped below the surface of the water, Draven could no longer contain his growl, and their eyes locked in understanding. Eden was moving toward him at the same time as his hands shot out to grasp her about the waist and pull her into his lap, seating her properly atop him.

Draven was now fully hard, his length trapped beneath the spread of her thighs, aching to feel her wet heat accept him. He pulled her flush against his chest, claiming her mouth in a hungry kiss that stole away any chance for words, the glide of his tongue over hers tugging whimpers from Eden instead.

Drawing away from the kiss, Draven moved his lips along her jaw, and throat, nipping and suckling gently on the flesh so readily at his disposal. Eden's head fell back, exposing the full length of it to his exploration. His hands dropped from her waist to her hips, angling her so that as he shifted his own, the breadth of his phallus pressed between her folds, finding the hidden pearl nestled there.

Rocking himself against her, Draven felt the shudder of pleasure that swept through Eden's body and took delight in the gasp that escaped her lips. Draven, himself, groaned against her throat, the glide of her only increasing his own hunger to feel her properly envelope him.

Eden's hands were in his hair, tugging against the short strands as they found purchase, her hips moving of their own accord, seeking the stimulation of his firmness. Draven moaned, his fangs dropping in response to his need; lust for body and blood wrapped so sweetly together.

"Draven . . ." Eden breathed his name on a sigh.

Hearing it, Draven pressed a hand to her lower back and arched her over the water so that his head could drop and claim a nipple between his lips. Eden made a sound of pleasure as he did so, which only fueled him. Allowing his tongue to glide over the hardening peak, his hand dropped below the water to the valley between her thighs.

His fingers found her clit, rolling over it, much to the delight of her body. The hungry press of her hips urged him to continue, and he did so gladly.

Trapping her nipple between his teeth lightly, he tormented it with the flick and swipe of his tongue, while his fingers rolled and pressed the little nub of pleasure between her thighs. Draven listened intently, as Eden's breathing increased, her heart tripped erratically, and her body was left trembling and grinding into his touch.

When she was there, on the precipice, he ceased his actions, wringing a ragged wail of protest and frustration from Eden's throat.

Her eyes opened for the first time in a while, head lifting as she looked at him questioningly. "Why?"

Draven's only response was to claim her lips for himself once more. His hands swept beneath her thighs, crushing her against him so that he could hoist her up on his hips as he stood. Water streamed from them, leaving a puddle across the floor as he climbed from the tub and carried her to the door.

His lips did not leave hers as he carried her swiftly down the hall toward her chambers, a trail of water and chattering goblins left in their wake.

Eden's arms wound around his neck, clinging to him as fiercely as did her legs.

Throwing open her bedchamber door, Draven carried her into the room and quickly slammed the door shut behind them with his foot. There would be no disrupting them this time.

With swift strides, Draven moved to her bed and laid Eden down along its length. He took but a moment to gaze on her flushed features: lips swollen, lids drooping, eyes begging for him to continue.

Settling himself between her thighs, Draven's hands rested on either side of her shoulders, holding himself up. "You said that you wished to make use of the time we had." His voice was husky, throat tight with desire.

"Yes. Please, Draven."

He sealed her words with another kiss, moaning as her hands reached for him, exploring the breadth of his shoulders and down along his back.

Draven kissed back down her throat, making his way over her lightly freckled chest to tease between the valley of her breasts. Her warm scent flooded his senses, increasing his craving for not only the pleasure of her body but the taste of her blood. He wanted to consummate the bond between them. To not only have the light presence of Eden in the back of his mind but for her to feel the connection as well.

He kissed lower, over her slender torso, nipping

teasingly at her navel before traveling farther. His own body shifted backward on the bed as lips brushed over the curve of one hip, then his fangs lightly grazed the other. Above him, Eden's breath hitched, and when he looked up at her, he found her eyes on him.

"Y-you . . ." She swallowed, halting her words as she struggled to catch her breath. "Drink from me."

Draven looked at her in shock. "What?" he whispered.

Eden's hand rose to cup his cheek, the pad of her thumb parting his lips to scrape along the sharp tip of one fang. The action made him shudder, his eyes closing for a moment.

"I know they're linked." Even in her inexperience, she had come to understand this about him. That hunger and lust were one and the same for a vampire. "I trust you, Draven."

He groaned at her words, a searing, glorious pain shooting through his heart as his hand grasped her wrist and he turned his head to kiss it. She had no idea what those words meant to him, coming from someone as pure as her.

"I'll feel your pleasure if I do," he explained, voice raspy with emotion. "It'll connect us more greatly because you've already had my blood." Draven looked into her eyes, making sure that even in the midst of her lust, she understood. "And should you drink more of mine, you would begin to feel my emotions."

Eden nodded. "Drink from me. Please."

"Thank you," he said, rather than trying to explain exactly what this meant to him. But his eyes remained locked on hers, and he hoped that Eden could read it there within their depths.

Draven dipped his head then, nuzzling against her tender inner thigh. He released a harsh breath, his desire and hunger now an overwhelming presence inside him. His tongue scraped lightly over the vein there in her thigh, and with as much gentleness as he could muster, Draven bit lightly into her skin.

Eden's breath hitched, an indrawn hiss of pain through her teeth, before the subtle venom of his bite spread pleasure through her form. Draven could tell when it flooded her, for she gasped a surprised, "Oh." Her fingers sunk into his hair, pulling his lips more tightly against her.

Draven was in his own world of bliss as the first drops of Eden's blood hit his tongue. It dazzled and sang along his taste buds, tasting like bright rays of sunlight and fresh spring flowers. Her blood was the essence of pure life, sparking memories of warmth and bliss. Draven groaned, his lips fastening onto her thigh as he drew a mouthful from her, losing himself, for just a moment, to the flavor of heaven washing over him.

It was intoxicating. Awakening every cell within his body, washing over him with pure energy. Draven felt as if he could fly, run from one end of Andhera to the other without stopping, and rut the night away.

He could not, however, allow himself to become carried away. And so, after that first delighted swallow, he swept his tongue over the wound, encouraging healing. Licking at his lips, Draven nuzzled against the mound between her thighs.

"By the moon . . . you are delicious," he rasped, and then his tongue swept between her folds with another moan of pleasure.

Eden's knees drew up a fraction as Draven began a

gentle assault on the little bead of pleasure between her thighs. His tongue lapped over it, encouraged by the gasps of delight issued from Eden with mounting frequency.

Draven lifted his eyes to watch her as he sunk two fingers into her silken depths, feeling her body instinctively tighten around him. He groaned, delighting in the heated wetness he found there. She was so very ready for him.

With a gentle coaxing, Draven's fingers stroked Eden, pulling further moans from her mouth. Each one he received only increased his own desire and spurred on his actions.

Nipping the bud between his lips, Draven growled in appreciation as Eden's hips rocked against his mouth in response, her fingers tightening on the bedding. Soft whimpers of pleasure slipped from her, and Draven felt himself desperate to hear her cries of completion once more. To taste her as she released.

His fingers pulled from her so that his tongue could replace them, his thumb rolling over her clit instead. Eden's response was instant, her hips arching more desperately into him. Draven's thumb rolled in quick pulses over the bead, and when her cries rang out, his tongue was there to tease the last of her pleasure out of her.

When he lifted his head, Eden had an arm over her eyes, soft pants issuing from her chest. Draven kissed his way back up her body, settling his hips between her thighs once his lips found hers again.

"That was . . . that was . . . " Eden sought for words.

"Just the beginning," Draven responded, and silenced any further discussion with a hungry kiss, letting her know he had not yet had his fill of her.

Eden

Eden's eyes wrenched shut as Draven's mouth clashed with hers again. Every nerve ending in her being had ignited as she came undone moments ago. Yet, she still craved more. Her body yearned to unite with him fully.

When had her trust in him grown so much? She surmised it had happened alongside the love that blossomed within her chest. It drove her actions, and when she was still enough, she could feel it humming in the back of her mind, in a voice that wasn't her own but Draven's instead.

Perhaps it was silly of her to think Draven could grow to love her. He was the king of Andhera, and she was a naive fae from Lucem, who belonged to the dark world as much as a fish belonged on land. But she could dream, and while she was in this bed with him, she'd allow herself to.

"The beginning?" she rasped out with laughter, and it soon turned into a moan as the tip of Draven's length nudged her center. Her heart thrummed wildly in her chest, and Eden wondered if he could feel her desire as it spread through her limbs. This time, it had little to do with his blood in her system and everything to do with how *he* made her feel, that in his presence, beneath his gaze and his touch, she came to life.

Draven's lips slanted into a grin against hers. "I'm not through yet, Eden." When he pulled back, his fangs gleamed in the golden light of the room, and while they may have inspired fear in many, they were simply part of him and no longer frightened her.

He lifted his brows in a silent question, to which Eden replied by hitching one of her legs around his slender waist.

"Wait." The word slipped out from her, stilling both of their movements. If Eden could have read his thoughts, she assumed he would have groaned in frustration. But Draven didn't utter a word, nor did he move. "I want to feel you here too." She lifted her hand, fingers splaying against his firm chest.

He sucked his bottom lip into his mouth, letting his fang graze it enough to cut into the tender skin. When a drop of blood formed, he lifted his hand, wiping it away, then reached out toward her.

Eden parted her lips, and her tongue licked away the residue. She closed her mouth around his thumb and suckled.

Draven's blue eyes focused on her mouth, and he hissed the moment she pulled away. "By the moon, Eden, if you—"

She silenced whatever chastisement waited for her with a kiss. His blood, even in the smallest dose, melded with what was coursing through her already and heightened her arousal. Or was that his? By the sun, it was Draven's desire flooding her senses too.

Eden swept her hand down his shoulder, toward the small of his back, as she lifted her hips to meet his. "I need you, Draven." She panted as the silken tip of him pushed against her barrier.

"Just breathe. It'll hurt for a moment." Draven cupped her face with one hand, his forehead against hers, while his other lifted her knee as he pushed against the resistance.

Pain blossomed within her, hot and overwhelming. She exhaled as Draven sunk into her depths, filling her entirely. Her inner muscles were so tight, and his member stretched her, furthering the sting. However, his blood coursing through her dulled the pain.

He pulled his head back to gaze into her eyes, and when the pain faded a fraction, she nodded her head. Draven's hips shifted, which brought forth a moan from her. A delicious need blazed in her again, and the slow, torturous motion of his hips withdrawing only to surge within again drove her into maddening bliss.

Draven's lips trailed down her neck in heated, reverent kisses. Then his hands slid beneath her bottom, and he pulled her onto his hips at the same time he sat down. His length drove into her in a deliciously slow movement.

Eden moaned as he filled her more completely. Meeting his gaze, she leaned forward and brushed a kiss along his jaw and to his neck. His hands pulled her against him as he thrust upward, and it drew a hissing moan.

"Show me what to do," she whispered as she ground against him. The motion drew more pleasure from her as her sensitive flesh slid against him.

Draven captured both of her hands in his and squeezed

them before he lay lingering kisses against her knuckles. "I plan to do just that." He chuckled, and Eden had never wanted to hear a noise more than she did just then.

In the next moment, Draven twisted and lay backward, so that it was Eden straddling him. His hands tugged her hips forward and then lifted her, encouraging her to follow the motion.

Her fingers splayed on his chest as she gave in to following the rhythm of their bodies. With every one of his upward thrusts, she crashed down on him and ground her flesh into him. Her breaths grew ragged as the familiar intensity unfurled within, and she chased it until she felt as though she would burst. And then she did. In the most heavenly way. Her inner muscles tightened around Draven's length, and in the same instant, he groaned.

Her lips sought his out, even though she could scarcely breathe, but as the waves of her pleasure continued, she felt Draven meet his own release.

Every muscle felt spent. Eden sucked in a breath as she leaned down onto his chest. Her heart beat wildly, so hard that she thought it might gallop away from her. She closed her eyes, reveling in the feel of his flesh beneath her and the smell of him around her.

"If we spent the remainder of my time like that," Eden began, still breathless, "I'd be content."

Draven's fingers swept the hair away from her face, and he laughed. It was a throaty noise that Eden delighted in. "Just content? By the moon, Eden. What would it take to sate you?"

She twisted in his grasp and nipped at his neck, laughing. In return, Draven growled at her, and his fangs grazed her shoulder. Eden writhed on top of him, then his hands lowered to her bottom, and he squeezed.

"I could task you with finding out." She dragged her nose along his collarbone and kissed a trail to the tip of his pointed ear.

In a quick roll, Draven pinned her to the mattress, his hands seeking hers out to keep them occupied. "I could do just that." His head lowered and his lips circled around one hardened peak. "Did you not have your fill?"

Her body flushed at his words. She had, and in a moment, she could fall asleep if she allowed herself. But his mouth on her sensitive flesh awakened her desire again.

"Perhaps, but even if I didn't . . . I don't think I could possibly go again." She lifted her hand and cupped his face, her thumb brushing beneath his eye. "Do you have to leave?"

Draven ran his hand along her arm and to her wrist. "No. You have me all night." When he lowered his mouth to hers, he pulled on the blankets and lifted them over them. "I will be here."

His words constricted her heart. If she could freeze this moment for a lifetime, she would. Never had she felt so at peace or so cherished.

"And if I wake?"

"If you wake, I'll still be here . . . And if you find yourself wanting more, we can see what it takes to fill your appetite." He fairly purred his words as he settled onto the mattress and pulled her against him.

"And if you can't keep up with my needs, what then?" It was a playful question, but in return, Draven growled. Eden rested her cheek against him, one arm curling around him.

"Your lack of faith in my abilities is insulting. However, we will cross that bridge when we come to it." He swept his hand along the back of her head and down her back. "Now please, for the love of the sun, moon, and sea, get some rest." It was quiet for a moment, then he added, "Because you'll need it."

Exhausted as Eden was, she laughed and let the pulse of their twined emotions, coupled with Draven's fingers combing through her hair, lull her into a restful slumber.

28

Draven

Draven stared down at the wrist in his hold, the man standing at his side whimpering in a fearful manner. The fingers of the hand trembled lightly, a shiver of fear that moved up the arm to the body it was attached to.

"Is something displeasing to you about this one, Your Grace?" Seurat asked from where he stood across the room, arms folded behind his back.

"No," Draven replied, and brought the wrist up to his mouth, biting into the flesh. The human gasped in pain as his fangs tore through his skin. The trembling lasted until the venom from his bite spread, then he was silenced.

The last drops of blood to pass his lips had been Eden's, and a part of Draven didn't want to chase it with the essence of a Midnivian criminal. Yet, food was necessary. Draven took what he needed, feasting on the warm, heady liquid, then pulled away from the wrist and released it from his hold. Wiping at his lips, he motioned to Seurat, who came forward to take the mortal and pass him off to the harpy waiting outside in the hall.

Leaning back in his chair, Draven folded his hands in his lap and shut his eyes, taking a moment to let the fresh blood sweep through his system. He caught flashes of the mortal's last few days trapped down in the dungeons with the others, flickers of his journey in the prison carts through the Veil from Midniva, and a quick burst of the life he had lived before his crimes had been discovered.

But Draven wanted none of that. He wanted only the memories from the night before. The taste of Eden on his tongue. The feel of her around him. The hungry press of her lips to his as he wrung pleasured cries from her throat.

He shouldn't have given in, because he was aware that at the end of the six months, she had to return to Lucem. And already he was questioning what it would be like should she stay.

"Your Majesty, I wondered if I might have a word?"

Draven opened his eyes to find Lord Esruiit standing in the doorway. Straightening in his chair, he beckoned the man forward.

"Enter."

"While I have never been one to question your decisions, you have made a grave error in judgment, Your Majesty," the vampire wasted no time in saying. He was a portly man, who had chosen to come to Andhera with his family because he felt it was his duty to help bring a civilized culture to it.

Draven's brow lifted in disgruntled offense. "Excuse me?"

"Lord Capala was not guilty of going against you and creating a hive in Midniva."

Draven steepled his fingers over his chest, eyeing the

other man. "He was accused by a woman about to be executed. She had no reason to lie."

"But she did," Lord Esuriit insisted.

"Esuriit, Forstuss only supported it. Capala and his son were guilty."

Esuriit shook his head and stepped farther into the room, beginning to pace a little. "They hated being restrained, that I will admit, but Capala was always loyal to you as a ruler." He looked to Draven. "He would not have done this. Did you feed from him? To be certain?"

"Aamanee led me to him without any pressure on my part. This was not simply me looking to be rid of opposers. Their actions were bringing scrutiny from Midniva upon my kingdom. That will not be tolerated."

"And death was your only solution? You could have sent him through Sollicitus. Allowed him to face the torments in that cave and come out a free man. Execution was not your only recourse."

"You know the law. Death of a mortal means a punishment of death for the killer."

"But what of you, My Lord? What will be your punishment when the truth comes out?"

Draven merely stared back at the nobleman, a muscle ticking violently in his jaw.

"There are mutters. Dissatisfaction. If you cannot be trusted to find the truth before you act, how can they trust it won't be them next?"

Draven stood up quickly, slamming his hands down on the desk before him. "Enough! I followed the information, and it led me back to Capala. We're not having this conversation any further."

Esuriit shook his head. "Very well, Your Majesty. Heed my warning or not, it has been delivered." The vampire bowed and backed out of the room.

Feeling the weight of the last few days, Draven leaned on the desk with both hands, his head bowed.

"And here I thought I had some battles to fight at home."

Draven groaned as he heard his brother's voice. "Zryan. Why are you here?" Lifting his head, he looked across the room to see his brother leaning against the doorframe.

"Is that any way to greet your little brother?"

"Yes." Zryan very rarely stepped foot in Andhera, and when he did, even less often was it a good sign.

Zryan rolled his eyes. Pushing off from the door, he strolled into the office and dropped down into one of the chairs opposite the desk. "Your words are like an arrow to my heart." He placed a hand over his chest, then lifted his legs up to rest his feet on the edge of the desk, crossed at the ankles. The fabric of his light green tunic slid up his bare thighs to expose the curvature of his ass, which Draven didn't appreciate.

Sighing, Draven dropped back down into his own chair. "I repeat, why are you here?"

"Can I get some food? I know you don't eat . . . but you feed the young lady, right?" Zryan gave a shout, and a revenant appeared before him. "I'd love something to eat, and a nice cold glass of pomegranate wine."

Draven simply sat, glowering at his brother as he placed his demands with the revenant, who disappeared shortly afterward. Of course Zryan would arrive and make himself at home without thought.

"How long does it usually take? I know they're not used to getting orders for more than blood, but—what?" Zryan finally halted, staring over at him.

"Why. Are. You. Here?" Draven's voice was firm and cold.

"Naya told Alessia of my latest pretty treat. I had to hide her in Midniva before my wife decided to viciously maul her mind and/or kill her. I figured it would be best if I came this way for a little while and gave Lessie some time to cool down."

Draven stared at his brother. "I don't have time for you."

"Excuse me?" Zryan's brows shot up.

"I don't have time for you or any of your nonsense. You heard Lord Esuriit, I have furious nobles due to the execution of another, I have vampires and lamia in Midnivia—"

"I've heard. I really thought you and Travion were better at doing your jobs," Zryan cut him off.

Quickly, Draven reached out and swatted Zryan's feet off the desk, upending him in his chair and sending him tumbling onto the floor. Just at that moment, the revenant reappeared with a tray of food for Zryan. Startled, the girl looked from the king sprawled on the floor to her own sovereign seated unfazed in his chair.

"Is everything all right, sire?" she asked uncertainly.

"Everything is just fine," Draven replied calmly, crossing his hands back over his abdomen as he watched his youngest brother pick himself up off the floor and shoot him a withering glance as he righted his chair.

"Your king is an *ass* is what is going on here," Zryan grumbled.

"Oh, don't fuss, Zry, your food will get cold."

Once the food was spread out on the desk and Zryan had settled himself once again, the brothers resumed staring across the desk at each other.

"I would have thought that sending that untouched ball of sunshine your way would have shed a little light on your mood. Apparently not."

"Leave Eden out of this."

"Oh, the defensive tone in your voice." Zryan fairly cooed the words.

Draven said nothing. Zryan only smiled more.

"Or maybe things *have* gotten better with you because of the sexy little nymph. Has the dark king personally welcomed Naya's daughter into womanhood?" There was glee shining in Zryan's eyes.

Draven growled, his lids lowering over his eyes dangerously. "Do not speak of her in such a manner." His brother may treat the females of his kingdom like an endless stream of playthings for his own amusement, but Draven would not have him lumping Eden into that mix.

Zryan leaned forward, elbows on his knees and a broad grin spreading over his lips. "Ohhhh, you *have* found your pleasure with the maiden."

"Get out."

Zryan laughed, waving him off. "Calm down, brother. I'm merely happy to see that you've finally allowed yourself to find some pleasure. I could see it in your eyes that night, that you wanted her. It's why I knew you wouldn't fight me too hard on bringing her back here with you."

Draven could only glare at him. What Zryan was saying couldn't be true. Surely he hadn't given in to Zryan and pulled Eden from her life because deep down he'd wanted her. His brows pinched with a frown as he thought it over.

"Seriously, Draven. You're the only creature I know who admits he's enjoyed a female's body and still ends up frowning over it."

"I'm not frowning over it."

"You are . . . Does this mean you'll be pleased when she goes home? Was she too innocent for your taste?"

Draven shot him another perturbed look. How he managed to spew insensitive sentiments every other breath was both remarkable and infuriating. "It doesn't matter whether I want her to go home or not; she must. It isn't safe for her here. It never was."

"Whether or not?" Zryan's eyebrows shot up, then his face became more serious, and Draven found himself being studied by his brother.

Draven never did like when his brother actually took the time to look into the reality of a situation. He had a tendency of reading a person correctly when he bothered to try.

"Draven, do you care about her?"

"I meant what I said, Zryan. Eden cannot stay here. Her life will be altered if she does. She will become either a vampire or something else. We have no right to take her life from her. She has already spent most of her life controlled by her mother. She does not need the two of us telling her what she must do with the rest of it." Draven shook his head and glared down at the desk.

The truth was, if he had the choice . . . No, he would not send Eden home. Her presence here was more than just a fresh breeze in stale halls. She was a spot of life in the constant shadow of death.

"Fascinating." Zryan picked up a piece of bread, dipping it in oil before he took a bite. He chewed slowly as he contemplated something.

This time, it was Draven who studied Zryan. His brother appeared calm on the outside, but there was something about the subtle shift of his body that indicated otherwise.

"Why are you really here, Zryan?"

He gave Draven a laugh, waving a hand to brush him off, but the truth rested in his eyes.

"Zryan?" he growled.

"The Creaturae is missing."

Draven stilled, a chill coursing down his spine. "What?" he asked carefully.

"Ruan found the griffins guarding its tomb dead. No easy task, mind you. When he went in, the book was gone."

Draven cursed. Pushing his chair back abruptly, he stood. "How could you be so foolish to lose The Creaturae?"

"Foolish? I've kept it protected for how many millennia?!"

Draven forced his fingers angrily through his hair as he paced out from behind his desk. "So you came to bring me word of this, but what do you expect me to do? I cannot look for it. I'm unable to even step foot into Lucem."

"I thought you should know. You and Travion both, in case it has something to do with what is taking place in Midniva and Andhera now."

Turning, Draven swept the items on his desk onto the floor.

There was more in the works than any of them were

aware of. They were all being played as fools by someone who remained several steps ahead of them. The mayhem, the disorder, the death; it couldn't be all pure coincidence. But where was the common link they were missing?

Eden

Small red seeds sat in Eden's palm. She plopped one in her mouth, and the sweetness burst on her tongue. Tulok playfully sparred with an imaginary foe as he showed her one of his infamous moves that had apparently won him a fight when he was younger. She tried to listen intently, but it was difficult when her mind raced and her body still hummed from last night's turn of events.

Eden could still feel Draven's fingers trailing over her body and his tongue exploring her mouth. She ached in a way that reminded her of their time together. As Draven had promised, when she woke, he had tested her limits until Eden was certain she would shatter into oblivion.

Just thinking about it caused her heart to flutter. Was this what her mother felt for her father? And if it was, could she convince Draven she wanted to remain with him instead of returning to Lucem? The notion of returning to the kingdom of light wasn't appealing any longer if it meant she'd never see Draven again or feel his firm body against hers.

Maybe it was foolish to feel so strongly already. But

with his blood in her veins, she knew it wasn't just her, that he felt it too.

"And then it didn't matter anyway, because I slammed his head on a chair, and he was snuffed out like a candle." Tulok smashed his fist into his palm, pulling Eden from her thoughts.

If she had just arrived in Andhera, his outburst, let alone the whole story, would have startled her. Eden would have stared at the were-wolf, mortified, and run far away. But now, she shrugged. The move had been fair since the other creature had stooped to using a chair first and struck Tulok in the back. He was only retaliating with more force to put a stop to the fight.

She wrinkled her nose. "I don't foresee myself in a tavern, let alone getting into a fight in one."

"That's not the point, my lady." He turned to face her, his lips tilting in their typical grin. "I'm only reinforcing what I've said before. Use what you have. Your fists, or if it's a chair, use the sharpest corner. A weapon doesn't have to be a knife or an arrow." Tulok tapped his temple and nodded. "Using your wit and what is presented to you can save your life. You've told me on more than one occasion you could never be a warrior." His dark eyes flicked from her head to her boots. "Not all warriors battle on a field."

Eden's lips twisted as she doubted his words, but he was sincere in his belief at the very least. What about her said *warrior*? She laughed and plopped another seed into her mouth, ignoring his dry expression. Dusting her hands off, she let the remaining juicy red beads tumble to the ground, and ravenous sprites grabbed at them.

"That being said, Dhriti is switching guard with me. I

have somewhere to be." An almost sheepish glint entered his eye. "I can stay until she arrives."

In the garden? Eden shook her head. "Don't be silly. I don't need anyone hovering over me while I'm gardening. I have my new blade . . . " She shoved the fabric of her waistcoat aside. On her hip hung a secured long dagger in a baldric sheath. "I can use what I have at the ready should I need it." Eden laughed, then turned to face a glowing flower. When she touched the feather-like petals, it closed, and as she drew away, it opened again.

Tulok's boots scuffed the stone walkway as he stood next to Eden. "Only if you're certain." He seemed hesitant to leave, and she surmised it had something to do with an order.

"Tulok, I will be fine. I've been in the garden alone before. And besides, Alder is with me." She looked around for her pet, but he was currently buried deep in the brush, likely hunting sprites.

Whatever notion Tulok had been warring with, he came to a conclusion and bowed to Eden. "Dhriti will be here shortly." And with that, he backed away and turned down the winding path of the garden.

At least in the silence, Eden could attempt to muddle through what she felt and how exactly she could convince Draven to let her stay past her six months. She could endure whatever Andhera turned her into if he would allow her to stay and ease into the role Eden had thought was hers all along.

A rustling by her feet drew her attention toward Alder. He sneezed, then his leathery wings lifted him into the air so he could light on Eden's shoulder. As her fingers ran through his silky pelt, his tail curled around her neck. It dawned on her that she couldn't take Alder home with her if Draven chose not to keep her. Not because the sun would harm him but because he was no longer a creature of Lucem.

Could she not have one thing she wanted in life? Frustration, anger, hurt—they all collided within her.

His ash-colored nose twitched as he smelled the air. Alder stomped his back feet against Eden's neck, which was promptly followed by a low clicking noise.

"What are you upset about?" She lowered herself to the ground and let her pet hop down. "Did you see more sprites? Then go. I won't stop you." She scratched the top of his head and watched as he hopped down the path, his whiplike tail slashing back and forth in annoyance.

Eden turned to a rose bush. The petals were a combination of bloodred and white. As if someone clumsily bled all over the pristine flowers and they were now stained. More bouquets were needed for her room, so Eden slid a pair of gardening shears from her pocket and clipped away several stems.

In the next moment, a strange sensation unfurled within her stomach, as if someone were watching her. Eden spun on her heel and found Mynata approaching. Unfortunately, the vampiress' feet had made no sound on the ground to alert Eden of her arrival. Eden was in no mood to deal with Mynata's meddling, but she wasn't so foolish as to turn her back on her.

"So you've managed to wheedle your way into Draven's arms." The statement was cold and bitter, much like the speaker. "You have the whole castle twittering over your union with him." She sneered.

Eden would have flushed if it weren't for the anger

steadily rising in her. "I'm not discussing my personal life with you." Eden tightened her grip on the stems, and while the thorns pressed against her skin, they didn't yet pierce it.

Mynata strode forward and ran her fingers along the blinking flower Eden had planted in the garden. There was something ugly blooming inside of her chest. Mynata didn't belong here, touching the flowers Eden had planted and cared for or baiting Eden into a fight.

Mynata hissed. "You're a passing fancy, and an unsuitable one at that. Before long, he will be in my arms again, and you will be nothing more than a faded memory." She pulled her hand back and ran a black nail along her chin as she assessed Eden. "Nothing more than a king's strumpet."

Anger sprung loose within Eden. She squeezed the rose stems as she strode forward, and with her free hand, struck the vampire across the face. "Get out of here now, Mynata. Your lies and your manipulation will not work on me. You know *nothing* about me, and certainly not how Draven feels about me."

A low growl emitted from Mynata. Then she laughed. "Do you? Do you know how he feels, Eden?" The vampiress turned her blackened eyes on Eden, and her fangs lengthened over her lips. "I can see why he chooses to feed on you . . . you do smell so good." Dark laughter erupted from her again as she leaned closer. "But tell me . . . how do you enjoy tasting him? Do you prefer it straight from the source? Or in a goblet?"

It had been Mynta. It had to have been. She had dosed the goblet with Draven's blood and fed it to Eden. Had she enlisted poor Gruff to do her bidding? "Did you . . . ?" Not even the vampiress could be so bold as to act against her king—yet the smirk on Mynata's face said otherwise.

"Goblins are stupid little creatures." She sighed as if bored. "Unfortunately, my plan didn't go as I'd hoped."

That was enough. Eden wouldn't endure her taunting any longer. "Get out of my sight before I tell Draven everything." But the words died on her tongue as Mynata's hand shot out and squeezed off her air supply. Eden's hands lifted, and she clawed at the one arm holding her in place.

"I'm afraid there is only room for one of us, Eden. And you don't belong in Andhera . . . Draven needs a capable queen, someone strong and able to fend for herself. Not a damsel constantly in need of aid." She tightened her grip. The prick of her nails digging into Eden's neck burned as she tried to suck in precious air.

This couldn't be how Eden died, not by Mynata's hands. She refused. The flowers had long since tumbled from her grasp, and her hands pushed at Mynata, who was as solid as stone.

With her feet still planted on the ground, Eden kicked at Mynata's knee, and it was enough to make her loosen her grip. Then Eden dipped low and sprung to the side.

Mynata launched at her and tore her nails across the tender skin of Eden's neck, which only heightened the vampire's frenzy as blood seeped from the deep scratch. She slammed Eden's back to the ground, forcing whatever air she'd sucked in back out. Mynata hovered over her, but she was too preoccupied with the bleeding neck to notice Eden slipping her dagger free.

It was too awkward of a position to impale Mynata

properly, but she could inflict enough damage to scurry away again, perhaps buy time until Dhriti arrived.

She slid the dagger free and plunged it into Mynata's chest, low enough to avoid piercing her dead heart but deep enough so that Eden could scramble away and crawl into the foliage.

A shriek escaped the vampire, melding in with a growl as she plucked the dagger free. "Oh, you little wretch. I'm going to enjoy drinking you dry."

Drink me dry? Eden's eyes widened. The vampiress could try, but Eden wouldn't make it easy. Mynata was a hunter; she would find Eden hiding within the trees, and then what? She swallowed, trying to soothe the rising panic. If she felt this way . . . surely Draven . . .

Draven would sense her distress, and the vampiress would die by his hand.

A snarl erupted beside her. Mynata's face came into view, and Eden launched forward, only to be tripped by her foe. She smacked the ground hard and instantly grew dizzy. Nails bit into Eden's calf, forcing her to cry out in pain. The fabric of her breeches gave way, but that was the least of her worries.

"You are a temporary plaything, Eden. A taste of the past, bitter and acidic. He needs someone of the dark, like him, not you—a silly nymph of the sun."

"Nymph?" Eden screeched. Anger, whether it was her own or not, filled her, chasing out her panic. Blood trickled down her forehead to her eyebrows and onto her nose, but Eden had the sense to flip around to face the looming vampire. Quickly, she assessed her surroundings. Behind her the carnivorous plant stretched, feeling the tremors in the ground and tasting the blood in the air. Mynata was far too focused on a meal to worry about a plant.

Eden allowed the pulse of her magic to greet the awakening creature, feed it the energy it so craved, and at the same time, Mynata sprung at her again. Her fingers wrenched Eden's head to the side, and she lay still until Mynata's fangs were about to pierce her skin. In a lightning-fast movement, Eden withdrew her energy from the plant, and the beast which yearned for it grew agitated. The rustling near its roots only furthered its annoyance, and as Eden looked up, its gaping, jagged maw opened.

With every thread of strength she possessed, Eden pushed her legs up against Mynata, shoving her upward into the opening mouth. The vampiress didn't know what was happening until razor-sharp teeth tore into her. Blood dripped onto Eden's face, and she rolled to the side, wide-eyed in shock and suddenly quite ill.

The beat of wings filled the air, and arms scooped Eden up. Dhriti's face creased with fury as she assessed the damage.

"My lady! Are you all right?" Dhriti's silver eyes flicked over Eden, assessing her.

Eden frowned and swallowed back the bile creeping up her throat. "Mynata," she panted. "Mynata, she came at me." Shakily, she swiped at her face, and her blood ran cold as she saw blood that wasn't her own on her fingers.

Dhriti spat a curse. "Eden, are you hurt anywhere other than your neck?"

As soon as her words left her, the plant spewed clothing into a steaming, bloody heap.

Eden stared at it, anger hardening the set of her jaw. "I don't know." Her entire body felt numb, bloodless.

"We need to get you to . . . "

To whom? Draven? Eden frowned at her. Draven would be on his way already. As far as she knew, he was in the castle, which meant there would be no time to clean herself up before he saw what she looked like. What *did* she look like? She glanced down at her breeches, only to find a tear in them, and a line of blood from where Mynata's nails had torn into her calf. The waistcoat's tail whipped around Eden like a battle-tried banner and just as tattered as one.

With shaking fingers, Eden lifted her hand to her head and swept a stream of sweat away. Anger washed through her in waves, but it wasn't her own.

"You don't have to. Draven has found me." She turned as he rounded the corner of the garden and in quick strides made it to her.

At once, his hands gingerly tilted her face up to his. His blue eyes darkened as worry blended with fury. "Are you all right?"

No. She wasn't all right. Mynata had assaulted her, attempted to kill her, and as her adrenaline abated, every muscle throbbed. "I will be." Eden's gaze slid to a figure just beyond Draven's shoulder, and to her surprise, it was Zryan.

Draven

The sensation of Eden's fear had swept through him like a vicious wave, making Draven feel sick and furious all at once. He hadn't even stopped to say anything to Zryan before storming from his study. Draven had taken the time only to ask one revenant where Eden had last been seen before hurrying off to the garden.

He hadn't been sure what he would find when he arrived. Eden was both worse and better off than he had been expecting. Blood, scratches, and bruises littered her body, but she was alive. And she was whole.

"Who did it?" His voice sounded harsh even to his own ears, and the anger coursing through his blood was enough to set the entire garden on fire if he did not restrain himself a little.

The notion that someone had dared to place their hands on Eden said that his kingdom was far more out of his control than he had originally thought. How could anyone have thought they would get away with harming her?

Eden appeared almost hesitant to tell him, and he realized he was looming over her with a deep scowl on his face. Taking a moment to gather himself, Draven released her chin so that he could step back a little and inspect the rest of her body.

She loosed a breath, then said shakily, "It was Mynata." Still, Eden's shoulders didn't drop from her ears. She remained tense, and Draven couldn't blame her.

Draven growled, his eyes darting around the garden, landing accusingly on Dhriti, who looked shamefaced and apologetic. "Where is she?"

Something like a grimace formed on Eden's face, an expression he'd never seen on her before. "Dead."

Draven looked down at Eden. "What?"

"She's dead. I killed her." It was spoken so simply, he wondered if he was hearing correctly.

Once again, Draven looked around the garden. He found no Mynata, only a steaming pile of bloody clothes.

"What did you do?"

"By the sun, moon, and sea . . . " Zryan had stepped around them and moved over to the pile of clothes. He toed it gingerly with the tip of his sandal. "Is this all that's left of that beautiful vampiress?" Zryan peered over at Eden in awe and amusement. "It looks as if she's been regurgitated."

"She was devoured by the venandi flower, sire," Dhriti supplied.

Draven gently brushed his fingers along the wound on Eden's forehead, seeing if the bleeding had stopped. "Tell me what happened," he demanded.

"Mynata attacked me after saying that I wasn't fit to be with you. She was the one who put your blood in my wine. She's been attempting to undermine me this whole time."

"She was trying to feed from her when I arrived, Your

Majesty," Dhriti added. "Lady Mynata was on top of Lady Eden on the ground."

"Wish I could have seen that," Zryan said offhandedly. After receiving a glare from Draven, he lifted his hands and walked a little farther away.

"I thought that you said you killed her? But if the plant ate her . . . ?" Draven looked her face over once more, wishing that he were able to break one bone in Mynata's body for every mark he saw there.

Eden lifted her hand, her brow furrowing as she looked at her fingers. "I used my magic to draw it toward us. I've been feeding it energy for weeks; it responds to me." She swallowed roughly. "Tulok said anything could be a weapon."

Draven's hand cupped her cheek, and she pressed her face into the touch, their eyes meeting. "Remind me to thank him," he said softly. Then a thought struck him, and he lifted his head to pin Dhriti with a stony glare. "Where *was* Tulok? How was this able to happen?"

"I was on my way to relieve him, sire. She came upon Eden before I arrived."

Draven growled. "What part of 'do not leave her unattended' did I not make clear enough?"

"Draven," Eden called. "Don't be angry with her. It's not her fault. Nor is it Tulok's. I told him it was okay to leave. I thought I would be safe here in the garden."

"Well, you thought wrong. Do you have any idea what is going on right now? I have beasts invading Midniva as they please, vampire nobles wishing to see me unseated, and now Zryan has gone and lost the Creaturae book."

"Hey," Zryan interjected with a grumble.

Draven continued as if his brother hadn't interrupted.

"Eden, it is no longer safe for you here. Your ties to me cannot keep you protected. In fact . . . they may make it far more dangerous for you to be here than it has been."

She was frowning, as if realizing already what he was going to say. Eden's hands lifted to grasp at his arms, but Draven stepped back, putting much needed distance between them.

"You're going to return to Lucem with Zryan."

"What?" She looked as if he had struck her.

"What?" Zryan echoed. Hearing his name, he stepped closer. "But her mother—"

"Damn you and her mother!" Draven growled. "I don't care about you feeling the need to punish her mother for spilling your secrets to Alessia."

"Draven," Zryan hissed.

"She knows. I already told her," Draven informed him as he watched his brother's eyes dart to Eden's face. "And your petty games no longer matter. I cannot keep Eden safe here."

"Well . . . I can't argue with that part." Zryan's eyes passed over the disaster that was Eden's form at the moment.

"Draven . . . no." Eden moved toward him once more, putting herself between him and Zryan. "I don't want to go back to Lucem. I want to stay here. With you. Mynata was the threat, and now she is gone. It's no longer an issue." Her hand reached out to grasp his arm.

"Things are only going to become worse, Eden," Draven insisted, feeling his anxiety to have her somewhere safe mounting.

"But I can help. I've found my place here with you, Draven."

"You are going to be more of a target tied to me. The unrest will only grow with Mynata's death. There is no choice. You must leave with Zryan when he goes." Draven kept his voice cold. He pulled his arm free of Eden's hand and stepped back once more, turning from her.

"Draven," she said firmly. He recognized that tone from the night he'd been drunk, and she'd browbeaten him into submission. "I am going to stay here. This is where I want to be. I've seen every side of you, and of Andhera. I know what is waiting for me here and I wish to stay. I belong with the man that I love. With you."

It took all of his control to keep his face devoid of emotion as he heard those words coming from her lips, a plea for him to admit that he wanted her here at his side as well.

"No, you don't," he replied coldly.

"What?" It was barely a whisper.

"You do not belong here. You never did. Andhera is not a playground for you to frolic and play around in. It is a serious, dangerous land. And it will be the death of you." Draven kept his face turned away from her, his eyes focused on a plant in the distance.

"Draven—" Zryan began, but Draven lifted his hand to cut him off. He didn't need to hear whatever it was his brother thought to add to this.

"Why would you—" Her voice started out soft, pained, but Eden cut herself off. "Do I even get a say in the matter?" she asked, tone hardening.

"No," he said simply.

"No? That is all? Simply, no."

"Yes," he said through gritted teeth. "Simply, no." It didn't matter what either of them wanted.

314

Andhera was not a safe place for her to be. It never had been, and Draven had allowed himself to foolishly think for a moment that perhaps he could forget all that. That Eden could be safe here with him if he surrounded her with protection and allowed her to see the true darkness of Andhera. But he had been fooling himself.

This land would never allow him to keep someone such as Eden.

"You know . . . I had allowed myself to believe you were better than Ludari, better than all those who told such horrid tales of you. But you are no better. You lie and manipulate, just like everyone else. Expecting everyone to bend to your will but never compromising." The words were cold and bitter, and he hated hearing them come from her.

The spot of sunshine he had found here in Andhera was now slipping out of reach. Hidden behind dark furious storm clouds of his own creation.

Draven turned his head to look at her face. Her green eyes swam with angry tears, and her hands were clasped in fists at her sides.

"Are you surprised?" he asked. "I am my father's son after all." He hissed the words at her, then turned to Dhriti. "Take her to her chamber to be cleaned and her wounds tended to. Then have Loriah pack her things. She and Zryan will be leaving before the fall of the day moon."

"Draven," Zryan began. "I can't leave yet. We haven't even had a chance to discuss the book!"

Draven shot him a glare as he turned from Eden and the harpy, already starting back across the garden. His brother fell into step beside him.

"You were a little hard on Eden, were you not?"

315

Draven did not respond as he stepped into the castle once more. There was no room for softness when a man was destroying his own happiness in one fell swoop.

"Draven . . . rethink your decision. Anyone can see you care for her."

It didn't matter what he wanted for himself. It never had. There was always someone to protect. Someone to safeguard from the dangers of this world that never seemed to end. He had been foolish in thinking there could be any light in his days. Draven may have been freed from the dungeon, but he was still trapped in that cell, and he always would be.

He spun on Zryan, forcing his brother to take a step back in surprise. "And that is the reason she must leave. My feelings for her will only drive my enemies to destroy her. It nearly happened in my very own garden! If I cannot keep her safe in my own walls, how can I keep her safe at all?" He snarled viciously. "You will take her back to Lucem, and I will keep an eye out for that *damn* book."

Storming away from his brother, Draven found Seurat and ordered him to summon Mynata's family. They would have to sort out this latest disaster before anyone could be sent home.

They were all assembled in the throne room. Draven stood before his throne, Eden at his side but far enough away from him that the separation was noticeable. While her clothes were no longer torn, and the blood had been washed away, her injuries were still obvious and even more numerous now that he could clearly see them all.

Mynata's mother and father had been brought before them, led into the room by a reserved looking Seurat, who remained by the door, ever attentive, ever watchful. Captain Channon and his pack lined the sides of the hall. Though they sat back casually on their haunches, Draven knew from experience each was primed for attack should this go badly.

Lord and Lady Perfidiae gazed up at him, their expressions calm but bewildered.

"I have called you before me today to inform you that your daughter, Lady Mynata Perfidiae, was found guilty of treason. She admitted to the theft of my blood, which she then gave to Eden against her will. To make matters worse, today she attempted to feed from and kill Lady Eden."

Lord and Lady Perfidiae stilled, their eyes filling with understanding and dawning fear.

"Where is our daughter now?" Lord Perfidiae asked.

"She is dead." Draven watched Lord Perfidiae's face blanch, and his wife's eyes shut tight. "She was eaten by the venandi flower."

Lady Perfidiae gasped. "*Why?* Why have you taken my daughter from me in such a manner?"

Before Draven could respond, Eden was speaking. "Lady Perfidiae, I am sorry that it happened in the manner it did, but in that moment, she earned such a death. She left me no choice." Eden spoke gently but firmly.

Draven watched her from the corner of his eyes and could admit only to himself that he was proud of her. Had this been another time, and another land, she would have made a wonderful queen.

317

Eden

Loriah frowned as she packed the last of Eden's belongings. As requested, this included only what she'd received *from* Lucem. Everything else was to remain behind, and Draven could do as he wished with it. The gowns she'd commissioned, the trinkets she'd picked up in the shops, everything that belonged to Andhera would remain in it.

Even Alder.

Eden sank to the floor. She welcomed the inquisitive creature into her arms and nuzzled into his soft pelt. "You can't come back with me. Loriah can take you to the garden, and perhaps you'll find you prefer her to me." Eden dragged her hand across his head and swallowed the lump in her throat. As much as she wanted to cry, she wouldn't give in.

She refused.

Andhera took freely and gave nothing in return. Eden wouldn't give Andhera or its king anything more. For all of his tenderness and the quiet moments they'd shared, Draven had turned his back on her when she pleaded with him. He may as well have taken a knife and embedded it in her heart.

Worse than that, she felt like such a fool for allowing herself to fall.

"You'll make certain he has adequate attention, Loriah?"

"Of course, my lady. He will want for nothing."

Eden released Alder, then stood and walked to her handmaiden. "Thank you for listening to me and being there when I had no one else." She wrapped her arms around the revenant in a gentle embrace.

Loriah squeezed her in return. "Be well, my lady."

"And you." Eden pulled away as the door opened, and in came two male revenants to retrieve her two bags. She took the moment to walk to her mirror and inspect her reflection. The cut on her forehead had healed, but a scabbed line remained. Bruises littered her neck from where nails and fingers had pressed in, but they'd healed for the most part, courtesy of her ability.

Eden assessed her features. Her green eyes were still bright, and her face still smooth, but something about her had changed. Not in the way Andhera could distort an individual but something unseen.

She wasn't the fae who had sat in the Midnivian castle's sitting room, tearful and terrified. In a short amount of time, Eden had grown because she was allowed to. Perhaps Andhera had gifted her something after all, and if it weren't for Draven, she'd never have blossomed as she did.

Without looking back, she left the room and followed the revenants outside. Zryan was already inside the chariot. His team of gray horses stomped in agitation from waiting.

Behind the chariot, a separate carriage had been

prepared with a team of kelpies, and Eden stared at it in confusion. Was she not meant to ride with Zryan?

"Place her belongings in the carriage." Zryan motioned with his hand, then turned to Eden as she approached. "Unfortunately, I didn't know I would have company. Someone will be driving the carriage with your things to Lucem, but you'll be with me through the Veil."

Eden wasn't sure whether or not to be comforted by that notion. The last time she'd been in the Veil, she had fainted. What would it be like this time? Although, as she locked eyes with Zryan, Eden refused to succumb to whatever terror lay inside the in-between.

She walked up to the chariot, refusing the offered hand, and stepped inside. Eden realized belatedly she was one of his subjects. No matter the situation, he was still her sovereign. "Thank you, Your Majesty, but I can manage."

Zryan's eyebrows lifted as he entered the chariot beside her and held the reins. "Of that I have no doubt, Eden." His lips turned up into a smile that reminded Eden of a cat waiting to eat a canary.

Aurelie had told Eden of all the rumors circulating about Zryan, and her mother had taken it upon herself to let Alessia know of his indiscretions. She frowned and pressed herself against the railing of the chariot. Much of Lucem was in disarray because of Zryan and Alessia's quarreling.

With the jostling of the reins, the horses departed the courtyard, and Eden did her best to shut out the kingdom she'd allowed herself to fall in love with. If she thought about it, no doubt tears would fall, and she had promised herself not to cry.

By the time they reached the woods where the

manticore had rushed them last time, it was almost quiet, except for the beat of their harpy guard's wings overhead, and the shrill scream of something dying in the distance.

Eden turned to look in the direction of the sound but didn't flinch.

"You can move closer to me if you want. I won't bite." Zryan paused, then chuckled. "That was poor timing on my part." When this garnered no response from Eden, he sighed. His shoulders lowered, and although his eyes remained trained on the path, his demeanor softened visibly.

"I know what it's like . . . to fall so hard, to feel so deeply, then to have it ripped away." Zryan glanced down at Eden and caught her eyes for a moment. "To be separated from who you love is the worst. And for what it is worth, I am truly sorry." Silence filled the minimal space between them before he added, "If I could have changed Draven's mind, I would have."

She had seen Zryan's false sincerity in Midniva, but this was different. And he, for whatever reason, was allowing her to see another side of him. Did he speak of another, or was the one he loved Alessia? Eden didn't want to think on it. Her life was crumbling again, all thanks to the royal family.

Eden lowered her head. She gripped the rail in front of her and squeezed. "I hope you can find your way back to each other." It was the truth. When someone felt that deeply for another, why should they be apart?

Zryan sighed again. "Time will tell. But as for you, try not to think badly of my brother. He has his reasons, and nothing he does is without a purpose."

"I'm well aware of court politics. Everyone is a pawn to play with."

Zryan's jaw shifted, and he shook his head, his dark hair tumbling into his green eyes. "No, you're not. You've known Draven for a little over a month, and maybe you've touched the surface, but you don't know." He didn't say it unkindly, but Eden still frowned. "You know so little." The words were soft, almost a whisper.

Zryan turned the chariot down a path, and it burst through the Veil. They went from the dark of the day moon of Andhera to a hazy sky with an abundance of shadows.

Eden kept her eyes trained ahead. The whipping wind howled and pulled her hair free of its pins.

"I'd feel more comfortable if you stood next to me."

At first his words annoyed her, as she assumed he only wanted to feel her body against his. However, Zryan didn't glance down at her, and his voice didn't hold a playful edge, either.

"What? I am close enough, Your Majesty."

"No." Zryan reached out, and when Eden leaned farther away, he cursed. "Listen. Do you hear *anything?* Outside of the wind . . . do you hear anything?"

Eden focused on the noise around them, but unlike the wails she had heard before, it was only the wind. No screeching or growling pierced the air.

This time, Eden willingly stepped closer to Zryan and clung to the rail. "What would make them grow quiet?"

"Nothing good."

After that, they were silent for the duration of their journey through the Veil. Neither one seemed to want to test the beasties that lurked in the haze. It wasn't until they emerged from the Veil and into Lucem that Eden made any noise at all.

The sun blinded her. She covered her face with her hand and winced, but oh, the warmth of the sun's rays against her skin felt wonderful. In no time, her faded freckles would surface like a sky full of stars.

"Oh. That'll take some getting used to again." Zryan cocked his head and squinted as his eyes adjusted too.

But the light felt like a pick to her head. Even as it reflected off light patches of dirt, it stung her eyes. However, she could see more than just shadows and vague outlines.

When the chariot met the main road, Eden peered up, still shielding her eyes. She recognized it as the way into Edessa, the town she lived in. The fragrant blooms filled the air, carried on the warm breeze, and tickled her nose.

"Aren't you bringing me home?" Eden twisted as she watched the side road pass by, the very road that led to her manor. She frowned as she turned to look up at Zryan.

"No. You're coming with me to the palace. Your mother will receive word once we arrive."

The obvious question hung on the tip of her tongue, but she stopped herself from asking. Of course Zryan would make her mother come to the palace. She was still being punished for telling Alessia the truth about where he'd been. But why, then, did he make the comment earlier? It only caused Eden to wonder further if it was Alessia he'd spoken of.

When the road gave way to Celeia, the capital city, it was obvious. The bleached stone buildings grew more numerous, and the mansions were larger than those in the neighboring town. The open fields lessened, and even the blooming trees grew sparse, only replaced by fountains or statues.

Even at the entrance of the city, one could see the palace perched on top of a hill. Eden had been there once, when her father had been alive, and she'd clung to his leg the entire time. But she still remembered the brightly lit palace and its opulent nature.

Little by little, Eden's eyes adjusted, though they still burned from the excess light. Mercifully, by the time they arrived at the palace, the sun had shifted to cast shadows in the courtyard.

Zryan stepped down from the chariot, and this time, Eden accepted the offered hand. As she glanced behind them, the carriage from Andhera pulled up beside them. The team of kelpies chomped on their bits and pawed at the stone beneath them. They were so out of place amidst the pink and white blossoms of Lucem and stuck out like a sore thumb.

Zryan turned to the approaching driver. "Bring the bags inside and then you're free to go." He glanced down at Eden and nodded toward the palace.

Eden spared the carriage a lingering glance, frowning, before she followed Zryan into the palace. Fortunately, the lighting was dimmer inside, giving her eyes a reprieve from the bright sun.

Zryan turned toward Eden, his lips parting as he readied to say something, but the sound of sharp footfalls caught the attention of both of them.

Eden wanted to shrink backward as Alessia stormed toward them. She had a commanding presence, one that demanded respect. Eden lowered her eyes a fraction, but the gauzy gown of gold did little to hide Alessia's slender curves beneath. Had it not been for her waves of ebony hair, Eden would have seen the mounds of her breasts. She was beautiful and harsh at once.

"So, it is true. You were in Andhera, Zryan." Alessia clucked her tongue and clicked her nails together at her sides. "But to steal your brother's bride?" A mirthless laugh escaped her. "Was it not bad enough you betrothed them in front of Midniva's court? You now *abduct* her?"

"What? No!" Zryan spat out.

Dark luminous eyes shot from her husband to Eden, then raked over her figure. In a blink, Alessia was in front of Eden. "What have you done, Zryan?" Her hand hovered above the bruising at Eden's neck. Rage colored the queen's golden cheeks a deep red.

"No! That isn't from me!" Zryan sputtered. "And honestly, Less, as if I'd steal *Draven's* bride? Much less harm her. You know me, Less, I would never."

Eden's gaze darted from Zryan to Alessia. The queen looked ready to pounce on her husband, and while it may have been his fault Eden was in this predicament to begin with, he had shown her genuine kindness in the chariot. "He is right, Your Majesty. It isn't from him; it was from a fight with a vampire."

"A vampire?" Alessia squinted and looked to her husband, no doubt asking for confirmation.

"Yes . . . She's dead." And a dark piece of Eden wished she could have done it again. If that wretched vampiress hadn't attacked her and hadn't made a point to make her stay in Andhera more difficult, perhaps she'd still be there.

"Then why are you here?"

"Because Draven no longer wishes for me to remain in Andhera." Eden clenched her jaw and lowered her eyes.

"Alessia." Zryan stepped forward, whether to catch his wife or to shield Eden, she wasn't certain.

"What?" Disbelief crept into the queen's eyes, but then she turned a glare on her husband. "For how long?"

Eden wondered if she was purposely rubbing salt on her wounds, was surprised, or just didn't believe them. "Indefinitely."

Alessia stepped around Zryan and gently grabbed Eden by her bicep. "Come with me. Zryan, go send for her mother." She cut him a look, leaving no room for an argument.

At once, Eden wished she was at Zryan's side instead. Alessia, though perfectly amiable at the moment, had a presence about her that set Eden on edge. Like at any moment she would turn on her and reduce her to shredded fabric and flesh on the marble floor.

"I want you to be honest with me, Eden, and tell me all of what happened. My husband has a way of leaving things out or prettying them up, but I can tell you'll do none of those things." Alessia's expression softened, and it reminded Eden of a mother comforting a sullen child. "It's still too fresh, isn't it?" Alessia stroked a hand down the side of Eden's neck, where a bruise no doubt was. Quickly, her gaze hardened, and she retracted her hand. Without a word, she walked away.

If she'd answered at that moment, she would have choked on the lump in her throat. Instead, Eden nodded and followed Alessia to a quiet, dimly lit room and told her the majority of what transpired once she found herself able to.

By the time she finished, she had, in fact, cried. To

Eden's surprise, Alessia fetched a silk kerchief and stroked her back in a motherly fashion.

"Dear girl, shed your tears now, but not again. Draven is not unlike his brothers, which is complicated to say the least." Alessia plucked the pins from Eden's hair, then stroked her fingers through it. "If Draven sent you away, I believe it was purely to keep you safe."

"But he . . . "

"I don't need to know what he said or how he looked. I've been around since before Draven ruled Andhera, while he still sat on one of the gilded thrones of Lucem." Her head tipped back, and she sighed. "Trust that I just know him, and if you know your history at all, you should know the truth."

Eden knew Alessia had been there. Anyone who knew anything of the stories, the historical recountings, and the legends knew. However, she'd foolishly grown detached from those, and knew only the Draven of the present day. The nightmare king. The fae turned *other*. She hadn't stopped to consider the one he was before. Lounging in the sun, the rays kissing his freckled shoulders. Eden shrunk in on herself and dabbed at her eyes with the handkerchief. She glanced at Alessia. "Which truth?"

"That Draven will sacrifice his very life if it means protecting those he cares about." Alessia turned to Eden again, her dark eyes intensifying. "Did he tell you of the book?"

Eden nodded. "It was one of the reasons why he cast me out of Andhera."

"That book . . . The Creaturae is a powerful weapon. It has the ability to create and destroy. To cast peace or destruction. The wretched old king used it to wreak havoc on the realms, and in the wrong hands . . . Could you imagine?" Alessia shuddered. Despite being a vision of strength, she looked frightened by the idea.

Zryan strode into the room, silencing the conversation. He looked from his wife to Eden, as if assessing whether or not any damage had been done. "Your mother is on her way . . . "

While Eden was happy to hear it, her heart didn't soar with joy, because it meant she was returning to a semblance of her old life, and it wasn't a life she wanted anymore. Nor did she know if she even fit in it.

Cast aside by Andhera's king, tainted by the dark realm, none would want her in their circles now.

"Thank you, Your Majesty." Eden bowed her head.

"Enough of that," Alessia cut in. "Between us, you've earned the right to call us by name."

Eden smiled. It was a small one, but for a moment, she felt comforted. The Zryan in Midniva was vastly different from the one staring out a window in this room. He was a quiet, solid presence. And his wife, although terrifying by reputation and certainly when she approached Eden, was not as she expected.

Though Eden wished she could doze off, she didn't. Instead, she studied a blank wall and attempted to silence her tumultuous thoughts and emotions. But it wasn't meant to be because not long after, a servant announced the arrival of her mother.

Eden sprang from her spot next to Alessia but came up short as Zryan held out a hand to stop her.

"Naya Damaris, thank you for coming." Zryan motioned to Eden.

"Eden!" Naya gasped, lurching forward.

Zryan barred her path. "I've called you here for an obvious reason. As a father, I can understand how difficult losing your only child must be . . . which is why I've decided to bring Eden back to Lucem. No strings, no tricks." He gestured for Eden to move forward. "Only a show of good faith between us both. No more nonsense on your part, and your daughter safely back in Lucem."

It was a lie. Zryan's only part in her return had been escorting her to the palace. But this was another game. One that she would play along with, if only to avoid Alessia's ire. Still, she wondered how the royal family refrained from tripping over each binding lie. It was dizzying.

Confusion warped her mother's face, as if she didn't quite believe the sight before her eyes.

Eden reached out and grabbed her mother's hand, which turned into a vice grip. "It's really me, Mama. It isn't a trick."

Alessia had moved to stand beside Zryan. Her gaze remained solely on Naya, and Eden had no doubt that her mother assumed it was a game put on by the two of them.

"Mama, it's truly me." She leaned closer, and her mother's free hand slid along Eden's cheek and into her hair.

"Why?" Naya hissed. Her green eyes flicked between the two rulers.

"It's as I said. I wouldn't want my child ripped away in such a manner." Zryan caught Eden's gaze, and he lifted a brow in the most subtle of gestures. If she hadn't spent a month and a half with his brother, she would have missed it.

"Please, let's go home and be done with this." She

could feel the prick of tears at the back of her eyes but refused to give in. It didn't matter if she knew Zryan's words were lies and that Draven had cast her off.

Naya curtsied stiffly. "Thank you for your kindness, Your Majesties. I will never forget it." She looped her arm with Eden's and led her out of the room. It wasn't until they were down the corridor that she halted and turned to face Eden. Quickly, her eyes assessed the one before her, and she must have realized it truly was her daughter. But a frown tugged at her lips.

"Who did this to you?" The question came in such a low tone that Eden's skin prickled. "No. Not here." Naya pulled Eden through the halls of the palace, and it wasn't until they were nestled inside their family carriage that she spoke again. "It was him, wasn't it?"

If she hadn't been so caught off guard, perhaps Eden would have laughed. Her mother didn't know Draven at all if she suspected him of harming her. "What? No. He would never."

Naya scoffed. "Wouldn't he? Did he place you in a trance while he used you for his purposes?" The words were cold, but the fury beneath wasn't directed at Eden. Regardless, the careless way she hurled her words stung.

The carriage lurched forward, and Eden stared out her window, shaking her head. "No. He wouldn't. No matter what you may think of him, he wouldn't have touched me against my wishes." Color rushed into her cheeks unbidden as she recalled the way he touched her.

"But he did touch you?" Naya asked lowly.

She couldn't lie, not with her mother watching her so closely. "Because I wanted him to."

"Oh!" Naya sat forward then rocked against the back of

her seat. If they were home, she would be pacing frantically. "You foolish girl. It isn't your fault—he is a monster after all."

Yes. No. No, he isn't. Eden's heart still ached from the abrupt departure, but hearing how her mother spoke of Draven grated on every nerve. "He is not a monster."

"And he has brainwashed you. My girl, it will all be well soon enough. We can work around the damage he's done."

"What damage?" Eden's voice bordered on hysteria. "If I had a choice, I wouldn't be here, Mama. I *want* to be in Andhera. I want to be with Draven, Mama. I love him." As soon as the words left her mouth, her mother gasped. Betrayal, confusion, anger—it all burned within her mother's eyes. A look Eden knew well, and she could feel herself inwardly stepping back, shrinking.

Naya leaned forward, hands coiled in her lap, but the motion still made Eden flinch. "And that is why I'll be keeping a close eye on you. You're to have a chaperone at every turn, and you are not allowed to leave without me knowing. I will fix this, like I promised in my letters."

Eden's bottom lip quivered, and she bit it with such force it began to bleed. "Just listen to me. I don't need protection." She wouldn't cry. Not for the loss of her love nor for the loss of her freedom. She would endure it until it was time to break free again.

Naya ignored her daughter's distress and instead dove into how life had been without Eden, what it would be like now, and how it would be different.

Different, she thought, *like a true prison.*

32

Draven

Draven had made the right decision. He fully believed that Andhera was currently too dangerous, too unsettled, for Eden to be safe in Aasha's walls. He had only ended their time sooner than expected. Eventually, for her own good, she would have had to leave. But it had been three days of hell. The vitality Eden had brought to his halls had faded, leaving only the emptiness that had always resided there. Gone was her warmth, her willingness to draw him from his own personal darkness.

His entire castle seemed to be at odds with itself, and he was at the core of it. The were-wolves growled and grumbled their way through the day, Loriah consistently shot him looks of reproof, and the goblins had taken to screeching at him whenever he passed them in the hall; Draven found himself actually missing their high-pitched nonsensical chatter.

Perhaps it was a benefit to his own sanity to not have time to dwell on it, to find himself embroiled in the misfortune of the realms instead.

"Your Majesty, welcome," one of the harpies stated as he drew Rayvnin up before the retinue standing guard over the gate into the Veil.

Draven nodded to the soldier. "Has there been much activity today?"

"A few manticore, Your Majesty. But nothing we haven't been able to handle," she assured him.

"Good," was his simple response.

It had been centuries since there had been a need to have guards posted at the gate to the in-between. But his carefully constructed laws could no longer be trusted to hold his subjects in check.

Draven lashed Rayvnin's reins and made his way through the gate and into the shadowed realm beyond.

After Zryan had returned to Lucem with Eden, he had made a point to contact both Draven and Travion to inform them of another matter. There was silence in the Veil.

Draven kept his eyes focused on the path before him as he drove through the Veil, but his ears remained open. Where desperate wails of misery would typically be, there was nothing but an eerie silence that truly bothered him more than the screams ever had.

As he approached the middle of the Veil, Draven could see Travion already there, waiting. Pulling up beside his brother, Draven climbed down out of his chariot.

"It's odd," Travion muttered by way of greeting. "But the silence is more chilling than the howls."

Draven snorted, finding his own thoughts thrown back at him—a common occurrence after so much time spent in the dungeons together.

"I think there were souls lost in this space long before we began venturing into the Veil," Draven responded.

Now firmly planted on his feet and not traveling, Draven turned so that he could cast his eyes out over the emptiness that was the Veil, watching the swirling tufts of fog as they drifted along the void.

"It is certainly not a good sign," his brother replied.

Both turned to look to the right as the sound of an approaching horse sounded. Zryan appeared as if out of nowhere, seated atop a gray pegasus and looking for all the world as if he had just run a race. His hair was a wild tangle, cheeks dusted with red, and his clothing thoroughly rumpled. Draven couldn't remember the last time he had seen his youngest brother looking so out of sorts.

Pulling to a halt, Zryan slid down off his stallion and moved toward them without his typical cheer.

"The clouds have only increased," he stated roughly to Travion before his eyes moved to acknowledge Draven.

"Dammit," Travion growled, rubbing the back of his neck.

"The clouds?" Draven asked, looking between his brothers.

"We haven't seen the sun in two days. The clouds rolled into Lucem the day after I returned, and they've just continued to grow darker and stormier looking. I've never seen weather like it."

"I even went to try and help," Travion added. "But it doesn't feel like any weather or storm I've ever felt before. It also doesn't seem to want to respond to me at all. It's as if someone has drawn it to Lucem rather than it having formed naturally."

Draven's face darkened, his brows knitting in a scowl. He had sent Eden to Lucem with Zryan to keep her away from the dangers overrunning Andhera, and now he was

334

learning that something was amiss in the light realm as well.

"Could this have something to do with the book?" Draven asked.

"Damned if I know, but likely," Travion grumbled.

They both turned their eyes on Zryan, who gave them a helpless look. "I'm looking for it!" he shot back, exasperated.

Draven simply shook his head. "Book aside . . . let's get this over with."

From his chariot, Draven produced a spool of rope. Keeping one end in his hand, he tossed the remainder of it into Tavion's. Wrapping his loose end around his waist, he tied it off.

"Should you feel a tug on the rope, pull me in. No matter what I may be shouting to you out there."

Travion nodded in understanding.

Beside him, Zryan crossed his arms over his chest. "Are you certain you don't want one of us to go in instead?"

"Can you travel by shadow?" Draven asked dryly. He received only an eye roll from his youngest brother.

Without another word, Draven called the nearest shadow to him and stepped into it, leaving the path to move into the emptiness of the Veil.

As he expected, the void rose up to surround him, swallowing him into the vast nothingness around him. If it weren't for the rope fastened around his waist, Draven would have quickly lost any sort of awareness of what direction his brothers lay in. Not allowing that to disconcert him, he continued to move from one dark shadow to another, keeping out of the brighter spots in the

Veil. While he did not think it was sunshine, he could never be certain.

The further into the void he traveled, the more emptiness and silence Draven found. While he had only come into the emptiness of the Veil once before, he could tell this was entirely different.

The souls hadn't been exactly tangible then, but he had sensed their presence all around him, even when their wails weren't sounding loudly in his ears. But there were no souls wandering lost within the Veil this time. All that he found was more emptiness and more deafening silence.

Something had freed the ones that had been lost in the Veil. Freed them . . . or taken them.

When he had searched as far as his tether would allow, Draven grasped ahold of it and made his way back, following the taut line.

Travion and Zryan did not become visible to him until he had physically stepped back onto the pathway and found himself once more in the center of the Veil. Travion looked relieved to see him.

"Anything?" he asked Draven.

"Not a soul."

Zryan pinched the bridge of his nose. "Well . . . at least this place isn't so bloody eerie any longer." He offered his brothers a tentative look, only to find them both frowning.

"I want to check out the gates into both your realms," Draven stated. "Perhaps there is some evidence of where the spirits have gone."

The three kings moved to grab their mounts, pulling them along behind them as they walked the distance toward the first gate, which led into Midniva. With a quick examination, they could spot no outward difference in its appearance.

"Do you think we'll actually find anything?" Zryan asked.

"I don't know. But something has pulled the spirits from this space and is also drawing the creatures of Andhera to my gate."

"What do you mean?" Zryan cast him a glance as they left Midniva's gate and took the path toward Lucem's.

"I've had to post guards at the gate leading into the Veil. Manticores, lamia, chimera, trolls . . . even some of the were-creatures have attacked the gate, looking to cross through into the Veil. Something is driving the inhabitants of Andhera mad with hunger. And whatever it is, it's pulling them in this direction."

Draven's words left both Zryan and Travion frowning deeply. Together, the three of them had taken down their tyrannical father, ending his reign of terror over the three realms and bringing a sort of order and peace between them. Their own reign over the realms had gone mostly uncontested for more centuries than any of them could remember. What was happening now perplexed all of them, and it wasn't a good sign.

As they approached the gate leading into Lucem, it didn't take long for them to spot the black coils of shadow wrapping around the giant pillars like tentacles. The shadows wound the entire way up the carved stone structure and seemed to disappear through the barrier into the light realm.

On the other side of Travion, Zryan cursed loudly. "What in the name of the sun does this mean?"

Draven didn't know. It was not something he had ever seen before, but it could mean nothing good.

Had he sent Eden away from the dangerous land he ruled in order to protect her only to land her in a realm becoming equally as dangerous, and which he was physically unable to enter?

"Zryan," Draven found himself growling. "You must promise me you will retrieve Eden and keep her under your protection." The barrier between Lucem and the Veil was too solid for their blood connection to tell him anything of her current state.

"What—"

"Swear it," he demanded. Dread crept through him at the thought of his own helplessness in ensuring Eden's safety. If he couldn't be there to keep her safe, then his brother and his family would have to see to it for him.

"Draven, I don't think that is nec—"

Draven turned his head to capture his brother's eyes in a fierce stare. "I said, swear it." His voice was low, threatening, leaving no room for refusal.

Zryan finally nodded. "I swear it, brother."

Eden

Her mother hadn't lied. Things were different, much different, now that she was home. Eden hadn't been allowed outside without a household chaperone, and when Aurelie came to visit, they weren't even alone in the gardens. It was stifling and ridiculous. Draven couldn't step into Lucem, and Eden wasn't about to run back to Andhera after she'd been cast off.

As Alessia had suggested, she spared no more tears, and focused on her current situation and how she'd convince her mother to loosen her control.

In the three days since she'd returned to Lucem, new drapes hung from her floor-to-ceiling windows, shielding her from the gray light. Despite the lack of sun, it was still brighter than Andhera, and she'd grown accustomed to the dark realm's moons. As if she weren't having a difficult enough time settling back in, the servants scarcely made eye contact with Eden, let alone spoke to her. She wasn't certain if they feared her or what potentially lurked beneath the surface. Or maybe it had very little to do with her at all, and everything to do with the one she'd been betrothed to.

It didn't matter.

The sky was dimming as the days passed on. A haziness that wasn't normally there hung around, which made the sky more bearable.

Eden plucked up her hairbrush, but the sound of scurrying in her room forced her to turn on her heel. "What was that?" she murmured, stilling to listen.

Another scratching noise, then a gurgling. Not just any gurgle . . .

Eden dropped to the floor and stretched beneath her bed, one hand scooping back and forth until she felt the clammy skin of the creature. She gasped and then pulled backward until she tumbled onto her bottom.

"Who came here?" she whispered, and her eyes grew wide as she recognized the flesh of a goblin.

After a moment, the little being slid out from under the bed. His ears drooped instead of perking up to the side as they normally did. Drizz.

"By the sun . . . What are you doing here?" Eden choked out. She plucked him up only to sit him on the edge of her bed. "It isn't safe here." She paused. It wasn't as if Andhera was safe either, but Lucem wasn't a place for little goblins. "This isn't Andhera. Besides, Draven will be upset with you." *So that's where my snacks had disappeared to,* she thought. All of those extra slices of fruit bread, honey cakes, and tarts had fed Drizz over the past few days. At least he wasn't starving.

Drizz's lips thinned, and he trilled a soft purr before pointing to Eden. She didn't know how to interpret their odd language, but she gathered he was trying to tell her something.

"I don't understand." She frowned.

His cool fingers wrapped around her hand, and he tugged on it. He chirped softly, then pointed to the window.

Eden laughed even as she felt the prick of tears. "No. I cannot leave. I have no place in Andhera, Drizz." Neither did she have a place in Lucem, it seemed. She sighed, closing her eyes as she stood. "Perhaps Zryan can return you . . . " She'd scarcely got the words out when Drizz squawked in protest. Eden lifted a finger to her lips and hissed. "Don't do that. Not here. I need you to promise me you'll hide when you hear someone coming. I don't want anyone to hurt you." And she had no doubt they would. Drizz's razor-sharp teeth didn't inspire warm and cozy thoughts, nor did his clawed hands. Although sometimes a thief, he was never malicious.

Outside her room, she could hear her mother calling her. Panicked, Eden lifted Drizz and helped him scurry under her bed. "Not a sound!" she whisper-yelled to him and quickly grabbed up her brush just as the door opened.

"Eden. Do you have wool in your ears?" Naya stood in the doorway, her brow furrowed and lips pinched.

"No, Mama. I was trying to grab my brush. It fell and slid under the bed."

Naya looked annoyed, but it faded quickly. "I will be gone all day. You're not to leave or have visitors while I'm out."

Eden frowned and twisted the brush in her grasp. "But Aurelie wanted to visit today . . . "

"She can visit another day. Surely you still need time to

adjust." Her eyes flicked to the heavy drapes on the windows.

"I am fine, Mama." Eden's tone hardened.

"I wish you were." Naya sighed, then left the room.

How Eden had lived her life this way for so long was beyond her. But after the experience of freedom in Andhera and the respect that came with it, to then come back to this was maddening. She couldn't remain cooped up in her home with little to no interaction except for staff.

Not to mention her mother's mood had grown increasingly odd. She spent hours holed up in her study, and when she wasn't there, she was running errands. There was very little time spent with her daughter, and when she did manage a meal with Eden, it was stilted and short. Had she truly even missed her?

When Eden finished preparing for the day, she opted for a soft pink sheer dress. Despite the sun's strength dwindling—which worried her—it was still warm, and the air thick with moisture.

Silence filled the manor. No chirping of goblins, no shouting from outside as harpies and were-wolves sparred. The sound of Eden's sandals clapping on the floor echoed off the walls, disturbing the quiet.

With a quick glance around, Eden turned the knob to the study, but it was locked. Her shoulders slumped forward in defeat, but she wasn't about ready to quit yet. She hurried back to her room and fetched a few hair pins, then back in front of the study door, she fiddled with the lock. It took longer than she would have liked, but thankfully, no one caught her.

When the lock clicked, signaling it had shifted, Eden sighed in relief. She opened the door and expected to see something drastically off, but nothing was. It was a brightly lit room, with several vases of flowers and potted plants. The same study she'd crawled around in when her father was writing letters or reading. But why then would her mother lock it? It didn't make sense.

She searched the bookshelves, the cabinets, and even the closet in the room. Nothing was amiss. Eden grumbled as she plopped into the chair at the tidy desk. Her knee bumped into the bottom of it. "Of course," she whispered. Hurriedly, she reached for a small, gilded statue and turned it upside down. Eden's father had always kept the key hidden beneath it, and it wasn't something she made a fuss over. Had her mother hidden it in another place?

As she glanced at the bottom, the bronze key stared up at her. Eden pulled it free and shoved it into the keyhole. The drawer sprung out, and in it, a leather book sat. Eden's hand hovered over it, and she felt a thrum of power surge from it.

"Mama, what have you done?" Eden whispered as her eyes caught the name etched on the worn cover. Horror washed over her. This couldn't be the book Draven and Alessia were talking about. That would mean . . . it was her mother that had stolen it? The notion didn't align with her emotions, but when she pushed those aside . . . The letters, her odd moods, her hatred for the kings.

Zryan needed to know immediately.

Eden jumped to her feet, then ran to the shelf in the study which held some herbs. She gathered them, then a bowl and water. As she murmured, she added each herb, some water, then pricked her finger on a letter opener for a drop of blood. The water rippled before her, glowing as she spoke Zryan's name. When a face appeared, it wasn't Zryan but Alessia.

"Eden?"

"Alessia! Where is Zryan?"

"He left with Ruan to inspect the portal to the Veil." Alessia's eyes narrowed. "Why? Are you all right?"

Panic crept up Eden's neck. She splayed her hands on the table as she peered into the water. "It was my mother, Alessia. My mother stole the book. I found it in the study." She sucked in a breath, trying to soothe the climbing hysteria. "You must tell Draven and Travion."

She peered out the window to the sky, which seemed darker than it had prior to her entering the room. How long had she been in here? "Hurry."

"Promise me that you'll—"

Whatever Alessia was about to say was silenced as the desk flew against the wall, splintering on contact. Eden managed to snatch the book away just in time, but her mother approached in quick, angry strides.

"You foolish girl," Naya said with a sad, strange smile. Her light green eyes darkened as she held out a hand and thrust a blast of power at Eden, which sent her back into a wall. She was pinned, unable to move.

"Mama, please." Eden's quaking fingers clutched the book with every ounce of strength she had. "You don't have to do this. Whatever you think you're doing . . . "

Naya strode forward and, with ease, plucked the book away from her. "What I'm doing is fixing everything. The kings are no better than their father before them, and they've ruled for far too long." She swept her hand through Eden's hair and smiled. "I told you I had a plan. You will be spared from all of this, and safe."

Eden fought against the hold of the spell but only grew frustrated with herself and her mother. "Please! Don't do this."

Naya released the spell and turned away. Eden lunged for the book, and a crack filled the quiet room. Pain bloomed against her cheek, then warmth trickled down her face. When she touched it, her hand came away bloodied. Hurt filled her eyes as she stared at her mother.

"Eventually, you'll come to see how this is the right thing. But don't get in my way, Eden." Naya tucked the book in the crook of her arm and grabbed hold of Eden's bicep. "You've left me no choice."

"What?" Eden dragged her feet as her mother led her up the stairs, down the hall, and toward the attic stairwell. "No. You can't! Mama, don't do this." She fought against her mother's grip but was thrown into the stuffy room. She stumbled backward, tripping on her skirt, and crashed to the dusty floor. "If you do this, they'll kill you," Eden rasped through tears.

"No, it isn't me who is going to die." Naya said no more and slammed the door shut.

She couldn't kill them! Eden lunged forward, pounding on the door. "Don't do this! Let me out!" With the book in her hand, her mother *could* kill every one of them, and that notion terrified Eden as much as it angered her.

When Eden was coated in sweat from her efforts and her throat sore from screaming, she crumpled to the floor. The stifling attic only grew darker as time ticked on, which could only mean the sky was darkening all the more.

A chirp from the rafters caught her attention. Eden glanced up and saw Drizz scaling the wall. He hurriedly ran to her and then eyed the door.

Eden frowned. "It's locked."

Drizz scampered away in the shadows. The sound of scuffling filled the space, then as Drizz grunted, an easel collapsed to the floor, exposing a small hexagonal window. He squawked and pointed to it.

Eden rushed up to it, pressing her fingers against the warm glass. "If I go . . . you must hide. I'll come back for you." She had to warn Alessia that her mother was on her way, if she wasn't there already. It dawned on her then that her mother could have emptied the Veil of its beasts and unleashed them on the two realms. At the same moment, screeches filled the air, and it wasn't a horse whinnying. Eden knew that sound well enough.

Drizz pointed to a chair, then the window again, and nodded.

She gathered his meaning and grabbed the chair. With a steadying breath, she slammed the chair into the window, which shattered on impact. Wind howled through the space, and in the distance, Eden saw a black sky. "By the sun . . . what have you done, Mama?" Fear spiked in her, then quickly, anger that was unlike any she'd felt before. No . . . that wasn't true. She'd felt it not a week ago.

Draven.

Draven was in Lucem?

Eden stuck her head out the window and surveyed the roof. If she could manage to find a spout or trellis, she could easily climb down the manor without snapping her neck. Time was of the essence, and with little more thought, Eden stepped out onto the roof. She crouched down and peered over the ledge. The trellis wasn't close enough to the ledge for her to safely make it, but as she lifted her gaze, she spotted her favorite tree. One she'd climbed more times than she could count.

Eden sucked in a breath. She could jump and chance missing the branch or slipping, or she could utilize what she had within.

She lost her footing, and tumbled onto her backside. But she slammed her palms out, catching herself. Above, Drizz wailed from the window, holding onto his oversized ears in dismay.

"I'm okay," she grunted as she sat up. This time, Eden remained still and extended her hand, allowing the thrum of magic to call to the tree. At first, nothing happened. But then the tree's limbs bowed. A slight motion to begin with, then, with a groan, they stretched forward, twining together to form a makeshift bridge.

Once it was secure, Eden clambered onto the boughs, and as she walked, two sturdy branches secured themselves around her waist. As if they were nothing more than hands, they passed her down the height of the tree until she safely stood on the ground.

"By the sun, I'd never thought I could do that . . . " Eden glanced up at the tree and placed her hand against it. Energy poured from her palm into the bark as a thanks for aiding her. The tree shuddered, raining white petals down on her.

A flash in the distance caught her attention. Lightning speared the sky in a mesmerizing spider web of purple and white.

Eden ran as fast as she could to the stable. Aiya frantically swirled in her stall, ramming her chest against the door. "It's okay, girl. We're going to ride out of here." She opened the stall door, readying to grab a hold of her frantic mare's mane. She did just in time, as the horse bolted forward. Eden pulled herself up and guided the mare down the drive and toward the palace.

To her horror, as Eden rounded a bend in the road, she saw a creature stalking toward Aurelie's house. "Oh no." She spurred Aiya forward, much to the horse's dismay. Eden searched for something, anything to use as a distraction or a weapon.

There was nothing.

Nothing except for the monstrous wisteria that loomed over the manor.

Aiya reared up as the Veil beast screeched. The sound was like a fork scraping against porcelain.

"I'm sorry, Aiya. You're not going to like this."

34

Eden

Aiya squealed in fear as Eden drove her toward Aurelie's manor. The shadowy creature's glowing eyes caught sight of them, and the same ear-splitting cry echoed. Much to Aiya's credit, she only balked instead of tossing Eden to the ground. She was thankful because it allowed her to ride directly to the front of her friend's home.

Dismounting, Eden knelt to the ground, and she saw a flash of someone's face in the front window. "Get away from the window! Go to your cellar, now!" She thrust her hands in the direction of the vines of the wisteria, coaxing her magic into them. With the direct connection, it spared her the time of finding the root system in the soil.

The snarling beast didn't hesitate to run at Eden, but she was prepared for it. She willed the wisteria to lash out, like an extension of her hand. It curled around the creature, impaling it with a growing snarl of limbs.

She realized too late that the beast had been calling for backup. Eden was tossed to the ground, on her back, and a foul-smelling maw opened wide above her, showcasing rows of razor-sharp teeth. Visions of Mynata grinning down at her flashed in her head, and she snarled at the beast.

"I'm not ready to die yet." She called a net of wisteria vines down, which thickened until they caged the beast.

Aiya squealed, kicking out at another creature near an ancient oak tree. The roots protruded from the ground, and Eden reached for them with her magic. They snapped free from the earth and shot forward, spearing the creature.

Gasping for breath, Eden ran to the front door, coaxing the wisteria to block it. "I'm so sorry, Aurelie and Tamas . . . " she whispered. If it weren't for her mother, none of this would be happening. "Aiya!" Eden kissed to her, and as the mare approached, she mounted. With the threat subdued near the manor, Eden needed to get to the palace.

Griffins soared overhead, which could only mean there was a battle ensuing somewhere. As if to echo her thoughts, a rumble of thunder shook the ground, and lightning stretched across the darkened sky.

By the time Eden arrived at the palace, it was as dark as night. True night. She'd never known a sunless sky in Lucem. She soothed the puffing Aiya and rubbed her lathered neck. The guards staring up at her waited expectantly.

"Take care of her, I need to speak to the queen." Eden didn't wait for approval. She turned away, but the sound of beating wings gave her pause.

"My lady!" Dhriti's low voice called to her.

Eden glanced over her shoulder to see Captain Hannelore accompanying Dhriti. She wasn't Andhera's lady, and after her mother's antics, she'd be lucky if she was seen as *lady* anything. "Walk with me, I need to find the queen."

"We were instructed to bring you to Midniva." It was Hannelore who spoke this time, her broad wingspan tucked behind her. "We need to leave now."

"And I said I need to find Alessia," she hissed. "It's my mother who has the book, and she took off with it." Hannelore shared a look with Dhriti, but they didn't try to stop Eden as she burst into the palace. There was little doubt in her mind that it was Draven who'd sent them, but he had no power over Eden, and she certainly wasn't going to stray from the path she was currently on.

As luck would have it, Alessia was in the foyer speaking to her daughter, Brione. Gone was the gauzy gown Alessia typically wore, replaced by knee-high boots, white leather breeches, and a golden leather vest. She wore golden vambraces and a sword strapped to her back. The same silken black hair that typically hung in loose waves was held back in a tight braid.

Alessia turned her gaze to Eden, then to the harpies flanking her. "Eden! I sent riders your way. Did they not . . . ?"

Eden's perplexed look must have said it all. She'd seen no corpses, but that didn't mean the beasts hadn't had their way with them.

"No, they didn't. Alessia, I don't know where my mother is . . . but she plans to wipe out the kings."

Alessia hissed. her face contorted in rage. "Not without the fight of her life."

"I expect nothing less." Eden lowered her gaze. "For what it's worth, I'm sorry."

"You have nothing to apologize for unless you plan on

falling during this battle." She inclined her head and cast Eden a challenging look. "I don't want to deal with that hell too. So, do us all a favor and live." Alessia nodded to the harpies, her eyes hardening. "Now, get out of here while you still can."

"I'll need a fresh horse. And proper attire." Eden motioned to the sheer gown she wore, which was hardly appropriate for battle.

"Whatever you need, I'll supply it." Alessia glanced at Brione. "Show her where to find some armor. You can have whatever you wish, just get yourself to safety, and fast."

The princess was nearly a replica of her mother. Golden skin, silken hair as dark as ebony, but her eyes were the same gem-like green as her father's, and there was a softness to her features where her parents had an edge.

"Hannelore, Dhriti, meet me outside with the horse."

"Come with me, Lady Eden, I'll see to it that you are properly equipped." Brione turned on her heel and led Eden down the corridor at a brisk pace.

As much as Eden often reflected on the time she spent in the palace with her father, she'd forgotten so many details. The alabaster columns stretching toward the impossibly high ceiling, the carved limestone embellishments, and the distant cries of peafowl.

Brione turned down another corridor, then pushed open double wooden doors. They opened to what looked to be a dressing room. A tall silver mirror sat in the corner of the room, and against the walls, several wardrobe doors were thrown open, empty.

The princess strode toward one, pulled out several pieces of armor, and motioned toward Eden. "Perhaps we can meet on better terms next time." She offered a small smile. "I remember when you were a little girl, hiding by your father's knees. You remind me of him, in your eyes." Brione set the armor down and fetched an undershirt from the wardrobe's drawer before returning to Eden.

That was something she'd heard a thousand times over. Although she was the mirror image of her mother, the shape of her eyes and the light within them was said to be the spirit of her father. Eden ached to hold him then. To have him whisper in her ear that all would be well.

But he was gone.

She tugged on the string at the nape of her neck, and the sheer fabric pooled at her feet. Eden took the cotton shirt and pulled it over her head, tying it at the hollow of her throat. Brione motioned for her to spin, then piece by piece, she strapped and tied the leather armor into place.

"No one wishes for you to fight, Lady Eden, but to ride into the unknown without precaution is simply asking for evil to strike." She paused as she finished the last of the stays. "My uncle would want you safe." Brione handed over the leather breeches, avoiding Eden's eyes.

That was why she was in Lucem to begin with, wasn't it? To be safe. Frowning, Eden pulled the leather bottoms on. Despite being adorned in leather, she didn't feel weighed down, it all felt like a second skin. Something she'd grown used to in Andhera. Fresh perspiration trickled at her temple. It was still so bloody hot.

"It's time for you to go." Brione offered her tall lace-up boots.

Eden took them and pulled them on as quickly as she could, then worked at the laces.

A loud crack of lightning lit the sky, and Brione stared out the window as if waiting for someone. Worry etched her brow, and Eden opened her mouth to speak, but the princess turned her gaze upon her, this time sternly.

"You must leave now." Brione strode toward the door but paused at a rack that held a short sword. "You'll need a weapon." She took it down and glanced over her shoulder, a small smirk tugging at her full lips. "Lady or not, I know my uncle, and I know you had training in Andhera. He'd have been a fool to not ensure that." She tossed the sword, watching expectantly.

When Eden caught the hilt of the blade, Brione nodded in approval, and they both left the room.

Outside the castle, the harpies waited with a fresh horse for Eden. The palomino was saddled and brought to her.

"A better choice in attire, my lady." Dhriti's dark eyes glimmered with approval.

Eden mounted, managing a small smile. "It reminds me of Andhera."

Hannelore and Dhriti took to the sky, then they were off to the Veil.

Not far into the ride, a beast leaped onto the path, but Hannelore quickly swooped down, sword in hand, and beheaded the threat. Thankfully they could see, because Eden was struggling to see the lighter dirt of the road in the darkness. Without a sun, without a moon . . . there was just enough light that it was similar to Andhera's night.

The ride to the Veil remained fairly quiet, save for a few more beasts, which were slain by the harpies. When they arrived, Dhriti lowered herself to the ground, wings folding neatly against her back, but Hannelore remained in the air.

"I must return to His Majesty's aid. Be safe." Hannelore

bowed her head, then, with a powerful thrust of her wings, she rode the winds away from them.

As she left, Eden bit the inside of her cheek. She should have passed along a message to Draven. But what was she to tell him that he couldn't feel? She stroked her fingers over her heart. "Just don't die," she whispered.

"Are you ready?" Dhriti's feathered hair whipped in the wind.

"As I'll ever be."

The Veil was still, even more so than before—it sent chills up Eden's spine. The shadows no longer writhed, and the howls were absent.

"I don't know what awaits us on the other side," Dhriti started, and almost seemed unsure of herself. It struck Eden as odd. Was it because she was afraid, or was it that she feared for Eden's well-being? "But I want you to be prepared. Remember all that we've taught you."

Eden's brow furrowed. "But Midniva should be . . . "

"Should be, my lady, but who knows."

Their journey through the Veil was uneventful, but as they emerged in Midniva, dread filled Eden. Howls filled the sky, as did the same screeching she'd heard in Lucem. Like a knife dragging down stone, the sound penetrated Eden's core.

"A nightmare, that is what awaits us." Eden gritted her teeth as guilt threatened to tear her apart. Her mother had done this. She'd thrust Lucem into darkness and brought chaos to Midniva. "We have to get to King Travion."

"Yes, but—"

"Draven isn't here, and our choices are limited, aren't they? Travion can't fall in battle. I won't have that on my conscience, Dhriti!" Eden spurred her mount forward. Dhriti's cursing brought a brief smile to Eden's face.

"No matter what anyone may think, you are suited to be Andhera's queen."

Eden snorted. Although it was a compliment, it still stung because Dhriti's king didn't see it that way. "Why do you say that?"

Dhriti peered down from above. "You are stubborn to a fault."

She laughed, shaking her head. "That is bold of you."

"I thought you'd appreciate it." Dhriti swooped down, her talons digging into the ground as she raised her sword and lashed out at a shadowed creature. It leaped out of the way and toward Eden, who'd grabbed her sword before the beast knocked her from the saddle. She landed on her back, the breath forced from her. The creature's teeth snapped inches from her face as she sliced the short sword through the air.

Dhriti flew above, but Eden was able to drive the blade through the soft underside of the monster's maw. In a swoop, the harpy kicked the beast to the side. A long, lizard-like tail curled around its back end, but its shaggy body reminded Eden of a wolf.

"I should have had it," Dhriti cursed.

"I'm fine." No, she wasn't, but she would pretend she was until this nightmare was through. "You can kill the next one, and the next after that."

"Deal."

The road to the castle was treacherous, and Dhriti made good on her word, cutting down the foes that presented themselves. Even the sea was angry with the state of the realms, for it struck against the stone barrier repeatedly.

The salty wind whipped across Eden's face, kicking dust and hair into her eyes.

Over the roar of the sea, Eden could hear shouting and the clash of swords, which didn't inspire much hope in her that the castle was safe. Whatever hope she had diminished when they reached the top of the hill and saw soldiers fighting against a horde of beasts.

"We have to find King Travion!" Eden wheeled her horse around as it shied away from the fight.

Midniva's soldiers poured down the hill from the castle, forming a wall—or at least they tried to. The sound of their battle cries bled into the roar of the sea as sword clashed with sword, and bellows met growls.

Dhriti grabbed the horse's reins in a lightning-quick reflex. "No. You need to be safe."

Frustration mounted in Eden. "I'm not arguing with you, Dhriti." Eden wasn't a soldier, and the combat skills she'd learned weren't enough to save her amidst a war, but she wasn't going to run and hide. Eden needed to warn Travion and see for herself that he was alive.

Dhriti's eyes narrowed. "I'll be killed if anything happens to you."

"Then I suggest you don't let anything happen to me." Dhriti's grip loosened on the reins until she released them completely. "There are plenty of things I can use here to my advantage." The castle was surrounded by old trees which were nearly as tall as the structure, and around it, smaller trees formed a wall. Flowers, both fragile and thorned, decorated the premise. If it weren't for the location, it would have reminded her of Lucem's palace, surrounded by vibrant blooms.

Pressing forward, Dhriti cleared the way, until a horned

357

beast charged Eden's mount from the side. Fortunately, Eden had seen it coming, as did Dhriti, so as Eden leaped from the horse, Dhriti caught her and whirled her away.

The horse was impaled on impact. As much as Eden wanted to mourn and cry for the brave mount, Dhriti wasted no time in sprinting forward and leaping onto the back of the chimera.

Eden lurched and sucked in air as a quick, burning pain spread along her back. Warmth trickled down her side, but with adrenaline coursing through her, her pain faded, at least for the moment.

If she ignored it, the wound wouldn't slow her down. That's what she told herself.

When she spun to face her foe, she saw a woman's youthful face staring at her. A *human*. Eden opened her mouth to plead with her, but as the woman lunged forward with her sword, Eden dropped to the ground and rolled out of the way. Roots sprung from the soil, lashing out at the assailant before twisting around her legs and snapping them.

Dhriti landed beside her, yanking Eden to her feet, and spun her away in another lethal dance.

Roses became instruments of death as beasts lunged for Eden. The stems grew thick, and their thorns with them, until they impaled and constricted the assailant in a gruesome death. It allowed Dhriti to continue on her search for Travion while cutting down foes.

"I found him!" Dhriti shouted above the melee.

Eden kept her eyes trained before her but walked toward the sound of Dhriti's voice. When she glanced to the side, she saw the harpy dive in to take care of the threat attacking the king.

He glanced up and focused on Eden, bloody sword in his hand. "By the sea . . . You shouldn't be here."

"I belong nowhere right now, apparently." Eden sucked in precious air and rubbed at her back where the woman had struck her. Her stomach dropped. Eden's fingers were wet, and she didn't have to look to know it was blood. She swallowed roughly and made a fist. Travion needed to be safe first. "Lucem is in the dark. Draven is there."

"Draven is in Lucem?" Travion's brows pinched together.

"Without the sun, he is able to be. My mother has the book, and we have no idea where she is!" Eden looked over Travion's shoulder and pulled him forward just as one of the lizard-wolf hybrids leaped forward. She used the rose bushes once again, which speared through the creature.

Travion barked out laughter. "And he worries about you."

"*I'm* worried for *all* of you." Eden drank in precious air. Adrenaline coursed through her still, but when her reserves of energy and abilities ran out, what then? "My mother wants all of you dead."

Travion eyed Eden, as if weighing her words, then nodded. "She has quite the battle before her then." He grinned, but it faltered as a manticore landed not far from them. "Shit. Not another one of these. I'll lure it away with a few of my men." With a wink, Travion barked orders to the nearby soldiers, then disappeared into the courtyard.

Fear for Travion threatened to overwhelm her, but with a new wave of attackers, she didn't have time to focus on it for long.

35

Draven

Draven gulped down the rich blood coursing through the prisoner's veins, feeling the warmth of it coat his throat on its way down. Upon his return from the Veil, he'd felt famished and in deep need of blood. Traveling through the empty wasteland that was the in-between had left him exhausted, so he fed greedily on the offered vein.

When he'd had his fill, Draven released the man's arm and waved to the harpy guard to take him away. Just as the soldier was walking him back out Draven's study door, General Ailith shoved past her.

"Your Majesty!" She was winded, and there was concern in her eyes. "Word has just come in from the gates: the guard there has fallen, and beasts are pouring into the Veil as we speak."

Draven froze for a moment, feeling the human blood flooding through his body in a rush of sensation and life, now mixed with a truly horrible sense of dread. "What?"

This was the last thing that was meant to happen.

Draven rose quickly to his feet, swiping a hand over his face. "Call your army and head for the Veil at once, we must try to cull the herd before it is able to do too much damage in Midniva." With a sharp nod, Ailith turned on her heel and was gone at once. "Seurat." Draven looked at the man in the corner of the room. "Send an owl to Travion. Give him warning of what is coming, but let him know we are on our way."

Draven barely had the words out of his mouth when the bowl on the edge of his desk hummed, and suddenly, Zryan's panicked face was shimmering on its rippling surface.

"Draven? Are you there?" Zryan called out.

"I haven't the time, Zry, there is trouble in the—"

"Lucem is in complete darkness."

"What?" Draven asked for the second time in as many minutes.

"The entire realm is pitch-black, and we are being overrun by unimaginable beasts. I think whatever was in the Veil is now here. It is madness and hell."

The fear that settled into his marrow was so intense, Draven found himself stunned for a moment.

Eden was in Lucem. And Draven had sent her there.

"I am coming," he growled to Zryan before striding quickly from his study. "Ailith!" His bellow carried through the halls of Aasha Castle, and soon his General was there before him once again.

"Yes, Your Majesty?"

"Prepare the full army, we're going into Lucem."

"Your Majesty?" Ailith questioned once more, confused.

"The entire realm of Lucem has been cast in darkness and they are being overrun with creatures from the Veil. Send half of the infantry through to Midniva to hunt down Andherian creatures that have passed through their gates. The rest will come with us to Lucem, where I fear the true battle is taking place."

Draven had braced himself for the turmoil he would find in Lucem. What he hadn't anticipated was the effect Lucem would have on him, stepping into the light realm for the first time since he had left for Andhera so long ago. Even in the darkness that now hid its eternal beauty from view, he could smell the fresh scent of florals and feel the residual warmth that came from the sun's constant shining on the land.

A wave of loss and homesickness swept through Draven violently. So violently, it brought the king to a sudden halt. This was the land he had been denied for so very long.

"Your Majesty?" General Ailith was eyeing him with concern. Around them, the armies of harpies, were-wolves, and were-panthers streamed into Lucem, swords and bows at the ready.

"Did the rest of the troops enter Midniva as ordered?" Draven rushed past the concern written in his general's eyes and forced himself to concentrate on the battle at hand.

"Aye, sir. The remainder of the were-infantry has passed through into the middle realm. They will hunt down any potential beasts that have slipped into Midniva."

Draven nodded. Then they both turned their heads sharply as a scream rang out.

A call of, "The dark king has arrived!" sounded from the darkened street.

"Don't let his creatures take your children!" someone added to the fray, followed by frantic screams of terrified people.

Draven frowned. Did they not realize he was here to help? His question was soon answered as a gathering of Lucemites suddenly surrounded a band of were-panthers, pitchforks and shovels in hand.

"Fools! We have come to aid you!" Draven felt a rush of fury as the citizens of Lucem viewed their presence as a danger. Did they think that he was behind what was happening now? Growling, Draven shouted out, "Protect yourselves, but do not harm them! We have not come here to kill the citizens of Lucem but to aid them!" Obeying his orders, the small flank of were-panthers surrounded the upset group of men, snapping at them to force them back toward their homes.

Draven turned to Hannelore. "Find Dhriti. Between the two of you, go and collect Eden. If Zryan held true to his vow, she should be at the palace. Once you have her in hand, Dhriti is to get her to safety into Midniva with Travion. This is your top priority. Understood?"

"Understood." Hannelore's arm came across her chest, and she bowed quickly before calling for Dhriti. Together, the two harpies launched into the sky.

Trusting that the two of them would see to Eden's safety, Draven waded through the chaos, his eyes easily seeing in the darkness around them. Ahead, he could make out the shapes of a group of beasts surrounding a home.

363

Already they had killed someone and were feeding on the corpse.

"Disperse!" he heard Ailith shout. "Fan out through the streets. The creatures will be attracted to the areas of most activity."

Draven descended upon the beasts quickly, stalking them with the quiet efficiency of one born of the shadows. His dark form was clad in a black leather vest fitted tightly to his chest. At his shoulders, he wore layers of added leather, but his arms were left free to swing his sword. Across his chest were a series of tight straps that held his sword strapped to his back, and at his shoulder was the customary gray cape.

His forearms were wrapped in black metal vambraces, sculpted perfectly by his nephew, Kian, to mold to his body. They shone still, despite the series of blade strokes they'd been subjected to over the centuries.

Reaching back, Draven wrapped nimble fingers around the hilt of his sword, and in one swift motion, he freed the black blade from its scabbard and brought it down upon the lizard beast's neck. A dull thud sounded out as its head dropped to the ground, followed shortly by the rest of its body. The first dispatched, Draven faced off with the second. This one was larger, and as its gaping maw opened, he could see the stoking of fire deep in its throat.

"Why must you creatures always spew flame?" he growled.

Draven leaped out of the way of the onslaught of flames just in time, feeling the singe of it along his forearm. Drawing on his invisibility glamour, he rushed the beast. However, the monster's eyesight seemed driven by heat rather than sight, and his tricks did not work on it.

Wolf claws scraped along the outside of his thigh just as his blade sunk deeply into the creature's chest. It released one final screech before joining its brother on the ground.

All around him, the sounds of creatures hissing and shrieking met with the responding whistle of an arrow or the thwack of a sword. Beyond, the sky was streaked with bright flashes of lightning dropping down from the clouds to strike at the ground below. Zryan had entered the fray, which meant the beasts had made their way to the palace. Draven could only grit his teeth and trust in Hannelore and Dhirti's efforts.

"Sire! Above!"

Looking up, Draven found the sky dotted with the light of several torches. As they drew closer, he could make out the image of his nephews, Ruan and Kian, perched atop griffins, with a number of their soldiers following. Draven lifted his hand into the air, signaling to them.

Ruan landed before him, a wide smirk on his bearded face. His dark eyes gleamed even in the darkness, his brown hair windswept back from his face. The eldest prince was dressed in a tan leather vest with thick straps rising over his shoulders. The front of the vest was woven with an intricate gold chest piece proudly bearing the emblem of Lucem. His forearms were wrapped in red fabric, clasped in place by gold vambraces that swept down over to cover his knuckles. Around his bare biceps were a series of gold bands, each proclaiming a different rank in the royal army he had achieved, or a particular battle won.

Ruan, otherwise known as the Prince of War, was ready to fight.

Behind him, Prince Kian climbed off his own griffin and stepped forward. The youngest prince had black hair that fell into his blue eyes. A look of unease on his features as he peered around them at the Andherian army in the midst of battle. On his right shoulder gleamed golden layers of armor that strapped on to his bicep and crossed over his chest to fasten beneath the opposite arm. His left arm was solid gold from fingertip to shoulder, a beautifully crafted piece to replace the one of flesh he had lost as a boy. The replica arm, imbued with magic, moved as if Kian had been born with it.

He wore a sword strapped to his hip, but unlike his brother who sought out battle, Kian was the fabricator of their weapons and preferred his place in the palace forge. While Ruan was the spitting image of Zryan, Kian held more of his mother's beauty.

"The creatures hunt by heat. Your torches are going to draw them directly to you and your men," Draven said by way of hello.

"Perfect. Then we'll have them right where I want them," Ruan responded, his hand moving to pull his blade free. Behind him, the sky lit with lightning once more.

Draven could feel frantic fear wash through him that he knew was Eden's. Rather than let it distract him, he only hoped Hannelore and Dhriti reached her before it was too late.

There wasn't time for more words after that. Draven and his nephews soon found themselves set upon by several of the Veil beasts, along with a number of chimera that had followed the shadows into the light realm. Dodging blasts of flame, Draven dove after a creature, grabbing onto one of its sharp snake fangs as it lashed at him and holding its head aloft while keeping out of the direct view of the goat head.

To his side, Ruan was wielding his sword with the fluidity and ferociousness that had earned him his title. A roar of victory spilled from his lips as he cleaved the head off one beast only to thrust his sword into the belly of another directly after. Kian, while not as blissfully in his element as his brother, was using his golden arm as well as his blade to fight through the onslaught.

Violently twisting the snake head off the scaled tail, Draven rushed forward to thrust his sword up through the bottom of the goat head, driving it through its jaw and up into its skull before more fire could be breathed. The chimera's lion head released a roar as it staggered. Doling out the death blow, Draven's hand plunged into its chest, pulling out a still-beating heart.

Bringing the organ to his lips, he bit into it, quickly gulping down the blood inside, then tossed it to the ground. While not his preferred human blood, it would help repair the gash in his thigh a little, enough to hopefully staunch the free flow of his own.

A series of snarls sounded to his right as Channon and his wolves surrounded a manticore. While the beast was violent, it had no chance against the pack. Beyond the wolves, Draven watched as three were-panthers chased a Veil beast between two homes. A flash of flame lit up the sky, followed by a harsh cry of pain. The harpies had taken up perch on the rooftops, firing arrows at whatever creature was in their line of sight.

They fought their way farther into town, chasing the beasts down and killing any they came across. Some of the soldiers continued to brandish the torches that lured the creatures out of the shadows and after them instead of the citizens. Their progress brought them into the town center just in time to see one home go up in flames as a beast went after a small girl who had escaped inside. Before Draven had a chance to say anything, Ruan had disappeared into the home.

"Go through the roof!" Draven shouted to one of the harpies closest to him. Understanding his command, she flew to the rooftop, using her sword to break through one of the upper windows and head inside.

Kian had fallen on the monstrosity, which had started the blaze, his gilded hand pinning the beast's head to the ground as he fought off a clawed foot. Trusting him to handle it, Draven moved to stand below the window, and caught the young fae his harpy brought to the opening and tossed out.

Setting the coughing female on the ground, he stood up in time to catch the young male who was dropped out next. Fortunately, the mother was aware enough to take her child from him, and Draven turned to see Ruan burst through another window, a small female clutched protectively in his arms.

Shaking his head at his nephew, his leather smoking lightly and soot smeared over one cheek, Draven pointed to one of the stone houses down the lane. "Get the family to safety over there."

Turning, Draven found Hannelore suddenly before him and realized he had lost himself to the bloodshed. Time had passed more quickly than he thought. The harpy was panting from the exertion of a long flight but seemed well overall.

"Eden?" he asked urgently.

"Dhriti has gone through the Veil with her to Midniva. They should be arriving at the castle soon."

"Had she suffered any harm?"

"We found her fending off beasts when we arrived. But she is okay, and Dhriti will get her safely to King Travion."

Draven grit his teeth at the thought of Eden battling the beasts that his women and men were falling to but nodded nonetheless. "Thank you, Hannelore." She had gotten Eden safely out of Lucem and hopefully to Midniva's castle, which should have been calmer and more secure.

"It was my honor."

"Now, join in where you can."

As the harpy took to the air once more, another replaced her. "Sire, we have contained the beasts on the outskirts," General Ailith informed him. "The army has fully closed around the village and are driving any that remain to the center where the prince's men await. We've sent any who can be spared to the outlying villages to dispatch any creatures that made their way there."

"Good." They might yet manage to deal with this before too many casualties were amassed.

"You should head to Midniva, Your Majesty."

Draven glanced narrowly at Ailith. "I am needed here."

"Prince Ruan has his men firmly under control. And we harpies were made for this sort of battle. You know this is nothing but a day of sport for us. Go to her, sire."

Draven contemplated this for a moment before he nodded. "Very well. But this does not stop until we are certain we have killed every last creature that has come through the Veil. Keep someone to guard and make sure no more come through."

"Already on it, Your Majesty."

Draven couldn't help but smirk a little. Of course. This

was why Ailith had been given command of the armies of Andhera. She knew how to handle a battle.

"I will see you on the other side, general. Be safe and . . . have fun." They shared a grin, then Draven headed back through the shadows, making his way toward the Veil.

His journey through the gate and across the vastness was swift, using what energy he could spare to make his movements faster than usual. Draven had no time to waste. If he could make certain things were fine in Midniva and Eden was safe, he would be able to return to Lucem and help finish off the battle that was underway.

It was early evening in the middle realm, so as he stepped through into Travion's kingdom, Draven was safe once more from the sun. However, it was not peacefulness that greeted him. A dead were-tiger lay on the path leading into the capital city, her body half-transformed back into a human. Cursing, Draven ran toward the main city, keeping his eyes open for any beast that may be lying in wait.

Passing through the streets of Caithaird, Draven was forced to stop to take down a lamia. She had already decimated a small house and discarded the parents as nothing more than things in the way of her true delight. She sat coiled around the bodies of the children she was feasting on. With an angry shout, Draven swung his sword, taking off her head so swiftly, it flew several feet away.

Growling through clenched teeth, he wiped some of the blood from his cheek. "Worthless creatures. I'll eradicate you yet." A wash of distress suddenly tore through Draven, strong enough that it caused him to stagger a little. "Eden."

Filled with a fresh sense of purpose, Draven left the bodies of the slain and ran through the pebbled streets, not stopping until the towering gates of Travion's castle came into view. A were-panther greeted him with a quick growl, flesh hanging from her jowls. But Draven paid little heed to her, his eyes searching for Eden. Through their blood bond, he could tell that she was near.

When he found her, she stood in the middle of what had once been decorative trees in Travion's courtyard but which now were a tangle of overly large roots shooting from the soil to wrap around the bodies of screeching manticores. A chimera lay dead to one side, its body speared by the large thorn of a rose bush.

Seeing the snarling beast behind her, Draven rushed forward, his arm slipping around Eden's waist to spin her out of the way as his sword sliced clean through the beast's jaw. It fell, its head now in half.

Panting, Draven looked down at Eden, his eyes quickly traveling over her body to make certain that she was fully intact. She was dressed in armor that he recognized as having once belonged to either his sister-in-law or niece, and his hand, when he pulled it away from her side, was coated in blood. The sight of it, and scent of it on the wind, froze him for a moment. Eden was injured, and that thought filled him with enough rage that he could have burnt away all the darkness currently clouding Lucem.

"Draven!" Eden gasped, eyes wide with surprise.

Her gasp pulled his attention away from his fury and up to her face instead. The sight of her for the first time in three days was like a kick to the stomach, making everything inside of him protest the loss of her. Unable to stop himself, Draven hauled her in tight against him and dipped his head to capture her lips in a fierce kiss, needing the reassurance that she was truly well and alive here in his arms. She stiffened at the initial assault, then leaned into it, her lips responding demandingly.

"You're okay," he rasped breathlessly when he finally pulled away from her. Pressing his forehead to hers, he took a moment to savor the feel of her in his arms once more. "*Are* you okay? You're bleeding."

"I'll be okay. And what of you?" Eden drew back, looking his body over. "You're covered in blood as well!"

"Most of it isn't mine."

"*Most* of it?"

Ignoring her concern, Draven spun, searching the courtyard to see who else was busy fighting creatures. "Where is Travion?"

"He's right over—" Eden's words halted, and she pointed to a corner of the courtyard that now lay empty. "He was right there when last I saw him."

Nodding, Draven took her hand in his free one, and with his sword gripped tightly in the other, pulled her into the castle. "Why were you outside?" he growled.

"I wanted to help. I *needed* to help."

Draven cast her a quick glance, his features tight. "And I sent you here to be safe." Shaking his head, he tugged her farther into the castle. "Travion!"

His shout was answered by the snort of a beast. Hurrying through the open doors of the throne room, Draven released Eden's hand and rushed forward. Travion lay crumpled on the floor in a pool of his own blood. A manticore hovered over him, its twisted human face bent on devouring him as his arms weakly fought it off.

Draven leaped at it, shoving the beast off of Travion. He rolled as the manticore slid across the floor, its clawed feet scraping at the stone. Jumping back up, Draven grunted in pain as one of the foot-long needles from the beast's tail caught him in the shoulder, piercing the area between collarbone and neck. Distantly, he heard Eden shout his name.

Hissing through his teeth, Draven ignored the pain and cloaked himself with invisibility. It was enough to confuse the creature and gave Draven enough time to rush it once more, this time stabbing it through the heart. As he withdrew his blade, the manticore collapsed to the floor. Draven dropped his invisibility and turned back to Travion.

His brother's torso had been torn open, leaving far more of his insides visible than what should be possible to survive. As he hurried back over to Travion, Eden met him, and together they knelt. Through his abdomen, which rose with short, shallow breaths, was an even deeper gash, torn open by the manticore's spiked tail or sharp claws. The sight of his brother in such a state made Draven feel ill. Too many times he'd been witness to Travion's pain. Too many times he'd been forced to be the cause of it. Once Zryan had helped them out of that dungeon, it was something he'd hoped never to have to witness again.

"By the moon . . . I thought you knew how to fight," Draven rasped.

Travion chuckled weakly, his breath hitching in pain. "We've been through worse, you and I. I've hurt more and less." His last words came with a rattling breath.

"I can . . . I can fix this." Eden's voice trembled as she spoke, and Draven thought she didn't sound quite as confident as she was trying to be.

"How quaint. One last family reunion before the end," a cold voice spoke from the doorway of the throne room.

Turning to look over his shoulder, Draven saw Naya Damaris holding a dark leather book in her hands.

"Mama?" Eden's voice was barely above a whisper.

Naya ignored her daughter, staring directly at Draven instead. "So convenient that you present yourself here to me just as one brother dies so that I might finish the job."

36

Eden

Thank the sun, moon, and sea, Draven is alive! Relief flooded her, however short-lived it was. It didn't matter that he'd cast her out of Andhera, only that he was here now. The press of Draven's lips had been enough to reassure Eden that it was no dream, but now was not the time to dwell on her feelings, not as the king of Midniva lay in a pool of blood.

Kneeling by Travion's side, horror washed over her.

Eden's blood cooled against her skin as her wound healed, but the throbbing pain remained. It wasn't a mortal injury, and she would live to see another day, but by the sun, as she beheld the state King Travion was in . . . His pale freckled skin was a shade of alabaster no one amongst the living should have been. The thick leather armor he wore had been torn away from his torso, exposing more than a cotton shirt. Blood oozed with every beat of his heart and spilled onto the marble flooring.

Eden could handle this. She had to. She wouldn't let her mother stain her conscience and take away Travion's life. She *would* save him, even if it drained the rest of her power. Eden had managed to heal herself on the way inside the castle, which, coupled with her fighting, had drained the well of power considerably.

"Hold on, Travion." Eden's nimble fingers gently pulled at the tattered remains of his armor and shirt, but as the crooning voice of her mother filled the space, she blanched and stood upright.

"Mama . . . please, don't do this." Sorrow filled Eden for what her mother had become, what her bitterness had twisted her into. This wasn't the mother Eden had known when she was a little girl. Not the same mother that had held her and read her stories, wiped away her tears, or cleaned a scuffed knee.

No. The fae who stood before them, with a scowl and her fingers tapping against the leather book, was a monster. But in her heart, she was still Eden's mother, and if she could use that to their advantage, she would.

Naya's eyes flicked to Eden's wound. "Eden . . ." She choked on a frustrated sob as she took a step forward, then stiffened as she halted. "You should have stayed in Lucem. I left you there to keep you *safe.*"

That was the running theme it seemed. But how safe was Lucem, with the threat of beasts ravaging the light realm? However, in her mother's mind, she was useless and therefore shelved away so someone could pull her out and dote on her later. Eden was more than tired of being shoved away so everyone else could handle things. She was aware of Draven's emotions colliding with her own, which was, for the most part, a roaring rage.

"I know," Eden said softly as she walked forward. "But this isn't right. This isn't at all what Papa would want. You know that." She shook her head and felt the prick of tears sting her eyes. "In his name, you'd do this?"

"Eden! What other options do I have?"

Briefly, Eden wondered what she would have done in her mother's position. Before? She'd have mourned, grown angry, and learned to cope with the hollowness. But now? Tearing three realms apart wasn't what Eden would've done. "Mourn and live as Papa would have wanted you to." Eden continued to move closer. Her mother didn't step forward, but neither did she pull back.

Naya's face twisted with grief and a hint of regret. "It's far too late for that." Her eyes flicked toward Draven, and she shook her head. "I cannot forgive what has been taken from me."

"No! You can end this now. Draven has taken nothing from you, and Travion took nothing from you. Please, Mama." Eden stood in front of her mother, blocking her view of Draven. One of Eden's hands lifted toward her mother's cheek, and she cupped it gently. Guilt tugged at her heart, because while she wanted nothing more than for her mother to relinquish the book, she knew she wouldn't, and Eden was merely attempting to distract her.

Naya leaned into her touch, but the moment Eden's fingers curled around the book, she stiffened. "You've always been honest to a fault, so I will blame this attempt at deceiving me on another." She hissed and shoved Eden away from her. In the same instant, she held out her hand, and a familiar blast of power hurled Eden to the floor.

An unearthly growl erupted from behind her. Draven rushed forward, teeth bared and poised to rip into Naya, except the same spell brought him to his knees. It was difficult to watch as he fought against the binding.

377

Eden clawed at the tiles, unable to lift herself. "Mama!" She looked to her mother, then at Draven. Anger colored his face as he fought against the restraint. Seeing him in such a state infuriated Eden. She wanted to reach out to the earth, call upon vines, but she needed her strength for Travion.

Still, tiles quaked beneath her as she reached out to the potted tree. The roots shattered the porcelain container, then erupted toward her mother. Except they shriveled before connecting with her. Eden deflated.

"Foolish girl." Naya ignored Eden's pleas and muttered unfamiliar words beneath her breath as she flicked through the book until she landed on a page that gratified her. A new round of unfamiliar words spilled from her mouth. An ancient, old tongue. With a snap, Naya closed the book.

Draven sucked in a harsh breath as he clutched at his chest. At first, he made no sound, then a gut-wrenching howl of pain erupted from his lips.

"Stop!" Eden cried. "Stop! You're hurting him." Eden pressed her forehead against the marble. A torrent of anger poured into her that belonged to *her*. Fear bled into the anger too.

"I imagine feeling the sun from within when you're a creature of the night *does* hurt."

The sun? Cold filled Eden as she glanced over at Draven. Her mother was going to kill him in front of her. "I will never forgive you." The hold on her faltered, allowing Eden to rise to a kneeling position. "Ever." The muscles in her jaw tensed as she narrowed her eyes on her mother. "And if you think I will choose to remain with you, think again, because I won't. I am not your pet, and I certainly wouldn't choose to be your companion in life." Eden strained against the wall pressing her down.

Unlike before, Naya didn't allow her hold to lighten. Tension hardened the already harsh angles of her face. "I don't need you to love me, but I need you to live in a different world. One without the taint of the kings."

A manticore strolled in behind Naya, its nails clicking on the floor before it sat on its haunches beside her. The spiked tail flicked in annoyance, or perhaps in anticipation of its attack.

Eden twisted to look back at Draven, who had slumped to the floor and was now convulsing. If hate alone were an ability, she'd have torn her mother to shreds. "Let him go!"

Naya motioned toward Travion's still body. "I think it's poetic. A creature belonging to Andhera has slain Midniva's king. Draven, in some fashion, is responsible for his brother's death, and that very beast will be his end."

Eden dragged her gaze back to the beast, and for a moment, she thought it winked at her. "I hate you." She had no more words for her mother, only hatred. She'd slaughtered so many, pinned deaths on Draven, then sent Midniva into chaos.

Naya stepped to the side, the book clutched against her chest. "End him," she ordered the manticore. Her icy tone was like a spear through Eden's heart.

The manticore snarled as he stood, muscles coiling as he readied to leap, but as he launched forward, much to Eden's confusion, it wasn't at Draven but at Naya. She crashed to the floor hard, knocking her chin on the ground at just the right angle to render her unconscious. The book slid across the floor, beyond Travion's prone body.

The pressure on Eden disappeared, and in an instant, she was scrambling toward Draven. She gathered him in her arms, her hand cupping his cheek. "Draven, look at me." Eden swallowed against the burn in her throat. She slid her fingers down the back of his neck and spread them so she could allow a flood of healing to surge into him. What damage had been done?

Draven mumbled against her chest. His limbs sluggishly pushed him upward, and when his blue eyes caught hers, her heart clenched. He was alive. But how long would they be alive with the manticore in the room?

Eden looked over her shoulder. The pacing beast's image shimmered, and in another moment, a very naked Zryan stood over Naya, scowling down at her.

"Zryan?" Eden blinked. "Don't kill her. We're not done with my mother yet." Eden ground her words out, then lifted her wrist to Draven's mouth. "I need you to be more than okay right now. Drink."

His fingers curled around her wrist as his fangs popped out. A familiar sting, then nothing as he fed off of her.

Draven's grip tightened as his strength recovered, and when he'd sampled enough to return an ample amount of his energy, he released her wrist. "Travion."

Eden didn't need to hear more than that. She rushed to Midniva's king and felt for his pulse. A faint thrum beat in his neck. "Travion, I'm not going to give up on you, so don't give up on us."

"Tell me why I shouldn't kill her for what she has done to us?" Zryan muttered behind Eden, and when she glanced at him, he was bent over, tying her mother up with one of the drape's ropes. It seemed it was a question he didn't want an answer to. He twisted to look over at Draven. "Are you all right? Is Trav . . . "

"I'm alive," Draven muttered. "Travion is . . . " He swallowed roughly.

Turning back to the fallen king, Eden peeled away the shredded articles of armor and clothing. Blood had clotted in the short amount of time, but with Travion's torso torn open, there was little good the clotting would do. By no means was Eden a trained physician, and aside from nicks and cuts, or a fractured bird's wing, she'd never healed anything as gruesome as his wounds.

"I need a bowl of water and clean linen right now. And for the love of the sun, remove my mother from this room." She turned her gaze to Zryan and wondered if the same fire she felt blazed within her eyes. "I can't move Travion until the open wounds are healed. Any movement . . . " And it would be his true end. But she didn't want to voice her concern, not that she had to. "If he has a healer, grab them too."

Eden ran her hand along the tip of the wound, which started at his shoulder. It was less severe there, so she allowed her ability to rush in. The skin pulled taut as she moved her hand down, and she imagined the skin healing layer by layer, weaving together again, much like a tapestry.

By the time she reached the more severe location, a bowl of water and clean linen had been brought to her. She dabbed at the wound, then realized she needed help. "Draven, I can't keep my hands on him and tuck his vitals back in at the same time." Eden's hands and ability moved of their own accord as she allowed her mind to travel far, far away. She didn't want to focus on the hot blood coating her fingers, or the nearly dead king laying on the floor.

Draven knelt beside her, shaking his head, but his eyes focused intently on her. "Tell me what to do."

Eden mopped up fresh blood, then started to tuck Travion's flesh in as it should have been. "Hold this down, because as I move, his skin is going to seal." Her stomach lurched, but she thought of the sun beaming down on her, feeding nutrients to the flowers, and nymphs playing in ponds.

Draven caught her gaze, and she saw a silent question: *Can you do this?*

"I'm not going to give up on him, okay?" As exhausted as she was, Eden was prepared to give the last ounce of her energy supply to Travion if it meant saving him.

Heat poured from Eden's palm as she raked it down his torso, and as the warmth spread across Travion's flesh, it healed. She swept her hand downward, applying enough pressure that more blood rushed forth. Eden intensified the outpour of energy on the more crucial area, and Draven nimbly tucked flesh and organs back inside.

By the time she was finished, blackness framed Eden's vision, and she swayed. Just as she leaned forward to check Travion's pulse, he sucked in a wet breath and coughed. Although he didn't stir as much as Eden wanted, hope blossomed within.

Draven shifted his bloodied hand to rest against his brother's rising chest, and the tension which had creased the corners of his eyes eased. "You've done it," he murmured, then frowned before he snaked an arm around her. "Eden?"

"I'm fine," she murmured, leaning against him for support. "I need rest. The healer will need me later." Between her efforts in Lucem, outside the castle, and nearly reviving Travion, Eden was fighting to keep her eyes open. Exhaustion pulled at her, weighing her down.

Draven leaned forward and pressed his forehead against hers. "Whatever you need, you'll have it."

Concern filled her, and she wondered if it was her own or his. "Draven, are you—"

He slanted her a look, then pressed a quick kiss to her lips. "I'm here."

Eden knew better than to press for more of an answer. He wasn't well, she could see, but he was alive, and that was something both of them could be thankful for in the moment.

Draven

There were no words to explain the pain that had blossomed within Draven as Naya's spell had unleashed sunlight inside him. He had felt parts of himself beginning to disintegrate, harden, and turn to dust. While he no longer required his organs as other creatures did, the pain had been unnatural, and even Eden's offering of blood—while it had stemmed the most severe edge of pain—had only been enough to get him back up.

However, with Travion's blood still coating his hands, and Eden's slumped figure pressing into his side, Draven knew there was no time to dwell on the pain lancing through him. There was still a devil of a woman to deal with, three kingdoms to settle, and peace to restore to Lucem.

"Zryan, call the servants. We need to get Travion to his chambers." Draven pulled back from Eden a little, his hand cupping her cheek. "And you into bed."

"I'm fine—"

"No," he interrupted. "You need rest."

"So do you." She gave him a firm look.

"Kings rest when the battle is over," was all that he said.

Rising to his feet, Draven grit his teeth at the internal protest of his body. He needed a great deal more blood to heal the injuries Naya had inflicted on him, but that would have to come later.

Zryan, who was still standing naked in the chamber, had shouted for servants as well as guards. Soon enough, men arrived to carefully collect Travion. Not even a grunt escaped his lips as he was moved.

"See to it that the palace healer is called in for him," Zryan instructed as they began to carry him out.

"Of course, Your Majesty."

Eden was still at Draven's side, and he could tell that she didn't wish to leave him. "Go," he stated softly. "Zryan and I will handle the rest."

"Very well, but please . . . don't overtax yourself."

Draven merely cupped her cheek in response. He could promise her nothing. "Please take Lady Eden to a guest chamber to rest, and fetch her clean clothes," he said to a servant nearby. "I'm sure Lady Sereia has left clothing somewhere amongst Travion's things."

The servant bowed slightly and led the reluctant Eden from the room. With her gone, Draven stepped up to Zryan, who was watching a couple of soldiers gather the still mostly incoherent Naya and lead her from the room.

Draven watched her go, wanting very much to slowly peel the flesh from her body, then heal her with his blood just so that he could begin the process over again. If given the chance, he'd do that until he'd taken every piece of flesh from her to make up for all the lives lost in this fiasco.

"We can't kill her yet," he muttered, having to remind himself. Draven placed a hand to his stomach, pressing against the fresh wave of pain radiating through him.

"Once we've dealt with all of this nonsense, we can." Zryan glanced around. "Where did The Creaturae go?"

Draven turned his head to look about the room, a deeper frown forming. Slowly walking the perimeter of the room, he found nothing. Looking over at his brother, Draven found Zryan's face pinched with a similar frown.

"She had it when I knocked her down . . . t should be right where you're standing."

Turning on the spot, Draven hurried to the edge of the room, stepping into one of the arched alcoves that led to the servant's passageway, which ran along the outside of the room. There was no one in the wings, just a lingering scent that was both familiar and unrecognizable all at once.

From inside the room, he heard Zryan calling for the palace guards, giving them orders to seal up the castle and search everyone for a leather-bound book.

Draven stepped back into the main throne room, his eyes meeting Zryan's. "It's gone. How?"

"If Naya had a partner, the guards will hunt them down. This is not over."

Draven cursed. The book had just been here. They *had* it back. But with Naya . . . healing Travion . . . who would have noticed someone else stealing in to take the book?

"Why am I not surprised to find you naked, even now, in the midst of battle?" a voice asked from behind them.

Both men turned to see Alessia standing in the archway, a tall harpy just behind her. Stepping into the room, Alessia scanned Zryan over before her eyes turned to Draven. Ailith moved from behind the queen, her taloned feet clicking lightly on the stone floor.

"I was a manticore," Zryan stated proudly, by way of explanation.

Still holding on to his stomach, Draven moved up to Ailith. "Lucem?"

"Mostly contained, sire. But with the complete darkness, we cannot be sure we've hunted down all of the creatures. Those that did remain seem to only be growing more bloodthirsty by the minute. The princess has the palace and most of the capital secured. I've left Captain Hannelore and Captain Channon closer to the Veil to aid the princes in continuing the search, but—"

"But they need the sun back." Draven looked to Zryan and Alessia, who had torn one of the long red drapes out of the window to toss at her husband.

Busy wrapping the piece of velvet around himself, Zryan glanced over quickly, then dropped his attention back to his hips. "Do any of us know what spell was used to douse Lucem in darkness?"

"No. I've never seen anything like that. Not since Ludari's reign of terror," Alessia responded with distaste.

"Good thing we kept the wench alive," Zryan stated cheerfully. Finished tying the drape around himself, he rested his hands triumphantly on his hips.

"She's not going to simply hand over the information willingly, you fool." Alessia's lip curled.

Draven looked at Alessia, face darkening. "Then we make her. But first, I need blood."

The book had not been found. After a thorough search of the castle, through every hiding place Travion's captain of the guard could think to look, they had come up empty handed. Whomever had been in the servants' corridors outside of the throne room had managed to not only slip in undetected but to leave as if they had never been there.

It left a foul taste in the back of Draven's mouth. The Creaturae was not something they wanted out there in the world, in the hands of a foreign enemy. For now, however, they would concentrate on the thing that they could control, and that was Naya Damaris.

Draven had found three who were willing to give him blood, though it wasn't enough to fully heal the damage that had been done to him internally. With or without the blood, the healing process was going to take a while. But it took the sharp sting of the pain away, leaving only an ache that he could look past.

Once again gathered in the throne room, they waited for the guards to bring Naya up from the dungeons. Eden had been called to join them, and she now stood looking a little lost. Draven felt himself drawn to her side, and his arm slipped around her. He pressed his hand to the small of her back.

"You don't have to be here if you don't wish to be. We may be required to do things to get your mother to talk that you shouldn't see." Draven saw no point in hiding their intentions.

"No, I need to be here."

He merely nodded in understanding; Eden did not balk at tough situations. She no longer ran when she was afraid but faced that fear head-on. Feeling pride at the thought of it, Draven kept himself close to her side as the guards ushered Naya back in before them. Her hands were cuffed and chained together behind her back. Even in irons, her chin remained lifted with defiant pride.

"Naya Damaris, you have committed treason against all three realms," Zryan began. "Death is on your horizon. However, if you tell us how to bring the sun back to Lucem, perhaps we can be persuaded to be lenient with you."

Naya didn't bother to even acknowledge Zryan. Instead, her eyes bored into Draven, staring at him so close to her daughter, an angry tick at the corner of her lips.

"Lucem will remain plunged in darkness until I see fit to lift the curse. Kill me if you wish, but you shall never be free of it." Her tone was even and without fear.

It made Draven's eyes narrow. Naya did not seem concerned with her own fate, nor that of any of the innocents that lived in Lucem whom she had sentenced to a vicious death by beasts.

"We have ways to make you talk," Zryan stated, then motioned to Alessia, who smirked at the thought of being able to unleash her abilities on the other woman.

Naya stiffened mildly but still did not pay her king and queen any mind. Instead, her unblinking gaze never left Draven. That was, until his arm shifted once more to lift from Eden's back and rest on her opposite hip instead.

The woman's eyes dropped to watch the movement while her lips thinned out. Draven could tell she wished to speak, wanted to tell him to take his hand off her daughter and step away from her.

Suddenly, Draven was behind Eden, his arm wrapping around her body to pin her arms to her sides and his free hand gripping her hair. He pulled her head to the side, exposing her throat. Over Eden's shoulder, he locked eyes with Naya.

"Tell us, Naya, or I will take Eden back to Andhera with me, and you will never see her again," he growled lowly.

Alessia halted, leaving Draven to play out his threat.

Though she paled, Naya remained firm in her stance. "I will always find my way back to my daughter. I will always get her home where she belongs."

"Do you truly think you can take her back if you are in prison?" Draven brushed his lips along Eden's throat, his eyes staying on Naya. In his arms, Eden shuddered; while it may have looked as if it were from revulsion, he could feel Eden's emotions in the back of his mind. She was not frightened of him.

"I will never give up," Naya insisted coldly.

"You will if I make it so that she can never return." Slowly Draven's face split with a cold smirk, his blue eyes glinting with a darkness that was often only seen by those about to be slain. Naya blanched beneath it, swallowing roughly.

"What—"

"She's already had a little of my blood. Did she tell you that?" He pressed another kiss to her throat, his hand sliding down over her stomach possessively. "If I take hers, and replace it with more of my own, she will be one with me. One with the night." Without hesitation, Draven bit into Eden's throat.

At the sensation, Eden whimpered, a sound of fear and pain, her hand lifting to clutch his wrist. "No," she gasped out.

Naya visibly jerked, held back only by the guards holding on to her chains.

"You beast! Unhand my daughter now!"

Draven made a show of feeding from Eden, when in actuality he had already retracted his fangs and lapped the holes clean. But Eden, willing to follow his lead, began to slump in his arms, relying on him to hold her weight.

Seeing her daughter visibly wilting before her, Naya unleashed an animalistic howl, struggling against the chains that bound her.

"Enough. *Enough!*"

Draven lifted his head and flashed her a bloody smile. "Do you have something to say?" He wrapped his lips around Eden's throat once more, growling in a sound of blissful bloodlust as he did so.

"Yes! Just stop." Still struggling, Naya released a sob of despair. "I'll tell you. Just don't turn my daughter into an abomination!"

Keeping his mouth on her, Draven lifted a brow at Naya, indicating she could continue.

Naya's eyes never left the space where his lips were fastened onto her daughter. "There is a talisman in my study. A brass medallion hung on a chain. It has a raven etched into the front of it. You need only destroy it. *Now for the love of the sun, stop!*"

Draven finally lifted his lips from Eden's throat but kept his arms around her, holding her back against his chest. Eden didn't move much, leaving her weight leaned back into him, but her head lifted, and she peered back at her mother.

"You better not have lied," she stated firmly.

Naya blinked in confusion, her frantic struggles ceasing as she looked at her fully responsive daughter. Draven watched Naya's eyes drop to Eden's throat, then lift up to meet his eyes before they returned to Eden's face.

"Wh-what?" she stammered.

"Return her to the dungeons," Draven ordered the guards. "And Naya, if you're found to be lying, I swear you have never known wrath until you've seen mine. I vow Eden *will* become a vampire, and I will make certain you are there to watch the entire process."

Naya released a shriek as the guards pulled her from the throne room. Draven released Eden, allowing her to step back into her own personal space. Their eyes locked for a moment before both looked away.

"Shall Alessia and I see to this? If Naya was telling the truth, we don't need you burning to a crisp." Zryan's eyes dropped to Draven's torso.

"Yes. I've had enough sunlight for today."

Eden

The last thing Eden wanted to do was sleep while others battled, but she had nothing left to give, and without her magic, she was nearly useless. Unable to beckon the flora to her, Eden would only serve as a distraction and endanger Draven. And the paltry moves she'd picked up during her combat training would not serve her well against a manticore.

Her back ached, but luckily, one of the servants in the castle could heal too. Eden had suffered a stab wound in the back, but she'd been so focused on everyone else and on simply surviving that it had nearly been forgotten.

Once she was cleaned, healed, and changed, she nestled into an oversized bed. She was assured the palace healer was tending to Travion, and without the constant influx of adrenaline coursing through her, Eden gave in to the heavy pull of exhaustion.

There had been hope within Eden when she had awakened that everything would turn out to be a dream. But unfortunately, it was reality. As her mother stood before her, she found herself wishing that she was still asleep. Despite the grogginess tugging at her, the adrenaline coursing through her once more roused her enough to keep her very much awake.

Naya lifted her chin, clearly unrepentant. With one assessing glance at her mother, Eden knew she was determined to defy them and would gladly die for her cause.

What would make her rethink it? she wondered as she listened to them speak. But when Draven shifted his hand, Eden knew at once he'd found a vulnerability to expose. No matter what had passed between them, Eden trusted Draven with her life.

She gasped as he pinned her arms down, straining against his hold to bring the playact home. When he exposed her neck, the shudder that wracked her body wasn't a farce, but it also wasn't done out of fear. Every inch of her flesh knew him, and the last time his lips had been against her neck had been in her bed.

If playing along would make her mother speak, so be it. Eden only needed to follow Draven's cues, which he guided her through.

A part of Eden detested the trickery, but seeing as how her mother had left them no choice, it was the only way. Since Naya didn't believe her daughter could possibly come to love the king of nightmares, it made it all the easier. Although it wasn't easy on Eden, not as the scent of Draven invaded her senses, his hands on her body and his lips secured to her neck.

It was the slumping in his arms that finally sent her mother over the edge. Eden could almost feel her hysteria mounting before she burst with the information. If she was lying . . . Eden would have to rethink allowing Alessia to tamper with her mother's mind.

"Eden! Eden!" her mother howled the entire way out of the throne room.

When Draven relinquished his hold on her, she longed to say something and yet didn't. With the moment gone, she averted her eyes, then glanced toward Zryan. "The medallion," she murmured. "I saw it in the study when I was there. I didn't think anything of it." Eden shook her head. If she'd known . . . "It's hanging on the third shelf in a glass display on the far side of the room. At least, that's where it was last." Eden flinched, recalling how her mother had thrust her against the wall without a care. "Wait. While you're there, go to my room and find Drizz—he's my goblin friend."

Alessia lifted an eyebrow. "Thank you, Eden. I will retrieve your friend for you." She inclined her head toward her husband. "Let's get this done. Mind your skirt on the doorknobs, Zryan." She leveled him with a look, then winked before strolling out of the room.

Left alone with Draven, Eden fidgeted in the strained silence, until finally she couldn't bear it any longer. "How did you know she'd bend?"

He lifted a hand and picked at his thumbnail. "Because you are what she holds most dear." Draven's blue eyes settled on her, not entirely free of the wall he often put in place. "And when people are desperate to protect the ones they cherish, they're willing to do anything to ensure their safety."

Eden turned, facing him. She kept her hands at her side, not trusting that she wouldn't continue to fidget beneath his gaze. There was far too much between them that had gone unsaid, and now alone with one another, Eden felt the weight of it.

"Draven, I . . . "

"We don't need to do this now." His expression said he would prefer it *wasn't* now, but Eden knew better than to let the moment slip away. Draven had a way of retreating far into himself, and she knew there was a point at which she wouldn't be able to reach him. It was now or possibly never.

"We do," she started, then rushed into her next words. "I said things I never should have, and I need to apologize for that." Eden's shoulders slumped forward, but her eyes never left his. "Draven, you're the most selfless person that I know, and to say otherwise is simply a lie." She chewed the inside of her cheek and shook her head. "You've been nothing but honest with me all along, so to call you manipulative was simply cruel." With her hands spread out, indicating to the throne room, Eden sighed. "For my words, I'm sorry. And for all of this. I wish I could have stopped it . . . that I'd known . . . "

"You had nothing to do with this. Don't apologize for the evil your mother has done, and don't for one moment let her deeds taint you." Draven closed the distance between them in two strides. He lifted his hand to brush back her hair, then tilted her head back. The shaky walls he held up crumbled in an instant as his head dipped forward and he pressed his forehead against hers. "Eden, you have been my greatest comfort. My wish was to keep you *safe*, because if I lost that, don't think for one moment I wouldn't tear the world apart as punishment." His lips tilted at the corners in a subtle smile. One that was wholly for Eden.

Her heart fluttered in response to his words, to the smile, to the earnest expression in his eyes.

"Excuse me," a voice came from behind them. "His Majesty is requesting Lady Eden's presence."

Both Eden and Draven twisted to look at the intruder, who seemed to notice his presence was very much unwanted. He quickly bowed and dipped out of the room.

"We are not done," Draven murmured, then claimed her lips in a firm, drawn-out kiss that ignited Eden's bones.

Reluctantly, she pulled away from him. Eden nodded, touching her fingers to her lips. There was hope blossoming in her chest that this wasn't the end and that they wouldn't part for good. "No, we're not," she finally said, then left the room.

By the time Eden reached the king's quarters, Travion had fallen asleep again. With no healer in the room with him, she eased the blankets down from his chest and examined the healed wounds. A nasty scar would remain from his shoulder all the way to his hip. Eden grimaced as her fingers spread across his abdomen. *Mend*, she thought. There was little power in her, but what she possessed from the hour of rest she gave to Travion.

Whatever her mother's punishment would be, Eden would make sure it was befitting of the crimes she'd committed in all of the realms. For Travion, Draven, and Zryan. For all the realms' sakes.

When Travion woke, he jolted from the bed and immediately groaned in protest. No doubt his muscles ached from being stitched back together.

"Easy," Eden murmured, gently pressing on his good shoulder, and was met with a grumble. Travion's furrowed brow and mutterings made her think of Draven, which brought a wave of complex feelings to the surface. Every time she looked down at Travion, it was as if she were seeing Draven in a similar position. "We have worked very hard on you. It'd be a shame to put that all to waste." Eden lifted an eyebrow as she lightly reprimanded him. "How are you feeling?"

Travion's eyes raked over her face, then her clothing. An unreadable expression clouded his gaze as he settled against the mound of pillows. "I'm not dead."

Eden squinted. "Besides that?"

"That's all I've got." He chuckled, then promptly winced. "It feels like my innards were used to tie an anchor hitch. Is that better?"

Eden pinched her nose and shook her head. "No. I'm sorry I can't do more—"

"No, Eden. Don't apologize. You've done more than enough." Travion reached for her hand and squeezed it. "You saved my life, and I owe a great debt to you." He drew it toward his mouth and laid a soft kiss to her knuckles. "For one who was so haphazardly tossed into chaos, you have done exceedingly well." A tired, lopsided smile touched his lips. "For what it's worth, I think you are what this family needs, what *my brother* needs."

Eden smiled at his words, squeezed his hand, and opened her mouth to reply, but the sound of approaching footsteps stopped her.

A moment later, Alessia entered the room, golden cheeks flushed. "It worked. The talisman has been broken, and the sun is returning to the sky." Her dark eyes shifted toward Travion and Eden. "Your friend is in the kitchens eating everything in sight."

Oh, Drizz. He must have been terrified and hungry. Then Eden stilled. The sun had returned to the sky—the spell had been broken. Relief flooded her, but also dread for what was to come.

Travion gritted his teeth. "Then bring the witch in here. I'm not missing her judgment."

Eden remained quiet as Alessia left. Her mother's punishment drew near, and although she knew that Naya Damaris deserved whatever they deemed fit, she was still her mother. Albeit a twisted version of the woman she once was, but she was still the same flesh and blood that Eden possessed.

The quiet was disrupted as Zryan strode into the bedchamber, still wearing his drapes as a robe. He grinned widely as he stood next to the head of the bed. "You're awake. You slept through the best part of it all."

"I wasn't sleeping," Travion bit out.

"Right, laying in a pool of blood and *resting your eyes.*" Zryan winked. His dark brows lifted as if he were waiting for something.

Travion narrowed his eyes. "No."

"Yes. Come now." Zryan waited patiently.

Perplexed by the exchange, Eden watched them until Alessia entered the room again.

Travion shifted his jaw, shaking his head as he stared up at the ceiling. "Thank you for saving my life, Zryan." The words had barely left his lips when Zryan bent down to half embrace his brother.

Out of everything thus far, this was what broke the dam of Eden's tears. She swiped away the trail as quickly as they formed. If Zryan hadn't been there . . . both of his brothers would be dead.

The tension in the room surged the moment Draven and Naya entered. Guards flanked her as she came to stand at the end of the bed. The royals, including Eden, remained at the head of it, staring Naya Damaris down.

Despite his current state, Travion stubbornly willed himself to sit upright. Even Eden could tell it pained him. "Naya Damaris, your crimes are impressive. You've committed treason against your sovereigns, nearly committed regicide twice over, and in unleashing your hordes in Lucem as well as Midniva, you've slaughtered countless innocents. What have you to say for yourself?"

"I am not sorry. You're all wretched, all of you. My crimes pale in comparison to those of *King Zryan*." She spat her words. "Sending my Lelantos to his death, stealing Eden from me. What of *these* crimes?"

"We are not judging Zryan," Travion bit out.

"And it is no excuse to turn around and kill hundreds of people!" Eden leaned forward as tension coiled within, ready to spring forth. How could her mother still excuse her actions? "Papa would be ashamed of you and what you've done. You know that." Eden's tone remained crisp and cool.

Naya flinched at her words as they hit their mark, and her bottom lip quivered. "Eden I . . . "

Eden lifted a hand to silence her mother. "No. You are not here to beg us for forgiveness or plead your case. You are here to receive your punishment." Eden glanced in Draven's direction. He cocked his head, and his brows dipped inward in question, but when she looked back at her mother, and Naya still wore the face of defiance, Eden settled on a growing idea.

Death was too kind.

Death was too swift.

Death was a reward.

"I know it isn't up to me to decide, but I offer up my opinion to Your Majesties that Naya Damaris doesn't receive a punishment of death."

At once, all eyes were on Eden. Draven's anger rose within her, but he was quiet, waiting for an explanation, waiting for Eden to continue.

"You would let her live?" Alessia scoffed.

Travion, not so quietly, swore a blue streak but waved Eden on. "As you were."

Rightfully, they were all upset, but a dismissal of her mother's crimes was never the intention. Eden believed she deserved a punishment most befitting of the crimes she'd committed and the stain she'd left on each realm.

"For tormenting Andhera, Midniva, and Lucem, I bring forth the motion to imprison you indefinitely. Trapped by iron and mind. To live in the prison of chaos you thought to unleash on the realms." Eden lifted her chin, watching as her mother's face hardened into a scowl. Gone was her caring mother. No doubt she now saw Eden as in league with the royals. To her mother, Eden was likely as monstrous as the rest.

"Death is too swift, too kind of a punishment," Eden added.

"I must say, I wasn't expecting that," Travion offered. "But I agree." He paused for a moment, then, "It seems, Naya, that Andhera has done your daughter well, and she isn't as weak as you thought."

Eden glanced down at Travion, catching his blue gaze, which was so familiar and yet not. In his eyes, beyond the hardness, there was a playful glint.

"What say all of you? An indefinite imprisonment of mind and body?" Travion posed the question to the room.

Eden shifted her gaze from Travion to Draven. She could feel the war within her, the one he battled. He'd want blood for blood, flesh for flesh, and even doling the punishment out himself, it didn't seem equal to what a mental punishment could inflict on her.

After a pause, Draven shifted from his rigid stance. "I was picturing a slow, torturous death, but I suppose an unrelenting mental torture would be fitting."

Zryan chuckled behind Eden. "Well, darling, what do you say?"

A dark smile tugged at Alessia's lips as she stared intently at Naya. "I will gladly do it." She turned to look over at her husband. "And I have just the punishment in mind."

That was it. It was over . . . at least for now. But with the book missing, Eden wondered how long it would be until they faced a similar situation—or worse.

Draven

I t wasn't exactly what he wanted. Not being able to inflict the punishment himself grated even further, but Draven could accept it. Especially since it was one that Eden herself had chosen.

"Don't take her down yet," he commanded the guards.

Feeling the eyes of the room on him, Draven ignored them as he stepped up to Naya. Grasping her wrist, he pulled her arm up near his mouth. The woman struggled, eyes widening with uncertainty.

"I will not give you the opportunity to lie about this," he growled, then bit into the vein in her arm.

Draven sorted through her memories as the blood flowed from her wrist. Searching through the images, he growled at a memory of her locking Eden up and wished, not for the first time, that he were able to extract his pound of flesh. The look of betrayal on Eden's face at what her mother had done hardened his heart, while the echoes of her begging and pleading mirrored the ones Draven himself had caused, sending a wave of guilt through him. Forcing himself away from those flashes of thought, he sorted through all the memories of her plots and plans, searching for familiar faces.

When he pulled away, Draven bore a deep frown on his features. Capala had not been among the many faces in her mind. He now knew who she had really been dealing with in Andhera to help spread the madness. Draven had been led purposefully in the wrong direction to stir up chaos and dissension amongst his nobles.

He had killed the wrong man.

Dropping Naya's hand, Draven waved the guards off. Pressing a hand to his brow, he wondered how he was supposed to atone for this. Esruiit was right; he had thought himself infallible. "Take her away," he rasped to the guards.

Watching her being led from the room, Draven fought to keep his emotions in check. His head lifted to take in Alessia as she stopped to place a hand on his shoulder.

"Is everything all right, brother?"

Draven's face hardened as he contained his emotions, and he nodded. "Make sure whatever horror you instill in her mind, you make it a truly terrible one."

Alessia's face curved into a dark smirk. "You know me, Draven. I keep all the truly good ones for those who deserve it most." Her hand lifted from his shoulder to cup his face. "I'll give her a few twisted images specifically for you."

She then trailed after the guards, following Naya into the dungeon to dole out her specific brand of warped punishment. Zryan was not far behind.

"You can come and watch if you'd like," he suggested.

"No need. I trust you two to handle it."

Zryan nodded. "Why didn't you drink from her earlier? Why that whole charade?"

"I wanted to make her suffer." Call it him extracting his pound of flesh.

His brother chuckled, then before he slipped from the room, he looked back at Eden, who was bent over Travion once more, fussing with his wound. "The two of you are going to make peace, correct? Don't let a foolish disagreement stand between you, Draven. There is no easier time to make it right than right after it's happened. Time . . . "does not heal all wounds."

Not waiting for an answer, Zryan stepped out and continued on the same path as his wife.

Sighing, Draven took a moment to gaze over at Eden and Travion. Could an apology make it better? Solve all the issues facing them? Eden was all of the things Draven didn't realize he'd needed in his life, until suddenly she'd been there, bringing him love and acceptance. Who could have imagined a sweet fae from Lucem would be the one able to look past the monstrous casing created by thousands of years of rumors and gossip, and see instead the man? He wanted nothing more than to bring her back to Andhera with him, to make her his queen and keep her tucked safely by his side for all the rest of their days.

She had said she loved him, and there was no denying his love for her, no matter how he had tried.

But was love enough to protect them from all that still remained to be dealt with in Andhera? What of the change that would come over her? Draven was still determined to leave Eden untampered with. He wanted her to remain fae, to be able to cross into Lucem when she desired the sunlight on her skin. That would require her spending only six months in Andhera at a time and leaving before it had a chance to settle within her. Could they make such a life work?

And what of his people? What would they think of their king when the truth of his misjudgment was made known?

Unable to control his own convoluted thoughts, he stepped from the room and out into the hall. Moving to lean against the wall, Draven pinched the bridge of his nose. He would need to make reparations to Capala's family and do something to show to all of his people that he took it very seriously that he had erred in such a way.

Andhera was built on the foundation of a life for a life . . . "That did not exclude him, king or not.

"Draven?"

He glanced to the side at the sound of Eden's soft voice. There was concern in her eyes as she looked up at him.

"Is everything all right?"

His reflex was to tell her everything was fine, that there was nothing for her to be concerned about. But Eden didn't need to be coddled. She had proven herself more than strong enough to handle whatever the world sent her way. So instead, Draven allowed himself to reach for her hand so that he could pull her into him. Wrapping his arms around her, he simply held her for a moment, finding relief in the knowledge that she was safe. The darkness had not taken her, nor had her insane mother.

"Lord Capala was not involved in the forming of hives in Midniva," he rasped softly into her hair. "Your mother set him up in order to set me up, so that I would execute the wrong man and feed into the unrest."

Eden made a muffled noise of distress, and he could feel

the upset brimming in her at further knowledge of her mother's crimes.

She lifted her head, green eyes studying his. "What does this mean for you?"

Draven sighed and shook his head. "I don't know yet. I have to make amends somehow. We have laws even I am not immune to."

"Draven . . . "

"I took the life of an innocent vampire and his son, Eden. I must atone for that in some manner. I cannot hold my people to an expectation that I am not also bound by."

She nodded, though the frown remained. "You don't have to face this alone."

Draven lifted his hand to cup her cheek, his thumb brushing lightly over her satin skin. "Did you mean it?" he asked. "When you said that Andhera was where you wished to be? Because I spoke the truth when I said I would never force you to remain at my side . . . "especially now that the Damaris family home will be in your control. You can live whatever life you choose now in Lucem."

His need to have her return with him to Andhera was so great that he was certain she could feel it zinging through her own blood. He didn't have the answers for how any of this would work, but he was done telling Eden what she should do. She would decide where she wanted to be.

"Draven," she grumbled with frustration. "Have you not listened to anything I've said? Can you not *feel* it within you?"

He could, even though it was hard to allow himself to trust in it. Instead of responding right away, Draven dipped his head to kiss her, tasting the love there on her lips.

Feeling the way her body melded obediently into his own, as if there was no other place she would rather be than pressed against him.

"I am sorry I forced you away. I wanted nothing but to protect you from the dangers that were growing, and in that need to do so, I failed to listen to your wishes. I never wanted to be another person in your life who silenced you and shut you away." Draven closed his eyes in remembrance. He had understood why she was upset, as well as the words she had spoken to him in anger.

It was Eden who initiated the next kiss, pulling a soft moan from Draven's lips as he felt the emotions swelling up in him. This time, she was honey and yearning. He felt the deep need to reconnect and bury whatever hurt lay between them.

"I know, Draven. I do."

Their lips connected once more, and Draven's arms wrapped tightly around her, lifting her off her feet as he ignored the protests of his own body and allowed himself to drift off into the peace Eden brought to him.

"Do you know that the first time I saw you in that garden, I thought your smile was like the very sun itself, and I longed for nothing more than to bottle it up so that I might feel its rays in the darkness of my hall?" he whispered, fingers threading through her hair and forehead pressed to hers. "Eden, if I have made you think for one moment that I do not love you, I apologize."

Her breath hitched a little at his words, and her eyes remained unblinking upon his own.

"I want nothing more than for you to return with me, for you take up your place by my side and bring your light eternally into my days."

Eden smiled softly up at him, teeth biting at her bottom lip a little before it fully broke out into a broader grin. "Draven, are you saying that you wish for me to be your queen?" There was a teasing but hopeful sheen to her eyes.

"Yes," he responded in all seriousness. "We can figure out a way to keep Andhera from transforming you, whatever it takes to keep you yourself. But I do not want to live the rest of my days in that darkness without you by my side." He was done resisting it. If it was what Eden wanted, then together, they could make a union between them work. "You have already proven yourself Andhera's queen."

Eden's laughter was a burst of happiness to his own heart, and as her arms slid around his neck and she responded by kissing him once more, Draven knew that he did not deserve such a beautiful fae as her in his life. But he would do whatever was necessary to make certain she never had reason to regret her decision to stand at his side.

"There is still so much to be done." Eden sighed from the security of his arms as she drew back just a fraction to rest her head on his shoulder.

It was true. Before they could even consider a proper union between them, much had to be done, and each realm needed time to heal in its own way after this ordeal.

Draven nodded, dipping his head to press a kiss to the end of her nose. "There is. But we will do it together."

Epilogue

Draven

"We have to move faster," Draven shouted over the roar of flames, grasping Eden's hand tightly.

He could feel the heat of the fire on his cheeks, and his skin threatened to sizzle along with it. Draven feared what this could mean for Eden and pulled her more closely to him, hoping to shield her from the heat.

"Where has Zryan gone?" Travion shouted from beside them, his words stunted from the exertion of running.

Draven stopped, a new sense of fear gripping him. Where *had* Zryan gone? He'd been right behind them. Draven had promised he would get them out of this, that he would not fail them. But where had they lost Zryan in their mad dash away from the castle?

A thunderous sound shook the very earth they stood on, and only his tight arm around her waist kept Eden from falling. Looking back the way they'd come, Draven found to his horror the gigantic form of his father cresting the hill. The furious face was much like his own, only more rigid and worn. In his large fist, he held Zryan, his body already slack and lifeless.

There was a roar of fury, one which Draven thought for a moment had come from himself, only to realize that it was coming from Travion. Putting out his hand to stop him, Draven could do nothing but watch as his brother drew his sword and charged at the giant form of their father.

He wasn't sure how he knew, but Draven was sure if he allowed him to do this, Travion was going to die too. Turning back to Eden, he clasped her arms firmly. "You have to stay here. Do you hear me?"

"But I can help!"

"No! Stay here, *please.*" He wanted to kiss her, but there was no time.

Leaving Eden behind, Draven raced over the rocky ground, avoiding the flames that were only growing more intense. He chased after Travion, who was hell-bent on facing Ludari. He didn't make it in time. Instead, Zryan's lifeless body collided with his own, sending them both careening into the flames.

Fire licked at him, lighting his clothes with hungry orange fingers. Scrambling away from the flames, Draven dragged Zryan's form along with him and watched in horror as Travion was swept up by the hand of Ludari. Before his brother could react, the fierce tyrant brought him to his mouth and bit him clean in half.

Draven could feel the raw edge of the scream tearing from his throat as he was helpless to do anything to stop it. Forced to abandon Zryan's lifeless form, Draven staggered to his feet and only then realized that Eden had disappeared.

Spinning on his heels, he called out for her, ignoring the thunderous steps of his father approaching.

"Eden!" he shouted. "Eden, where are you?!"

She was gone. No matter where he turned, he could not find her amongst the flames lapping away his kingdom.

"Eden?" Was that her voice he had just heard, calling over the roar? A scream, piercing the darkness illuminated by the flames. "Eden!"

As the flames drew nearer, and Ludari approached from behind, Draven's eyes locked on the horizon before him just as the sun began to dawn in Andhera for the very first time.

"H-how . . . " Draven found himself rooted to the spot as the sun's rays washed over the land, and he was captured in a world of pain and torture as the sunshine began to eat away at the flesh of his face and hands. Behind him, the fire licked at his ankles.

There was no point. He could go no farther. His end would be met here in the light of the sun or at the hungry maw of the flame.

Draven sank to his knees, letting himself drown in the pain as it consumed him. This was how he ought to go. This was the fate he deserved. Turning his face up into the sunlight, Draven grit his teeth and gave into the approaching death.

But Eden's voice was there again, sounding out over everything else. Calling to him. Begging for him to find her.

Draven began to crawl his way over the earth, forcing himself through the flames, breathing in the heat that singed his insides and burnt them away just as the sunshine overhead tore at the flesh now bare from the fire. Fingers clawed at the earth, bending nails back in his fight to keep crawling, keep moving in the direction of that sweet voice beckoning to him.

If she were still alive . . . "If he had not yet lost her, there was a reason to keep going.

When Draven finally staggered out of the mouth of Sollicitus Cave, his clothing was muddied and torn, but intact. He felt as if his flesh had been peeled from his bones and hastily stitched back on, leaving him exposed and raw. But he also felt unburdened. In the rawness of the pain, there was now room for fresh growth.

Eden was there, anxiously waiting, and as he cleared the stone and stepped out into the bright moonlight, she ran to him. Draven wrapped his aching arms around her and buried his face in her neck.

"Are you okay?" he heard her whisper. "The screams coming from the cave . . . "By the sun, Draven. I thought you would never come out."

Draven pulled back enough that he was able to lift his hands to cup her face, looking down into the concerned eyes that greeted his. "I promise that I am okay," he rasped wearily. His body, mind, and soul had been scoured by the powers of the Sollictus Cave, but he would be okay. His debt had been paid. "I'm sorry that I gave you cause to worry."

They shared a kiss, one filled with great relief and promise. With Eden ever there to brighten his path, he could find relief from anything.

Slipping his arm around her waist, Draven turned to the others that stood there, waiting for him. Lord Esuriit stood alongside Capala's widow, the two, while not smiling, looked vindicated at least. Draven nodded to them and received a bow of their heads in return.

As a group, they took the stone steps that led back up to the castle grounds from where Sollictus sat, nestled at the mouth of the great black pit.

It was not rest nor a warm goblet of blood that awaited Draven at the entrance to his castle but Travion. Seeing him standing there was like a sudden punch to his abdomen, the image of his brother being bitten in two still fresh in his mind.

"Travion, what brings you here?" Draven asked, his arm tight about Eden, keeping her tucked into his side.

"I wish I came bearing good news, but I am afraid that is not the case." Travion looked him over, frowning as he took in Draven's haggard appearance. "But perhaps now is not the time."

"No, go on," Draven prodded as they stepped into the candlelit hallways of Aasha Castle.

"Reports have been coming to me of large sea creatures attacking and sinking ships all along the eastern coast and into Tribonik. I believe this to be the work of whoever stole The Creaturae."

Draven halted in his steps, eyes locking with Travion's. "Do you plan to go looking for it?"

Travion offered a grim smile. "If things continue this way, I fear I might have to."

ACKNOWLEDGMENTS

Firstly, we want to thank every Hades and Persephone fan that picked up this retelling to give our version a try. We hope that you enjoyed reading about Eden and Draven's love blooming in Andhera as much as we enjoyed writing it. Being huge admirers of Greek mythology ourselves, this book was a labor of love. The first draft was written in just two months. Neither of us was able to step away until the tale had been told.

None of this would have come to fruition if it weren't for Candace Robinson encouraging us to write a vampire-related novel which inspired Elle to approach Tiss with the thought of a Hades and Persephone retelling. Thank you for the push, Candace!

Of course, a newly edited first draft is nothing without beta-readers. We couldn't have done it without our wonderful team, Lou and Candace, you two are gems! A final draft is also nothing without proofreaders, Tanya and Amber H., you're amazing! Thank you all so much for your help.

We also want to send out a massive thank you to our comma goblin, Meg Dailey! Without you, our novel would be a sad pile of misused commas, and missing semi-colons. You helped bring the proper inflection to our word, and we love you for it!

To the loyal Patreon supporters, Donna and Sanem, thank you for your support and believing in the various stories tumbling in our heads. You're the reason why we continue to write.

Lastly, we want to thank our friends and family who continue to push us toward our dreams. It's the unconditional support of our inner circles that help to keep us going. We started reaching for Andhera's moon with this story, and plan to keep going until we've grabbed Lucem's sun.

THE OFFICIAL PLAYLIST

Want to listen along while you read and immerse yourself into the world of Seeds of Sorrow? Listen to the playlist below!

1. City of the Dead by Eurielle
2. Who Wants To Live Forever by Breaking Benjamin
3. Release Me by Crystal Skies Ft. Callie Fisher
4. Fallen Angel by Three Days Grace
5. Wake Me Up by Tommee Profitt Ft. Fleurie
6. Iris by Kina Grannis
7. Come Away To The Water by Maroon 5 Ft. Rozzi
8. Innocence by Nathan Wagner
9. Don't Fear The Reaper by Denmark + Winter
10. Monsters by Katie Sky

ABOUT ELLE BEAUMONT

 Elle Beaumont loves creating vivid and fantastical worlds. She lives in southeastern, Massachusetts with her husband and two children. When not writing or chasing around her children, she enjoys making candles. More than once she has proclaimed that coffee is the lifeblood and it is how she refrains from becoming a zombie.

Stay up to date and receive some free books by signing up for her newsletter! ellebeaumontbooks.com/newsletter

Join Elle's Facebook group and hang out with her
facebook.com/groups/ElleBeaumontStreetTeam

For more information visit
www.ellebeaumontbooks.com
Follow Elle on social media!

f facebook.com/ellebeaumontbooks
⊙ instagram.com/ellebeaumontbooks

MORE FROM ELLE

Standalones

Die From A Broken Heart

The Dragon's Bride

The Castle of Thorns

Demons of Frosteria

Frost Mate

Frost Claim (Oct '22)

Immortal Realms Trilogy

Seeds of Sorrow

Tides of Torment (June '23)

The Hunter Series

Hunter's Truce

Royal's Vow

Assassin's Gambit

Queen's Edge

Secrets of Galathea

Brotherhood of the Sea

Bindings of the Sea

Voice of the Sea

King of the Sea

Anthologies

Link by Link

Something in the Shadows

Stories for Nerds Vol. 1

Beyond the Cogs

Emporium of Superstition (Oct '22)

ABOUT CHRISTIS CHRISTIE

 Christis Christie lives on the east coast of Canada, in Nova Scotia. She gets most excited about diving into a new fantasy world while writing, but also loves a good supernatural plot. Tiss, as she is affectionately called by her friends, enjoys being creative in any way she can, so if she's not writing then she's crocheting or she's embroidering. Her favorite animal is the sloth, and her favorite retellings are anything Beauty and the Beast related.

Follow Christis on social media!

f facebook.com/ChristisChristieWrites
⃝ instagram.com/tiss.writes

MORE FROM CHRISTIS

Standalones

Spun Gold

The Dragon's Bride

Immortal Realms Trilogy

Seeds of Sorrow

Tides of Torment (June '23)

Reaping Series

Ephesus

Anthologies

Something in the Shadows

Emporium of Superstition (coming Oct '22)

SNEAK PEAK!

Continue reading for the first chapter of The Dragon's Bride by Christis Christie & Elle Beaumont!

IMARA

With a slight press of the blade tied to her belt, the stem of the witch hazel snapped between her fingers, coming away from the body of the plant to be placed in the small pile in her lap. Overhead, the sun shone down upon her shoulders with an almost blistering heat—unobscured by even the smallest of clouds. Imara couldn't remember the last time the noonday sun had been pleasant, rather than a sweltering force to abide, the days trying to hold on to the last dregs of a fading summer as fall approached.

"Oh, this won't do," she murmured to herself, examining the sprig, then the bush as a whole.

"What was that?" came a voice from over her shoulder.

Leaning back on her heels, Imara lifted her hand to brush the back of her wrist across her forehead, ending with a swipe of her fingers through the blond strands of hair at her temple, tucking them behind one delicately pointed ear. The grass-covered roof beneath her had seen better days. Where once thick, luscious green blades had grown, now yellow spiky strands fought to stay alive. What life was left in the soil had been driven toward the herbs and flowers Imara had planted several years ago, her father doing what he could to keep her garden alive.

"This witch hazel is dry as a bone. I don't know that I'll

get much more than this harvest out of it," she stated, glancing over at her sister currently struggling to draw water from the soil around the house, sprinkling it over the rooftop garden once it had gathered upon her fingertips in small, perfectly formed spheres.

Words hardly free of Imara's lips, a spray of water splashed over her face and down the front of her. "Asta, the garden, not my face!"

Imara shot an irritated glare at her sister, who released a giggle of surprise before offering an apologetic smile.

"I'm sorry, that wasn't intentional, I promise. I wasn't paying enough attention to where I was pointing," Asta explained, reaching out to brush a few drops of water from Imara's face. Collecting them with a soft tickle of magic upon her skin, she turned to sprinkle them over the bush of witch hazel.

"Fortunately, it was rather refreshing." Imara cast an accusatory glance toward the sun. Whatever relief could be found from its rays was welcomed.

Brushing a trickle of water along her own temples, Asta turned and plopped down at the edge of the roof, her feet braced where the roof became actual ground. "When do you expect Birger today?"

Clipping one last branch from the bush, Imara turned to sit beside Asta, her eyes drifting over their lands. Situated just a stone's throw away from the village of Omdahl, their little farm was immersed in a breathtaking landscape of rolling hills dappled with tall, branchy trees and split below by a winding river that reflected the blue skies above. The seidr had chosen this valley to settle in many moons ago due to the snow-capped mountains that loomed on either side, majestic giants of protection that graciously supplied fresh spring water to the village and its inhabitants. The valley had also been a land of opportunity, its soil rich and fertile—the perfect place for a people known to cherish the earth and all that she supplied to take root themselves.

Their family plot had been the ideal location for raising sheep and growing cotton—the supply for Dagny Hjelmstad's beautiful woven fabrics and tapestries. Erlend had seen in these fields everything he had hoped to give his new wife: the home, the opportunity, the prospering family. It was everything—until the rains stopped coming, the river began to dry up, and the soil turned to dust beneath their feet.

"He usually arrives about midday, once he has passed through Omdahl proper and spoken to anyone who has dealings with him there." Imara glanced down at the small pile of witch hazel in her lap—not nearly the offering she had hoped to have once he arrived but the best that she had to give.

Asta peered up at the sun, gauging the time by its position in the sky. "It's half past two, but is there time for a quick drink before we need to bundle and prepare that?" she asked, eyes flicking quickly to indicate the witch hazel.

Nodding slightly, Imara pulled up the corners of the blue apron-skirt layered over her green shift, containing all of the branches she had cut, and rose to her feet. Having been outdoors for some time now, a break from the sunshine was more than warranted by both.

"Yes, let's fetch ourselves some water and perhaps run some down to Father. He's been working in the fields since early this morning." Keeping the corners of her apron-skirt swept up, Imara walked off the roof and down the small bank to the front of their home, the curved white frame set just inside the hillside as familiar to her as her own self.

Toeing the partially opened door all the way, she stepped into their home. Her mother, Dagny, stood before a loom, a finger tapping idly upon her lips as she contemplated it. Moving easily to her side, Imara pressed a soft kiss to her cheek.

"It looks beautiful, Mother, as all your pieces do. Jorunn will love it," she murmured in passing, slipping by to deposit her collection of branches onto the table.

"Thank you, Mari," was her mother's contemplative response.

Behind her, Asta came into the house with a flourish of cotton skirts and the scent of spring rain, her elemental affinity so strong she wore it like a mantle upon herself. As Imara brushed a few lost yellow petals off her skirt, her sister got busy pouring them glasses of water from the tap in the wall.

"Is Father down in the western field today?" Imara asked, reaching for the clay goblet Asta held out to her. The fresh mountain water was crisp and cold, sending a blessed chill through her body. A grateful sigh escaped her lips, shoulders relaxing as she soaked up the moment of relief.

"No, he took the sheep to the north pastures, so he ventured to the southern field instead to see how it is faring," Dagny murmured in a distant tone, her attention remaining more on the tapestry before her than on the girls.

Her questions answered, Imara finished her goblet of water and placed it on the counter beneath the tap. Freeing a water flask from the cabinet below, she worked on filling it with water, the tap squeaking softly in her grip.

"I'll take Ishka down," she said to Asta, letting her know there would be no need to walk down with her. "Should I take him a bite to eat as well?"

Her sister plucked a ripened apple from the basket on the table and brought it over to her. Once upon a time, Magnhild's apples had been so large one needed almost to hold it up with two hands to take a bite. Now, the crisp fruit nestled easily in her palm as she accepted it and slid it into the pocket looped around her belt.

"If Birger arrives before I've returned, please ask him to wait. I will be but a moment," she asked of Asta, who nodded with understanding.

"Of course."

With a smile of thanks, Imara stepped out the door and back into the bright sunshine, the ground crunching beneath her soles with every step toward the paddock. Sensing her approach, Ishka wandered over, her snowy coat gleaming against the backdrop of hills, mountains, and sky. There was a brief moment of nuzzling as girl and horse greeted one another, and then Imara mounted the mare and they were off, down the lane leading to the cotton fields closest to the river.

Fingers twined lightly in the horse's mane, Imara started her in the right direction, then left the rest to Ishka. This trek down to the lower fields had been made so many times in days past that both horse and rider could have made it in the dead of night without even the glow of the moon to light their way. While communication with animals was not an elemental strength, nor could she have tapped into it if it were, there was an unspeakable bond between them, a way of understanding each other that had been there since Ishka had been a foal and given into Imara's care.

It was a swift, and easy ride down to the southern field. Spotting her father kneeled down with his hands in the soil, Imara slid off the horse's back. Smoothing a soft touch down the side of her neck, she praised Ishka for a job well done.

"Stay here, girl." With her parting words, Imara pulled her skirts up above her ankles to keep them from sticking to the cotton as she went by and headed down the row her father was in.

Down on one knee in the brown soil, his palms on the earth itself, Erlend Hjelmstad was muttering softly beneath his breath. While she could not make out the words, Imara instinctively knew that they were words of summoning, and her father was trying desperately to pull nutrients and life from deep within the ground and up into the topsoil their crop was planted in. Sensing her behind him, Erlend stopped. His head lifted and he gazed back at her over his shoulder, blue eyes a mirror of her own, shining with love as he took her in.

"Imara, haven't you a trader to meet with this afternoon?" he asked, running a soiled hand through short-cropped blond hair.

"It isn't quite time for that, and I thought you could do with some fresh water." Her hands were already upon the flask at her waist. Loosening it from her belt, she uncapped the top and held it out to him.

A look of gratefulness came over his features, and without further prodding, he stood, taking the water flask from her and tipping it back. As her father drank, Imara held a hand to her forehead, shielding her eyes from the sunlight so that she could survey the area around her. While the soil was meant to be brown, the cracked nature of it was worrisome. Both her mother and sister had been down here the day before, pulling what water there was left to the surface. It looked as if nothing had been done at all.

"It's not going so well, is it?" she asked, eyes returning to her father at last.

Erlend swiped a hand across his lips.

"No, it is not. I'm doing what I can, but there is simply nothing left in the ground to pull out of it." His hand motioned to the grounds around the cotton field. Just two months ago, they had borne green grasses and wildflowers; now they were withered, yellow, and barren.

"Is it even worth it anymore?" Imara questioned, taking in the sight of the cotton plants, perhaps only a third of them bearing anything worth gathering.

The decline had started gradually, beginning with hotter-than-typical days and a lack of fresh rain. With two water elementals in the family, fewer rainy days had never been an issue before. But then the grounds dried up faster than what had made sense. The grasses withered, flowers began dying, and everywhere one looked, the world was turning brown.

There had been difficult farming years in the past, but elemental abilities had always been able to combat it.

"To be honest, I'm not so certain. This won't be enough to supply what your mother needs for her fabrics . . . The yield simply isn't there this year." Erlend shook his head, his frustrations melting away into something resembling defeat.

It would have been nice to reach out a comforting hand and reassure him. However, reassurance wasn't something that Imara had to give. Not when, everywhere they looked, their neighbors were fighting the same effects. Each day seemed to bring new struggles, and with the lack of crops this harvest, people were beginning to question if they would have enough to get them through the winter, let alone hold over until next year for planting.

"Will there be enough wool to compensate?" They had not lost any numbers from the flock, the sheep hardy enough to withstand poorer grazing. Whether their coats had held up would be the next question.

"We'll see when we start sheering in a couple of weeks." The look in his eyes wasn't necessarily hopeful, which was difficult to see.

"What of our offerings for the Dragon Master? Do we need to lessen the amount we give?"

Each Fallfest, the residents of Omdahl welcomed Lord Lajos the Dragon Master to their celebrations. A powerful being who resided in the forests surrounding the mountains, he had centuries ago come to an agreement with the founding Elders of their village. At the commencement of the fall harvest, each household in Omdahl would provide a portion of their yearly produce, cattle, or craftmanship to him, and in return, he would keep the dragons in the woods from raining fire down upon them all.

It was a burden felt heavily by each citizen this year.

Erlend sighed. "We cannot, you know it. Each family offers up the same portion of their goods. We are not the only ones suffering this season. There can be no leniency for us if it is not offered also to them." His features were pinched with concern.

Imara's father had always been a lighthearted man.

While he worked long, hard days to care for their crops and the flock, he had always upheld a cheerful countenance. Worry was a weighted cloak that had come only recently to rest on the Hjelmstad family's shoulders.

"Something will work out," Imara assured him, feigning confidence she did not feel. Pressing a soft kiss to his cheek, she left him to his work and returned to Ishka, who awaited her patiently.

As Imara came up the hill to the family house, she was welcomed by the sight of a small horse-drawn cart covered by a canvas tarp that hid several items beneath. It was a sight that brought a smile to her lips, and without thought, she urged Ishka on a little faster. The days of splurging were behind them, but her trade relationship with Birger was the one allowance Imara still afforded herself. It came at no cost to her family, her small rooftop garden supplying the barter items Birger required for their exchanges.

The cart's seat sat empty, his horses standing unattended and unconcerned. Releasing Ishka back into the paddock, Imara was drawn toward the open door of their home, familiar voices sounding out from its depths.

Inside she found her mother and sister seated at the table with Birger, who was in the midst of sipping tea from a clay mug. Her presence did not go unnoticed, and all three turned to look her way, greeting her with three unique smiles.

"Miss Imara!" Birger called. Setting down his tea, he held his hand out to her, which she took as she approached. The rough fingers used to holding leather reins gave hers a fond squeeze. "As always, it is a pleasure to see you. I managed to find not two but three of the volumes you were seeking."

Smiling at the warm greeting, she pulled out the wooden chair beside him and took a seat, noticing that the witch hazel she had picked this morning was neatly bundled in cheesecloth and tied with twine—Asta had been kind in her absence.

As they began to speak, her mother left the table to fill their little teapot with more water from the tap. As she turned back toward the table, her hand rested upon its ceramic side until steam rose from the white spout. A mug with tea leaves nestled in the bottom was placed before Imara, and then her mother poured in the now steaming liquid, leaving the perfect amount of room for a dollop of cream to be added once she was ready. Imara waited for the leaves to settle at the bottom, then added a tiny portion of cream from the small jug on the table. Letting it all steep for the time being, she peered over at their guest.

"That is wonderful to hear, but I don't know that what I have is worth three hard-sought-after books on mage medicines. Try as I might, I couldn't keep the witch hazel from drying out," she explained.

"Nonsense," he replied. "Our arrangement has always been my books for one bunch of witch hazel, and that is what you've offered up."

"Yes, but—"

"Imara." He reached out to rest his hand over the top of hers on the table. "I've seen the state of Omdahl." He shook his head before continuing. "I'm not looking for more than what you are able to give right now."

THE DRAGON'S BRIDE BY CHRISTIS CHRISTIE & ELLE BEAUMONT

If you loved the first chapter, you can snag it at
books2read.com/thedragonsbride

Available in ebook and paperback

MORE BOOKS YOU'LL LOVE

If you enjoyed this story, please consider leaving a review!

Then check out more books from Midnight Tide Publishing!

Maddie by Candace Robinson & Amber R. Duell

She's a mad hatter. He's a loyal brother. Together they must survive a world steeped in blood.

Maddie has been trying to rescue her sister from the Queen of Hearts' prison for two years. When her last hope to infiltrate the palace fails, Maddie is left with no choice but to join forces with a sexy man from outside of Wonderland.

Noah's life has become a repetitive cycle ever since breaking up with his long-time girlfriend. But then his sister, Alice, arrives at his doorstep sporting a new pair of fangs. Noah vows to cure her, even if it means sacrificing himself.

Tensions rise when the Queen of Hearts threatens to take down Maddie and Noah's sisters, putting both their worlds in peril. They must combine their strengths to bring their enemy to her knees and protect their hearts...or risk losing them.

Maddie is the first in a series of sizzling romance, sexy vampires, and devious villains.

Available Now

Come True by Brindi Quinn

A jaded girl. A persistent genie. A contest of souls.

Recent college graduate Dolly Jones has spent the last year stubbornly trying to atone for a mistake that cost her everything. She doesn't go out, she doesn't make new friends and she sure as hell doesn't treat herself to things she hasn't earned, but when her most recent thrift store purchase proves home to a hot, magical genie determined to draw out her darkest desires in exchange for a taste of her soul, Dolly's restraint, and patience, will be put to the test.

Newbie genie Velis Reilhander will do anything to beat his older half-brothers in a soul-collecting contest that will determine the next heir to their family estate, even if it means coaxing desire out of the least palatable human he's ever contracted. As a djinn from a 'polluted' bloodline, Velis knows what it's like to work twice as hard as everyone else, and he won't let anyone—not even Dolly f*cking Jones—stand in the way of his birthright. He just needs to figure out her heart's greatest desire before his asshole brothers can get to her first.

Available Now

Made in United States
Orlando, FL
18 June 2022

18912329R00248